Praise for *Panacea*

"This thriller will grip you to the end."
—*Suspense Magazine*

"The best part is the possibility of a new series."
—*The Nameless Zine*

"The narrative is quick, the characters enthralling . . . intense and gratifying."
—*Tor.com*

"Grabs readers and holds on tight until the very end."
—*RT Book Reviews* (4½ out of 5 stars)

"Imaginative and well-paced, with a good mixture of action and fantasy."
—*Booklist*

"Complex, entertaining, smart . . . An intelligent, intriguing, fast-moving blend of science fiction and thriller."
—*Kirkus Reviews*

"It would be easiest to describe it as a lovechild inseminated by authors Dan Brown and Robin Cook."
—*Diabolique* magazine

"The plot is fascinating . . . Think *The Da Vinci Code* meets *Indiana Jones* meets *Parasite* by Mira Grant."
—*GeekDad*

"It's a lean, swift thriller with a core of cosmic speculation, and its pace and suspense may steal your breath."
—Ramsey Campbell,
award-winning author
and World Fantasy Grand Master

ALSO BY F. PAUL WILSON

REPAIRMAN JACK NOVELS*
The Tomb / Legacies / Conspiracies / All the Rage / Hosts /
The Haunted Air / Gateways / Crisscross / Infernal /
Harbingers / Bloodline / By the Sword / Ground Zero /
Fatal Error / The Dark at the End / Nightworld

THE TEEN TRILOGY*
Jack: Secret Histories / Jack: Secret Circles /
Jack: Secret Vengeance

THE EARLY YEARS TRILOGY*
Cold City / Dark City / Fear City

THE ADVERSARY CYCLE*
The Keep / The Tomb / The Touch / Reborn / Reprisal /
Nightworld

OMNIBUS EDITIONS
The Complete LaNague / Calling Dr. Death (Three Novels
of Medical Mayhem)

EDITOR
Freak Show / Diagnosis: Terminal / The Hogben Chronicles
(with Pierce Watters)

THE LANAGUE FEDERATION
Healer / Wheels Within Wheels / An Enemy of the State /
Dydeetown World / The Tery

OTHER NOVELS
Black Wind* / Sibs* / The Select / Virgin / Implant /
Deep as the Marrow / Mirage (with Matthew J. Costello) /
Nightkill (with Steven Spruill) / *Masque* (with Matthew J.
Costello) / *Sims / The Fifth Harmonic / The Proteus Curse*
(with Tracy L. Carbone) / *A Necessary End* (with Sarah
Pinborough) / *Definitely Not Kansas* (with Tim Monteleone) /
Family Secrets (with Tim Monteleone)

SHORT FICTION
Soft and Others / The Barrens and Others* /
The Christmas Thingy / Aftershock and Others* /
The Peabody-Ozymandias Traveling Circus & Oddity
Emporium* / Quick Fixes—Tales of Repairman Jack* /
Sex Slaves of the Dragon Tong

* See "The Secret History of the World" (page 463).

PANACEA

F. PAUL WILSON

TOR

A TOM DOHERTY ASSOCIATES BOOK • NEW YORK

This is a work of fiction. All of the characters, organizations, and events portrayed in this novel are either products of the author's imagination or are used fictitiously.

PANACEA

A Tor Book
Published by Tom Doherty Associates
175 Fifth Avenue
New York, NY 10010

www.tor-forge.com

Tor® is a registered trademark of Macmillan Publishing Group, LLC.

ISBN 978-0-7653-8517-8

Our books may be purchased in bulk for promotional, educational, or business use. Please contact your local bookseller or the Macmillan Corporate and Premium Sales Department at 1-800-221-7945, extension 5442, or by e-mail at MacmillanSpecialMarkets@macmillan.com.

First Edition: July 2016
First Mass Market Edition: June 2017

Printed in the United States of America

0 9 8 7 6 5 4 3 2 1

ACKNOWLEDGMENTS

The usual suspects plus a newbie: my wife, Mary;
David Hartwell, Jennifer Gunnels, and
Becky Maines at the publisher;
Steven Spruill, Elizabeth Monteleone,
Dannielle Romeo, Ann Voss Peterson, and my agent,
Albert Zuckerman.

Thanks for all your efforts.

There never was an idea stated
that woke men out of their stupid indifference
but its originator was spoken of as a crank.

—OLIVER WENDELL HOLMES, SR.

I can believe anything, provided that
it is quite incredible.

—OSCAR WILDE

PANACEA

SOMEWHERE IN QUINTANA ROO . . .

Laura Fanning's sense of something terribly wrong had grown as she'd walked through the silent, empty Mayan village. She found the inhabitants standing in a circle in a clearing by a tall ceiba tree, staring up at the body swaying in the breeze.

Someone had set him on fire and hung his blackened remains from a thick branch. Whoever had done this had tied wire around his neck, looped it over the branch, and secured it to the trunk. The flies hadn't wasted any time getting to work.

She felt her gorge rise. Used as she was to death, this struck home—and hard. She hadn't known him well—hardly at all—and hadn't particularly liked him. But she'd *known* him. He hadn't deserved to die, and certainly no one deserved this.

Laura hadn't signed up for anything even remotely like this. The deal had been to fly to the Yucatán Peninsula, talk to a local medicine man, gather information on a supposed miracle cure, return home, collect her money, and return to her daughter and her quiet, uneventful life.

She wished she'd never agreed, wished she were back home with Marissa or even at work on her cadavers, teasing a cause of death out of them one at a time.

In fact, the Suffolk County morgue was where it had

all started: with a charred corpse like this one and an unknown cause of death. Who would have dreamt when she'd been called out to a crime scene Wednesday morning that it would lead to . . . *this*?

1

"Got a crispy critter for you, Doc."

Laura Fanning nodded absently as the deputy sheriff led her through the early morning light toward the smoking embers of what had once been a three-bedroom ranch on the fringe of Sunken Meadow State Park.

Crispy critter . . . she hated the way the term casually objectified a dead fellow human being. Same with the ever-popular *DB*.

But she suppressed a sanctimonious comment. No point in getting all holier-than-thou on him. She understood the defense mechanism involved, especially in cops and morgue workers: They saw so much death, so many horrendous examples of man's inhumanity to man, or the results of simple stupidity, or the random assaults by nature and machinery on the human body, that they had to erect some sort of emotional firewall. Those unable to raise that barrier didn't last long.

Laura made do with *victim*. Or *vic*.

"How's Marissa doing?" the deputy said.

His name was Philip Lawson and he looked like he'd been plucked from central casting's file of deputy sheriffs. Thinning hair under his black Stetson, florid face, button-stretching gut. But a good man. One of the first deputies Laura had met when she joined the Suffolk County Medical Examiner's staff five years ago. He was already a veteran then. She figured he'd been with the sheriff's department close to twenty years now.

He'd guided her through her first crime scenes. An easygoing man with a generous spirit. Her only problem with him was that he seemed to like her a little too much. He could get a bit clingy at times.

Oh, and he had this thing he did with his neck: rotating it back and forth until it cracked—like popping a giant knuckle. Very annoying after a while.

"She's great," she said. "Bored as all get-out with staying home all the time."

"You'd figure she'd be used to it by now."

"Would you be?"

He laughed. "I can't wait! When I retire, I'm never leaving home. Not even for the paper. I'll have *Newsday* and the *Post* delivered right to the front door every goddamn morning."

Natasha, Marissa's tutor, had agreed to come early today so Laura could get out to the crime scene. Being a deputy ME allowed her a normal work schedule on most days—except when she was on crime-scene call. And Wednesday was her call day. Accidents and murders always seemed to happen during the off-hours. Death tended to be inconsiderate that way.

"Not much left," she said, looking around at the blackened ruins. "You suspect arson, I take it?"

He popped his neck. "Oooh, yeah."

"The squad's been out?"

"Nope."

"But all-knowing Swami Lawson's got it pegged."

He smiled as he shrugged. "Seen enough of these. The smoke was reported around two A.M. By the time the fire crew got here, it was pretty much over. This baby burned hot. I mean *real* hot. Hotter than wood and fabric will burn on their own. I don't catch any odor of gas or kerosene, but some sort of accelerant was at work here. And you know what that means."

Laura knew. Arson meant she'd be posting a murder victim. At this point, the legal subsets—first degree, manslaughter, felony murder, whatever—didn't come into play. But later on the designation would hinge on her final report. The burden had now fallen on her to establish the cause of death—not just beyond a reasonable doubt, but beyond *any* doubt—because her findings would help determine the charges brought against the perp or perps when they were caught.

"How'd you get involved?"

"Well, the fire did threaten the state park, and that's the sheriff's turf."

But murder wasn't. The staties and local Smithtown cops would be handling that. Still, Laura knew how Phil liked to worm his way into any investigation that involved a murder. Deputy Lawson: detective wannabe. He probably would have made a good one. He liked to talk about vegetating through retirement, but she wouldn't be surprised if he didn't end up doing some PI work.

They stepped through a leaning rectangle of blackened steel—all that was left of the front door. The walls were gone too.

"Do we have a name?"

"Not yet. We figure it's a winter rental—found a 'For Rent' sign in the backyard. We're tracking down the owner." Phil stopped and made a flourish toward the floor. "There he be."

Laura stepped closer and bent over the victim. He lay on his back and was indeed crispy—skin blackened and flaking and the air around him redolent of burned flesh. The fire had vaporized whatever hair he'd had, giving her a clear view of his scorched scalp. No obvious entry or exit wound. His face was gone, but his jaw hung open, revealing a mouth full of white teeth. Good. She could use dental records for identification. With his limbs bent into flexion contractions, his position was almost fetal. Not unusual. Intense heat shrank the muscles, contracting the limbs.

"This how you found him?" she said.

"Haven't touched him."

"No signs of foul play on the body?"

Phil shook his head. "Nothing obvious. No knife sticking out of his chest, no dents or holes in his head. No sign of ligatures, but the fire could have burned those away."

"So he's one big mystery for now."

"Yeah, but maybe the motive isn't so mysterious."

"Meaning?"

Phil pointed to some of the charred debris. "He had lots of dirt inside the house. I mean *lots.*"

Laura knew what that meant. "Weed?"

"Can't be a hundred percent sure, but you're looking at what's left of big wooden trays filled with dirt, and a shitload of lighting fixtures. So either he was filming mud wrestling or he was growing something. I'll go with growing. The crop, whatever it was, is ash now, but I got a feeling it wasn't orchids."

Laura raised her eyebrows as she turned to him. "Horning in on someone else's business, you think?"

"That's my take. Turf wars tend to turn nasty real quick."

Another reason for Deputy Lawson to be here: He was attached to some sort of joint task force between the DEA and the sheriff's office. He'd told her it offered a nice break from serving warrants and eviction notices.

"When are they going to legalize that stuff, Phil?"

"Can't be soon enough for me. I waste so much time busting people who just want to get high. If they don't do it on county property, it's not my business. But if folks could grow it and smoke it in their own backyards, you and me wouldn't have to deal with shit like this."

Her stomach gave a little lurch as she thought of her eight-year-old Marissa toking on a joint when she got to middle school. Although the poor kid sure could have used some form of it during her chemotherapy.

"People worry about their kids."

Phil snorted. "Show me a kid these days who wants it and can't get it, and I'll show you a kid who's still being potty trained."

Laura couldn't argue with that. As she turned to signal the morgue attendants who'd come along, she heard someone say, "Who's the MILF?"

She looked over and found one of the firefighters leering at her.

"Punk!" Lawson muttered behind her. He popped his neck. "I'm gonna—"

She put out a restraining hand. "I've got it."

She was aware that her looks attracted attention. Her mother was Mesoamerican—full-blooded Mayan—and her father lily-white Caucasian. Their mingling had left her with a slim, five-six frame, black hair, mocha skin, and startlingly blue eyes. Attention was fine; bad manners were not.

As she walked toward the man, glaring, his leer faded. A newbie, no doubt. The others knew better. He'd been standing with a buddy, both in firefighter PPE, but now his buddy faded too. The guy was all of twenty-five, if that. Laura had a good dozen, maybe fifteen years on him. She stopped and looked him square in the eyes.

"What did you call me?"

His brown eyes darted left, then right. "Uh, nothing."

"I heard 'MILF.' I know of no such word, so it must be an acronym. What does it stand for?"

"Nothing. I was just talking to—" He turned to look at his buddy who was no longer there.

"M-I-L-F . . . let's see . . . " *DOLAN* was stenciled on his yellow rubberized jacket. "What could that stand for, Mister Dolan? Morsel I'd Like to Fondue? Mignon I'd Like to Filet?"

"You weren't supposed to hear."

"Oh, yes I was. I'm not a MILF, Mister Dolan. I'm a deputy medical examiner for Suffolk County. Do you know what can happen when one public service employee sexually harasses another public service employee? In front of witnesses, no less? There's *alllll* sorts of regs and nasty consequences for that sort of behavior."

"Hey, I wasn't—"

"Yes, you were—six ways from Sunday, as the saying goes. I'll send a copy of the regs to your chief so he can explain them to you."

With that she turned and continued her trek toward the morgue attendants. Lawson was already with them.

He grinned. "Carved him a new one?"

"I went easy on him."

"But I bet he won't be mouthing off anytime soon."

"His type never learn. But, on the bright side, one of the perks of my practice is that my patients have impeccable manners."

She told the attendants to tag and bag the victim. She'd post him later this morning.

2

Nelson Fife rubbed his temples but the fingertip massage did nothing for the headache. He was suffering more and more of them lately. No time was a good time for a headache, but now was especially inconvenient.

"Can we get on with this, Fife?" said Arnold Pickens from behind his desk.

Pickens was a deputy director of the Office of Transnational Issues. They were using his office to view the recording of last night's bust. Nelson blinked back the pain and focused on his superior.

"Of course. Just a little prelude, if I may. We traced the suspect to a house on the north shore of Suffolk County and began questioning him."

"He's one of these 'panaceans' you talk about?" He said the word like it tasted bad.

"You'll hear him admit to it."

Nelson knew he was viewed as a bit of an eccentric. Usually the Company would ease out someone like him, so he'd learned to compensate. His talent for astute analysis had earned him the rank of senior operations officer in the Special Activities Division of the Central Intelligence Agency's National Clandestine Service, and made him damn near indispensable. So, because he never let it interfere with his assigned duties, the Company allowed him what they considered his one harmless eccentricity.

He was an analyst, not a pitchman, but he had to sell Pickens. He'd need extra funding and a certain amount of leeway to track down the panaceans. To get those, he needed Pickens on board.

He remembered Alec Baldwin in that depressing movie about salesmen: *Always be closing.*

He plugged the thumb drive into the USB receptacle on the side of the flat-screen monitor set in the wall and it flickered to life. The time display in the lower right-hand corner read *1:38 A.M.* Not even eight hours ago. Seemed like days.

A shirtless man sits on a chair among plant-filled trays crowding the front section of the small ranch house he's renting. They bask in artificial sunlight from the lamps strung above them. Marijuana growers use this method with great success, but these specimens are not Cannabis sativa.

In a grating voice he says, "Who the hell do you think you are?"

A man in a suit—Nelson—steps into the frame.

Nelson admired his suit from the rear—a dark-blue pinstripe, drape cut in the classic British style. He never got to see it from this angle and it looked good. Damn good. He especially liked the way the center vent fell. Nineteen hundred dollars well spent. He'd switched to a three-piece wool herringbone for this meeting.

On the screen, he yanks one of the plants from the soil and holds it up to the light for the camera. At first glance, from a distance, it resembles garden-variety pachysandra. As it's brought closer to the camera, the leaves show smooth edges and a rounded tip.

Pickens said, "That's the plant you've been rattling on about?"

Nelson refused to respond to the verbal slap.

. . . rattling on about . . . as if he'd been raving like a madman.

He studied the image. Such an innocent-looking plant. And yet so dangerous. Despite the resemblance, its genome was far removed from pachysandra. This abomination was like no other plant on Earth.

He watched the shirtless man on the screen. Nelson had run his prints before the confrontation and knew lots about him: Cornelius Aloysius Hanrahan, age thirty-two. Born and raised in Des Moines. High school graduate. No criminal record. Lutheran by birth but never attended church as an adult. Worked as a mechanic until he seemingly dropped off the face of the Earth for two years. Resurfaced three weeks ago as a panacea dispenser under the guise of an orderly at Franklin Hospital in Valley Stream.

"You can't just march in here without a warrant!" Hanrahan says.

He's not bound to the chair, yet he offers no resistance. Nelson does not reply. Allow a suspect to blather long enough and they often let secrets slip.

"This is crazy!" he adds. "I ain't broke a single damn law! But if you want my plants, take 'em."

Nelson can't suppress a smile. "As if I needed your permission. And rest assured, I care not a whit about your tawdry plants. I—"

Hanrahan laughs. "'I care not'? Really? Who talks like that?"

Nelson ignores this. "I already have more of your plants than I can count. I'm here for answers."

"I'm all ears."

As Nelson opens his mouth to speak, Agent Bradsher emerges from the rear rooms.

Behind Nelson, Pickens groaned. "You got Bradsher involved too? Jesus! Do I have to remind you—?"

"I'm well aware of the restrictions, sir." Of course he knew the CIA was not allowed to operate on U.S. soil. "But this is a matter of national security."

Bradsher was an operations officer assigned to Nelson. Built like a fullback and an excellent field agent, but dressed in an awful, sack-cut, off-the-rack gray cotton suit.

"That is still up for debate," Pickens said. "But even if it turns out to be true, we have something called the Department of Homeland Security to handle that."

"Do you trust DHS, sir?"

Pickens didn't answer. No one trusted the heavily po-
liticized DHS with anything sensitive.

On the screen, Nelson asks Bradsher, "Anything?"

Bradsher shakes his head. "Nada."

*"Just what is it you're looking for?" Hanrahan
says.*

*Nelson turns to him. "Answers. First question: Why
have you returned?"*

*Hanrahan frowns. "Returned? I didn't know I'd
gone anywhere."*

*Bradsher steps forward and makes to backhand
him across the face, but Nelson raises a palm.*

*"We don't need that." He looks at Hanrahan again.
"Don't be obtuse. Your cult has been quiet for decades. Why return now?"*

Nelson wanted to know this most of all. The last time
the panaceans made their presence felt was post–World
War II during the polio epidemic, before his time. The
plants and the man in the video were proof positive of
their return.

*"Why now?" Hanrahan's tone is matter-of-fact. "Be-
cause the All-Mother says it is time."*

*The All-Mother . . . how can such pantheistic
bullshit exist in this modern age? Anyone can ascribe
anything to the so-called All-Mother.*

"Did this goddess of yours say why it was time?"

*He shakes his head. "She's all-knowing. She doesn't
need to explain. If she says it's time, then it's time."*

*"Does she speak to you in dreams? Does she whis-
per in your ear?"*

"Word comes through channels."

"Channels?"

"You know: the grapevine."

No, Nelson did *not* know. The cult is fragmented, cellular, acting as individual operatives with only the most
tenuous interconnections.

*"How exactly did word reach you to begin dispens-
ing your potion?"*

*"The mail—a packet of seeds in my mailbox. That
was all I needed."*

"And of course you disposed of the envelope."

Hanrahan smiles. "Of course."

"And where do you store your potion?"

*The smile holds as he speaks without hesitation.
"In the fridge."*

*Nelson glances at Bradsher, who shakes his head.
"Nothing there."*

"And no sign of any elsewhere?"

"Sorry, no."

*Hanrahan says, "You want some for yourself, is
that it?"*

*"I want it for many reasons, none of which involve
me."*

*He shrugs. "Whatever the reason, Mister Pleeceman,
you're outta luck. The batch was small and I used it
all."*

"How many doses did you dispense?"

"Four. But don't ask who to. I'm not allowed to tell."

*"I know all four—that's how we found you. But
I'm not interested in them. I'm interested in you . . .
the brewer of the potion."*

Nelson now turned to Pickens, a shadow in the darkened room. "Please listen carefully. Here is where he ad-
mits to making the panacea."

*Hanrahan's eyebrows lift. "Brew . . . so you know
something about the process."*

"*I know everything about the process except the missing ingredient.*"

The eyebrows rise higher. "Missing ingredient? You got me there, pal."

"*Don't lie. We know that you boil the plants, roots and all, but you add something in the process. What?*"

"*I have no idea what you're talking about. Seriously. Like you said, we brew a tea from the plants, but that's it.*"

Nelson knows there's more to it. "You will tell us."

"*Or what? I can't tell you something I don't know.*"

"*Maybe you've just forgotten," Bradsher says. "We'll jog your memory.*"

"*You can't get away with this.*"

"*But we can," Nelson says. "And we will.*"

Hanrahan's features grow bleak. "So that's it, then? Torture, then what? Death?"

Nelson tells him, "You're familiar with Exodus 22:18?"

"*The Bible? I don't read your Bible.*"

"*You should. The passage leaves no wiggle room: 'Thou shalt not suffer a witch to live.'* "

"Are you fucking kidding me?" Pickens said. "You're quoting the Bible?"

Maybe he should have cut that out, but Nelson hadn't wanted the recording to appear edited in any way.

"Just playing head games. He belongs to an ancient pagan cult, so I thought I'd take a shot at putting a little Inquisitional fear into him."

"Jesus!"

Nelson winced as he turned back to the screen.

"*I'm no witch! I'm just a guy who cooks up plants and doles out the tea they produce. Where'd you guys come from? The Dark Ages? You're crazy. Totally bug-fuck nuts! What's it gonna be? Thumbscrews? Got an iron maiden waiting outside?"*

"Don't be melodramatic. We have injections now."

"Right," Bradsher adds. "You'll tell us everything. Even stuff you don't know you know."

"And then you kill me?"

"It doesn't have to be that way."

"Now a death threat? Jesus, Fife. You're heading off the reservation at ninety miles an hour."

"Just a little theater," Nelson lied.

Nelson speaks softly to Hanrahan. "Tell us the ingredient and I'll let you go."

The sudden tears in the man's eyes startle him.

"I can't do that. I'm pledged to the All-Mother."

"Stop that!" Nelson shouts, causing even Bradsher to jump. His face contorts. "There is no All-Mother! You are pledged to a fiction!"

"No," Hanrahan says, sobbing. "You are. And now . . . I've gotta go."

"You're not going anywhere," Bradsher says.

"Good-bye."

So saying, Hanrahan closes his eyes and takes a deep breath. As he lets it out, his head drops forward and his body slumps to the floor.

Bradsher looks from Nelson to Hanrahan, then back again. "What's he doing?"

"Passed out. But that's not going to change anything. Wake him up."

Bradsher kneels by Hanrahan and lifts his head. Dull, lifeless blue eyes stare ceilingward.

"What the—?"

Jabbing two fingers against the side of the man's throat, Bradsher waits, then says, "No pulse! He's dead!"

"He's *what*?" Pickens said. "What did you do to him?"

Nelson had intended the recording to capture every nuance of the interrogation. But now it exonerated him from doing any violence to the man—the main reason he wanted Pickens to see it.

"Absolutely nothing. As you've seen, neither of us touched him. He simply keeled over dead."

"How?"

Bradsher says, "He must have had some cyanide—"

"No," Nelson says. "Not cyanide, but check his mouth anyway."

He's seen people die of cyanide poisoning and it's anything but a peaceful death.

Bradsher finishes his inspection and lets the head drop. "No sign of a hollow tooth or the like." He shakes his head. "He said 'good-bye' and then . . . "

Nelson turned back to Pickens. "Almost as if he willed himself to die."

"Is that possible?"

"I've never heard of it, but I think we just witnessed it."

Nelson steps around the plant trays and checks for a pulse himself. Not that he doesn't trust Bradsher, but this is too uncanny. He finds the carotid artery lying still beneath the already cooling flesh of the man's throat.

Damn him! They were so close!

Nelson motions to Bradsher. "Bring the camera over here. I want this on record."

*The image wobbles and blurs, and then refocuses
on Hanrahan's back, revealing a black-ink tattoo.*

*Nelson owns photos and drawings of similar tat-
toos, but this is the first time he's seen one on a human body. It looks much like all the others: the
shooting star behind the staff and snake of Asclepius,
all bisected by a straight line. The only variation has
been the angle of the line. Nelson assumes that's a way
to individualize the tattoo.*

*A foot comes into frame and turns the body over
onto its back. The chest area is unmarred and—*

*Suddenly the image flares white and the screen goes
dark.*

Nelson tugged the thumb drive from its slot as Pickens said, "What just happened? Where's the rest of it?"

"That's all we have. The place burst into flame. We
barely got out with our lives."

He walked to the window and twisted the wand on
the blinds, angling the narrow slats to let in the day. He
suppressed a groan as the light jabbed into his brain,
intensifying his headache. Squinting, he saw Foley
Square basking in the sun fifteen stories below. And beyond that, the roof of the hulking New York City Supreme Court building.

"So, he had the place rigged to go up, taking him and

everything else with him. And I'm supposed to believe that this is the guy with the secret to a cure-all?"

Yes, you are, Nelson thought. And I'll have you convinced before I leave here.

Always be closing.

Nelson wandered the office. Brown industrial carpet, beige walls adorned with blah photos of Manhattan streets. The sign on the door said *Asian Studies*. The directory down in the Federal Building's lobby didn't list the room at all.

"I don't see an incongruity. We're dealing with a member of a hyper-secretive cult. The incendiaries he had rigged destroyed all evidence, including his plants. From his end it makes perfect sense: His secrets are safe."

Pickens motioned to the chair before his desk. "Sit down, will you? We have to talk, and your wandering around gets on my nerves."

Pickens was a dozen years older—mid-fifties—red-faced and balding. He had his suit jacket off, revealing black suspenders. Most of the men Nelson knew who wore suspenders were fat, and Pickens was no exception. His suit was of only slightly better quality than Brother Bradsher's, but at least he'd had the good sense to choose a jacket with side vents to accommodate his girth. He'd let himself go the past few years, developing a big gut that stretched his shirtfront.

Nelson prided himself on not gaining an ounce in the past decade. He still had a thirty-two-inch waist and a healthy head of dark, gray-free hair. Clean, righteous living did it—no meat, lots of fruit and veggies.

"Look," Pickens said when Nelson had settled himself, "this panacea thing of yours was all fine and good when it was just some theory you were investigating on your own time. It's been all speculation, all cloud-cuckoo-land stuff till now. But last night changes things.

You ran an op—and an illegal one, at that—without clearing it. You should have come to me first."

Nelson repressed a smile. Pickens's bald statements about things they both knew perfectly well made it obvious he was recording the meeting. Fine. Nelson understood and appreciated CYA. So why not help get Pickens off whatever future hooks might come his way via Nelson Fife?

"The reason I didn't clear it was I knew you'd quash it."

Pickens blinked at having been handed the proverbial Get Out of Jail Free card, then visibly relaxed.

"Well, I . . . I think we could have found a legal path. By the way, is this place you were at the same as the fire I heard about on the news this morning?"

Nelson nodded. "Unfortunately."

"Look, Nelson, it's time we laid some ground rules. I know you caught this bug from your uncle who was, as I've said many times before, a fine, fine field agent. But Jim Fife had this obsession—"

"It exists, sir. The panacea is real. My uncle saw the cures."

"I know he thinks he did, but . . . " He leaned back and took a deep breath. "Let's just say for the sake of argument that a panacea exists. Why is this cult keeping it secret?"

"That was what I was hoping to learn from Hanrahan. But it's pretty much a truism, isn't it, that cults don't have to make sense, and it's wrong to expect them to. People believe the strangest things. Look at Dormentalism's core beliefs. You wonder how anyone can buy into that stuff about aliens, but it has thousands of devoted followers. I would guess offhand that these panaceans—"

"Is that what they call themselves?"

"Frankly, I don't know what they call themselves.

That's my uncle Jim's term for them and I think it's a good one. From what I've gathered, they keep the panacea secret because they think their goddess—they call her the All-Mother—wants it that way."

"All right. They've got a religious reason. Fine. It doesn't have to make sense. But *how* do they keep it secret? You're talking about the legendary cure-all—as in cure-*all*. You can't keep something like that secret for long."

"You can if the ones who are cured don't know they've been dosed with anything."

"And what does it do? How does it work?"

"Uncle Jim learned that one dose cures any illness you have—infection, cancer, autoimmune, everything."

Pickens laughed. "So we're talking immortality here?"

Was he being obtuse on purpose?

"No, of course not. It cures whatever's wrong with you at the moment. That doesn't mean you can't come down with the flu or have a tumor start in your prostate the next day."

"But if you took another dose, you'd be free of those as well?"

"Correct."

"Well, then, if you had an endless supply, wouldn't you be immortal?"

"Aging isn't a disease."

"You say your uncle told you all this? How did he learn? Take a dose?"

"He would never do that."

"Then how *did* he learn?"

"From panaceans he interviewed."

"Interviewed how? Or do we not want to go there?"

Nelson shook his head. "Probably better not to, sir."

James Fife, his father's older brother, had been a young OSS officer who migrated to the SSU at the end of World War II; from there he moved to the CIG, which was redesignated the CIA in 1947. He became a legend in the Company, especially in the area of psychological warfare.

"All right. So it cures what ails you, no matter what. And you think you traced it to the fellow on Long Island."

Nelson clenched his teeth. He didn't *think*—he *knew*.

"Cornelius Hanrahan worked as a hospital orderly. In the three weeks he was at Franklin, they had four so-called 'miracle cures.'"

"And you know this how?"

"Our friends at NSA. Remember my request to add a few terms to their ECHELON search list?"

Pickens frowned. "I thought that had to do with biologicals."

"It did. But I included 'miracle cure' and 'spontaneous remission' to our list."

Pickens opened his mouth, then shut it.

Right, Nelson thought. Don't say anything.

He'd shoved the list in front of Pickens, who'd only glanced at it before scribbling his signature.

"In its scanning of phone calls and texts and apps, they picked up scattered hits on the terms all over the country, but also clusters in and around certain hospitals. One of those was Franklin, and since it was so close, I did a little investigating."

Pickens scoffed. "Miracle cures are reported all the time."

Nelson gave him a knowing smile and nod. "Exactly. Leukemia cells fading away, wasted kidneys starting to function again, a miraculously shrinking brain tumor. Doctors come up with convincing medical jabberwocky like 'spontaneous remission' and such, but they have no idea what happened."

"Did you ever hear of Occam's razor?"

"Of course."

"Then apply it. Because Occam's razor will lead you away from the idea of a panacea."

Nelson bottled his frustration. He understood the natural resistance to accepting a supposed myth as real, but he had to sell this.

Always be closing.

"Let me say this again: four 'miracle cures' in the three weeks he's been there. Three weeks."

"Are you going to tell me they had no 'miracle cures' before he arrived?"

"No. But the four previous so-called 'miracle cures' occurred over a three-year period." *Three weeks versus three years* . . . Nelson let that sink in for a few heartbeats, then added, "And hallway video footage shows Hanrahan entering their rooms the night before each 'miracle' occurred."

Looking perplexed, Pickens drummed his fingers on his desk. "I still don't see . . . I mean, really . . . why die to protect the secret of a cure-all? It's not as if it endangers anyone."

Nelson had to rise from his seat for this. He spoke better on his feet.

"On the contrary, sir: Widespread use will delay countless deaths that, over the course of a single decade, will cause a population surge that will bring economic chaos. Even worse, letting it fall into the wrong hands could prove disastrous. We can't allow anyone but the U.S. to control it."

"It's a *cure-all,* Fife. You can't weaponize a cure-all."

"Oh, but you can, sir. Whoever controls the panacea effectively controls the world."

"Okay. You've lost me now."

"Consider, just as a for-instance, North Korea or a jihadist group mutating the H_7N_9 bird flu to an airborne pathogen. They can release it worldwide and decide which populations they want to protect with the panacea and which they want to let die. Or simply release it and sell the panacea to the highest bidder. Do you see the possibilities?"

From the slow slump of Pickens's features, Nelson knew he did.

Got him!

But then the director shook himself. "Wait-wait-wait. You inherited your uncle's persuasiveness. When he was my superior I had to listen while he went on and on about this. He almost had me convinced back in the day, and now you're doing the same. But you've got as much proof as he had—which is *none*."

"I'm sure he would have found some had his injuries not forced him to retire."

"Yes, well, we're all sorry about that, but my point is, all these scenarios assume your panacea is real. That's a huge leap of faith. Have you ever seen it work?"

Nelson had to be honest here. "No."

"Have you ever spoken to someone who has seen it work?"

"My uncle—"

"I'm not talking an after-the-fact spontaneous cure, but a controlled test where this panacea was administered and worked a cure where everything else had failed?"

Again . . . "No."

"Well, then—"

"But, sir." Nelson wasn't giving up—*couldn't* give up. "If it *is* real—and I am sure it is—can we afford to allow it to fall into anyone else's hands?"

Pickens shook his head. "I'm not ready to head down that road. It's way premature. Prove to me this thing exists, and then we'll talk priorities and strategy. Until then, it's just a pipe dream."

"What will it take to convince you?"

"A 'miracle cure.' Right here." He tapped his desktop. "Right in front of me."

"And then what?"

"If you can prove to me beyond a reasonable doubt
that you've found something that can cure any and every illness, I will find a way to put the whole fucking
Company at your disposal."

Fife smiled. "I'll hold you to that, sir."

He already had another panacean under observation.
And if things went his way, he'd have Pickens's sample
by this time tomorrow.

And then he'd close the sale.

3

"He didn't die of *anything*?"

Deputy Lawson stood on the far side of the autopsy
table sipping coffee—leave it to Phil to know the places
that still served it in the classic Anthora paper cup. His
Stetson has been replaced by a paper surgical cap; an
aqua paper gown and booties protected his uniform
and shoes. The unidentified vic lay supine between
them, hidden by a green plastic sheet. Laura had already
opened and closed the chest and abdominal cavities.

Phil had stopped by to tell her who had rented the
now destroyed ranch house near Sunken Meadow State
Park. Perhaps *stopped by* was an understatement. He'd
driven from Riverhead to the Suffolk County municipal
complex in Hauppauge to tell her, confirming a more
than casual interest in the case.

The rental papers had been signed by one Cornelius
Aloysius Hanrahan. That didn't mean the vic was
Hanrahan, but it gave her a place to start checking den-
tal records.

She wanted to show Lawson something so he'd subjected himself to the protective wear and come down to the tiled autopsy room in the basement.

"Well, the blood and vitreous tox screens are pending, but the best I can say now is cardiac arrest."

He popped his neck. "You've always told me cardiac arrest isn't an acceptable cause of death because every DB has a stopped heart."

"Right. It's whatever did the stopping of the heart that's important."

"So?"

Laura shrugged. "He's got a perfectly healthy heart. His valves are fine. Aortic stenosis could cause sudden death, so could the so-called widow-maker lesion in the left main coronary, but . . . all his coronary arteries are pristine—like a newborn's."

"Newborns can die suddenly, right?"

"Sure. Sudden infant death syndrome. But the brain stem is the culprit in SIDS—it controls breathing and heart rate—and this fellow was not an infant."

Phil was nodding. "Brain . . . right. So, a stroke."

She shook her head. "No sign of stroke, no concussion or subdural, and his brain stem looks fine. No blunt trauma. I've got slides prepared that'll have to be stained and scoped, but I don't have high hopes of finding anything."

"Y'gotta give me *something*. The arson boys say the place was definitely torched. They haven't identified the accelerant yet, but no question it's arson. Can we say the heat of the fire stopped his heart?"

"Afraid not. He was dead before the fire started."

"Shit, Laura. You're not helping at all here."

She shared his frustration. Her boss, the CME, would be expecting a cause of death, especially where a crime was involved. She'd be unhappy if Laura could not deliver one. And Dr. Henniger could be a real beast when she wasn't happy.

Laura spread her hands. "I can only report what I find, and there's no sign of heat or smoke damage to his oropharynx or trachea. The fire didn't kill him."

"Okay, then the blaze was started to cover up his murder."

Laura wanted to help him, really she did, but he wasn't going to like her final report.

"I have no evidence of murder, Phil. Not a single penetrating wound—no bullet, no blade, nothing. No organ damage, not even a hint. No internal bleeding. No sign of any violence at all, for that matter."

"Then poison."

"Well, that'll show in the tox screen, but I'm not holding my breath."

Another neck pop. "So you're telling me a potential charge of drug-related arson-murder just got reduced to simple arson?"

His addition of "drug-related" to the charge did not escape her. A drug motive was the only way he could stay involved.

"Looks that way."

He drained his cup and tossed it in a nearby wastebasket.

"How about signs of gang affiliation?"

"You mean colors?" She shook her head. "Whatever clothes he was wearing are ash or scorched beyond recognition."

"I guess it's useless to ask about tats."

"Not at all. That's what I wanted you to see. Pull a pair of gloves from that box and help me roll him over."

Laura removed the sheet while Phil stretched the latex over his beefy fingers. As they eased the vic onto his belly, she said, "He was lying on his back while the fire razed the house, so the skin there was somewhat protected."

"You call that protected?" Phil said, gazing at the expanse of blackened flesh once they had the body prone.

"I said 'somewhat.' But look." She pointed to a dark outline vaguely visible through the scorching. "You can make out some sort of image here."

"Gotta be a tattoo."

"Big one—twelve and a half inches from top to bottom. Looks like some variation on the caduceus."

"The what?"

She smiled. "Caduceus. It's the winged staff with the coiled snakes that you see on medical offices and the like. Only I can't make out any wings on this one, and only one snake."

"Don't know of any gang tattoo like that. You think he thought he was some kind of doctor or something?"

"Doctor of weedology, maybe. Marijuana does have medical uses, but it may have a personal meaning. I took some high-res photos. We may be able to get a clearer image through them."

Phil was nodding. "We cooperate with Immigration and Customs on a joint task force involving gangs of illegals. They've built a nice database of tats. If we get a decent sketch we can run it through and see if we get any hits."

He stepped back, looked at the vic's back from a couple of different angles, then shook his head.

"You've sliced and diced him and all we've got is a charcoal-broiled tattoo?"

"I'm telling you, Phil, this may just be the healthiest man I've ever posted."

And that gnawed at Laura. Not just because it would put her on the wrong side of the CME, but because no one that healthy should drop dead.

Sure, it could happen—a perfect storm in the heart's

electrical system could cause a fatal arrhythmia or sudden cardiac arrest. But his myocardium showed no signs of distress. She'd put the heart aside for sectioning of the AV node and bundle branches, maybe even selected Purkinje fibers.

She had a feeling she'd never know what killed this man. And she didn't like that. That was one of the reasons she'd taken the pathology residency. Living bodies too often refused to reveal their secrets, but cadavers always gave them up.

Or almost always.

4

Nervous, Chaim Brody stepped up onto the Cochrans' narrow front porch and stood rubbing his hands together. He glanced around, up and down the quiet street. Like next to zero chance that anyone he knew would wander by, but still . . . he was breaking all the rules by coming here—not just his job's rules but the All-Mother's as well. But he couldn't allow this to go on any longer.

The Cochrans lived in a small two-story colonial that had seen better days, but was still light-years beyond Chaim's digs. He knew Mrs. Cochran and her son Tommy from the Moriches Physical Therapy Center where everybody called him "Chet." Chaim's idea. Less ethnic and all that. People heard "Chaim" and expected a yarmulke and tzitzis. He'd left all that stuff behind when he embraced the All-Mother.

He rang the doorbell and Mrs. Cochran appeared almost immediately—a plump woman in her mid-thirties with a round face and short brown hair.

"Chet?" she said as she opened her front door. "What are you—oh, did Tommy forget something?"

"No, Mrs. Cochran. I . . . I wanted to, like, speak to you in private about Tommy."

Her smile faltered. "Is something wrong?"

"Nothing you don't already know. May I come in?"

She hesitated a second, then pushed open the storm door. "Of course. It's chilly out there."

"Downright unseasonable."

He pulled the storm door closed behind him but did not move any deeper into the house. He stood in a super-short hallway that opened into a small, crowded living room. She looked nervous about letting a relative stranger into her home. They'd had a few conversations at the PT place where he helped out with the clients, but that was it. No reason she'd ever expect to find him on her doorstep.

Not a terribly warm person, she tended to be totally arm's length. Cordial at best. He'd pulled his piercings but he'd caught her looking askance at his short ponytail—she should have seen it before he'd trimmed it and sent it off to become a cancer wig. Not too much he could do about the tattoos and the old track marks except keep them under wraps, but every so often some ink would peek out.

"I'll get right to the point."

"Please do. You said it's about Tommy?"

"Yes. I have something I think can help him."

Although he'd said "think," he *knew* he could help.

"Help him how?"

"With his arthritis."

"Oh, Chet, you have been helping him. The exercises—"

"No-no. I mean with like a medication of sorts."

She frowned. "He has a rheumatologist for that."

"I know, I know, and I'm not saying anything against Doctor Sklar, but I'd just like Tommy . . . " He reached into the pocket of his parka and pulled out a small glass vial with a red rubber stopper. "I'd like him to try this."

Her frown deepened as she took the vial and stared at the half ounce of cloudy fluid within.

"What is it?"

"An ancient herbal mixture." More true than untrue. "From the Orient."

Totally untrue.

"Oh, dear. I don't know about this."

"One dose. Please, Mrs. Cochran. One dose and you'll see a miraculous improvement in Tommy."

He didn't want to say "cure," because no way she'd buy that. Worse, she'd think he'd gone shuggy. Juvenile rheumatoid arthritis wasn't curable—at least not by accepted medical practices. But the *ikhar* in that little vial operated far, far outside those accepted boundaries.

Her eyes narrowed. "Does the PT center know you're going around selling—?"

"Oh, no. I'm not going around and I'm not selling anything. This is, like, strictly from me to you for Tommy—no strings, no cost."

And speak of the little devil, look who just rolled around the corner in his wheelchair. Jeans covered his swollen knees and his rashes were hidden under a blue Giants sweatshirt.

Chaim's heart swelled at the sight of the little guy. He didn't know what it was about Tommy, but he'd bonded to this kid. An instant thing—*bam!*—on day one of working with him. He was sweet and brave and tough. His limbs were all stiff and getting more and more twisted by the day, but he never let it get him down. He kept smiling and kept trying. The kid was a fighter. Lots of the kids had attitudes about the therapy, but once Chaim told Tommy that the exercises would keep his muscles from wasting away, Tommy was *there*. When the kid had told him he was gonna ride his bike again someday, Chaim had gotten totally *verklempt*.

"Hey, Chet!" Tommy said with a big grin that revealed a missing tooth. "What are you doing here?"

He caught Mrs. Cochran's warning look as she enclosed the vial in her hand, hiding it, but Chaim hadn't intended on saying anything about the *ikhar*.

"Hey, buddy. Just talking to your mom. You know, like checking up on you. You missed therapy yesterday."

"Yeah. Got this cold and Mom doesn't want me going out."

"Don't take that tone, young man," Mrs. Cochran said. "You know the medicine makes your immune system weak."

"I know."

Chaim had tried every trick he knew to slip him a dose of the *ikhar* during therapy, but his mother was a total helicopter—no, make that a flying saucer, always hovering within a ten-foot radius so she could keep Tommy in her tractor beam and haul him up at any moment. She had hand cleanser ready at all times and never let him eat or drink anything at the therapy place—like everything was germy or something.

That had left Chaim no choice but to take the proverbial bull by its proverbial horns.

So far in his life he'd caused a ton of bad feelings and misery and harm—to himself and others. But he'd gotten clean, quitting the shit he used to squirt into his veins—H, meth, even tried Berzerk, but only once. Now that he had the means to make up for all his past failings, he was determined to take it seriously. Tommy needed—no, more than needed—Tommy *deserved* the *ikhar,* and by the All-Mother, he was going to get it.

"Tommy, dear," Mrs. Cochran said, "why don't you set up the chessboard on the kitchen table and we'll play."

"Chess at eight years old!" Chaim said, avoiding the grown-up gosh-wow enthusiasm that kids instinctively scoped out as phony. "What are you, like some kinda prodigy?"

He grinned. "I'm getting there."

"He's a natural," his mother said. "Beats me all the time." She shooed him away. "Go ahead. Chet and I will be finished in a minute."

"Are you gonna be talking about me?"

You got it, kid.

"Damn straight," he said. "We're talking about changing your therapy and such like."

No way could Chaim make changes—he was just a helper, not an RPT—but Tommy wouldn't know that.

After a long pause with a nakedly suspicious expression, the kid turned his chair and wheeled away.

"See you tomorrow, Chet," he said over his shoulder.

"You got it, buddy!"

As soon as he was out of sight, Mrs. Cochran tried to press the vial back into Chaim's hand. "I know you mean well, but I can't take this."

But he wasn't having any of it. "You've got to, Mrs. Cochran. It's his only chance for a normal life. Just promise me one thing: If, like, he suddenly gets a whole lot better, don't mention my name, okay? Just say it's a miracle and leave it at that."

"Miracles come from God, Chet. This isn't from God."

He'd spotted her crucifixes and rosaries when she brought Tommy to PT and knew she was Catholic. A praying Catholic. Didn't see a whole lot of those these days.

"Th . . . God works in mysterious ways, Mrs. Cochran."

Whoa! He'd almost said "the All-Mother." That would have totally blown it.

He backed out the storm door onto the porch, pleading as he moved. "Just one dose, Mrs. Cochran. Half an ounce. I'm begging you for Tommy's sake. One dose is all it will take."

He closed the door and hurried away. His first glance back showed her staring at him through the glass, her hands clutched around the vial. When he looked back again the door was closed.

She had to believe him. She *had* to.

5

A miracle . . . Tommy had stopped right around the corner from the front hall and listened. He'd heard Chet and Mom mention a miracle. Tommy *craved* a miracle.

As soon as he'd heard the door slam, he'd wheeled his chair up behind his mother. The rubber wheels made no noise, so when she turned and saw him there she jumped and gasped—and almost dropped the little glass tube in her hand.

"Tommy! You startled me!"

"What did Chet give you?"

Her fingers tightened around the tube, hiding it. "Nothing."

"Mo-om." He drew out the word. "I heard him say 'miracle.' If he—"

"Oh, Tommy, dear," she said, kneeling beside his chair and getting eye to eye with him. Usually he liked when she did that, but he had a feeling he wasn't going to like this. "Chet means well. I'm sure he believes his folk remedy can help you, but it's just some herbs and things that might do more harm than good."

"Chet wouldn't hurt me."

"Not on purpose." Now she showed him the tube, holding it up between them, just inches away. Tommy had to admit the liquid in it looked yucky. "But I'm sure even he doesn't know all the ingredients in this stuff. It might not hurt a regular person, but who knows how it will mix with the meds Doctor Sklar is giving you. It might even cause an infection."

"But what if it really can cure me?"

"Don't you think Doctor Sklar would know about it? He's spent his whole life treating children like you." She shook the tube like she was shaking a finger at him. "All this is is false hope. If you drank it, you'd be expecting a miracle that would never come. And when it didn't, you'd be so terribly disappointed. I don't want you to go through that."

"But—"

Tommy couldn't help it . . . he began to cry. He was tired of the swollen knees and the bent fingers and being in a wheelchair and hurting ALL. THE. TIME.

Finally, when he found his voice, he said, "I don't want to be like this forever, Mom! I'm sick of riding the short bus! I wanna play soccer, I wanna ride my bike, I wanna WALK!"

Now she was crying too.

"I want that too! This is why I sent you to set up the chess. I don't want anyone making promises that won't come true, because it's so much worse when they don't." She pushed herself to her feet. "Now . . . we won't talk about this anymore."

The glass tube disappeared into the pocket of her sweatpants.

Tommy wiped his eyes on the sleeve of his Giants shirt. "Okay."

"Want to play chess?"

He didn't. Not really. But since she'd kept him home from school today . . .

"I guess so."

"Good. Set it up and we'll play, okay?"

He set it up, and they played, and he won only one

out of three games because all he could think about was
that tube in his mother's pocket.

Afterward he kept an eye on her. He pretended to go
watch *SpongeBob* in the living room, but peeked back
around the corner and saw her shove something deep
into the kitchen garbage pail.

He bided his time, waiting until she went upstairs to
use the bathroom. As soon as she reached the second
floor he wheeled himself into the kitchen and opened
the cabinet under the sink. He pawed through the wet
paper towels and remnants of breakfast until he found
the glass tube. His gnarled fingers had trouble with the
rubber stopper, but finally it came free with a soft pop.

He hesitated for a second—what if Mom was right
and it made him sick?—then upended it into his mouth.

Gah! It tasted awful!

He forced a swallow, then restoppered the empty tube
and jammed it back into the garbage. By the time his
mother returned he was playing *DNA Wars* on his old
PS3 . . .

. . . and waiting for the miracle.

6

"He's *dead*?" Nelson Fife said, staring at Chaim Brody's
body, facedown on the floor.

The inside of the run-down, double-wide trailer was
almost a carbon copy of Hanrahan's front room: virtually no furniture and the same array of long wooden
trays filled with strange little plants basking in artificial
sunlight.

He'd rushed out here to the North Fork from the city,
fighting traffic on the LIE, then following his GPS onto
secondary roads, then this gravel path to a double-wide

trailer on the edge of what would be a potato field when growing season began. All to question a dead man.

Add that to his endless headache and his patience had just about reached its limit.

Nelson didn't know who he wanted to kick more—Bradsher or Brody.

Brother Bradsher, dressed in the same sack-cut suit he'd worn in the recording, nodded. "Just . . . keeled over. I don't think I was here ten minutes when he said, 'Good-bye,' and he was gone. Just like Hanrahan."

He turned on Bradsher. "What did you say to set him off?"

"Nothing. I swear. I didn't even get a chance to set up the camera. But he knew we were coming."

"He told you that? How—?"

"No." He pointed to the side of one of the growing trays. "Look."

Nelson stepped around and stared in shock. Someone had written a number in black Magic Marker on the unfinished wood.

536

"But how could he know?"

Bradsher shrugged. "Maybe he saw what happened to Hanrahan's house and guessed."

Uncle Jim had studied these panaceans. He'd said they were like the old communist cells—independent functioning units, minimal knowledge of each other, connected by third parties. Maybe that was changing.

"Perhaps. But I still don't understand why he died so quickly. You sure you didn't—?"

Bradsher held up a pair of glass test tubes. "Maybe it was because I came up with these."

Nelson felt his knees wobble. "You've found some?"

"I peeked in before I entered and saw him with his arm behind the refrigerator. So that was the first place I looked."

Finally . . . finally!

Thrilled, he cupped his shaking hands before him to receive the vials. Each was three-quarters filled with a cloudy fluid. He had it . . . he finally had the panacea.

"What are we going to do with them?"

"I'm going to use them to prove to someone high up that we're not crazy. And once we convince him the panacea is real, we'll have all the resources we need to track it to its source."

Bradsher gestured around. "And what about all this?"

"Same as with Hanrahan."

With a curt nod, Bradsher hurried out. Nelson wandered over to Brody's cooling corpse. The NSA phone-and-text surveillance had found a number of "miracle cure" hits connected with a Moriches physical therapy facility. Chaim "Chet" Brody had been easy to trace. The backgrounding had made a good case for his being the panacean connected with the cures, and the trays of plants confirmed it. But Nelson needed to see the final piece of the puzzle.

He pulled a knife from his pocket and unfolded it as he knelt beside the corpse. He grabbed the back of Brody's long-sleeve T-shirt and slit it top to bottom, then spread the edges.

Well, well, well . . . another of those strange tattoos. The final confirmation.

Bradsher returned with a red metal can.

"You know the protocol," Nelson said.

The fumes that filled the air as Bradsher began sloshing the accelerant onto the plants bumped the intensity of Nelson's headache from four to six. He headed for the door. Outside in the twilight, he seated himself behind the wheel of his car and dug into the pocket of his suit jacket—the same herringbone he'd worn to the meeting with Pickens—for the bottle of Advil he'd taken to carrying everywhere.

As with last night—or rather, early this morning—no trace of the plants would remain, and the panacean himself would defy identification for a while. Not indefinitely, but it would take time to determine that he belonged to no gang and was not connected to any drug traffickers. As the local yokels scratched their baffled heads, Nelson would be well on his way to tying up the panacea and its makers once and for all.

Less than a minute later the trailer burst into flame with a loud *woomp!* Nelson saw Brother Bradsher hurrying across the yard, silhouetted against the flames. They'd faked the incendiary booby trap on the video he'd shown Pickens. No need for a repeat performance. Tomorrow he'd report a similar story: The panacean dropped dead and then his incendiaries exploded, taking the camera along with everything else. The only new wrinkle would be that Nelson had obtained samples of the panacea before everything blew to hell.

Nelson dry-swallowed three of the Advil as he put the car in gear and drove away. Was that irony? Taking Advil when he had something in his pocket that would cure his headaches forever?

He thought about it—he could take one dose and use the other to convince Pickens. No more headaches. Even better, the panacea wouldn't limit itself to his headaches. It would cure Nelson of *everything*—these migraines and all other maladies, known and unknown. Really, who knew what was lurking in one's body? He took care of himself, got a checkup every couple of years, and led a life rigorously free of risky behavior: didn't smoke or do drugs, ate a vegetarian diet, drank only wine, and that sparingly. But that didn't mean a cancer couldn't be smoldering somewhere in his body—say, his pancreas, for instance—hiding, waiting until it had progressed to a terminal stage before revealing itself.

Tempting, but no. That would be just plain wrong. He had a higher calling. But perhaps . . .

He exited the LIE and took the Northern State Parkway toward East Meadow . . .

7

"We've got to stop meeting like this," Deputy Lawson said. "Three times in one day. Tongues will be wagging."

You wish, Laura thought, as she surveyed the chaotic scene before her.

She was tired. She wanted to be home. But instead she'd felt compelled to drive out to the North Fork to view another crime scene. Jeff Hager, one of her fellow MEs, had been on deck to take this one, but Deputy Lawson had said the scene was so damn near identical to the Sunken Meadow fire that Laura just had to see it.

Long Island's South Fork was the crowded home of all the sundry Hamptons—South, East, West, and Bridge—and their moneyed inhabitants. The North Fork was still relatively rural and had reinvented itself, morphing from corn and potato farms into wine country.

Smoke drifted from the charred ruins of a double-wide trailer situated on the southwest corner of a ten- or twelve-acre rectangle of plowed earth. Two fire trucks and an EMS rig idled around it, red and blue flashers lighting the night. Their work done, the Cutchogue firemen were winding up their hoses while the EMTs hung out.

Waiting for her most likely.

What appeared to be a corpse lay on the brown grass under a plastic sheet.

Also waiting.

Phil waved toward the firemen. "These boys were just on their way back from Southold when they spotted the smoke and turned in for a look-see. Good thing they did. They managed to pull the body from the trailer but weren't able to kill the blaze. We don't have a crime scene—well, not in any useful sense—but at least you've got an uncooked DB to work with."

"Was he growing something too?"

"Yep." He popped his neck as he led her over to the embers. "And it looks like the same kind of super accelerant as before."

"So we still don't know what he was growing."

Phil looked at her. "Really? You think he was growing geraniums or something? He had big light racks. It's an indoor pot farm."

She wasn't convinced. "*Cannabis sativa* grows how tall?"

"Eight, ten feet. Oh, I see what you're getting at: Too tall for a trailer. But these were probably seedlings he was getting started to transplant somewhere else. Or maybe some shorter strain. You won't believe the hybrids some of these pot farmers are developing these days."

Laura shook her head. "Don't they know GMO is politically incorrect?"

She'd heard of cannabis hybrids. But something about this didn't sit right.

"Forget the plants," Phil said, reaching for the plastic sheet on the ground. "They just go to motive. Check out the vic."

A male corpse lay facedown on the ground. His T-shirt had been sliced open to reveal a strange tattoo in the center of his back.

As she squatted for a closer look, she noticed other tattoos running up and down his arms, which lay straight at his side, palms up. That was how she saw the number scrawled on his palm.

536

It didn't look like a tattoo. When she noticed the cap of a black Sharpie protruding from the back pocket of his jeans, she had a pretty good idea how it got there. How long ago had he written that? Might be nothing, might be the last thing he did before his death. She turned her attention to the tattoo.

Phil said, "Are you thinking what I'm thinking?"

"I'm thinking I am," she replied.

Yes . . . this certainly shared features with what she'd been able to discern on the back of the burn vic.

"Is that the caduceus or whatever you mentioned?"

"No. But neither was the other one, and what we

could see of the burn vic's tattoo was missing the same features. This is the same size and looks to be the same variation on the caduceus, which means . . . "

". . . the vics are connected. And owing to the similarities of the crime scenes, the deaths are connected."

Laura rose to her feet. "I think that's a safe assumption, Sherlock."

He popped his neck again. "Hot diggity."

Laura had to laugh. "I don't believe I've ever heard anyone say that."

"Something my grandfather used to say." He rubbed his hands together like a miser contemplating wads of cash. "The joint task force is going to want to hear about this: new gang in town."

"That's a bit of a leap, isn't it?"

"Not at all. Two growers with matching tattoos, both murdered among their plants—"

"Hold on now with the murder bit. I couldn't find a cause of death on the first."

"But you will. I have faith in that. And in both cases the rival gang committed arson to destroy the evidence. Drug-related felonies galore."

She didn't know where the rival-gangs idea came from—probably just frosting on Phil's story—but no question about the felonies.

She stared at the body of the dead grower. Despite the colorful tattoos on his arms and shoulders, the black lines of the snake and the staff stood out.

Wait . . . staff? That looked more like a bone . . . like a femur. And what was with the shooting star? She'd have to do some digging online after she'd posted him tomorrow.

She sure as hell hoped she could find a cause of death for this one.

In East Meadow, Nelson pulled into the parking lot of an assisted-living facility run by the Catholic church and called the Advocate. Ceil, the receptionist in the lobby, recognized him and said, "He's in the common room."

He found Uncle Jim in his wheelchair playing pinochle. Some sort of jury-rigged clamp attached to his paralyzed left arm held his cards. He tossed them on the table with his good right.

Uncle Jim . . . At age seven, after Nelson's parents were snuffed out in a head-on crash on the Jersey Turnpike, he'd had no one. So he'd wound up in the care of Child Protective Services with a round-robin of foster homes looming in his future. Then a man calling himself James Fife showed up—his father's brother, older by two years. He'd never known he had an uncle. Apparently the two of them had had a catastrophic falling out before Nelson's birth and hadn't spoken since.

James had himself declared executor of the estate and moved Nelson into his Brooklyn apartment where he raised him like his own son. His boyhood lacked any and all frills except the live-in housekeeper who saw to his daily needs during his uncle's frequent absences. But Jim always brought Nelson interesting little artifacts when he returned from his trips.

As Nelson grew, Uncle Jim taught him the lore and the ways of the Brotherhood.

Nelson owed Uncle Jim everything—*everything*.

"Nelson?" Jim said in a slightly slurred voice as he looked up. His smile didn't reach the left half of his lips. "What brings you here at night? Everything okay?"

"Everything is finally right. Can we talk?"

"Sure. This hand should put me and Jerry over the top. Meet you in my room as soon as I'm done."

Nelson had to cut through the lobby to reach Jim's quarters. He noticed someone different at the reception desk.

"Where's Ceil?"

The new gal looked up from her rosary beads and said, "Just left. Her shift was over."

Nelson nodded at the beads in her hands. "Nice to see such devotion. Not enough people say the rosary anymore."

"I'm flying to California tomorrow," she said with a shrug and a smile. "I'll need all the help I can get."

"I'm glad to have a good Catholic working in a Catholic facility."

Another shrug. "I don't know how good I am, but I am a Catholic."

Interesting, Nelson thought. "In what way might you not be so good, may I ask? Do you go to church every Sunday and on the Holy Days of Obligation?"

"Oh, I do all that, but I just can't get behind some of the stuff the pope says."

Uh-oh. He ran into these folks all the time, but rarely were they saying the rosary.

"Like what?"

"Well, you know, birth control, like the pill. I don't believe—"

"You don't get a choice what to believe," Nelson snapped, feeling his ire on the rise. "The Catholic faith is not a Chinese menu—'I'll take that one from column A and these two from column B.' No-no. When the pope is speaking on matters of faith or morals, he is infallible."

She blinked. "Yeah, but—"

"There is no 'but.'" He was aware of his voice rising. "If you don't believe in papal infallibility, you aren't a Catholic. You'd do better calling yourself an Episcopalian or maybe a Presbyterian, because you most certainly are *not* a Catholic! Which means you're wasting your time with those beads, so put them away. Or better yet, give them to a *real* Catholic!"

With that he stormed away.

He managed to calm himself by the time he reached Jim's room. The "room" was more like a studio apartment with a full bath, a small kitchen equipped with a little fridge and a microwave, an electric bed nestled in the rear section, and a small sitting area at the front. Jim might have been able to live on his own, but it wouldn't be easy, what with his left side totally useless. He had no family but Nelson, who would have been glad to take care of him. But Jim wouldn't hear of it. He'd found the Advocate, moved in, and was adamant that he liked it here. They served three meals a day down in the dining room, they cleaned his quarters, made his bed, changed his sheets, and he'd made a lot of friends. They bused him to the local Catholic church every Sunday to hear mass.

As basic as it was, the Advocate was not a step down from how he'd lived before the accident. Despite a decent income from the Company, he'd stayed true to his vow of poverty and always lived below his means—like the monk he was.

The Lord does everything for a reason, Jim kept saying. *I'm in His hands.*

Because he was injured while on assignment, the Company paid the monthly fees. Twenty years now . . . the injuries fell into the "shit happens" category: The police report had said a teenage girl applying mascara behind her steering wheel ran a stop sign and plowed into him as he crossed a street in Salt Lake City, of all places.

James Fife was why Nelson had joined the CIA, and why he had become a member of the 536 Brotherhood monastic order. He'd inculcated the truth behind the

Scriptures in Nelson from the moment he entered his care. But though the Brotherhood was a cenobitic order, dwelling—or perhaps hiding—in plain sight in the community, his uncle was fond . . . No, that wasn't the right word. *Attached* was better. Uncle Jim was attached to the old ways.

Nelson would never forget the day he found Uncle Jim scourging himself. He'd gaped at the bloodied flesh of his back as his uncle explained that through the course of Nelson's life his faith would be tested by both the Serpent and the Lord Himself. He would have to be strong to pass those tests. The scourging was a form of discipline, but also punishment in advance for future lapses.

Nelson had never been able to bring himself to engage in the scourge. For that reason, perhaps, he would never ascend to the head of the Brotherhood as his uncle had.

The abbot of the 536 Brotherhood wheeled himself through the doorway. All the other members of the Brotherhood called him "Prior." Nelson called him Uncle Jim.

"Well, Nelson, you certainly did a good job upsetting Mavis."

"Who?"

"The late-shift receptionist."

"Oh. The apostate."

"You can't hold everyone to our standards, Nelson."

"I can if they call themselves a Catholic but are anything but."

"Let's drop it, okay?" Jim smiled. "To what do I owe this pleasure?"

Nelson took a deep breath. Right. He had not come here to argue with a lowly receptionist. He had something so much more important. His hands trembled with anticipation as he pulled the vials from his pocket.

"These."

Jim's eyes went wide. "Is that . . . ?"

"Just found them hidden in a panacean's home."

Jim reached out a shaky right hand.

Just don't drop it, Nelson thought as he placed one in his uncle's palm.

Jim held it up to the light, a look of wonder suffusing his lopsided features as tears filled his eyes.

"This is it . . . really it?"

"Yes."

"Praise the Lord."

Nelson felt his throat thicken and tears start in his own eyes . . . so proud to be able to offer his uncle this moment.

"The essence of evil," Jim whispered. "After all these years . . . with our dwindling numbers and resources, I was beginning to fear I'd never live to see the day."

Nelson knew what he meant. The Brotherhood had once numbered in the thousands, but times had changed. The world became more secular as science pushed God farther and farther away. The quiescence of the panaceans hadn't helped. The Brotherhood existed to oppose them, but with no visible opponent, their ranks had dwindled until they now numbered fewer than two hundred world-wide. Those brothers were well placed to act in case the panacean threat returned—which it had—but still . . .

"I know it's been looking grim," Nelson said, "but you never lost faith."

"I confess that it wavered at times. We were never assured victory. And we still haven't won."

"Not yet, no." Nelson pointed to the vial. "But that is going to lead me to the source so I can remove this scourge once and for all. I just wish . . . "

Jim's gaze flicked toward him. "What?"

"I just wish you could be with me . . . at my side when we win."

"That is not God's plan, apparently."

"As you've always told me, we can't know God's plan. Maybe He let me find two vials for a reason . . . maybe the extra is meant to heal you."

Jim shoved the vial back into Nelson's hands. "No. Never." His expression turned angry. "Why do you tempt me like this?"

"I'm not. I . . . I simply thought you deserved the option."

"To what? Circumvent God's plan?"

"No, of course not. I meant to get back in the fight, back to doing the Lord's work."

"The Lord is testing me. Haven't you been listening all these years? Every affliction has a purpose, every trial is part of His Divine Plan. You've disappointed me terribly, Nelson."

"Sorry. I—"

Jim stared off into a corner of the room. "Leave me now. And take those abominations with you."

Crushed, Nelson pocketed the vials and turned to leave.

"Finish this, Nelson," said his uncle behind him. "You were put into my care for a reason. I was struck down for a reason. Everything in our lives has happened so that you could finish this battle. God has chosen you as his instrument, his sword. Do not let him down."

"Yes, Prior," Nelson said and hurried out.

He'd simply wanted to give his uncle a chance to regain the use of the dead half of his body. Was that so bad?

Yes . . . yes, it was. Jim was right. He should not have tempted his uncle that way. He had acted like the Serpent in the Garden.

And it was good that his uncle had been strong in his heart and faith. Nelson still had two vials, and he knew that two miracle cures would be far more convincing than one. A single cure could be written off as a case of good timing and nothing more. But two . . . a pair of simultaneous cures would put Pickens in the palm of his hand.

9

By the time he'd reached Park Slope, Nelson still hadn't shaken off the bad residual feelings from his visit to Uncle Jim. He parked in his rented spot in an underground lot on 12th Street and walked up to Seventh Avenue. As he hurried along he was accosted by a well-dressed woman handing out fliers.

"Please donate to the NCLR."

"What's that?" he said, pausing.

"The National Center for Lesbian Rights."

Nelson couldn't help making a face. The neighborhood had become a sapphic circus over the past decade or so.

"Lesbians. How quaint."

"We serve the whole LGBT community."

He knew he should hold his tongue and move on, but silence was acquiescence. He felt compelled to speak out.

"Even worse. Why on earth would I want to help promote dykes and sodomites?"

She shook her head. "You can just say no. You don't have to be so intolerant about it."

"Yes, I do, actually. That's what I'm into. You people like to say 'Free to be you and me.' Well, this is me."

He left her with her mouth hanging open.

A few blocks away, he entered an apartment on the second floor of a 7th Street brownstone that still belonged to Uncle Jim, who'd bought it for a song back in the days before Park Slope had become trendy. Nelson had grown up here, and during that time its price tag had rocketed through the roof.

Nelson hung up his suit jacket and went to the refrigerator where he poured himself a glass of chilled white wine from a five-liter jug. He admitted to two weaknesses: good suits and a daily glass of wine. He didn't drink hard liquor, but Jesus approved of wine—even drank it Himself during His time in human flesh—so why shouldn't Nelson occasionally indulge? He favored Carlo Rossi Rhine. He'd tried more expensive varietals and blends but found he preferred the cheap stuff.

Not so with his clothes. The suits were an extravagance, he admitted, but part of the role he had to play in the CIA. The rest of his life was as Spartan as the one his uncle had lived.

Sipping the fruity blend, he looked around his empty apartment and felt a need for someone with whom to share tonight's success. But, like a snippet of melody from a car cruising past on the street, the feeling faded.

No woman in his life—his vow of chastity assured that. He didn't think he was meant for a relationship anyway. He knew many women, of course. Came into contact with them every day. But they didn't tempt him and he was sure most would find him dull. He couldn't argue with that. By current standards he *was* dull. He didn't have a life outside the Company and the Brotherhood and, quite frankly, didn't want one. He maintained a bland exterior that belied the iron will within. He liked an organized life—which translated as *dull*.

Take his taste in art. He knew most would call it "monotonous."

That was because the average person would be blind to its significance. Monotonous? Hardly. The walls were adorned with prints by Thomas Cole, Doré, Masaccio, two by Chagall, and others—even one by "Anonymous."

Someone with narrow vision might find the subject matter repetitious.

True, all the art depicted Adam and Eve's banishment from the Garden of Eden. But that was where the similarity stopped. They were all so different. Even the two Chagalls were nothing like each other—so dissimilar they could have been painted by different artists.

Nelson never tired of his prints. Each piece depicted *the* most crucial moment in human history, the turning point when everything changed and Mankind's fate was sealed for eternity. Most Christian scholars said the Crucifixion and Resurrection of Jesus were more important. But then, for their ilk, the Old Testament barely existed. Nelson took a broader view. In the panorama of Scripture, the Crucifixion and Resurrection would not have been at all necessary had not Eve succumbed to the Serpent's temptations and precipitated Mankind's banishment from the Garden into the outer world of sin and death.

Though Jesus' suffering might have gained forgiveness of Mankind's sins, it did not change God's Plan for Mankind after the Garden: Man was to know pain and grief and suffering and death. Chapter 3 of Genesis contained all anyone ever need know on the subject:

> *Cursed is the ground because of you! In toil you shall eat its yield all the days of your life. Thorns and thistles it shall bear for you, and you shall eat the grass of the field. By the sweat of your brow you shall eat bread, Until you return to the ground, from which you were taken; For you are dust, and to dust you shall return.*

Thus was Man's lot until the Second Coming announced the End of Days, the end of all suffering.

But the panaceans . . . the panaceans and their potion sought to subvert that. One look at their tattoo and who could harbor the slightest doubt that here was a servant of evil? The Serpent itself had center stage, coiling around the Tree of Life, waiting for Eve, while the star of Mankind began its precipitous fall from grace.

Uncle Jim had taught—and Nelson firmly believed—that tracking the panacea was part of God's plan too. But Nelson needed human help as well as divine. Deputy Director Pickens was key to that human help. And now he had the means at hand to bring him into line.

AN INCONVENIENT CURE

1

As soon as Tommy rolled over in bed to shut off his alarm clock, he knew something was different. He stared at his outstretched hand. The fingers had lost their sausagey look and were no longer crooked and twisted. He made a fist—*without pain*.

He jerked upright and checked his other hand: the same.

He swung his legs over the edge of the bed and pulled up his pajama legs. His knees . . . the balloonlike swelling was gone. He could see his kneecaps. Same with his feet. He could see his ankle bones.

"Mom?"

He slid off the bed and put his feet on the floor. Then he pushed his butt off the mattress and stood. His legs were shaking but he felt no pain.

I'm standing. I'm STANDING!

He took a wobbly step. And then another.

"Mom!"

He was halfway to the door when she arrived.

"What's—?"

She froze in the doorway with her jaw dropped open and her eyes showing white all around.

"Look, Mom! Look!" He still had his pajama legs up. "I'm cured! Chet was right! It's a miracle!"

Then his mother went all white and dropped to the floor. She didn't pass out, just landed on her knees. She wrapped her arms around Tommy and began to cry. Tommy cried too. He'd cried himself to sleep last night because nothing had happened and he'd thought Chet had lied. But these tears were different from last night's. Today was the happiest day of his life.

2

"I don't suppose I can go over to Emily's tomorrow night," Marissa said as she poked at her maple-flavored oatmeal.

Laura stood at the kitchen counter with the first of her many cups of coffee for the day and stared at her daughter. Marissa had her parents' blue eyes and her father's strong chin. Before chemotherapy had denuded her scalp, she'd had her mother's ebony hair. It had started growing back in patches but still had a long way to go. Thus the Mets cap that seemed grafted to her head—the first thing on when she arose and the last thing off before bed.

Laura managed a neutral expression even though this sort of thing broke her heart.

"The way you phrased that tells me you already know the answer."

Though Marissa was only eight, Laura did her best not to talk down to her.

"But everyone's gonna be there."

"You can be there by Skype. You're a whiz with Skype."

"It's not the same."

Of course it wasn't. Not even close. But . . .

Seeing tears start to rim her daughter's eyes, Laura moved over and squeezed next to her in the chair. She snaked an arm around her and hugged her close.

"It's not forever, honeybunch. Just till your immune system is running at full speed again. All sorts of viruses that your friends can simply brush off like dust will make you very, very sick."

"I don't care! Everybody's forgetting about me!"

When acute lymphoblastic leukemia struck a year and a half ago, Marissa had been misdiagnosed as having juvenile rheumatoid arthritis. Not unheard of because the early symptoms were so much alike.

But at least ALL was curable. Marissa's leukemia, however, didn't respond to the usual chemotherapy so she'd wound up with a stem-cell transplant—a successful one.

But that meant up to a year of isolation. Laura and Steven and the visiting nurses had had to wear masks around her for the first few weeks. Bottles of hand sanitizer became a fixture around the house.

Marissa's illness had altered not only Laura's quotidian existence, but changed her inside as well: It had shattered her sense of control. She had a medical degree, she should be able to protect her only child from a life-threatening illness. She knew how irrational that was, but still it rankled. She'd tortured herself with guilt—why hadn't she prevented it, what hadn't she done that she could have? Logical or not, a lot of her sense of control and some of her self-confidence had died with Marissa's diagnosis.

The good news was Marissa could be outside in the backyard as much as she wished. She wasn't a Barbie-doll type of girl. Her passion was baseball. Laura's sports growing up had been swimming and cross-country running, and tennis later. She'd never thrown a ball in her life. But she'd learned. Being a single mother—except on alternating weekends—hadn't left her much choice.

So, weather permitting, they played catch whenever

Laura had the time. She'd bought her a baseball return trainer—with a catcher painted on the net—so she could practice her pitching on her own.

Marissa's favorite team was the formerly hapless Mets. Absolutely *loved* the Mets—or "Metropolitans" as she insisted on calling them. And oddly enough, they began winning once she became a fan. She knew the stats of every player and had very definite opinions on who should be played and who should be benched for every game. Laura didn't understand a word of it. All she knew was that baseball players seemed to spend most of their time spitting. She found it disgusting—the dugouts had to be ankle deep in saliva—but it didn't seem to bother Marissa in the least.

"Nobody's forgetting about you. And anyway, Daddy's coming tonight."

A sudden smile. "That's right! I forgot."

Daddy could always trigger Marissa's smile, damn him.

"Right. You wouldn't want to leave him high and dry, would you?"

"No way!"

Right. No way.

Most children of divorce played musical houses between the parents. After the stem-cell transplant, Laura and Steven decided that Marissa should stay in her safe, hygienically structured home environment while they did the shuttling. Steven would arrive Friday for his weekend with Marissa and stay in the guest bedroom while Laura migrated to Steven's Manhattan apartment. Silver-tongued Steven, as he was known, was a big shot in a public relations firm, with a good salary and better bonuses. A lot of fathers would have objected to the arrangement, but Marissa had never been a pawn in the divorce. Steven Gaines—she was Laura Fanning on her medical degree and had kept her name—was sane enough to put his love and concern for his daughter's well-being above his ego. And really, with Laura out of the house, he had his daughter all to himself in an environment that protected her. He'd said he couldn't see the downside.

A sweet loving man. The loving part had turned out to be the problem. *Too* loving. His roving eye and silver tongue had shattered their marriage. Laura hadn't forgiven him for what eventually came to light as not an isolated affair, but a string of them. But she'd put that behind her.

While he was probably still bedding a string of women, Laura had yet to cross paths with any man she found even remotely interesting. She wasn't looking for a relationship anyway. Her daughter and her job filled her life right now.

She and Steven had already gone their separate ways when Marissa fell ill. The leukemia had necessitated more contact with her ex than Laura had wanted, but proved best for Marissa. Laura's hurt and animosity at being betrayed abated, but nothing could bring them back together. The past was past and they'd buried the proverbial hatchet . . .

But Laura knew exactly where.

Her ME salary had been extra money before the divorce and the leukemia. Now, even with generous child support, the regular paychecks and benefit package proved critical for Marissa's extraordinary expenses.

Laura still managed to treat herself now and again. Like the ticket for a new Broadway play Saturday night. She didn't remember the name now—some Irish drama. She didn't care. She loved the theater and didn't mind going alone. She'd seen pretty much everything on and off-Broadway. The ticket was in her shoulder bag.

This was her life now. She'd been in a bridge club, had a circle of women friends who played round-robin tennis. All that stopped when Marissa fell ill. She missed them, but only a little. Marissa was what mattered. Life would be back to normal—whatever that was—before long. Until then, her life was focused on the little girl huddled next to her.

"And doesn't the Subway Series start tonight?"

Laura thought "Subway Spitfest" a better title but kept that to herself. Marissa lived for the Yankees-Mets games. She hated the Yankees almost as much as she loved the Mets.

"Mom," she said with her I-can't-believe-I-have-to-tell-you-this look, "that's not till Monday."

How could I ever forget?

Marissa's tutor, Natasha, arrived then, sparing Laura further embarrassment.

3

"Damn!"

Nelson had never been to the Walter Reed complex before and realized he'd just sailed past the front gate.

He'd shuttled down from LaGuardia to Reagan, then driven a rental into the hills of Bethesda. He was far more familiar with northern Virginia—Langley was there, after all—than Maryland.

He doubled back. No wonder he'd missed it. Hardly his idea of what a world-famous medical center should look like. Maybe because a portion of it was given over to apartments for the wounded warriors. He'd read that if a soldier lost a limb in the line of duty, this was where he was treated, fitted with a prosthetic arm or leg, and trained how to live with it. The apartments were used to help acclimate to the activities of daily life in the real world.

The guard at the gate gave him a map to a parking

area near his destination. Nelson found a spot near the rear of the lot. As he walked toward the front entrance of the red brick building, he began to pray.

Forgive me, Lord, for what is about to transpire. I know the ends do not justify the means, but I am sworn to protect Your Plan, and this is the only way I know to keep my vow.

An MP let him through the glass doors. He checked Nelson's ID, then escorted him to the fifth floor where Pickens waited. Nelson had called him last night with the news that he had two doses of the panacea. Pickens had called back to say he'd set up a test in Ward 35 where the results of the trial could be observed and reported by a disinterested third party.

The deputy director had shuttled down earlier and his expression now mixed anxiety and impatience.

"I can't believe I'm going along with this," he said in a low voice. "The more I think about it, the more foolish I feel."

Already setting us up for failure, Nelson thought.

But he'd been expecting that. By this time tomorrow, one of them would be eating crow for breakfast, and Nelson was planning on scrambled eggs.

"I'm sorry you feel that way, sir. But this is a means to settle our question once and for all, and perhaps do some good in the process."

Pickens gave a dubious grunt. "Ward Thirty-five should only be so lucky."

Ward 35 was reserved for CIA agents injured in the field. Their wounds weren't always from blades or projectiles. Overt murders of agents too often provoked retaliation in kind, and streets littered with dead operatives were to no one's advantage. So removal methods that looked like an illness or an unfortunate accident were devised. The nastiness of the method tended to rise in proportion to the enemy state's rogue status.

"Who did you choose?"

"We had six volunteers," Pickens said. "Doctor Forman helped pick the two sickest. One is Jason Kim. He was dealing with a North Korean group working out of Shanghai when he became infected with a strain of staph that's resistant to every antibiotic they've thrown at it. It's spreading and the docs don't give him a week. The other is Leo Ashcroft: acute radiation poisoning."

"Russians?"

Pickens nodded. "He's tested positive for polonium two-ten. The Russians swear up and down they had nothing to do with it, but the FSB is partial to polonium."

Right. Nelson remembered how they'd used it to kill Alexander Litvinenko back in '06.

"Bastards."

"Ashcroft has less than a week as well."

Nelson knew neither man, but he felt for them.

"Then we've no time to waste, sir. What did you tell them?"

"An experimental treatment. They don't care what it is, they'll try anything. They're desperate, even for something that even you don't know will work."

"It will work."

"Goddamn it, Fife. If—oh, hell, here comes Doctor Forman." He lowered his voice further as a balding, lab-coated man approached down the hall. "I told him the same: experimental and hush-hush. None of your panacea talk, Fife. If asked, just say that you're not at liberty to discuss the treatment."

"Very well."

Nelson never had any intention of mentioning the panacea. The fewer who knew about it, the better. He even wished he could have avoided this little demonstration, but he knew of no other way to get Pickens on board than to rub his nose in the reality of it.

After introductions, Dr. Forman gave Nelson a hard look. "I'm against this, you know."

"I understand," Nelson said.

And he did. Perfectly. If positions were reversed he'd feel the same.

"Just let me make sure I've got this straight," the doctor said. "You say you've got a single compound that's going to treat two completely different conditions."

Nelson nodded. "That is correct."

"The whole idea is preposterous. One man is dying from cellular damage due to acute radiation exposure while the other is infected with a virulent strain of bacteria. So let's just say, for the sake of argument, you have something that can repair genetic damage from alpha radiation. That same something is not going to act as an antibiotic as well. It's crazy."

"If you have something better . . . " Nelson said.

"You know damn well I don't. That's the only reason I'm allowing this trial. That and the fact that they're volunteering. Where is this compound?"

Nelson fished the two vials out of his pocket and held them out.

"Please be careful with them. It's all we've got."

Dr. Forman took the vials and held them up to the light. "This is it? Two doses?"

"One each," Nelson said.

"Insane," the doctor muttered. "Completely insane. What's in it?"

Nelson flicked a glance at Pickens. "I'm not at liberty to give specifics. I can tell you it's herbal."

"Herbal, shmerbal." Forman looked at Pickens. "I know you guys have got your own labs and such, but I expected something a little more scientific."

Pickens shrugged. "It is what it is." He glanced at his watch. "Can we get on with it?"

"I took an oath: 'First, do no harm.' I need to know this stuff is safe."

"Guaranteed," Nelson said.

Pickens added, "We have no wish to see further harm come to Ashcroft and Kim."

The doctor gave them a dubious look. "I've heard that before."

"They're terminal, damn it," Pickens said, flaring. "You said so yourself. We can't do any worse than what has already been done."

Nelson said, "But I will need to witness the dosing."

Forman handed back one of the vials. "You can dose Ashcroft yourself, but Kim is in isolation. You can watch through the glass."

Forman led them along a labyrinthine path to a private room in the bowels of Ward 35. Pickens held back at the door.

"Is he . . . ?"

"Radioactive?" Dr. Forman shook his head. "The polonium gives off alpha particles. Won't even penetrate skin."

"Then how . . . ?"

"We've concluded that someone slipped ten micrograms into a beer he drank."

"Ten micrograms?" The amount startled Nelson. He knew people had been poisoned with polonium-210 before, but . . . "That's next to nothing."

"It's a couple of hundred times the lethal dose when it's in your gut."

They entered and he introduced them to Leo Ashcroft, a pale sickly man propped up in bed with monitor wires running out of his hospital gown. He appeared completely hairless—even his eyebrows were gone.

"You know why we're here, Leo?" Pickens said.

Ashcroft's nod seemed to sap most of his energy.

Nelson held up one of the vials. "You need to drink this. One dose, that is all."

"It'll help?" His voice was a faint croak.

Nelson and Pickens spoke simultaneously.

Nelson: "Yes."

Pickens: "We hope so."

Achcroft raised a shaky hand. "Give."

"Tell you what," Nelson said, suddenly afraid the man might drop the vial. "Let me pour it into your mouth. We don't have any backup doses."

Ashcroft opened his mouth as Nelson pulled the rubber stopper, then poured the fluid onto Ashcroft's tongue and watched him swallow. His eyes bored into Nelson's with a pleading look, then glanced away.

Nelson felt a tug on his arm: Dr. Forman. He followed him into the hall.

"Kim is next. Let's get this charade over with."

He saw Pickens holding out his hand. "The tube. Give it."

"But—"

"Now."

Nelson had no choice but to comply.

They then followed Forman on another twisty-turny path to an isolation area. Through the glass behind a nurses' station, Nelson saw an Asian man lying on a hospital bed, a sheet drawn up to the bottom of his rib cage. His upper body lay bare except for patches of yellow-stained gauze adhering here and there to his arms and torso. The areas without gauze were marred by golf-ball-size swellings, angry red, occasionally oozing. A capped, gowned, masked, gloved nurse attended him. The hand-lettered card on the wall next to the door read *J. Kim.*

Jason Kim and his super-resistant staph.

Dr. Forman said something to the nurse at the desk.

She handed him a small plastic medicine cup into which he emptied the second vial of panacea. The nurse took it, then placed it on a tray jutting from a slot in the wall. She pressed a button and the tray slid through the slot, carrying the cup with it.

The nurse inside must have been expecting it. She took the cup and upended it between Kim's lips. He swallowed, then closed his eyes. Tears slipped from beneath his lids as his chest heaved in a single sob.

"Doctor Forman," Pickens said. "The tube, please."

Forman handed it over and Nelson watched Pickens pocket it. Why was he collecting the tubes?

"I'll never forgive you for this," Pickens said, leaning close and speaking through clenched teeth.

Nelson was more concerned with a Higher forgiveness, but the vehemence in his superior's tone startled him.

"I don't understand. I'm—"

"You're giving them hope where there is none."

He realized he'd lost all credibility with this man. Well, that would change.

"Let's wait until tomorrow, shall we?"

Tomorrow, Lord willing, he would force a one-eighty spin on the deputy director's attitude.

4

Mom had gone a little bit nuts. The first thing she did was call Dad. They'd split right after Christmas last year. Tommy guessed that Dad had stayed around till then so as not to ruin the holidays for him, but they fought so much over every little thing that Christmas was pretty much ruined anyway.

Dad had said he was coming over on his lunch hour

to see for himself. He didn't visit very often, so that was kind of cool.

But nothing was as cool as being able to walk all alone on his own two feet with no crutches or wheelchair. He wanted to go for a run but his legs were too weak. That was why he'd been going to physical therapy. Chet had told him it would keep his muscles from getting astrofeet . . . or something like that. It meant weak and wasted.

Good old Chet. He'd been telling the truth about that magic potion. Tommy had been wrong to think it would work in a flash. It took a whole night, but it could have taken a week or two for all Tommy cared. What mattered was it got the job done.

He owed Chet big-time. Which reminded him . . .

"Hey, Mom," he said, walking—walking!—into the kitchen. "Can we call Chet at—?"

"I already did, honey." She held the phone with her finger poised over the keypad. "I called his work and they said he didn't show up today. They wouldn't give me his home number."

Oh, no. "You didn't tell them what happened, did you. Remember Chet said not to mention him if—"

"I remember. I did tell them you wouldn't be in today, though."

"Why not?" He wanted to see Chet. If he wasn't in now, he'd come in later.

"Because I want you to see Doctor Sklar."

"Awww. I wanna ride my bike."

"Oh, no. You're not ready for that yet."

"Am too!"

"Don't talk back to me. We'll let Doctor Sklar decide. I'm going to call him right now and have him see you. And I'm not going to be put off. He's going to see you *today*."

As she started punching in Dr. Sklar's number, Tommy sidled toward the laundry room. Not a room, really, just a short hall that led to the garage. He heard her start to argue with the receptionist about getting an appointment.

Good. With all her attention fixed on the phone, she wasn't watching him. He pulled his jacket off a hook and slipped into the garage. As he closed the door behind him he reached for the overhead door button—but stopped himself just in time. Mom would hear it and come running.

He pulled on his jacket and wriggled his bike from behind the plastic garbage cans. His folks had wanted to give it to some charity but he'd cried so hard they backed off. He loved this bike, and giving it away . . . that was like giving up hope he'd ever ride it again.

Tommy had never given up hope. And now look at him: back on his feet and ready to roll.

He eased his bike out the rear door into the backyard. Staying close to the garage, he wheeled it around the side to the driveway. It took effort to swing his leg over the rear tire, and he almost fell. But he caught himself and got settled on the seat.

He took it slow down the asphalt driveway and wobbled as he turned onto the sidewalk. His balance seemed a little off at first, but he soon got the hang of it. His legs were weak—astrofeet?—and he had to work extra hard on the pedals, but by the time he reached the end of the block he was flying like someone who'd never been off his bike—nothing like someone who'd been stuck in a wheelchair yesterday.

He wished this was a Saturday instead of a school day. He'd zip over to Eddie Roe's house and show him that the old Tommy was back and they could go biking together again. Maybe he'd head over there anyway. Leave him a note for when he got home from school.

He imagined Eddie's face when he read that Tommy Co-chran had ridden by for a visit.

He made a hard left off the curb and didn't see the truck until its horn blasted in his ear.

5

Deputy Lawson, as was his wont lately, had shown up at the morgue looking for information on the second grower. Gowned and bootied, he'd arrived, manila folder in hand, just as Laura was finishing the postmortem.

"Me again," he said, adjusting his surgical cap around his ears. "I'm very interested in this guy."

Yes. Phil. Again. She hoped he wasn't interested in her as well, because he was destined for disappointment.

Not her type. Sooooo not her type. The neck popping only made it worse. The thought of spending the rest of her life hearing that dull *pop!* every few minutes . . .

"Well, did you find a—?"

"Don't ask."

"Aw, no."

"Aw, yes. As healthy as can be."

She felt his frustration, because it mirrored her own. She'd just finished dictating her preliminary findings. The voice recognition software would have transcribed it into her computer by now. She'd edit it later.

"But he was a pot grower, a druggie. He had to—"

"*Used* to be a druggie," Laura said. "And a big-time user at that."

"How big?"

"Very big. A ton of old track marks, and look at this."

She took a probe and stuck it in the corpse's left nostril. It came out the right.

Phil gave an uneasy laugh. "I'll be." Then he popped his neck.

"This was one hard-core user with emphasis on the past tense: *was*. All the scars are old. We tapped his bladder and ran a quick seven-drug screen on his urine. Not a trace of anything. But that's not the real problem. What's got me stumped is that hard-core IV users ruin their veins, yet his show no sign of sclerosis. And they inevitably pick up a variety of infections along the way, like hep-B, hep-C, HIV that cause all sorts of organ damage, especially to the liver. This guy's liver is like a baby's. I haven't seen the slides yet, but I bet they'll be clean."

The deputy was looking a little seasick. "And the rest of him?"

"Just like the previous. No apparent cause of death beyond cardiac arrest of unknown etiology."

"Don't you find that just a little strange?"

Laura had to laugh. "A little? I find it a *lot* strange. I've never seen an adult body with perfect internal organs. There's always *something* wrong. But to find two adult males—drug growers to boot—back to back with pristine organs?" She shook her head. "Uh-uh. That's . . . that's almost science fiction. That's getting into *X-Files* territory."

An exaggeration . . . she hoped.

"And those tattoos . . . "

"Right. I've got something on those." She whipped the sheet back over the corpse. "My office."

After shedding their protective wear, she led him up to the top floor. A hand-lettered sign on the wall next to her office door read WELCOME TO THE JUNGLE. An old joke, but she'd left it there because it was so apropos.

"Wow," Phil said, staring at her array of tropical plants as he entered. She'd never invited him up before. "That sign isn't kidding."

Half a dozen lush ferns of varying sizes—*Achrosti-*

chum, Dicksonia, and other species—rimmed her office. Her window faced east, allowing the plants to feast on the morning sun and bathe in filtered light the rest of the day. Dr. Henniger, the CME, liked the department on the warm side year-round, so all Laura had to do was keep the plants watered and they grew like crazy.

"They're all from Mesoamerica," she said as she moved behind her desk and awaited the inevitable question.

"Where's that?"

Right on cue.

"Roughly central Mexico down to Costa Rica."

She motioned to the chair on the far side of her desk. As Phil doffed his Stetson and seated himself, she wiggled her mouse to wake her computer.

"One of the assistants here is a graphic artist on the side, works with photos . . . manipulates them every which way. I gave him a couple of high-res shots of the burn vic's back to see if he could clean them up some way that would bring out the tattoo." She opened a desktop folder and clicked on the first jpeg icon. "Here's the best he could do."

A rectangle of burned skin appeared with the tattoo vaguely visible. She clicked the *NEXT* arrow and the same image appeared except that the tattoo had been outlined in yellow, showing the snake, the staff, and the comet. It also showed a horizontal line through the middle.

Next she opened a photo of the second vic's back. No photo tricks needed on this one: all the same elements, except the line here was angled, running through four o'clock and ten o'clock.

"Well," Phil said, leaning forward for a closer look, "that clinches it, doesn't it."

"Something is certainly clinched," Laura said. "But just what remains to be seen."

A neck pop. "The killings . . . they're related."

"I prefer to say 'deaths' for the time being. But I don't think there's any doubt about a relation. But what do these tattoos mean? And why the bisecting lines at different angles?"

"Who knows? Maybe it's a rank insignia."

Laura doubted that—tattoos were not easily changed—but didn't press the point.

"A gang tat that's a variant on the caduceus? Don't they go more for bloody daggers and skulls with flames shooting from the eye sockets?"

"Well, yeah. Usually."

"The caduceus reference implies healing and . . . oh, God." A thought hit her like a punch.

"What?"

"Caduceus . . . healing . . . and the two healthiest corpses I've ever seen. There's a crazy symmetry to it."

"I'm not following."

Just as well that he wasn't . . . too crazy.

"I'm rambling. Don't pay any attention." She moused up another photo, this one of the vic's left palm—the one with 536 drawn on it. "Does 536 mean anything in gang terms?"

"Not that I know of." He leaned closer. "A tattoo?"

"No. Done with a Sharpie. Shortly before his death, from what I can tell."

He shook his head. "Doesn't ring any bells. But I can look into it. In the meantime, I've got a present for you."

He opened the manila folder he'd brought with him and handed her an eight-by-ten color photo. It showed a bare-chested man and a short, dark woman standing before a wall of dense, lush greenery.

"Where did you get this?"

"Believe it or not, the vic had a fireproof lockbox. The arson guys found it in what was left of his bedroom. This was inside it. The original is out for finger-printing. If our guy's in the system, we can ID him."

"Just this? No insurance policy or birth certificate?"

Lawson shook his head. "Not a single identifying document."

She stared at the photo again. "Must have been very important to him."

"I'll say. Um, correct me if I'm wrong, but that sure as hell looks like our second vic in better times."

Laura nodded. The facial resemblance was remarkable, but . . .

"I wouldn't say 'better.' He looks sick and wasted."

Like someone with AIDS . . . because those sure looked like Kaposi's sarcoma spots on his chest.

Phil said, "I meant the living-and-breathing kind of better."

Laura stared at the photo and felt her palms grow just a tiny bit sweaty. This was vic number two, no question. In the photo he appeared to be dying of AIDS. But the man in the cooler downstairs had been hale and healthy and carried none of the stigmata of the disease.

He'd been cured . . . healed. And his tattoo hinted at healing.

What was going on?

"You know something?" Phil said, looking around. "The plants in the picture sorta look like these."

Laura snapped out of her mini daze and shifted her gaze from the man to the background.

"Good eye," she told him. "A couple of them are the same."

"I just wish we could identify the woman he's with. They look pretty chummy. She could give us the low-down on him, I'll bet."

Laura studied her. "She's Mayan."

"Really? You mean like the ancient Mexican Mayans?

I visited one of their pyramids on a side trip when I was in Cancun. How do you know?"

Because I'm half Mayan.

"I just know. Trust me on this." She didn't want to get into her lineage.

"I didn't think they were around anymore."

"They never went away."

"They're still in Mexico?"

"Not Mexico—Mesoamerica."

"Strange how things keep repeating themselves here."

"More than strange. Downright eerie."

A tap on her doorframe made her look up. A sixtyish woman stood there holding a folder. Highlighted hair in a short bob, face prematurely aged from sun exposure, she had a runner's physique with thin, tanned arms poking out of a sleeveless blouse.

Doctor Susan Henniger, Chief Medical Examiner for Suffolk County.

"Sorry to interrupt."

Deputy Lawson, ever the gentleman, leaped to his feet. He knew the CME—he seemed to know everyone— and they exchanged a few pleasantries.

"I'm checking up on those two dead pot growers," he told her, then popped his neck.

Henniger flinched. Obviously she'd never heard him do that.

"Oh, um . . . yes." She turned to Laura. "Were you able to establish a cause of death on the second?"

"Same as the first, I'm afraid: extremely healthy and no detectable trauma."

The chief ME's usually flat expression turned dour. "That's not acceptable."

"I'm well aware of that. Let's hope the myocardium slides shed some light."

"Yes, let's."

She's ticked, Laura thought. She wants answers and I don't have them.

"In the meantime, we have a new arrival. I know you'd rather not do children but we have no one else available."

Posting a child always got to Laura and she ducked it whenever possible.

"How old?"

"Eight. MVA."

She shuddered—just a little—as she took the folder. Marissa's age. At least a car accident vic wouldn't be an involved case. Head or visceral trauma. A quick in and out.

Henniger added, "And besides, the mother asked for you."

"What? Really? Why?"

"Haven't the faintest. At least the cause of death on *this* one won't stump you," Henniger said pointedly, then turned and left.

Laura peeked inside the folder. Tommy Cochran? Why did that name sound familiar?

"A real sweetie, that one," Phil remarked after Henniger was gone.

"She can't help it. It's not an easy job. Everyone wants a cause of death yesterday."

"Or the day before," Phil said. "Gotta get moving. Tell you what. Do me a favor: Scan that photo and see if you can pinpoint the location of the plants."

Laura already knew it was taken on the Yucatán Peninsula, but she said nothing. Her office printer was a three-in-one, so she scanned the photo and returned it to Lawson.

"Great," he said. "I'll crop the girl out and see if one of the papers'll run it. Maybe someone'll recognize him. And can I get copies of those tat photos? And the 536

on his palm? And a little case summary if you've got one.
I'll need to show them to the gang task force. Maybe
someone has seen something like them."

"Sure. I'll email them."

When he was gone, Laura returned to the folder on
the young MVA vic. She read the name again.

Tommy Cochran . . . slowly it came to her. She did
know a Tommy Cochran. She checked the address.
Mastic. Yes, that would be about right.

When Marissa had first fallen ill, her initial diagnosis
of juvenile rheumatoid arthritis was soon proved wrong,
but not before Laura met Tommy and his mother
through a rheumatologist. Tommy's JRA had been well
along by then.

She read further.

" . . . *struck by a truck while riding a bicycle* . . . "

Riding a bike? The Tommy Cochran she'd met
couldn't even walk.

6

"I left the house and the panacean in your hands," Nelson said, pacing his office. It looked much like Pickens's,
only half the size. He fought to keep from screaming.
"All evidence up in smoke: That is the protocol."

He'd left for the airport first thing this morning, never
imagining that the panacean's body hadn't burned.

Brother Bradsher stood by the window, hands in his
pockets. "I'm well aware of that, sir. It's the worst imag-
inable luck. But what was I to do?"

Nelson had no answer for that. The early arrival of
the fire trucks had left Bradsher no choice but to flee the
scene.

"At least the plants were destroyed, right?"

Bradsher nodded. "Completely. They received the bulk of the accelerant."

Good stuff, that accelerant. Burned hotter and cleaner than anything like it. A Chechen terrorist had developed it. The Company had disposed of the Chechen but kept his formula.

"Then we should be good. They may have the panacean's body but there's nothing to find there."

"The ME working the cases has already matched the back tattoos."

"But the first body was immolated."

Brasher shrugged. "She managed."

"You're so sure?"

"We're into her office computer. She has comparison photos."

Nelson didn't like that. He'd never doubted that the cases would be connected, but he hadn't wanted the tattoos made public. They indicated too intimate a link.

"Who is she?"

Bradsher pulled out his smartphone and did some screen tapping.

"Name's Laura Fanning, MD, Deputy Medical Examiner, Suffolk County."

Laura Fanning . . . the name had an oddly familiar ring.

"Have we dealt with her before?"

"Not that I'm aware of."

"Is she going to be a problem?"

"I don't think so. She did discover something we missed." He tapped some more on his phone, then passed it to Nelson. "I took this off her computer. The panacean wrote something on his palm."

A photo: The sight of 536 on the dead skin startled him.

Nelson shook his head. It wouldn't be an issue if his

body had been immolated as planned. This was not
good . . . not good at all. Dissemination of the photo of
the tattoo would put all other panaceans lurking about
on alert. If this 536 photo got out, however, it would
send them scurrying into hiding.

As for the medical examiner, she'd obviously connected the tattoos, but she had no way of knowing about
the panacea or the two corpses' connection to it. That
was the prime concern: Hide all evidence of the existence
of a panacea. It had to remain in the realm of myth until
Nelson had tracked it to its source. He had to be the first
and only to find it. As for the number on the second
corpse's palm, that would mean nothing to her.

So, the ME was not important, though the photo
was.

"We have to disappear those photos."

"Not so easy. I can delete them from her computer,
but the originals may remain in her camera. And she's
already emailed copies to the sheriff's office in Riverhead."

"Do what you can."

"I'll get right on it." But instead of leaving, Bradsher
stood there, shifting from foot to foot. "I had a thought."

The comment struck Nelson as odd. Bradsher was an
excellent field agent—competent, efficient, obedient. He
rarely offered an opinion unless asked.

"What, pray tell?"

"Not a pleasant one."

"All the more reason to voice it."

"All right . . . if the 536 on the panacean's palm
means he knew we were coming—"

"He might have heard of Hanrahan's death, then he
could have seen you getting out of your car and put two
and two together."

"I hope that's the case."

"If not, what's your unpleasant alternative?"

"That he knew he might be next, and so he hid his real panacea and left dummy samples for us."

Nelson felt as if someone had dumped a bucket of ice water over him.

No . . . not possible.

He leaned against the desk as he realized it was indeed possible. And if that were the case . . .

He'd been so sure and in such a rush to convince Pickens of the existence of the panacea that he hadn't done a preliminary experiment.

If the panacean had worked a switch . . .

But why would he do such a thing? What benefit to him?

And yet . . . he'd known they were coming for him— the 536 on his palm left no doubt—and so he might have concocted a placebo as a diversion.

Should that possibility prove true, then Nelson's credibility—and Pickens's opinion of his mental stability—would be forfeit.

"Is it too late to test it?" Bradsher said.

Nelson nodded. "The deputy director and I dosed two of the sickest on Ward Thirty-five."

"Then we can only pray . . . "

"Yes!" Nelson said, dropping to his knees. "Pray with me, Brother."

Bradsher knelt opposite him. They joined hands, and Nelson led them in prayer.

7

Laura sat in the first-floor lobby and waited for Dr. Sklar. The rheumatologist had been treating Tommy Cochran for years; he had been the one to determine that Marissa wasn't suffering from juvenile rheumatoid arthritis but leukemia instead.

Laura remembered how hope and horror had warred at the news. Acute lymphoblastic leukemia was potentially fatal but the newest therapies offered up to an eighty-percent chance of a cure to ALL victims Marissa's age. JRA was incurable.

Dr. Sklar hadn't believed what she'd told him about Tommy's autopsy and had insisted on seeing for himself. So she'd invited him to Hauppauge and called down to the basement to have Tommy's remains removed from the cooler. When Sklar arrived she escorted him downstairs to where a small body waited on a gurney.

After they were both gloved and gowned, she unzipped the top half of the body bag, revealing Tommy's damaged face. Dr. Sklar crouched and inspected the undamaged side.

"That's him," he said with a slow shake of his head. "First JRA, now this. Some kids never get a break. You're absolutely sure he was riding a bicycle?"

"I spoke to a uniform who was on the scene, who spoke to the driver of the truck that hit him: not a doubt."

"This is so bizarre. Let me see the hands, if I may."

Laura unzipped further and bent both arms so Tommy's hands lay on his abdomen.

"This . . . " Dr. Sklar said, a tremor in his voice as he inspected the fingers. "This can't be. He had the typical fusiform swellings last time I saw him."

"Let me show you the knee I opened."

She pulled the zipper the rest of the way down, then snipped the few quick sutures she'd used to close the incision she'd made in the joint. She angled the overhead surgical lamp so he could have a good view.

His voice dropped to a whisper. "The synovium . . . it's pristine. And the cartilage . . . "

"Smooth as a baby's cheek. I wouldn't steer you wrong."

"No-no, I never meant to imply . . . it's just that it's so . . . " He seemed to run out of words.

Laura zipped up the bag again. "I know. Impossible." That word was popping up a lot today.

"But . . . but even if the disease process were somehow miraculously arrested—I'll go so far as to say *cured*—the damage wouldn't be reversed. The articular cartilage would remain pitted, the synovium would remain thickened. But this . . . it's like he was never sick, like he swapped joints with another child." He pulled off his gloves. "Have you spoken to his mother?"

"No. I need to, but I thought I'd give her a day, at least."

"That's good of you."

"I'm a mother too."

"Yes, yes, of course. She called today for an appointment, said he'd been cured. I didn't believe her, of course. If only I hadn't put her off."

"She asked for me to do the post."

Sklar frowned. "That's odd, isn't it?"

"Almost unprecedented. But now I realize that she knew I was an ME, and knew that I'd seen Tommy in a wheelchair-bound state. Any other ME would simply report death by trauma. Only I would wonder what happened to his arthritis."

"Yes-yes. That must be it. Will you let me know what you find out?"

"Absolutely."

He laid a hand on Tommy's bagged body. "Something extraordinary has happened here."

"Tell me about it."

"You need to find out everything you can."

Her gaze wandered to the drawer where the unidentified second grower lay.

"I intend to."

GREEN LIGHT

1

Nelson pulled his rental to a stop in the Walter Reed parking lot. This morning's spot was right next to yesterday's. He turned off the engine and rubbed his temples. Another killer headache. They were always worse in the morning—sometimes they woke him. Lack of sleep wasn't helping. He'd spent the whole night wondering if he'd been played for a sucker by that second panacean. Giving up on sleep, he'd risen before dawn and caught another shuttle to Reagan.

If the two sick agents he'd dosed yesterday showed no improvement, what was his next step? He hadn't a clue. Pickens would never give him a second chance. Might even section-eight him out of the Company.

He looked up and was shocked to see the grim-faced deputy director striding toward him. Pickens had stayed overnight in the D.C. area, so he was undoubtedly fresher. Nelson practically leaped from the car.

"About time you got here," Pickens said.

Nelson checked his watch: *8:52*. Friday morning traffic from Reagan had been hell, but he'd still made it with time to spare.

"I thought we agreed on nine o'clock."

"We did but Forman's been on the phone with me all morning—three calls already. Wants to talk to you."

"About what? What did he say?"

"We'll just have to find out, won't we."

He had a feeling Pickens already knew. Why wasn't he saying anything?

To torture me?

Dr. Forman was waiting in the lobby. He bounded from a chair as they entered, grabbing Nelson's arm and practically dragging him to the elevator.

"What was in that solution?" Forman said as soon as the doors pincered closed.

Nelson glanced at Pickens. "I told you, I'm not at liberty to say."

Forman's face reddened. "Damn it, don't feed me that bullshit! This could be the most important medical find in history. I'm not going to stand by and let—"

"You will do as you are told," Pickens said in a stern headmaster's tone. "You are not in private practice. You are employed by the United States government and when you went to work on Ward Thirty-five you signed an airtight NDA with harsh penalties for breaking confidence. Penalties that will be pursued to the limit should word of what has transpired here slip out."

"But—"

"*But* nothing, Doctor. This is a matter of national security . . . "

As Pickens droned on, Nelson leaned back against the wall of the car and braced himself on the handrail. A surge of relief left him feeling a little weak. The temperature in the car seemed to jump twenty degrees. He loosened his tie and unbuttoned his collar.

"Are you all right?" Forman said, staring at him with a concerned look.

"Just a migraine."

Not a complete lie. The headache still throbbed, but he couldn't very well say he'd been agonizing all night over whether or not the solution would work.

And it *had* worked. Dr. Forman hadn't said it in so many words, but the message was clear: The two agents were better. Just how much better, Nelson could only guess, but right now it was enough to know the solution had worked. He hadn't been duped with a dummy concoction. Those two vials had contained the real thing . . . the real deal.

When the doors opened on the fifth floor, Dr. Forman led them through the halls at near race-walk speed. He first took them to the nurses' desk in the isolation area. The blinds were open and through the glass Nelson saw Jason Kim sitting up in bed, eating from a breakfast tray. He'd been bare-chested yesterday, but now wore a hospital gown. He smiled and waved when he saw Dr. Forman.

"That's Agent Kim?" Pickens said in a hushed tone. "He looks so . . . "

Forman was motioning to Kim to pull his gown down. The agent nodded and complied.

Nelson repressed a gasp. The crimson abscesses and oozing sores of yesterday were gone. All that remained were slightly reddened areas.

"What you're seeing is impossible, gentlemen," Forman said.

Nelson could only stare. His uncle Jim had drilled the existence of the panacea into him since he was a child. But Jim had never been able to secure a sample. He'd seen the results of the panacea post-facto but had never witnessed a cure firsthand. Nelson wished he were here now to bask in this.

"Not impossible if we're witnessing it," Nelson said.

Forman shook his head. "I won't argue that. Seeing isn't always believing, but I'm seeing and I'm believing. The infection is gone. A super staph that thumbed its nose at every antibiotic we threw at it just . . . just upped and cleared overnight."

"I don't see why that is impossible," Nelson said.

Forman turned on him. "Because even if we'd administered a totally new class of antibiotic to which the staph was exquisitely sensitive, it would take time, even after all the bacteria were dead, for the skin inflammation to go down, for the purulence to be reabsorbed. Even if the antibiotic worked instantly, Kim's skin would not—could not look like it does this morning."

"But it does," Nelson said.

He glanced at Pickens's stiff, expressionless face. If his superior was feeling anything, he hid it well.

"It's a fucking miracle," Forman said. "But not the only one. Let's go see Ashcroft."

A slower, shorter walk this time. They entered the room of the agent who had been poisoned with polonium-210. Instead of a pale, drawn figure, fading into his sheets, barely able to lift a hand, they found a bright-eyed man sitting on the edge of his bed and shoveling scrambled eggs into his mouth.

Agent Leo Ashcroft dropped his fork when he saw them. "My God, what did you do?"

Not God's doing, I'm afraid, Nelson thought. But instead of answering, he said, "How do you feel?"

"Wonderful! Weak, sure. I mean, my muscles are deconditioned from all the time in bed, but on the whole, it's like I was never sick. And look." He ran a hand over his scalp. "My hair's growing back."

Nelson leaned in and thought he could make out a faint fuzz in the morning light pouring through the window. He didn't touch it, though.

"What did you give me?" Ashcroft asked.

Pickens jumped in. "A new experimental anti-radiation treatment. All very hush-hush. You're not to mention it to anyone, not even family."

"Anything you say. I . . . " His lips trembled and tears rimmed his eyes. "I thought I was going to be leaving here in a box but Doc Forman said the scan this morning showed no sign of radiation anywhere in my body."

He quickly dabbed his eyes with his napkin. "It's a miracle."

"No," Pickens said. "Just science—hard work and good research."

They left him to finish his breakfast and let Forman lead them to the empty doctors' lounge.

"Two miracles," Forman said. "Two overnight miracles." He jabbed a finger at Pickens. "And don't sling that 'science' bullshit at me. That will work on Ashcroft and Kim because they don't know they were treated with the same compound. They each think they received something specially tailored to their condition. But we three know different. It's not science—it's *anti*-science, because the same compound cannot possibly treat staph and acute radiation poisoning. And no placebo effect in the universe could reverse their conditions overnight. So we've left science and entered the realm of the supernatural now."

Pickens snorted. "Really, Doctor—"

"Really nothing. I'm a devout agnostic but I'm pretty damn sure I've just witnessed a miracle. *Two* of them."

A miracle . . . two of them . . .

Nelson's first instinct was to call his uncle, the abbot of their order, and tell him of the morning's events. But he could almost hear his reply: *You expected something less?*

With a stab of guilt he realized now that somewhere deep in his unworthy heart he had harbored doubts about his uncle's tales of the panacea. He'd thought he believed, and he'd pursued the panacea with unquestioning zeal. But if he'd truly believed all along, why this profound sense of shock at seeing objective proof?

Clearly he had failed a test of faith. He could not go back, for faith was no longer required in the face of such incontrovertible evidence. He could only go forward.

And he would, with greater fervor and resolution than ever.

"Have you got any more of that stuff?" Forman said. "Because I've got patients who need it."

Nelson shook his head. "Sorry. That was it."

"Well, you can make more, can't you?"

Nelson looked away. "It's complicated."

"'Complicated,' my ass! Either you can or you can't!"

"We are tracking the source. We hope to be able to secure more in the near future."

"Hope? *Hope?* How can—?"

"You'll just have to trust us," Pickens said.

Forman laughed. "That's a good one!" He pointed to Pickens again, then Nelson. "You've found something that defies logic as well as analysis."

"Analysis?" Nelson said. "What do you mean?"

"I took a droplet left in Kim's dosing cup and put it through the center's spectrograph."

Nelson wanted to shout *NO!* No one must know the components.

"You had no right!" Pickens said, reddening. "I'm going to have to impound—"

"Relax," Forman said. "There's nothing to impound."

Pickens said, "I'll decide what—"

"We found nothing." He began pacing the lounge, flapping his arms like a chicken. "The analysis was a complete bust. Oh, we got water, of course, and believe it or not, we found clay, sand, and humus—in other words: dirt. Really, gentlemen . . . dirt? Under what conditions did you mix that stuff? But the machine kept crashing. I don't know how you did it, but you've got a compound that we can't break down into its components—at least not with the equipment available."

Nelson dropped into a chair to hide his relief. Maybe he would never learn the mystery ingredient, but at least Forman didn't know.

"You'll be under review," Pickens told the doctor. "Count on that. In the meantime, remember the consequences for letting any of this out."

Dr. Forman had wandered behind Nelson.

"First off, I'm loyal to my word. Second, I would only be jeopardizing my reputation as a rational human being by repeating this madness. I—"

He stopped and Nelson realized he was bending closer, staring at the back of his neck.

"What?"

"Have you had that looked at?"

"Had what looked at?"

"That mole on the back of your neck. Looks a bit sketchy to me."

On its own accord, Nelson's hand darted to his nape. "Sketchy? What's that supposed to mean?"

"Well, it's on the big side with an irregular border, and it's got three shades of dark brown, one almost black. Have it looked at."

"Never mind that," Pickens said. "Remember what I said." He turned to Nelson. "My car. Now."

They made the trip to the parking lot in silence. Nelson hadn't been able to read Pickens through all this. After what the deputy director had just seen, he couldn't go on denying the existence of the panacea. Or could he?

As they walked he found his hand drifting to his nape. A "sketchy" mole back there? He'd had no idea.

Pickens broke the silence as soon as they'd slammed the doors of his Navigator.

"I suppose you feel you're owed an apology."

Damn right, he was, but this was hardly the time for *I told you so*.

"Not at all, sir. I'd have been deeply dubious myself were positions reversed."

"Yeah, well, I've got to admit I did think you were a

few fries short of a Happy Meal." A quick, mechanical grin. Was Nelson supposed to laugh at that? "But after what I saw today, I'm a believer."

"It's incredible, isn't it."

He shook his head. "No argument there, Fife. Whatever it is, *we* have to control it. But what *is* that stuff?"

"That's what I'm working to find out."

"Yesterday I had our own lab run an analysis on the residue in the tubes. I'd like to think we have better equipment than Walter Reed—in fact, I like to think our equipment is second to none. But whatever that stuff is, it crashed our system as well."

"How is that possible?"

"The lab boys say its molecular structure does not compute. It's totally different from anything they've ever seen. Like it's from outer space."

If you only knew, Nelson thought.

Pickens shook his head. "We've run into a wall on that approach, and that's a goddamn shame. Because if we can't nail down its molecular structure, we can't synthesize it."

Nelson balled his fists. Excellent. How could he wipe it out if the Company could synthesize it?

"That leaves going to the source and bringing in one of these . . . these . . . "

"Panaceans."

"Right. We need one of these guys alive to find out how they make it."

"We know the process up to a point, sir."

Pickens looked at him. " 'We'? What 'we' are we talking about here? The only 'we' is you and me and the Company."

Had to tread carefully here.

"Sorry. I was referring to my uncle Jim and me. He—"

"Jim Fife again. We keep coming back to him."

"Well, he was the one who identified the panaceans.

He managed to grow some of their plants in his backyard and he would cook them up just like they did, but
the results were worthless. They *must* add something,
but they've all denied it. Even under . . . duress."

"Interrogation methods have improved quite a bit
from your uncle's time—as you well know."

Nelson nodded. The Company had a new infusion
that could make the most reluctant interrogatee positively loquacious.

"Not much use when they drop dead rather than
talk."

"You need to Taser one as soon as you find him—
knock him out before he can stop his heart or whatever
they do."

"I'll need manpower and resources, sir."

"Don't worry. You've got them. I'm stopping at
Langley. As soon as I get there I'll clear you for a black
account."

After all these years—a green light and a black fund.
That was something he could report to his abbot. But
instead of giving a mental cheer, he was thinking about
the back of his neck.

A "sketchy" mole? Really?

2

"There's a Helen Cochran on line three-two," said the
front desk receptionist. "Says she must speak to you.
Very insistent."

Laura frowned. Helen Cochran? Who—oh, God. She
jabbed the 32 button.

"Hello, Mrs. Cochran. I'm so sorry about Tommy."

"*Oh . . . yes.*" A muffled sob. "*Thank you. It's been . . .
hard.*"

"I can't even imagine."

"And your daughter. Is she . . . okay?"

"As good as can be expected, thanks. She had a stem-cell transplant and so far so good. She's still got a ways to go."

"Why does God try parents like He does?"

Parents? Laura thought. It's not exactly a picnic for the kids.

Mrs. Cochran heaved a sigh. *"I won't keep you. I—"*

"No-no. I was going to call you."

"You were?"

"Yes. I . . . " This was so hard to say to someone she knew. "I did the autopsy on Tommy."

"Oh, I was hoping you would. I asked for you because you'd met Tommy a few times. You knew of his condition. Is that why you were going to call me? What did you find?"

"Only injuries from the accident. It was what I didn't find . . . "

"You didn't find any arthritis, did you." A statement, not a question.

"No. Not a trace."

"That's why I'm calling you. I saw the article in the paper this morning with the picture of the unidentified dead man. I recognized him."

They'd published the photo? She must have missed it. Laura grabbed a pen, wondering how this middle-class woman from Mastic would know a member of a pot-growing gang. But this job had long since got her used to the weird connections between the most disparate individuals.

"You know his name?"

"I do. He's Chet Brody. He was helping with Tommy's physical therapy."

A name . . . she finally had a name.

But wait. A guy with a respectable day job didn't jibe with Lawson's drug gang theory.

"He's a physical therapist?"

"*Just an assistant. And maybe more. He's the one who cured Tommy's arthritis.*"

What?

"How-how-how did he do that?" Listen to me—stuttering like Porky Pig.

Mrs. Cochran told the story of Chet showing up at her door two days ago with a vial of strange fluid that she threw away but Tommy drank. The next morning, Tommy awoke arthritis free.

"*It was a miracle,*" she said. "*That's the only way I can explain it.*"

Dr. Sklar had called it impossible. But "miracle" and "impossible" were codependent, weren't they. Couldn't have one without the other.

As Mrs. Cochran had been telling her story it slowly began to dawn on Laura that here was her fantasized connection between the arthritic child with perfect joints and the world's healthiest ex–drug addict.

"What did Chet say was in the vial?"

"*All he said was that it was herbal.*"

Herbal . . . maybe he hadn't been growing *Cannabis*. But if something else . . . what? What on Earth?

"You wouldn't happen to have the vial it came in, would you?"

"*It's in the county dump, I'm afraid. I put the garbage out that night. After seeing Tommy the next morning I went to look for it but the truck had already come by.*"

Laura gave her desktop a quick double pound. Damn. She would love to know the chemical composition of that "miracle" potion.

Laura extended her condolences again and thanked the woman for taking the time to call despite the tragedy of her son.

"*How could I not call? Chet allowed Tommy a few*

*pain-free hours of happiness before he died. I couldn't
let him go to an unmarked grave.*"

Some people . . . Laura thought as she hung up . . .
some people are too good for this world.

She'd decided not to ask her in to identify Brody's
body. Better to track down some family member or a
coworker for that.

As for the name, she went straight to Dr. Henniger
with the news.

"We've had a hit on that photo in the paper," she said
as she entered the CME's office.

Henniger gave her a sour look. "Well, at least we're
getting a hit on something. No cause of death yet?"

She knew damn well there wasn't. "Not yet."

Henniger slapped her desktop. "We look like ama-
teurs here, Laura." She drummed her fingers, then, "All
right, what about the photo?"

"A caller said his name is Chet Brody and he works
for a Moriches physical therapy place."

Henniger was nodding. She held up a slip of paper.
"That matches with a call from a Miriam Brody in Williamsburg. But she says his name is *Chaim* Brody and
he's her son."

"Chet . . . Chaim . . . close enough."

"The wrinkle is she's Orthodox and it's Friday and
she wants to get him in the ground before sundown.
You ready to release him?"

Laura nodded. "We've got all the tissue we need. If
it's okay with the PD, we can let him go as soon as she
gives us an official ID. I'm ready to release Tommy Cochran too."

"The MVA boy. Good."

"I found a strange connection between Brody and the
Cochran child."

She gave her chief a quick rundown of her conversation with Tommy's mother.

"Odd," said Henniger. "Very odd."

"I feel I should write it up for the record—for future reference and so the connection doesn't get lost—but I don't know where to file it."

"Attach it as an addendum to both reports. By the way, what about the burn victim?"

"Beyond the fact that he and Brody are connected by arson, tattoos, and indeterminate cause of death, all we have is the name on the rental agreement. We'll have to wait on Hanrahan's dental records to confirm the ID."

"Put a rush on those. I want this tied up ASAP."

Laura wondered if they'd ever fully tie up these cases.

3

Nelson read the newspaper article and wanted to scream.

Before shuttling back from D.C., he'd wrangled a same-day appointment with a surgeon in Forest Hills who had been doing clandestine freelance work for the Company for decades. She was mostly retired now, but liked to keep her hand in. He'd said he just needed her to take a quick look at the mole on his neck to see if he should be concerned.

Forest Hills was a short ride from LaGuardia and he'd arrived a little early. To pass the time in her empty waiting room he'd picked up a copy of *Newsday* lying on an end table. He was glad he did, but almost wished he hadn't.

Nothing surprising in the first few pages: Police were investigating the suspicious suicide of a local woman named Christy Pickering, the author of some new best-seller called *Kick* was speaking at the Massapequa library, blah-blah-blah until he'd come to the photo.

This nobody county deputy medical examiner, this Laura Fanning, had released a photo of the second dead panacean, Brody. The man in the photo looked thinner and frailer than the Brody he'd seen in the trailer, but fill out those gaunt cheeks and no question they were the same person. He didn't know where she'd found it, what with his trailer burned to ashes.

This was bad. Nelson didn't know how many of Brody's fellow panaceans knew him by sight, but if they did, they'd hightail it into hiding. The only thing worse would be publishing the tattoo on his back. Even panaceans who had never heard of Brody would know that tattoo. The result could mean a long, long time before Nelson tracked down another.

A door opened at the end of the narrow waiting room and an elderly woman appeared. She motioned to him.

"Come."

He entered an examining room where she indicated an odd-shaped table at its center.

"Where is this mole?" she said in her French accent, so it came out *Whair eez zis mole?*

Dr. Adèle Moreau was in her seventies if she was a day. Painfully thin with very short, almost mannish orange hair.

"On my neck." He'd removed his tie and now he pulled down the back of his collar. "Right there."

She adjusted an overhead light and stared.

"Remove the shirts."

"Can't you see it? It's right there."

"It needs biopsy. You want blood on your shirt?"

"Biopsy? Really?" He pulled off his dress shirt and T-shirt. "You're going to do surgery right now?"

"Just punch biopsy. Little piece. We send it out for a look."

"You really think it needs it?"

"*Mais oui.*"

He wasn't too crazy about the certainty in her tone.

He heard her rattling instruments behind him. "You have no jokes about my name?"

"Sorry?"

"Doctor Moreau—everybody makes the jokes."

"I apologize. I don't know what you're talking about."

"*The Island of Doctor Moreau*—a famous novel."

"I don't read fiction. Made-up people, made-up events. Waste of time."

She *tsk*ed. *"Quel dommage."*

Let's stick to *me,* he thought.

"What do you—?"

"Hush while I sterilize the skin."

He felt something cold and wet on his neck.

"Hold still," she said, then a sharp, stabbing pain.

"Damn!" he cried, trying not to jump. "What did you do?"

"I told you: biopsy."

"You ever hear of local anesthesia?"

"That is for babies."

He turned and saw her dropping a tiny bit of bloody flesh into a specimen jar half filled with clear fluid.

"What do you think it is?"

"Does not matter what I say, only what microscope say, *n'est-ce pas?*"

She taped gauze over the biopsy site, then felt around his neck. As her questing fingers lingered in a spot, she made a *hmmmm* sound.

"What?"

"Feel here."

He reached up and pressed the area. "I don't—"

She guided his fingers. "Little lump, *oui*?"

He felt it. Like a lima bean under the skin. "What—?"

"A lymph node—enlarged lymph node. Get dressed."

His fingers lingered on the lump, then he pulled his undershirt back over his head.

"But if you had to guess, could my mole be a—what do they call it?—a malignant melanoma?"

"If it is not, I shall change my name to Anke and speak German only for the rest of my life."

Nelson felt a coldness seep through his stomach. A malignancy . . .

"No, really."

"Really." She began scribbling on a prescription pad. "Also I am sending you for chest X-ray."

"Why?"

"You will want to see if it has spread."

He noted the "you" rather than "I" or "we." Not her problem.

"Why the chest? You didn't even listen to my chest."

"It spreads to the lungs."

"The tumor?"

"Of course the tumor. What else do we talk about?"

"You're that sure?"

"The lungs are the Riviera of melanoma. An easy trip so it goes there whenever it can." She tore off the script and handed it to him. "Go to any hospital or imaging center. No appointment. They will do this as a walk-in."

"But what if it hasn't spread?"

"That is good. Wide excision on your neck may give you cure."

"But—"

She shoved the biopsy jar into his hands. "Take this to CIA lab. Much faster than commercial."

"But—"

She held up a hand. "I can tell you no more because I know no more. We are *finis*."

She guided him to the waiting room and shut the door behind him. Josef Mengele had probably had a better bedside manner.

Nelson stood in the close, empty space and took deep breaths to gather himself.

Okay. If the mole was malignant, he'd deal with it. Do that "wide excision" she'd mentioned if it hadn't spread—although he'd be damned if he'd let her touch him again. And if it *had* spread, well, medicine was doing amazing stuff with cancers these days.

As he headed for the outside, his gaze fell on the copy of *Newsday*. He snatched it up and tucked it under his arm. Time to refocus on what was really important. That medical examiner . . . Laura Fanning . . . she'd gathered too much evidence that needed to be neutralized.

And why did her name sound so damn familiar?

As soon as he stepped outside he put in a call to Bradsher.

4

Laura looked up at the knock on her doorframe. Juan, one of the morgue attendants, stood there: dark, twenty-something, with one of those dorsal-fin hair combs.

"Sorry to bother you, Doc," he said.

"What's up?"

He held up a leather belt. "Word came down that the family didn't want two-oh-three's clothes."

"Two-oh-three?"

The attendants tended to refer to the cadavers by the number of their cooler locker.

"Brody."

Chaim Brody's mother and brother had come by to identify the body. Miriam Brody told her that Chaim had been disowned by his father for being gay and was unsuccessfully treated for non-Hodgkin's lymphoma—common with AIDS.

"If that's his," she told Juan, "you can just toss it—or keep it if you like."

Some of the attendants weren't squeamish about taking discards from the dead. Sometimes, when it came down to a choice between their closet and the landfill, their closet won.

"I ain't got no use for it, but as I pulled it out of the loops I noticed there's something written on it."

That piqued her interest.

"Let me see."

He handed it over. "On the inside."

A string of letters ran the length of the inner surface of the leather, vertically along the line of the belt. She held it up by the buckle and let it dangle.

L
O
A
ī
X
O
ī
i

ī
L
X̄
i

i

i

v

She turned it around for the attendant to see.

"Mean anything to you?"

He shook his head. "Just a bunch of letters."

She twisted it back toward her. Yes, just a bunch of letters, but somewhere in the back of her mind a little voice screamed *CODE!*

Brody's body was gone but the mystery of his death, and the mystery of the solution or elixir or whatever he gave Tommy Cochran, remained. Not to mention the disappearance of his AIDS, his lymphoma, and his sarcoma. She'd notified the police that she was releasing the body and the detective she spoke to said they'd been unable to develop any leads on who had torched the two growers' digs.

Still an open case—very open.

"I'm going to keep this," she said. "Might be evidence."

Juan shrugged and waved as he left. "All yours."

"Oh, and thanks for bringing it by."

He was gone but she heard a faint *"De nada"* from down the hall.

She stared at the letters. Definitely a code. But why so repetitious? And why vertical?

She rolled it up and stuck it in her shoulder bag.

5

Looking rather military—after all, he'd spent time in Iraq with the First Brigade of the 82nd Airborne—Bradsher stood before Nelson's desk, giving his report.

"As instructed," he was saying, "we penetrated the medical examiner's LAN. Wiped both Brody's and Hanrahan's tattoo images from the system. Same with the sheriff's office. I should mention that this ME woman seems very interested in the tattoo. She's accessed the Brody tattoo many times since loading it into the system."

"What's her name again?"

"Laura Fanning."

Again the feeling that he'd heard her name before.

"What do we know about her?"

Bradsher fiddled with his phone, then began reading: "Laura Fanning, age thirty-seven, divorced, one female child, age eight. Did freelance bioprospecting in Mexico and Central America after medical school, then married and took a pathology residency at NYU."

"Where'd she go to school?"

"BYU, then Stritch Medical at Loyola in—"

"Wait-wait! BYU? Is she from Utah?"

Bradsher nodded as he stared at his phone. "Born and raised in SLC. Is that important?"

Could it be her? Twenty years after turning his life upside down, was it possible she was back to complicate it again? He shook it off. Later . . .

"Nothing. So you've seen to it that she won't be accessing it again."

"Let's hope not, but we can't say for sure."

The faint buzz of relief Nelson had felt that the photo was gone dissipated like steam.

"What's that supposed to mean?"

"Well, there's always the matter of a printout. And our other problem is that we don't know where the tattoo photo originated. Did she use a department camera or her smartphone?"

"I'd assume a department camera."

"That's logical, sir, but the newer phones take high-res photos and are always close at hand, so it's possible she used hers. The photo might still be on the camera's SD card."

"Which will allow her to upload it again. Any suggestions?"

"I've arranged for someone to visit the medical examiner's premises tonight."

"Someone from the Company?"

"Yes. Very competent. I'm thinking of having him

bug her office while he's there—in case she's got any more surprises."

"Excellent. Do it." This was why he liked Bradsher: thorough and efficient. "But what about the potential of photos on her phone?"

"I wanted to discuss that with you. We could have someone steal it, make it look like a mugging."

That was always an option, and in this case it felt like a good one. Smartphones were a popular target.

"Very well. But I'd rather not have the Company involved in that."

"I agree, sir. One of our own?"

"Yes. Find a brother who's fit for the job."

"I'll see to it."

"And speaking of photos, the one of Brody in the paper looked cropped."

Bradsher nodded. "Good eye, sir. I saw the original on Fanning's computer. He was with a native woman."

"Do you have it?"

"I saved it along with the others."

"Good. See if we can identify her, and where the photo was taken."

"You think she might be connected to the panaceans?"

"Well, look at it this way: He appears sick in the photo, and yet he looked perfectly healthy when we cornered him. Remarkable improvement between the time the photo was taken and Wednesday night. It's circumstantial, but enough to make me suspicious."

"Then she might be a panacean as well."

Nelson nodded. "My thoughts exactly. Perhaps Brody's gateway into the cult."

Bradsher's expression turned grim. "I'll get right on it."

6

When Bradsher was gone and Nelson was alone, he slumped back in his chair. It had taken every iota of will to stay focused on the problems at hand. The headache had calmed since this morning—still there, but bearable. The potential time bomb lurking on his neck kept intruding on his thoughts, usurping his concentration. He could almost feel it growing. He knew that wasn't possible, of course, but still . . .

He touched the bandage. Tender. With or without anesthesia, the biopsy spot would be sore now. But Dr. Moreau couldn't be bothered at the time. Called him a baby. Snail-slurping bitch.

But why had she been so quick to order a chest X-ray? Did she really think . . . ?

He didn't want to borrow trouble. He couldn't be seriously ill. But he'd gone to Forest Hills Hospital from her office anyway and presented her prescription to the radiology department. After a short wait they'd done the chest X-ray—turn this way, hold your breath, turn that way, hold your breath, good-bye. No one would tell him anything about the results. *Call your doctor tomorrow.*

But she wasn't his doctor. No way was that icy bitch his doctor. Still, she'd ordered the test, so the results would go to her.

He'd then called Dr. Forman down at Walter Reed to tell him he'd had the mole biopsied and was sending the tissue down to have him do whatever they do to biopsies. Forman had tried to slough him off, saying he didn't take private patients, but Nelson had pushed him hard, arguing that he was the one who had spotted it and the least he could do was expedite the diagnosis. Forman finally relented. As soon as Nelson had reached his office, he overnighted the specimen jar to Bethesda.

So now all he could do was wait. And while he was waiting, he could check out this Laura Fanning. The hunt would provide a little distraction from his health concerns.

With the help of the Internet it took only a few minutes to access the right issue of the Salt Lake City *Tribune* from twenty years ago—he would never forget that date—and the story about a pedestrian run down while crossing South State Street.

Yes! The driver's name was Laura Fanning. No picture of her but her age was given as seventeen. Fast forward to Laura Fanning, MD, with the Suffolk County ME. Same year of birth.

No doubt about it: The driver who'd hit Uncle Jim and left him partially paralyzed, ending his career, had performed the autopsies on the two panaceans Nelson had been chasing.

How does something like this happen? How did—?

His cell phone rang. He didn't recognize the number, but the 347 area code was local. Could be Queens . . . Forest Hills . . .

His finger shook as he tapped the *talk* button.

"Allo? This is Agent Fife?"

"Speaking, Doctor Moreau."

"You recognize my accent, oui?"

"Of course. You're calling to inquire how my neck is feeling?"

"Why would I do that? It is only a biopsy. No, I have your X-ray report."

So soon?

"And?"

"Not good. The tumor has spread to your lungs."

Nelson repressed a sudden urge to vomit.

"H-how bad?"

"Any spread to the lungs is bad. You must immediately see an oncologist."

"Can you . . . ?" His thoughts were scattering in all directions. "Can you fax me the report?"

"I have it in email. I can forward."

Email . . . that explained how she'd got it so fast. Those radiologists probably took one look and sent it right out. He gave her his private email address—he didn't want to use the Company's.

"Be aware, Mister Fife, that if it is in the lungs it is in other places as well. Good-bye."

The words themselves might have conveyed concern had they not been delivered in a better-have-that-taillight-fixed tone.

He watched his smartphone for the little @ symbol that indicated mail in his AOL account, then opened it. The phrases "mass in the right middle lobe" and "hilar adenopathy" from the X-ray report bounced around the inside of his skull without sticking, leaving no trace of meaning other than *This can't be good.*

He forwarded it to Dr. Forman. With the X-ray report plus the pending path report, he'd surely be able to offer an idea of what Nelson was up against.

He hadn't slept last night for worrying about whether the panacea would work. He knew he was looking at a second sleepless night, but this time for an entirely different reason.

But he had an important stop to make before he reached his bed.

7

At the Advocate, Uncle Jim greeted him cordially, saying, "We shall forget Wednesday night ever happened."

That was perfectly fine with Nelson. Hiding his continuing wonder at the outcome, he told him how the successful demonstration of the panacea had prompted an ops fund from Pickens. He withheld mention of the melanoma, instead producing a photo of Laura Fanning.

"Yes," Uncle Jim said, staring at the facial close-up. "That's her. No way I'd forget those eyes."

Nelson knew what he meant: Laura Fanning's pale blue eyes set in her dark face were striking, almost unsettling because they were so angelic. And yet . . . he sensed an air of sulfur about her.

"Do you think it's the Serpent's doing—involving her in the Brotherhood's quest—your *life's* quest?"

He shrugged his good shoulder. "Perhaps. But if so, I'm sure she's unaware."

The remark took Nelson by surprise. "She ruined your life, made it impossible for you to pursue the panaceans. How do we know she's not one of them?"

"I prefer to think of her as an instrument of the Lord to visit this trial upon me. Because that made you step up and be His sword."

As much as Nelson loved the idea of being the Lord's right arm, His archangel on Earth, he couldn't let Fanning off that easily.

"Still . . . "

"Do you know she visited me almost every day when I was in that Salt Lake City hospital?"

"To gloat?"

"Not at all. Mostly she cried and kept saying how sorry she was. She was a child and devastated by what she had done. I've forgiven her, Nelson. Apparently you haven't."

"I don't know if I can."

"You must. Even if the Serpent has manipulated events so that those two panaceans wound up on her autopsy table, it is not her doing. The Serpent is using her to distract you. Don't let it succeed. As your abbot, I am telling you to stay focused. Keep your eye on the prize."

"No worry about that, Prior. I'm close, and getting closer."

Jim leaned back and looked at him. "And what then, Nelson? If you succeed and send the panacea back to hell, what will you do with your life?"

The question took him by surprise. "I . . . I'll . . . "

"Do you even *have* a life, Nelson?"

He was totally off balance now. "Of course I do. I have the Brotherhood and the Company."

"But nothing else, right?"

"I've no room for anything else."

Especially not now with melanoma in his lungs.

"I and the rest of the brothers appreciate your zeal. But let me speak as your uncle now instead of your abbot. Your first duty is to the Brotherhood. Your second duty is to the Company because the Company provides access to intel that allows you to be proficient in your first duty. But you also have a duty to yourself, Nelson."

"I take care of myself."

"I don't mean staying in shape and eating right. I was like you until the accident. Then I no longer had the Company and, although I'm still abbot of the Brotherhood, my role is largely advisory. The accident left me facing a void."

"All the more reason not to forgive Laura Fanning."

"To forgive is divine, remember? But I'm talking about *you* not ending up like *me*. I look back and wish I'd done other things with my life. Besides raising you, I don't have any fond memories to look back on—I was so consumed by the Brotherhood and the Company, I didn't do anything else."

Nelson felt at sea. "But . . . I joined the Brotherhood and the Company to continue your work."

"And I appreciate that, I do, but I wish you'd get a life outside all that. Tell me, Nelson: What do you do for fun?"

"Fun?"

"Yes, *fun*. As in a pleasurable activity with no purpose other than the enjoyment it brings. Like scuba diving or hiking or playing basketball or reading a thriller. You know: *fun*."

Fun wasn't on his agenda. And fun was overrated. Mostly wasted time.

"A good job well done is fun." He knew that sounded lame even as he said it.

Jim shook his head. "You haven't a clue, have you? Trust me: If something disables you, you'll wish you'd taken a little time for fun. I know I do." He looked away. "I also wish . . . "

"What?"

"That I'd gone easier in my dealings with some of those panaceans."

"But they're pagans, servants of the Serpent."

"I know that, son, but I *hated* them with such a passion. You've heard the saying, hate the sin and not the sinner?"

"Of course."

"Well, I was blind to that. I hated the sinners as well. But as I look back I wonder if they were sinners at all."

Nelson couldn't hide his shock. "What?"

"Hear me out. A mortal sin requires a grave matter—which is met by attempting to sabotage the Divine Plan—full consent—which they certainly gave—and sufficient reflection. I'm no longer sure they met the last requirement."

"How can you say that?"

"It means you have to know you're doing wrong. I've come to realize that none of them believed they were doing wrong. They were dupes, servants of the Serpent, certainly, but *unwitting* servants. The ones I interrogated and condemned to the Leviticus Sanction . . . yes, they were pagans, they weren't saved, but they meant no harm. They only wanted to heal and I . . . I hurt them."

"You were doing the Lord's work."

"I keep telling myself that."

"'Thou shalt not suffer a witch to live.' Remember?"

"Oh, I remember, all right. I remember all too well." He glanced at the clock. "They serve dinner early here. I'd better get going."

Nelson rolled Uncle Jim to the dining room and then wandered back to his car in a daze.

What had happened to Uncle Jim? Was he getting senile? Wishing he'd been *easier* on the panaceans? He was the Brotherhood's abbot and their mission was to scour those pagans from the face of the Earth.

And his forgiving Laura Fanning . . . absurd. Maybe the injury she'd inflicted was softening the rest of his brain.

As soon as he reached the car, he phoned Bradsher.

"Have you chosen who will acquire the doctor's phone tonight?"

"*I was just speaking to him. He's on his way.*"

"Call him again. Tell him to plant a locator on her if he can. I want to know her every move."

"*Will do.*"

"And one more thing."

"*Yes, sir?*"

"Tell him to hurt her—hurt her bad."

8

It all happened so quickly.

Laura pulled into her driveway and stopped before the garage as usual. The motion-activated security light over the door came on, illuminating the area. A remote for the door clung to her visor but she didn't use it. The clutter in the garage had long ago banished her car to the elements.

She gathered up her things and stepped out onto the asphalt. She was shutting her door when a heavy weight rammed her back, slamming her against the car. The blow knocked the wind out of her, leaving her barely able to breathe, let alone cry out for help.

She felt her bag ripped from her shoulder and made a grab for it. She got a grip on the strap and was pulled around to face a thin man with scraggly hair and beard wearing a hooded sweatshirt.

"Give it, bitch, or you're gonna get hurt!"

A very aware part of her knew that was just what she should do—let him take it. Nothing in it was irreplaceable. But another, more primitive part was screaming, *This is mine and you can't take what's mine!*

So she hauled back on the strap.

And he swung at her face. She flinched away, allowing just a glancing blow, but still pain shot through her jaw, shocking her. Her fingers loosened their grip and he yanked the strap free. It took a second or two for her vision to clear, but he wasn't running. In fact he had his fist balled for another blow. But before he could throw the punch, someone grabbed his arm and spun him around.

Laura watched the second man push the first back to arm's length, then double him over with a punch in the gut, followed by powerful blow to the back of his neck. He dropped like a sack of cement, landing on Laura's shoulder bag.

The second man stepped toward Laura. He was wearing a dark blue warm-up with two darker stripes down the sides of the legs and arms. A pair of earbud wires dangled from his breast pocket. Dark hair and a square jaw.

"You all right?"

"I-I think so."

She wasn't. Not really. Her jaw hurt like hell and she was shaking from the adrenaline overload.

"Just happened to be jogging by and . . . " He shook his head. "You think of this happening in other towns, but Shirley?"

"I know. I mean, who's even heard of Shirley, right?"

He glanced back at the guy writhing on the ground. "At least he didn't have a weapon."

She gingerly rubbed her tender jaw. "He didn't need one."

She looked at her attacker. His right sleeve had ridden up, revealing a tattoo on the underside of his forearm. From here it looked like *DXXXVI*.

The stranger shrugged. "Didn't know what else to do."

"I'm glad you came along."

"Just hope I don't get in trouble for this."

"How could you get in trouble for stopping a mugging?"

"The law never sides with guys like me. This jerk'll probably sue me for pain and anguish or some such."

"Not while I'm around."

"I mean, calling and waiting for the cops wasn't exactly an option."

"Listen, you did just fine. But I think I should call them now. Oh, wait." She pointed to her attacker, still lying atop her bag. "It's under him."

"I'll do it."

He whipped out his own phone and tapped in three numbers. After a brief wait he said, "Hello, I'd like to report—"

Behind him she saw her attacker leap to his feet and start to run off.

"He's getting away!"

The second man spun and took off after him but the attacker had a good head start.

Damn! Her rescuer took his phone with him.

But then she noticed her shoulder bag crumpled on the ground. She darted to it and pawed through the mess within for her iPhone. Where was it? She dumped the contents on the hood of her car but no phone.

He'd left her wallet but run off with her phone.

What the—?

Just then a car pulled up to the curb. Laura recognized it in the wash from the security lamp.

Steven . . . her ex. With all that had been happening, his weekend with Marissa had been pushed to the background.

Sandy haired, tall and lanky, he unfolded himself from the car and swung a small overnight duffel over his shoulder.

"Laura?" his tone was light. "What are you doing outside?"

She felt a lump form in her throat, but she swallowed it.

"I . . . I was just mugged."

"Jesus God!" He hurried up to her. "You're serious?"

She nodded. The lump was back.

"Are you hurt?"

She shook her head. She couldn't remember being this glad to see him in a long, long time. She held out her arms. She needed a hug. He didn't hesitate. He dropped the duffel and wrapped her in a tight embrace.

It seemed before the divorce all they'd ever done was fight. Now, after years apart, they got along better than ever. They could never be husband and wife again, but they could be friendly parents.

"Did you call the cops?" he said after a few seconds.

"He took my phone."

He released her and pulled his cell from a pocket. "Let's get them rolling right now. You're going to have to call all the credit card companies and—"

"He left my wallet. All he took was my phone."

"That's weird."

"Maybe because that other guy didn't give him time to—"

"Wait. Other guy?"

"I'll tell you after you call the cops."

That other guy . . . where was he? And *who* was he?

STAHLMAN

1

"Toad in the hole!" Marissa cried as her father dropped one onto her plate.

"Well done, right?" Laura said.

Steven's mouth twisted. "Cooked through and through. I'm on board with the program, you know."

Of course he was.

"Sorry for being a pain."

With Marissa's immune system in a precarious state since the stem-cell transplant, Laura was taking no chances. Anti-contaminant kitchen routines were followed to the letter—fresh items scrubbed, cutting boards changed frequently, everything steamed or cooked to at least 160 degrees. She bought organic eggs but still worried about *salmonella* if they were undercooked. Long odds, she knew, but no sunny-side-up or over-easy in this house.

Steven slipped a three-egg Western omelet onto her plate.

"There you go."

She wasn't hungry, still hadn't bounced back from the mugging last night. She would have liked to have shielded Marissa from the scary truth, but with the cops around, asking for a statement, she'd had to tell her. The swollen bruise on her jaw was an ugly reminder. So was the pain. She was glad for the omelet. It hurt to chew.

"Looks great. As soon as I finish I'm off."

Steven smiled. "I'm not kicking you out."

"And I'm not going to hog your time with Marissa."

Laura took a bite—delicious—and looked around. Marissa digging into her egg-inside-toast combination, Steven at the stove, whipping up another omelet for himself. She couldn't remember the last time the three of them had had breakfast together. Their usual routine didn't accommodate that.

Breaking the routine, Laura had stayed over last night. She'd been too shaken to travel to Manhattan and hadn't wanted to be alone. Steven had been fine with that. He'd even come tapping at her door, asking if she needed company. She'd known what that meant, and shooed him away. Yes, she could have used a man in her bed, but not Steven. That bird had flown.

2

The morning sun was peeking through the trees when Laura wheeled her overnight bag toward her car through the weekend quiet. She couldn't help looking around to make sure no one was lurking. As she slammed the trunk she sensed motion behind her.

A huge, gleaming black van, somewhere between the size of a courtesy van and a touring bus pulled into the curb in front of her house, blocking her driveway.

Really? How did the idiot expect her to get out? As she approached with the intention of asking just that, a door slid open in the side and out stepped a man who reminded her a little of Nathan Fillion but with a thinner neck. Then she recognized him.

Her rescuer from last night.

"You! Where'd you go to last night? I was a little worried about you."

He shrugged with an easy smile that didn't seem to reach his eyes. She couldn't say his eyes were cold, exactly. More like cold lay *behind* his eyes. Hidden. What did that *mean*, anyway? If someone asked her right now to explain what she was feeling, she'd be at a loss. But something was *there*. Or maybe *not* there. Whatever it was, she didn't feel comfortable with it. He seemed distant. Almost removed.

"No need to worry about me. Tried to catch him but he was fast and had too much of a jump."

"Well, anyway, I want to thank you for intervening."

He angled around to her left and peered at her swollen jaw. "Too bad I didn't intervene sooner. Lousy punk." He thrust out his hand. "Rick Hayden, like the planetarium."

She shook it. Big hand. "Laura Fanning. And you're dating yourself with 'planetarium.' These days you should say 'as in Panettiere' instead."

"Nah. If people don't get the planetarium ref, I probably don't want to know them. But anyway, no thanks necessary. All part of the job."

Laura blinked. Did he say—?

"Job?"

"I was hired to watch over you."

Something in Laura's chest gave a quick, uneasy twist. "Who on Earth would—?"

"Name's Clayton Stahlman." He jerked a thumb over his shoulder. "He's inside. Wants to meet you."

"In there?"

"This is how he travels."

She peered into the darker opening in the black side panel of the van. "I don't know . . . "

"He's not very mobile. Even if your daughter weren't at risk for infection, your house isn't accessible to a man in his condition."

"His condition? What—hey, what do you know about my daughter?"

"You'd be surprised what he knows. He'd like a private powwow with you. Would have visited you in your office but he suspects it's been bugged by now."

"Bugged?"

"Please." He gestured toward the door. "I'm just the hired help. He can explain it better than I can."

He . . . this Rick Hayden, whoever he was, was so casual about it all. She'd never heard of a Clayton Stahlman but he obviously had resources. She couldn't guess how many hundreds of thousands this van must have cost. And he'd hired this man to "watch over" her? That meant he'd expected foul play. Why? Was last night's attack not the random act it had seemed?

Looked like the only way she was going to get answers was to go inside and talk to this Clayton Stahlman.

She took a breath. "All right. But you go in first."

She wasn't the suspicious type as a rule, but she didn't want this big man pushing her inside from behind and driving off with her. Yes, he'd come to her rescue last night but that could have been a setup.

Paranoid? Maybe. But something weird was going on here.

His smile was almost mocking but he preceded her through the doorway. Then he turned and extended his hand to help her step up from the ground.

"I can handle it," she said.

She found a railing and pulled herself up onto the bottom step where she stopped and looked around. The interior looked like the lounge area of a luxury airliner.

"Hello," said a weak voice from her right. An older man sat smiling at her from a wheelchair. A green oxygen cannula circled under his nose. "Doctor Fanning, I presume."

Okay. This looked on the level. And he looked anything but threatening.

"That's me," she said, climbing the rest of the way in.
"And you are . . . ?"

"Clayton Stahlman." He handed her a card embossed
with his name and a telephone number, then indicated
one of the sofas set against the walls. "Please, have a
seat."

Laura complied, slipping the card into a side pocket
on her shoulder bag. She made a quick assessment of
Stahlman: continuous oxygen, moon face, no barrel
chest. Probably pulmonary fibrosis. Hard to tell his age.
A knitted cap covered his scalp and the tops of his ears;
puffiness from long-term steroid treatment had flattened
whatever facial wrinkles he might normally have.

"Would you like some coffee?" He cocked his head
toward the driver behind the steering wheel at the front
of the van. "I'll have James pour—"

"No, thanks. What I would like are some answers,
starting with what this is all about."

He nodded. "Fully understandable. Where would you
like me to begin?"

She pointed to Hayden who stood in a stoop, too tall
for the interior of the van.

"Call me paranoid, but I never found 'Someone to
Watch over Me' a particularly engaging song. Why was
he?"

Hayden dropped into a seat toward the rear of the
van and looked bored.

"The simplest, most direct answer to that is 'because
I paid him to do so.' He's an ex–Navy SEAL and very
capable. But as to why I assigned him to you, that takes
a little background."

Laura leaned back and crossed her legs. "I'm off this
weekend. Plenty of time. I'm listening."

"First, about me: born at the end of World War Two,

a hippy in the sixties, earned an MBA in the seventies, retired with a gazillion dollars in the nineties before the dot-com bubble burst, and discovered a few years ago that the breathing trouble I was having was due to something called pulmonary fibrosis."

Laura nodded, pleased with the accuracy of her on-the-fly diagnosis.

"You're on high doses of prednisone, I take it."

"Plus immunosuppressive drugs. I'm almost as susceptible to infection as your daughter, Doctor Fanning."

Laura stiffened. "I'm not comfortable with you knowing about—"

"Please," he said, raising a bony hand. "You seem like a rational woman, grounded in reality. Certainly you don't still cling to the delusion that such a thing as privacy exists."

Laura sighed. "I guess not."

"I have money, Doctor Fanning. Tons of money. I'll never be able to spend it all. I can't even spend the interest and dividends I collect every quarter, so my principal keeps growing. In short, I can buy anything I want. And one of the easiest things to buy is information."

He spoke without bravado, appeared comfortable with his wealth. Used to it. Wore it like a favorite old sweater.

He smiled. "I know what you're thinking: Money can't buy health."

"Something like that. But at least you've got one fewer worry than most chronically ill folks."

"You said 'fewer' instead of 'less.' Thank you. Hardly anyone cares about grammar anymore. But that aside, I have children and I have grandchildren. With an average lifespan I should be able to look forward to ten or fifteen more years with them. But as things stand now, I've got two or three—if I'm lucky. So that's why I intend to buy—or rather, *try* to buy back my health."

Laura leaned forward. "I hope no one has told you they can cure pulmonary fibrosis."

"I know it's terminal. I've given millions to research but I've been told that if there's ever going to be a cure, it won't happen in my lifetime. Only something outside the mainstream can cure me."

Uh-oh.

"Have you been offered some sort of alternative-medicine cure?"

"I don't believe in alternative medicine. When you stick 'alternative' in front of 'medicine,' you mean it hasn't been proven to work. Once you can prove it works, it's no longer 'alternative' and joins the mainstream. Right?"

Laura nodded. "That pretty well sums it up. But if what you're after is outside the mainstream and yet not alternative, what are we talking about?"

His gaze bored into her. "You've heard of the legendary panacea, I assume?"

Laura shook her head. Had she heard right? Panacea? Long-term high-dose steroids could induce psychosis. Had his prednisone made him delusional?

He began to laugh. "Oh, I wish I had a picture of your face. It's precious. Just what I—"

His laugh broke up into a wheezing cough and his face reddened as he fought for air. Finally he controlled it and sat breathing deeply through his nose, sucking in the oxygen flowing through the cannula.

"I shouldn't laugh," he said after a while. "But I knew what your reaction would be: You think I've lost my mind, correct?"

Laura slung the strap of her bag over her shoulder and rose. Unlike Hayden, she could stand up straight inside the van. This had just run off the rails for her. But she'd give the sick old man the benefit of an explanation before she walked out.

"Mister Stahlman, the 'legendary panacea' is just that: a legend. Such a cure-all is impossible. No single concoction can cure everything. Disease processes are too varied, their causes are . . . are myriad, and their courses are different with every individual. What stops the out-of-control cell divisions of a cancer can't stop the progressive scarring and shutdown of the alveoli in your lungs. You see that, don't you?"

Stahlman sat watching her, a bemused smile undulating across his lips.

"Can I also suppose it couldn't reverse the effects of juvenile rheumatoid arthritis either?"

Laura could only stare at him. "What . . . ?"

"Young Thomas Cochran received a dose of the panacea on Wednesday morning."

"Tommy?"

"You speak as if you knew him."

"I did. I—"

"Wait." Hayden had straightened from his slump and was staring at her. "You knew the boy?"

"Yes."

"How?"

"My Marissa was misdiagnosed at first and—"

"So you'd actually *met* the boy before he showed up on your autopsy table?"

"I believe I've already said that. Why is that important?"

Hayden's gaze shifted to Stahlman. "One degree of separation."

Laura looked back and forth between them. "I don't understand."

"Mister Hayden has some unorthodox ideas about life, liberty, and the pursuit of coincidence. The two of us have had some lively discussions since he came to work for me, but his ideas need not concern us here. I was saying that young Thomas Cochran received a dose of the panacea on Wednesday . . . brought to him by Chaim Brody."

"That's not possible. There's no such thing."

"Explain the Cochran boy then."

"I can't."

"There's a gap in your knowledge, but you refuse to fill it with the idea of a panacea."

"I prefer to be honest and say I don't know rather than fall back on myth."

Stahlman was looking past her and nodding to Hayden. "Didn't I tell you?"

"Tell him what?" Laura said.

Stahlman said, "I've said I had a feeling about you. From your bioprospecting past I assumed you had a scientific mind and intellectual honesty—two indispensables for the job."

"Just what does a bioprospector do?" Hayden asked.

She gave him a quick glance. "Mostly we watch people's eyes glaze over when we answer that question." Back to Stahlman: "Job? What job?"

"I'm hiring you to find the panacea."

"Find a panacea?" She shook her head. "Why don't you simply go out and buy some sort of homeopathic cure?"

"I don't understand."

"They're both equally bogus."

"My, my. Your bedside skills could use some honing."

"My patients don't seem to mind."

"That's because they're all dead," Hayden said.

"Just the way I like them. Which brings me to an important point, Mister Stahlman: I already have a job."

"Does it pay you five million dollars just for trying? And an equal amount as a bonus for success?"

Laura felt her jaw drop.

"We've identified the girl in the picture with Brody," Bradsher said, placing a sheet of paper on Nelson's desk.

Nelson read it through squinted lids. He'd barely slept last night. He'd twisted and turned thinking about the black spot clinging to his neck and masses expanding in his lungs and spreading from there.

And then, this morning's headache—a killer. Virtually blinding . . . to the point where he wasn't sure he was seeing correctly.

Was that *Ix'chel Coboh* printed on the sheet?

"What kind of name is that?"

"Mayan, sir."

"How on Earth do you say that first one?"

"I was wondering that myself so I checked. Apparently you pronounce it like 'Michelle' but without the M."

Good old Bradsher . . . always anticipating.

"How did we find her?"

"We lucked out. She works as a translator in Chetumal."

"Pardon my ignorance, but where is that?"

"It's the capital of Quintana Roo . . . one of the Mexican states . . . on the Yucatán Peninsula."

"Yucatán . . . got it. But how . . . ?"

"Facial recognition software to the rescue. Mexican photo records aren't state-of-the-art, but they're getting better. I had a couple of Company people in Mexico City run through the criminal databases on the off chance that she'd been picked up for something. They came up empty so they tried government employees and bingo."

"Do we think she's a panacean?"

Bradsher shrugged. "She doesn't fit the pattern. She helps the local Maya deal with the government—a fair number of them still live in the jungle and don't speak Spanish. No connection to the health system that we know of."

"Phone-text monitoring no help?"

"Sorry. If she was in Mexico City, no prob. But Chetumal is in the sticks. Well, the relative sticks. Nothing happening there of interest to NSA and the Company."

Nelson drummed his fingers on the desk. "Assign someone to tail her for a day or two. See if anything pops."

"I know just the man."

"And what about last night?"

"The staged mugging nearly went south when a Good Samaritan stepped in, but Brother Simon managed to complete his tasks and get away."

He had to ask. "How bad are her injuries?"

"Negligible due to the interruption."

He hid his disappointment. An eye for an eye was too much to ask for, but he'd hoped at the very least that she'd be hospitalized.

"And the ME's office?"

"Mission accomplished: Our man wiped the SD cards on the three cameras they keep there, and placed two audio pickups."

"Excellent. Chaim Brody is in the ground, so she can't reshoot his tattoo, and Hanrahan's is deeply charred. It appears we have nipped that threat in the bud. Now we can concentrate on—"

The phone rang and he was informed that a Dr. Forman was calling.

"I have to take this," he told Bradsher.

The agent nodded and ducked out, closing the door behind him. Nelson's gut clenched as he punched the blinking button.

"Doctor!" he said as heartily as he could manage. "What news do you have for me?"

"Not good, I'm afraid, Agent Fife. That punch biopsy you sent me arrived first thing this morning. I put a rush on it as you requested. Good thing too—just got word that it's a malignant melanoma."

Nelson's gut tightened further. Dr. Moreau had indicated as much, but still . . . "That doesn't sound good."

"That's not the worst of it. Pathology here classes it as a grade four tumor."

"And that's bad?"

"The higher the grade, the more aggressive the tumor. Grade four is very aggressive. And that chest X-ray you sent indicates distant spread, which puts you at stage four."

"Grade, stage . . . I don't—"

"Grade four, stage four means an aggressive tumor that has already spread to distant organs. Get thee to an oncologist, Fife. Pronto. I'll overnight the slides to you."

"Tomorrow's Sunday."

"Oh, right. Well, then, I'll courier them up to you today and bill it to your people. You'll want them along when you see your oncologist. Sloan-Kettering is right there in the city. You can't do better than that."

"I don't have time for that right now. I'm in the middle of something important."

"You don't have time *not* to get started. At least let them start scanning you to see where else it's spread."

"Where might that be?"

"Anywhere."

Nelson rubbed his temple with his free hand. "Brain?"

"That's always a possibility. It's a frequent stop after the lungs."

"Oh, Lord."

"Why? You've been having headaches?"

"Daily."

A long silence, then, "Look, you need Sloan—now."

"I can't. Soon, maybe, but not now. Can you send me a script for a brain scan . . . just so I'll know?"

He supposed he could have asked Moreau, but she'd probably turn him down. No, not probably—he was sure she'd turn him down.

Forman said, "If it's positive, will that get you off your ass?"

"If it's spread to my brain, I'll go straight to Sloan. Promise."

A sigh. "All right. I'll order a no-contrast CT. It's not as detailed as an MRI but you can schedule it quickly without as much red tape, and if anything's there, it'll tell the story. I'll stick it in with the slides."

"Thank you."

"You said you didn't have any more of that miracle juice you brought me. Is that true?"

"Yes. As I told you, I'm working on tracking it down. That's why I can't start chemo or anything like that now."

"Well, I hope to hell you find some. And if you do, reserve the first dose for yourself. You need it. *Boy*, do you need it!"

As he ended the call, Nelson wanted to cry at the irony. If he did track down the panacea, he was forbidden from partaking of that devil's brew.

Uncle Jim's words echoed in his head: *Trust me: If something disables you, you'll wish you'd taken a little time for fun.*

He was beginning to fear that he might not have much time left for fun or anything else. If that was the case, so be it. Maybe he hadn't lived a full life by common standards—most people would consider it downright dull, he supposed. But he'd found it meaningful, and that was all that mattered.

As for fun . . . he sensed he was homing in on the panaceans and close to wiping them off the face of the Earth. Doing the Lord's work wasn't supposed to be fun, but in this case . . .

4

Did he say five *million*?

It took some time for Laura to overcome her shock. Then she said, "You can't be serious!"

"I am completely serious. Aren't I, Mister Hayden?"

"Believe him," Hayden said in a flat tone. "He's not kidding."

"But five million?"

"Chump change to him."

She looked at Stahlman. "I can't do that."

"Why not?"

"Because even if it's . . . chump change to you, I can't be involved in a sham."

He looked offended. "What do you mean, 'sham'? The offer is very real."

"Not the offer—the search. The search would be a sham. It has no hope of success. I can't be a party to that."

He smiled. "I do like you, Doctor Fanning. I admire your integrity, I truly do."

"Well, fine. You can also admire my back as I walk out. You'll have to find someone else."

He shook his head. "There is no one else with your unique qualifications."

She was curious now. "Such as?"

"You've got a medical degree—"

"Plenty of those around."

"—plus an expertise in exotic botany."

He seemed to know an awful lot about her.

"So?"

"So, the panacea is plant based."

"Do you know the plant?"

Stahlman gestured to Hayden. "Mister Hayden, would you be so kind?"

"Sure." Hayden grabbed a small ceramic pot from a ledge and handed it to Laura. "Here you go." When she hesitated, he added, "It won't bite. Not like it's a triffid or anything."

Stahlman said, "It's what your two dead growers were cultivating before their untimely deaths."

The pot contained a single, pale green stalk topped with five smooth-bordered leaves surrounding a central bud.

Laura had never seen this species before, but hazarded a guess. "Buxaceae family?"

"It would appear so, but it is genetically distinct. No one knows where it belongs in the scheme of things."

"Well, if your panacea is made from this, just grow some more and you're all set."

"Unfortunately it's not that simple. I have an acre of those plants on my estate in Duchess County. I put together a research team that has been working on them for years, to no avail. Nothing they come up with does a damn thing. We're missing some ingredient."

What you're missing, Laura thought as she placed the plant and its pot on the seat beside her, is a few of your marbles. No, make that a *lot* of your marbles.

"Then I don't see how you can expect more from me."

"Chaim Brody was a very sick man when he left New York City. I've seen his medical records from the free HIV clinic that was treating him. I know exactly how sick he was. He didn't have long to live. And yet he reappeared a year later hale and hearty, bearing the seeds of the same plant you just examined. He cultivated them and somehow used his crop to concoct the panacea, a dose of which found its way to Thomas Cochran."

Fantastic, she thought. Utterly fantastic.

"Okay, even if I believed that this panacea exists— and I don't—what do you expect me to do?"

"For five million dollars I expect you to follow in Chaim Brody's footsteps and learn what happened down there. He was terminally ill with AIDS, lymphoma, sarcoma, and an immune system that couldn't survive the common cold. Yet he was cured. I too am terminally ill. I too want to be cured. As I said, you are uniquely suited to the job."

"You have Mister Hayden here. Why can't he—?"

"While Mister Hayden is uniquely skilled in security and protection, he does not have a medical degree and wouldn't know a tulip from a daffodil. You have served as an ethnobotanist in the area of Mexico where Chaim Brody found his cure; you can gain the confidence of the natives there because your mother was Mayan and you speak the language."

She did speak one of the many Mayan dialects— Yucatec, specifically. But . . .

"H-how long have you been digging into my past?"

"Since you were called to the scene of Mister Hanrahan's death and—"

"Hanrahan?"

"The burned corpse: Cornelius Aloysius Hanrahan."

The name on the house lease. If he was right, she now had a name for the first dead grower. But . . .

"You've learned all this about me since Wednesday morning?"

"I knew ninety percent of it by Wednesday noon." He leaned forward. "Think about it: You and this task are a match made in heaven."

"You can say that again," said Hayden, staring at her.

"Better yet, I will: Made. In. Heaven. Or the likely equivalent."

What was he getting at?

"Doctor Fanning," Stahlman said, "I'm not just asking you, I'm *begging* you. You're my last hope. I'll die without it."

Her heart went out to him, but . . .

"I hate to burst your bubble, but there's no such thing as a panacea."

"Tell that to Chaim Brody and Thomas Cochran!"

Well, there was that . . . *something* had come out of Yucatán. But what?

She remembered Dr. Sklar with his hand on Tommy's bagged body. *Something extraordinary has happened here.*

"I have to think about my daughter. I can't risk a jungle trek."

"Life is risk—as was getting out of your car last night."

"I've engaged in my share of risky behaviors along the way and—"

Hayden snorted. "Really? Like what?"

He was getting on her nerves. Just to shut him up . . .

"How about skydiving?"

He shrugged. "Minimal risk. Done hundreds of jumps."

Was he really looking to start a pissing match? She wasn't playing.

"How about eating White Castle burgers?"

He stared, his lips rippling, then gave a low whistle. "Okay. White Castle . . . that's edgy." Totally deadpan. "Can't beat that."

Was he trying to be disarming? He'd almost succeeded.

"Can we get back to the subject at hand?" Stahlman said, sounding testy.

"That *is* the subject: I'm a mother now—"

"Whose daughter wouldn't have needed a stem-cell transplant had the panacea been available."

Laura bristled. "She's cured—a real cure by real medical science. But she's still a little girl, a little person in orbit around me who depends on a consistent gravitational pull. I provide it."

"Yes, a little person who has a devoted father, a visiting nurse, and a tutor. I'm offering you five million just to go and look. I guarantee the five million even if you fail. Think of what that will mean for her future. You won't have to deal with that chief medical examiner."

God, was there anything about her he *didn't* know?

He pressed on. "Don't do it for me. Do it for your daughter, do it for yourself, do it for humanity, but *do it*. And if you succeed . . . imagine if you succeed. Your name will be up there with Curie and Fleming and Salk."

The prospect of fame didn't faze her, because as far as finding the panacea was concerned, success was not in the cards. But she might be able to bring back *something*—if not of value to Clayton Stahlman, then maybe to someone else.

And the five million . . . after taxes she could put the remainder in a trust. Even with conservative management, five percent a year was doable, guaranteeing Marissa an income for life. She might well need it. A fair percentage of childhood cancer survivors faced physical and emotional challenges later in life.

Tempting . . . sooooo tempting.

But she had a feeling she was still missing something. And then she realized she was missing a *lot* of somethings.

"Wait-wait-wait! Did you burn that house and Brody's trailer?"

He gave his head a slow shake. "Absolutely not."

"Then there's someone else involved. Both those places were torched and the men in them killed by some means I've yet to identify."

Stahlman spread his hands. "Nothing I would have wanted more in this world than to sit down and talk to those two men."

"None of this makes sense to me. Let's just say that Chaim Brody came back from Mexico with the panacea. Why didn't he announce it to the world? He'd be a . . . a . . . "

"A god?"

"Yes! A god. He could have named his ticket. Yet he's sneaking a dose to Tommy Cochran and asking his mother not to mention his name. What gives with that?"

"The only reason I can offer you is that it appears Brody's cult wants to do it that way. One cure at a time."

"Cult or not, you can't keep something like a panacea—a *real* panacea—secret. At least not for long. What's the old saying? Three can keep a secret if two are dead. You're talking about something huge that's been kept secret for millennia."

"Not quite. But a good fifteen hundred years or so—since the Dark Ages."

"That hardly changes my point."

"Well, the word *panacea* comes to us from ancient Greece, and the concept has been floating around seemingly forever. A small cult of true believers *can* keep something like a panacea secret if they heed a code of silence, and if they're discreet in the ways they use it."

"You give a seriously ill person something to drink and the next day they're cured. Who's going to keep silent about that?"

"A person who is unaware that they've received the panacea. If it's slipped into their food or drink, they're aware only that they're cured. They credit their doctor, their god, or simply a reverse twist of the fate that made them ill in the first place."

"Brody wasn't exactly discreet."

"I believe he broke protocol because he was, at heart, a healer and he could not find a way to slip that boy a dose."

Laura could see that. She remembered his mother as a definite helicopter.

I'm probably one too, she admitted.

"You said 'cult.' What cult?"

He shrugged. "If they have a name for themselves, I don't know it. They're most certainly pagans, very low tech, completely off the grid and under the radar. I do know they're ancient, remnants of the Iron Age. They may be an offshoot of the Gaulish druids who somehow managed to survive the Roman suppression, but that's no help since we know next to nothing about the druids anyway."

"Didn't druids worship oaks and oppose Christianity?"

He waved a dismissive hand. "All inventions. They left not a single written record, so all that is fiction, concocted by tale-tellers centuries after they were wiped out."

Laura shook her head in disbelief. "So you believe this panacea is under the control of a nameless pagan cult left over from the Iron Age?"

"I more than believe it—I know it. They've been doling it out since the Dark Ages. I find it convenient to call them 'panaceans.' "

"Then who burned their plants and their homes?"

"Another sect."

Lara couldn't help rolling her eyes. "A rival pagan cult?"

This was getting more ridiculous by the moment.

"I don't think so. These folks might have their roots in Christianity, but I can't be sure."

"Do *they* have a name?"

"They might, but I have my own name for them: I call them '536.'"

Five-thirty-six . . . why did that sound familiar? Then she remembered.

"Brody! He wrote that on his palm!"

Stahlman was smiling and nodding. "Exactly. He knew he'd been found out and he knew by whom. I think he was sending a message to his fellow panaceans."

"Five-thirty-six," she said. "What does it mean?"

"It's an important number to the enemies of the panaceans—important enough to tattoo it or brand it on their arms."

Laura stiffened. "The mugger last night. He had something on the inside of his forearm."

"A Roman numeral, perhaps?"

"Yes! A *D* followed by three *X*s, I think."

"*D-X-X-X-V-I*, perhaps?"

"Yes! I think that's it. But I've forgotten what D stands for."

"In Roman numerals it's five hundred."

"So . . . " It took her only a second. The realization made her queasy. "Five hundred and thirty-six. He was one of them."

"What do you think he was after?" Hayden said.

"He took my phone." She hefted her shoulder bag. "Left my wallet, but took my phone."

"What was on your phone?"

"Nothing much. I'm not into my phone like most folks. I've got my contacts, a few apps, a few photos—"

"Of what?" Stahlman said. "Hanrahan and Brody perhaps?"

"No. I used one of the department's cameras to photograph them."

"But 536 couldn't know that," Hayden said, looking at Stahlman.

"No, they couldn't."

"Mostly I took photos of their weird caduceus tattoos."

"That's not a caduceus depicted on their backs. A caduceus has two snakes and wings—the staff of Mercury or Hermes. What they have is the staff of Asclepius, the Greek god of healing."

So what? bubbled to Laura's lips but she held it back. Instead, she shook her head.

"He's a new one on me."

"That's because Asclepius's staff has been replaced in the public mind by the caduceus, which in mythology has nothing to do with healing. The Greek god of healing had a number of daughters . . . one named Panacea."

Not quite a *eureka!* moment, but she had learned something.

"Interesting."

"From their habit of burning the houses and the plants and the bodies, it's clear 536 doesn't like to leave evidence. Only a stroke of bad luck—for them—preserved Brody's body unscathed. I suspected 536 would want to destroy any evidence you had. That was why I had Mister Hayden watching you."

"But it's all on my office computer."

"Don't be so sure," Hayden said. "Bet if you check your office you'll find all evidence wiped clean."

"But how?"

Stahlman said, "The 536 folk appear to be very high-tech—the polar opposite of the panaceans. Whatever you had is not important in the long run. Nothing I didn't already know about."

"Then why—?"

"I feared they might harm you in the process."

Laura swallowed. She wasn't quite sure how to respond to that.

"Why would they want to harm me?"

"Not on purpose, but they've proven as remorseless as they are relentless in their pursuit of the panaceans. If you stand in their way, they will run you over."

"That's comforting. All to control this panacea?"

Stahlman shrugged. "Who wouldn't want to? It's invaluable."

"Which brings up the question of who's funding them. Imagine what a pharmaceutical company would give to be able to sell a panacea."

Hayden's smile was dour. "This mean you're buying into it now?"

"No, Mister Hayden, I am not," she said in an icier tone than she intended. Something about him irritated her. "But if a company was convinced such a thing existed . . . "

"They'd do anything to control it," Stahlman said.

Laura leveled her gaze at him. "Is that what you want to do? Control it?"

"Before I became ill, I might well have wanted that very much. But spending time on the wrong side of a debilitating terminal illness causes a seismic shift in your perspective. Your illness comes to define you, consume you, and all you want is to get well. I'm not asking you to return with the secret of the panacea. I'm simply asking you to return with one dose. *One dose*—that is all I want."

She rose again. "Looks like I have some thinking to do."

"What's there to think about?" His expression turned alarmed. "There's not any time to waste."

"We're talking about my leaving my daughter and wandering around Mesoamerica in search of something that I do not believe exists. That's a tall order."

"I'll double my offer!"

"I'm . . . I'm not trying to drive up the price, Mister Stahlman."

"I know you aren't. I'm simply trying to make you an offer you can't refuse."

He was pretty much there, but she didn't say that. This was a decision she couldn't make on her own. Steven had to be involved, and Marissa too.

He added, "And you wouldn't be simply 'wandering around.' I have a lead on a jungle *curandero* who has performed some supposedly miraculous cures."

She took a step toward the door. "We'll meet again to discuss this further, Mister Stahlman."

"When? This is urgent."

"Later today." She stepped down and pushed open the door.

"My number is on that card, Doctor. Please don't delay."

As she reached the sidewalk, she glanced back and saw Hayden following her. He closed the door behind him.

"Think hard before you accept, Doc."

The warning surprised her. "I thought you worked for him."

"I do. But he's glossing over a few things."

"I suspected that. Give me a for-instance."

"Like 536. I don't know much about them, but they're on the hunt for the panacea—"

She remembered his snarky remark. "Have *you* bought into it?"

"I reserve judgment. *Something* is going on. But in practical terms, it doesn't have to *be* real to make me wary of people who *believe* it's real and are desperate to get hold of it."

"So, you're warning me?"

"Just want to make sure your eyes are open and you're aware of the risks. You're already on the 536 radar. If you go hunting the panacea, they may decide they don't want competition. Remember Hanrahan and Brody."

Laura felt the muscles at the back of her neck tighten. Good point.

"What I'm hearing is you think I should hire a bodyguard if I go."

He made a noise somewhere between a laugh and a grunt. "No need to hire. Stahlman has made it clear: If you go, I go."

Traveling into the jungles of Mesoamerica with this guy?

"I don't think so."

"Not your choice. Not mine either. Stahlman's. He'll want me along to protect his investment."

"I'm sure there are plenty of other—"

He was shaking his head. "I'm the best."

"Oh, really?"

"Really."

No compromised self-esteem issues with this guy.

"You mean ex-SEAL and all that."

"And all that. He'll want you to have every chance to succeed. You are, after all, the perfect match for this assignment."

Something in his tone . . .

"You say that as if it's a bad thing."

"It could be when you're *too* perfect."

"How so?"

"'Too perfect' doesn't just happen. It needs to be arranged."

She couldn't help taking offense. "Not by me. I assure you this morning was the first time I've ever heard someone mention the existence of a panacea with a straight face."

"Oh, I believe that. But that doesn't mean events weren't arranged. One degree of separation, remember?"

"You said that before. You mean between me and Tommy Cochran—because I knew him?"

"Exactly. How does that happen?"

"Simple. He died in Suffolk County. We have one chief medical examiner and three deputies—a one-in-four chance of his ending with me. Not exactly long odds. Besides, his mother asked for me."

"Asked for the same ME who just happened to autopsy the fellow who gave her son . . . whatever he gave him? What are those odds?"

Laura still wasn't impressed. "Nothing to write home about. What's your point? Who would be doing this arranging? Stahlman?"

"No. Not him. If you're interested, we can get into all that when you decide to go. If you don't, it's all moot." He gave her a hard stare. "You look like good people. Whatever you expect to be dealing with down there in Mexico, the reality will be worse. Think hard on this, Doc."

He waved and re-entered the van.

Though he seemed to have her well-being in mind, something about that guy still rubbed her the wrong way. Something was off.

She hadn't liked hearing that the reality she'd find would be worse than her expectations. What did he know about her expectations? But something else he'd said disturbed her more.

Too perfect . . . arranged . . .

Could it be?

She'd intended to totally veg this weekend. Now she had an irresistible urge to check in at her office.

She headed for her car.

5

Nelson almost knocked into Bradsher as he exited the elevator. He'd been thinking about tumors. He'd done some online research about metastatic melanoma. The prognosis for stage IV was grim but improving.

"I was just coming to see you, sir."

"And I was just going to lunch."

Nelson had been off his feed since hearing about the X-ray yesterday, and he'd wanted to vomit after talking to Forman, but his stomach had settled and was now insistent on sustenance.

"I have news."

"Can you tell me as I walk?" he said as headed across the Federal Building's lobby toward the front doors.

Bradsher fell into step beside him. "I think so."

"Good or bad?"

"Depends. The news itself is not good, but the fact that we know it in advance is good."

Nelson liked Bradsher's precision, but now couldn't help but find it annoying.

"Talk."

"As you requested, Brother Simon not only stole Doctor Fanning's phone but also managed to pin a pickup to the inside of her shoulder bag."

"Excellent. And I gather by your presence that our plant has borne fruit already."

"Yessir. A man named Clayton Stahlman has offered her millions to follow Chaim Brody's path into Mexico in search of the panacea."

The news brought Nelson to a sudden halt. So sudden that someone bumped into him from behind.

No doubt about it now. The Serpent was at work here.

"Who is this Stahlman?"

"We're referencing him now, but I gather from the recording that he's terminally ill."

Terminally ill . . . that had a too-familiar ring.

"A lot of that going around these days."

"Pardon?"

"Nothing. That would explain his zeal for the panacea. I don't foresee a deputy ME from Long Island posing much competition."

"Well, she did bioprospecting down there for years, so she knows the area well. She's also half Mayan and speaks their language."

"*What?*" Nelson stopped again. This time no one ran into him. "The stench of the Serpent is strong here."

He began moving again and pushed through the doors into the midday sun of downtown Manhattan.

Bradsher said, "In our favor is the fact that Doctor Fanning is a skeptic, believes the panacea is a fairy tale."

"God bless the skeptics."

They'd all rot in hell for eternity if they didn't see the Light before their final day, but in the meantime both the panaceans and the Brotherhood had benefited from science's offhand dismissal of the possible existence of such a thing as a panacea. It made it so much easier to keep the truth secret.

"This Stahlman says he's got a lead on a *curandero* in the Yucatán jungles who supposedly performs miracles."

Curandero . . . Nelson wasn't fluent in Spanish but he did know that word. It meant "healer."

"Well, if a civilian can find him, we certainly can. Get on it. Have our brother . . . what's his name?"

"The one in Chetumal watching the girl from the photo? That's Miguel."

"Have Brother Miguel leave the girl for now and start asking about a special *curandero* in the jungle. If he gets a hit he's to contact you immediately."

"And if this *curandero* has the tattoo?"

Nelson stopped and checked out the food carts lined up along the curb across the street as he thought about that. If this *curandero* had the tattoo, he was certainly a panacean. The Brotherhood had a set protocol for dealing with them, but this new wrinkle of willing themselves to drop dead had greatly complicated matters.

"If he's definitely a panacean, have Brother Miguel run a variation on the protocol: Be prepared to sedate him immediately, before he can stop his heart or whatever it is they do. Then proceed as usual."

"Including Leviticus?"

"Of course." A burnt offering, as mentioned in the Book, was an integral part of the protocol. "Why wouldn't he?"

"Just being sure, since we're talking about sanctioning a foreign national."

"He's a panacean. They have no nation, only their pagan goddess."

"What about sanctioning Doctor Fanning? That would allow us to take our time in Mexico."

Nothing Nelson would like better, but the Brotherhood had rules and he was obliged to follow them.

He gave Bradsher a withering look. "She's not a candidate for a Leviticus Sanction and you know it."

"But she's—"

"She's *chasing* the panacea, just like we are. If she starts *making* it, that's a whole other story. Then she becomes subject to Leviticus and we will not hesitate to invoke it. But . . . not being a panacean exempts her only from the Leviticus Sanction, not from simpler, more mundane methods of termination. And your suggestion about removing her from the picture has merit."

"Meaning?"

"Contact Brother Simon again. Maybe we should allow him to redeem himself by performing a quick, clean removal within the next few days."

Not only had she crippled Uncle Jim but she was a tool of the Serpent.

"I'll contact him right after lunch."

"Excellent." He rubbed his hands together. "Now that that's settled, let's get some food. My treat." He pointed to the pushcarts. "What do you recommend?"

Bradsher shook his head. "Oh, I don't think you'll like—"

"I'm having meat today, agent. *Meat*."

Bradsher's voice rose an octave. "Sir?"

Nelson almost laughed. He'd been a vegetarian for at least a decade now, believing it would increase his odds of living a long and healthy life. Well, fat lot of good that had done him.

Bradsher led him across to a cart labeled *Haque's Halal*, manned by a bearded Afghan who ladled chopped dark mystery meat—purportedly chicken—and long-grained rice from his griddle onto a pita, doused it with red, white, and green mystery sauces from squirt bottles, then folded the mess and placed it on a paper plate.

Nelson stared at it. This was everything he'd taught himself to avoid.

But he had a tumor on his neck and another in his lung, and he was pretty damn sure one was lurking in his brain too. So fuck it, he was gonna eat some *meat*.

Call it a celebration of the impending end of Laura Fanning.

6

"Well, look what the cat drug in!"

Laura recognized the voice. She swiveled from her computer to find Deputy Lawson standing in her office doorway.

"Hello, Phil."

She was feeling too unsettled to deal with him now, but she didn't see that she had much choice.

"I heard about what happened last night. You okay? I—oh, jeez, your jaw."

She touched the tender spot. "That obvious?"

"A little. The bastard got away, huh?"

"Yeah. With my phone. Might have been worse but for a Good Samaritan jogging by."

Yeah. Rick Hayden . . . Good Samaritan for hire.

"I read the perp's description in the report. We're keeping a special eye out."

"Thanks."

"Hey, I thought this was your weekend off."

She leaned back in her chair. "It is. What are *you* doing here?"

"They found a floater in one of the lagoons on Indian Island last night. Looks like it might be foul play. And since it's a state park . . . "

"You're involved."

"Yeah, just waiting on the autopsy. Looks like she's been wet awhile. What brings you in?"

She didn't want to get into that with him.

"Just needed to check my computer for something."

"Hey, that reminds me. Remember those photos you sent me? Well, they've vanished from the department computers. I must have erased them by accident. You think you could—?"

"Resend?" She shook her head. "Sorry. They're gone from our system too."

His eyebrows rose. "No kidding?"

"No kidding."

She'd just finished searching every jpeg uploaded since Wednesday. Not a trace. Same with the department cameras—nothing. Just as Hayden had said . . .

Bet if you check your office you'll find all evidence wiped clean.

Had Hayden known, or just guessed lucky?

Lucky for her she'd made hard-copy printouts of Chaim and the woman and of Chaim's tattoo for reference in case a third dead grower showed up. She'd checked her bottom drawer and found them right where she'd left them. Someone had been thorough but not thorough enough.

Someone . . . she kept coming back to Hayden's certainty. Could it have been Hayden himself?

"Can I ask you something?" she said.

"Sure."

"How hard would it be to run a background check on someone?"

"Well, anybody can do it through the Internet. Sites will dig up arrest records and court cases, but it takes time and patience and money, because the better ones don't do it for free."

"How about for someone like you?"

He grinned. "Easy peasy. We do it all the time. Why? Interested in someone?"

She'd looked up Clayton Stahlman. No trouble finding him. Wikipedia and other sources all told the same story he'd outlined for her in the van, but in much greater detail. The photos she found online weren't recent, but no question the man they showed was a younger version of the one she'd met this morning. If estimates of his net worth were anywhere near correct, the sum he'd offered her was indeed chump change for Clayton Stahlman.

Rick Hayden, however, was another matter. She'd found a listing for a business with the Hayden name, but that was about it.

Maybe she was being overly cautious, but . . . she hadn't decided to get involved with these two yet, and forewarned was forearmed.

"My Good Samaritan from last night. He stopped by this morning and I'm curious about him."

"We talking romantic interest?"

Oh, please.

"Just the opposite. He's kind of an odd duck and I'm curious."

"I can check him out, no prob. Where's he live?"

"No idea. I found a 'Hayden Investigations and Security' in Westchester, but that might not be him."

"You got anything on him besides his name?" He smiled. "A soshe would seal the deal, but his approximate age would help."

"He could be forty, forty-five tops. All I've got for you is his name and he says he was a Navy SEAL."

He laughed. "Don't count on it. That's a favorite pickup line."

"The way he handled that mugger, I wouldn't be surprised if really he was. And I don't think he was trying to pick me up."

God, if he was, he needs a whole new approach or he's going to die alone.

"Don't count on that either."

Did she detect some defensiveness in Phil's tone? He wouldn't be jealous now, would he?

"I don't think I'm his type."

She remembered Hayden's flat eyes, devoid of interest in her and pretty much everything else. Was anyone his type?

"Well, whatever. The SEAL connection at least gives me a place to start. I know an ex-SEAL runs a B and B out Montauk way. Goes nuts about phonies who say they were SEALs. He'll be glad to check. Probably want to open a can of whup-ass on him if he wasn't. Just jot down his name for me."

Laura wrote RICK HAYDEN on a sheet of paper.

"I think that's the right spelling."

Phil took it and folded it. "I'll give my guy a call today."

You do that, Laura thought. And then we'll see if Mr. Rick Hayden is the real deal.

7

"If I decide to go," Laura said, occupying the same seat in Stahlman's van as this morning, "we've got to set some ground rules."

By late this afternoon, after a long conversation with Steven and a lot of thinking, she'd made up her mind. She called the number on Stahlman's card and the van showed up in front of her house forty minutes later. As before, the driver stayed behind the wheel up front while the silent Hayden occupied a sofa toward the rear.

"Of course," Stahlman said. As before, a green cannula encircled his head, pumping oxygen into his nose. "I wouldn't have it any other way. What do you propose?"

"Well, first off, it can't be an open-ended trip. We have to set a time limit."

Stahlman nodded. "That's reasonable. What do you have in mind?"

"Two weeks." She waited for his reaction.

He rubbed his chin. "How did you come up with that?"

"Because right now my ex-husband says he's in a place where he can take a two-week leave of absence from his firm without making major waves. He'll move in while I'm away. If any rough spots come up at work, he can deal with them online or over the phone."

Steven had encouraged her to go. He knew what the dangling millions would mean for Marissa's future and wanted it for her. If he'd been half as good a husband as he was a father, she was pretty sure they'd still be married.

The trip itself hadn't been holding her back. She wasn't heading into the unknown—she'd been all through Mesoamerica. The coast was being overdeveloped, but the jungle interior . . . the terrain hadn't changed much since Cortez had slaughtered the Aztecs. Concern over Marissa had been the stumbling block. But now, knowing the child would have her father around 24/7 left Laura free to decide.

"I can't be gone longer than that," she added. "I'll give it my all while I'm out there, but when the sand runs out, I'm heading back home."

"All right. Two weeks it is. What else?"

"I want the money deposited into a special account to be paid immediately upon my return. Or, if I don't return, paid into a fund for my daughter."

Stahlman frowned. "I know the trip is not without risk, but the most dangerous part will probably be driving the LIE from here to JFK."

"Probably," she said, forcing a smile.

But Mexico had changed since she was last there—changed for the worse. The cartels seemed to be in charge of states along the northern border. She'd be way south of there, but still . . . she didn't want to stick her head in the sand about this. And if something happened—something as unlikely as a plane crash—she didn't want that money going back to Stahlman. She wanted it to go to Marissa.

"That's no problem to arrange," Stahlman said.

"What about expenses?"

"I don't want to be bothered with receipts and reimbursements. I'll authorize you to use one of my credit cards. Anything else?"

"I'm sure there is, but those are the big ones."

"Then it's settled," he said, slapping his thighs. "One small matter, and then we can shake on it."

Uh-oh.

"What 'small matter'?"

"You must leave tomorrow."

That jolted her. "Tomorrow? I couldn't possibly—"

"You must. We've not a moment to spare. The 536 crew will certainly pick up on Brody's trip, if they haven't already. You must get there first. I will have the name of the *curandero* and the location of his village by tonight. You must be face-to-face with him tomorrow."

Tomorrow? She'd have to call Henniger tonight and tell her an emergency had come up. She had the vacation days—no problem there—but the chief liked time to re-set the coverage schedule.

It seemed silly to worry about a job with millions coming in. But the money wouldn't be coming to her, so she still had to make nice with her boss.

She sighed. "Okay. It'll mean a lot of crazy juggling, but I'll get it done."

"Excellent." He extended his hand. "We have a deal then?"

She shook his hand. His skin had a cellophane feel, as if it would split with too hard a squeeze. A common effect of long-term prednisone.

"Deal."

He picked up the phone on his wheelchair tray. "I'll have my bank set up the account right now and—"

"But it's Saturday afternoon. How—? Oh, never mind."

He smiled. "One of the perks of being filthy rich. When I call money people, they answer."

She pulled Chaim's belt out of her bag and let it un-coil from her raised hand.

"This belt belonged to Brody. The writing has to be a

code of some sort. Do either of you have any idea what it might say?"

Hayden and Stahlman both stared at the string of letters and numbers.

Stahlman shook his head. "Give it to me and I can have cryptographers go over it."

"If I'm retracing his steps, I think I should bring it with me."

"Very well." He called over his shoulder: "James, please get a photo of this."

The driver left his seat up front and used a smartphone to take a couple of shots.

As Laura put the belt away, she took a breath. "One more condition, if I may."

She hadn't included it in her ground rules and was a little uncomfortable bringing it up in front of Hayden, but she had no choice.

Stahlman had been about to call his bank. He lowered the phone. "Yes?"

"I want to arrange my own security for the trip."

"You have a problem with Mister Hayden?"

Yes, she did, but she couldn't pinpoint exactly what that problem might be. Just a feeling.

She did not look Hayden's way. "Not specifically, other than I know nothing about him."

"I can vouch for him."

"I appreciate that, but still . . . "

"You've hired security before?"

"No. I usually traveled with a small team. My employers arranged security."

"Do you have someone specific you'd prefer?"

"Do I have a name? No, but—"

"Your problem is with Mister Hayden himself, isn't it?"

There. Stahlman had nailed it. But Laura said nothing.

"I can understand that." He aimed a wry smile over

her shoulder at the man in question. "Mister Hayden is not a warm presence. He does not light up a room, except perhaps when he leaves it. He does not have an engaging personality. He is not very talkative. Did I gloss over anything, Mister Hayden?"

"Forgot to mention that I don't like dogs, cats, children, or spectator sports."

"I was not aware of that," Stahlman said, smiling and nodding. "But come to think of it, I have never seen you in the company of a child or a pet."

"Or brussels sprouts."

Laura didn't consider this a joking matter. She spread her hands.

"Well, there you have it," she said. "You're not describing the sort of person I'd wish to be in hour-to-hour contact with for two full weeks."

Stahlman focused on Laura again. "On the other hand, once you get him started on the right topic, I can guarantee some interesting conversations. But he will not be along to act as your friend or confidant or soul mate. He will be along to guarantee your safe return. You *do* want to return, don't you, Doctor Fanning?"

"Of course, but—"

"*You* want to return, *I* want you to return, and I'm sure your daughter especially wants you to return. I daresay, even your ex-husband wants you to return. So the best way for me to assure that outcome is to put Mister Hayden at your side for the duration of your journey."

"But—"

"No 'buts,' Doctor Fanning. I thought it was understood. This account I am about to set up is your guarantee. I too need a guarantee. I am investing in you, and Mister Hayden is my guarantee, my insurance policy. This is a deal breaker."

Deal breaker . . . the term rocked her. She'd set her

mind on going, on setting up Marissa for life. Was all that going up in smoke because she had a *feeling* about Rick Hayden? Stahlman seemed to have supreme confidence in the man. Couldn't she go with that?

Yes . . . yes, she guessed she could. She'd have to, or not go at all.

"All right then." She turned to Hayden. "Looks like we're traveling companions."

He didn't smile as he twirled a finger in the air. "Yippee."

Laura sighed. This could be a long two weeks.

8

"Sir?" said the receptionist as Nelson pulled out his ringing phone.

She pointed to the *Please Turn Off All Cell Phones* sign attached to the front wall of her station.

He glanced at the screen: *Bradsher.*

"I need to take this," he said, rising and heading for the glass front doors. "I'll be right outside."

The courier had delivered Forman's slides and his prescription for a CT scan of the brain to Nelson's office at 2:40. Nelson had already been on the phone, calling various imaging centers around the city. He managed to wrangle a late-afternoon scan at a center on the ninth floor of an old building just off Columbus Circle. Like everyone else, they'd wanted to put him off till tomorrow—these places ran seven days a week—but he'd persisted. He saw no point in waiting.

As soon as Nelson reached the hall, he hit TALK. "What is it, Bradsher?"

"News, sir."

"Talk to me."

Bradsher told him that Dr. Fanning was leaving for

Mexico tomorrow morning to meet with a Mayan healer in the jungle. Nelson hadn't expected such a quick departure, but Bradsher already had a lead on the healer.

"Brother Miguel asked around and it seems the natives know of a curandero *in the jungles northwest of Chetumal. He's considered holy because of the miraculous cures he performs."*

"Sounds like our man."

"Miguel is already on his way."

"Alone?"

"No. He's bringing along a freelancer from Mexico City, someone the Company has used in the past. He's reliable and speaks a number of the native dialects."

Reliable . . . that usually meant an underworld sociopath who would do anything and keep his mouth shut as long as he was paid.

"Brother Miguel is prepared for the special circumstances?"

"Yessir. He's bringing a buzzer and joy juice."

That meant a Taser and a sedative. These were encrypted phones, but it never hurt to be circumspect.

"Good."

"Doctor Fanning will be traveling with a companion as well. Mister Stahlman insisted someone named Rick Hayden accompany her."

That name rang no bells, but a bodyguard might cause problems if Nelson waited until Mexico to dispose of Laura Fanning.

"The doctor will not be traveling at all. Tell Brother Simon he must get the job done tonight."

"Yessir. The doctor also mentioned a belt with a code on it—Brody's belt."

"Belt? With a code? Do you think it was unique to him?"

"Who can say?"

"We haven't seen anything like that on other panaceans."

*"Well, sir, that could be because of the Leviticus Sanc-
tion."*

True . . . they'd never had a belt to examine because
immolation destroyed whatever the pagans were wearing along with their bodies.

"We'll worry about that later. When Miguel calls,
conference me in. I have some last-minute instructions.
And book us into Mexico City tonight."

"Tonight?"

Tomorrow could be the turning point in a millennium-
and-a-half war. Nelson wanted to be on the front line.

"Tonight."

"Will do."

He glanced through the glass doors of the imaging
center and saw the receptionist waving to him.

"Gotta go."

He ended the call and turned off his phone as he re-
entered.

"We're ready for you," she said, indicating a burly
man in dark-blue scrubs waiting with a clipboard.

"This way," he said.

How strange, Nelson thought as he dutifully fell in
step behind him. In the outside world he could decide, in
given cases, who lived and who died—as he'd done just
seconds ago in Laura Fanning's case. But step through
those doors into a medical facility and he did what he
was told without questioning.

"Will you be reading the X-rays?" he asked.

"I'm just a tech."

"Well, when do I get the report?"

He glanced at the prescription on the clipboard. "It'll
go to your doctor. He's in Maryland, I see. He'll give
you the results. Call him on Monday. He'll probably
have it by then."

"Monday? But that's two days."

"Well, it's not a *stat* script, so the scan gets in line for the radiologist to read. Then he has to dictate the report, then it's gotta be typed up. Yeah, figure Monday."

Nelson ground his teeth, then wondered why he was so anxious for the report. It would only confirm what he suspected.

9

"You won't believe this," Steven said, stepping into Laura's bedroom. "Stahlman's bank just called to say the money's in the account, awaiting your return. Gave me an account number and all—on a Saturday night."

She pushed the last of her long-sleeved T-shirts into her rolling duffel bag. She should have felt excited about those millions but an indefinable *wrongness* about this trip nagged her. She didn't want Steven to see that, though.

"Money talks."

"What time do we leave for the airport tomorrow?"

"Stahlman's having a limo pick me up at the crack of dawn."

Steven gave a low whistle. "Wow. First class."

"Including the flight."

An eight A.M. Delta flight out of JFK nonstop to Cancún, then a private four-seater to Chetumal. She'd printed out her boarding pass.

"You're gonna be safe, right?"

"He's sending that ex-SEAL along as added protection. What can go wrong?"

He shook his head. "I hate it when people say that."

"Because it almost guarantees that something will?"

"Don't make me say it."

"I won't. Look, I'll be fine. I'm coming back in one piece. I promise."

She meant that.

Before he could say anything else, she picked up her new phone.

"I've got some last-minute calls to make, okay?"

"Oh, sure. I'll be downstairs."

When she was gone, she punched in Phil Lawson's number.

She'd already called Doctor Henniger. The CME hadn't been happy about losing Laura for two weeks on such short notice. But since no one else was away, and it *was* an emergency—Laura hadn't gone into detail, but implied it involved family—she'd okayed it.

"Hey, Doc," Phil said. *"Bet I know what you're calling about."*

"Any word on our SEAL?"

"Sorry. Nothing yet. My guy told me he probably wouldn't have anything till tomorrow."

Damn. Tomorrow she'd be gone.

"Look, I'll be in Mexico for two weeks starting tomorrow. Do you have international access?"

"The office landlines do. You didn't mention a trip."

"I just found out. All of a sudden I've got to visit my mother's people."

In essence, pretty damn close to the truth.

"Everything okay?"

"I hope so. But I'll be staying in the interior where the cell towers are few and far between if there are any at all. So if my voice mail picks up when you call, leave a message, okay?"

"Will do. Safe trip and safe home."

She thanked him and ended the call.

Yeah . . . safe home. Please.

10

The target entered the kitchen.

Finally, Simon thought. They're all in one room.

He'd found a good hiding spot in the thick shrubs at the rear of the backyard. His knees ached from squatting in one spot for so long. But he wouldn't be here much longer.

The target was the same as last night—the pathologist he was supposed to rob and hurt. His plan then had been to beat her unconscious, or nearly so, and plant the pickup/locator while he took her phone. The meddlesome passerby had nearly ruined everything. Simon's neck was stiff and his gut still ached from those two blows.

Luckily he'd fallen atop her bag and so was able to complete two parts of the assignment.

Tonight he would tie up the loose end—permanently. Brother Fife had said she was aiding the panaceans and was thus a threat to the Brotherhood's goals. That was all he needed to know.

He pulled the flash-bang grenade from his pocket. He'd watched the man—her husband?—grilling a steak on the rear deck. He'd been in and out of the sliding glass door numerous times without locking it. Perfect.

This was going to be easy: Pull the pin as he ran onto the deck, open the door, toss the flash-bang inside, inject the target while they were all disoriented or unconscious, then leave.

Clean and simple. Only the target would die. No unnecessary loss of life. The Brotherhood was not about needless killing. It did what had to be done with a minimum of collateral damage.

Simon didn't know what was in the syringe, but had been assured it was fatal within five minutes.

He patted his breast pocket where it rested, ready for quick deployment when the moment came.

Time to move.

But as he rose, something looped over his head and tightened around his neck with a vicious tug. He dropped the grenade as he tore at the strangling band but his gloved fingers were useless. Even bare, his fingers wouldn't have been able to squeeze around it.

"Two strikes and you're out," said a soft voice.

So tight! No air! Can't breathe! God help me—please!

He tried to pull away but was yanked off his feet and dragged by his neck through the underbrush. Darkness crowded his vision and he kicked and twisted, but that only hastened the steady weakening of his muscles. Finally his arms and legs went limp as the darkness claimed him.

THE LEVITICUS SANCTION

1

The only good thing about Mexico City as far as Nelson could see was the ease of finding a Catholic church. He and Brother Bradsher went to Sunday mass at the huge Metropolitan Cathedral with a host of tourists, then boarded a chopper to Quintana Roo.

They'd arrived in Mexico City late last night and moved into rooms at the St. Regis. As an analyst rather than a field agent, Nelson had had to let Bradsher guide him through the ropes of operating in a foreign country.

He'd waited all night for a call from Simon—a call that never came. Bradsher had tried his phone numerous times this morning but he wasn't answering.

That wasn't good.

And worse, a passport alert said Laura Fanning had used it as she passed through TSA this morning at JFK.

Simon had failed. The man traveling with her had been hired to watch over her. Stahlman had said he was an ex–Navy SEAL. Had he been watching last night and intervened again? If so, Simon wouldn't have had a chance.

Brother Miguel had phoned in the GPS coordinates of the village in the jungles of the Yucatán Peninsula and a charter pilot had found a clearing big enough for his small helicopter to set down.

Miguel was waiting for them when they landed. A tall, heavyset man, he gave a slight bow as he shook

Nelson's hand. He'd never met Miguel, but his reputation was that of a devoted and enthusiastic member of the Brotherhood as well as the Company.

"It is an honor," he said with a slight Mexican accent.

His handshake with Bradsher was quick and casual. They apparently knew each other well.

The jungle clearing where they landed was two miles from their destination, and Miguel drove them there along a bumpy, rutted road. Nelson's headache was murderous, worsened by every jostle of the Land Rover. Nevertheless, Nelson got straight to the point.

"The *curandero* . . . is he a panacean?"

Miguel nodded. "Most certainly—tattoo and all. Name's Mulac. We Tasered him, doped him up, interrogated him."

"And?"

"Nada. He denies being a panacean, even denies worshipping the so-called All-Mother. Says he worships Chac, the Mayan god of rain and lightning."

"That's odd."

When cornered, they might deny they were panaceans because they knew the penalty, but Nelson had never heard of one denying the All-Mother.

"You're sure of the tattoo?"

"Absolutely. The staff, the snake, the comet—all there. You'll see for yourself. After a little inducement, he became real cooperative. Showed us all his potions—"

"'All his potions'? They have only one."

"Not this fellow. He had quite a variety. Showed us his powders and plants too—but the plants weren't the panacea plants."

"You're sure you know what they look like?"

"I've got pictures. Nothing even close. We did find this patch of ground that looked like it was a garden or something. Somebody had ripped out whatever had been growing there. Nothing left but bare ground and a few weeds."

Damn. The plants would have been tangible proof. But then, the panaceans were said to rip up the plants by the roots to brew their concoction. A denuded garden proved nothing.

Or were the plants unable to grow in this climate? Was that why Mulac had reverted to local folk remedies?

"Look, we applied some severe techniques to him, if you know what I'm saying, and we've hit a wall. We can't get him to even admit he makes a panacea because he says there's no such thing—no one medicine that cures all. That's why he makes all sorts of different cures."

"This doesn't sound right at all."

"Tell me about it," Miguel said. "I've gotta say, if he didn't have the tattoo, I'd be pretty sure we had the wrong guy."

No, he wasn't the "wrong guy," but *something* seemed very wrong here. Nelson didn't even bother to ask if they'd found a sample of the panacea.

"What about the woman with Brody in that photograph I sent you? Was she there?"

"No sign of her, and nobody we showed it to recognized her or Brody. They could have been lying but who knows? We couldn't put the screws to everyone in the village."

"And the *curandero,* this Mulac? He didn't know Brody?"

"Said he didn't. We told him he was dead so there was no use trying to protect him, but he still said he'd never seen him. We didn't press him as hard on that as we did the panacea, but he didn't seem to have a clue."

Nelson couldn't see why this Mulac would suffer torture to protect a dead man.

Bradsher chimed in. "We'll need to tie this up before Doctor Fanning arrives."

"I don't think Mulac will last much longer," Miguel said. "Jorge, my associate from Mexico City, has been, shall we say, enthusiastic."

"You don't think you can squeeze anything more out of him?"

"We can always try, but I'm pretty sure that well is dry. You can judge for yourself. Here we are."

Nelson peered through the windshield at a cluster of huts that made up the *curandero*'s village: small thatch-roofed houses, with either hardwood or stucco walls, clustered in no particular order among the trees and along dirt paths. Here and there a battered off-road vehicle was parked in the brush.

They stopped before one of the huts. Inside they found Jorge with a bloodied man, curled in the fetal position, mewling like a sick kitten: the *curandero*.

Jorge, a squat man with Indian features, prodded him, tried to get him to speak, but his efforts only made the mewling louder.

This Mulac, this village healer, this dispenser of miraculous cures, had the tattoo. Nelson had never seen it anywhere else but on a panacean. Even though his story did not jibe with the customary practices of the cult, Mulac was certainly one of them. But Miguel had been right: They would get no more out of him.

"You must arrange for an act of faith."

"Leviticus?"

"Leviticus. And then I want you to stay around. Bradsher will send you pictures of someone who needs watching. She's looking for the panacea as well. And since she's half Mayan, she may be able to ferret out some things you missed."

Laura Fanning had forensic skills, whereas Miguel and his hired goon had none. Maybe it was a good thing

Simon had failed. The doctor could prove useful here. Perhaps she could sort this out.

Miguel looked offended. "I doubt that, but if she does?"

"Give her time to learn what she can, then confiscate whatever she finds and bring it to my hotel."

"What if she resists?"

"Obtain what she knows by any means necessary. And whether she resists or not, I want her and her companion to disappear. Forever. Do I make myself clear?"

"Perfectly."

"Good. Now drive us back to the helicopter."

He could *not* come away empty-handed here. According to his last report from NSA, phone and text chatter about "miracle cures" had dried up in the New York metro area. Obviously the panaceans has passed the word and were lying low. This village held the only lead right now.

But if it didn't pan out, what next? He'd worked so hard to get Pickens on board and had finally succeeded. He had his own project-specific black fund . . . but for what? With the panacean network gone to ground and silent, what was his next move?

And did it matter? He rubbed his temples. The headache was constant now. A tumor for sure. Would he even be around much longer to chase the panacea?

He sensed that the cult would not remain dormant long. Their goal in life was to dispense their infernal concoction. They'd be back at it soon. And Nelson would be ready for them.

He squeezed his eyes shut and massaged his scalp. He prayed he'd live long enough.

2

The rental company was called Top Car, one of three near Chetumal International Airport. A shuttle van had picked them up at the terminal.

"I imagine your Spanish is pretty good," Hayden said as they stepped off the shuttle into the midday heat and humidity of coastal Quintana Roo.

"You imagine correctly." And French and Yucatec too. But she didn't want to brag.

They'd hardly spoken during the entire trip. On the leg from JFK to Cancún, they'd both been in first class but across the aisle from each other. She'd watched Hayden chow down on mimosas and the steak-and-omelet breakfast. Nerves about the flight and the uncertainty about what would follow had killed her appetite. The only thing he'd said to her was, "You gonna eat that?" when he saw that she'd barely touched her food. She'd gladly handed it across.

Conversation on the noisy Cessna flight from Cancún to Chetumal had been possible only through headsets, and neither of them bothered.

"Maybe you should handle the rental counter then," he said. "Reservation's all set. And could you inquire about a package for me?"

"Package of what?"

"Some stuff I had sent down yesterday."

"What kind of stuff?"

"Stuff I didn't want to take on the plane."

She could tell she'd get no more information out of him, so she let it go.

As she started toward the counter, she pointed to the jumble of duffels and backpacks they'd brought along. "Watch those while I see what's what."

He saluted her, then pulled a fistful of clear plastic

strips from the pocket of the lightweight khaki safari jacket he wore.

"What are those?"

"Zip ties. Thousand and one uses."

He began looping them through the handles of their luggage.

"What are you doing?"

"Need to use the little boys' room. This'll keep any-one from walking off with one of our bags."

"How?"

"Because he'll have to carry them all at once, and that ain't gonna happen."

As he disappeared into the men's room, Laura stepped up to the counter. She went through the rental process, keeping an eye on the luggage. A couple of passing men slowed to give the zip-tied bags a curious look, but kept moving.

Noon now. She realized this was the perfect time to check her voice mail. Phil had had all morning to hear from his ex-SEAL friend. She checked the signal: four bars.

First she called home again. She'd checked in from Cancún and now Steven would want to hear that she'd survived the trip to Chetumal in what he'd called a "puddle jumper." After assuring him that all was going smoothly, she dialed her voice mail.

One call. Phil's voice: *"Hope all's well. My guy in Montauk can't find any record of an ex-SEAL named Hayden on any of the teams in the last twenty-five years. He didn't see any point in going back past that because you said he was fortyish. But he's gonna dig a little deeper, just to make sure he didn't miss anything. That's H-A-Y-D-E-N, right? Like that actress? I'll get back to you as soon as I hear something more."*

Laura chewed her lip as she put her phone away. Had Hayden lied about the SEAL thing? Stahlman seemed to have such high regard for him. Hard to believe he hadn't checked up on him. If he was lying about that, what else was he lying about?

Hayden came out of the men's room—wiping his hands on a paper towel, she noted with approval—then began to snip the ties with a little tool. When finished, he stood guard.

And yes, they had a package for Señor Hayden. The woman behind the counter put a cardboard box on the counter. Laura hefted it. Heavier than it looked.

She handed Rick the box then grabbed the handle on her duffel—which immediately snapped its connection. "Damn!"

This duffel had been her constant companion on all her trips down here, so she hadn't even considered replacing it. She guessed the wear and tear had finally got to it.

But Rick was suddenly there with one of his zip ties.

"Never fear." He looped it here and he looped it there, then pulled it tight and snipped off the excess tail. "That should hold it." He waved the tail at her. "Thousand and one uses."

"You've made me a believer," she said.

His zip-tie nerdiness, although she couldn't call it endearing, did make him seem a little more human.

Ten minutes later they had the luggage stashed in the back of a Jeep Wrangler Rubicon and were ready to roll. Having checked cellular maps for Mexico before she left, she'd added a satellite phone to the rental package. Coverage had vastly improved since her last trip, but the southern interior sections of Quintana Roo and Campeche—where they were headed—remained woefully blank. Despite an international calling plan, her cell would be useless there.

"I'll drive," she said. "You navigate."

He frowned. "I'd figured it the other way around."

"I've driven through this interior before, and you haven't."

Since the divorce she'd gotten used to driving herself everywhere and preferred to have the wheel when she was on the road. A control issue, she guessed.

"You're sure?"

"I haven't been tossing back mimosas."

"Only a couple. And that was hours ago. Besides, I've got a very efficient liver."

"You've also got the coordinates. Where's our first stop?"

He pulled out his phone, tapped the screen a few times and said, "Somewhere about forty-fifty miles southwest of a place called José María Morelos, wherever that is."

Laura started the Jeep. "Been there."

"Where? This José María Morelos?"

"Yep. And that area of the interior as well."

"Back in your bioprospecting days?"

"Exactly. We'll head north on 307, then take 293."

"Sounds like a plan." He cranked up the AC. "What about lunch?"

After two omelets and two steaks?

"I've got protein bars."

"Good enough. Let's roll."

Laura found her way to Route 307 where she hit the accelerator and got them moving along the worn, four-lane blacktop.

"Know what's missing from the map?" Hayden said, staring at his phone. "Rivers."

Very observant, she thought. Most people wouldn't notice. Or was he just trying to make conversation? He'd barely acknowledged her presence since boarding at JFK. Now that they were side by side, one-on-one, he decided to get chummy?

Lighten up, she told herself. We're stuck together for

two weeks, might as well make the best of it. She'd give him a little geography lesson.

"That's because there aren't any in Yucatán or Quintana Roo. Rivers need changes in elevation—hills and valleys—so they can flow. Look around you: flat as the proverbial pancake. The whole peninsula is like this. It's all limestone. The rain percolates through it. With no runoff into the ocean, the Carib is crystal clear around here."

"Flat all right," he said, gazing out the window. "If you woke me up and told me we were driving through bayou country in Louisiana, I wouldn't argue."

"Never been there but I'll take your word for it." She pointed to their right where utility poles and scrawny, scraggly trees flashed by. "You can't see it, but Laguna Bacalar is over there, just past the trees—a huge crystal-clear lake fed by underground streams."

He put down the phone. "How's it feel to be back home?"

Yeah, definitely getting chummy. Was he probing her? She should be probing him.

"This isn't home. The U.S. is home. Salt Lake City, Utah, to be exact."

"Thought Stahlman said you were Mayan."

"*Half* Mayan—on my mother's side. My father is Caucasian."

"Must have wound up with a lot of his genes, because you don't look Mexican. Not with those eyes."

"This is my mother's homeland. And if she were here you'd have caught yourself an earful for that remark about looking 'Mexican.'"

He made a face. "Is this where I get called a racist or something?"

Looking like she did and growing up in SLC, she knew racism firsthand, and this wasn't it.

"Not at all. But you'd hear all about Mexico being

nothing more than a political construct and the Maya being a *people*."

"The ones who built those pyramids, right? Visited Chichen Itza once. Talk about steep steps."

She couldn't resist: "An ex-SEAL who's afraid of heights?"

"Rather HALO jump than do those steps. You must have been up there at some time or another."

"They're closed off now, but yeah."

And yes, the steps to the top were scary steep. Not so bad going up, but coming down . . .

"Well, then you know: one missed step and you're wasting away in quadriplegiaville." He lifted the box that had been held for him and started pulling at the tape that sealed it. "So you're half Mayan. What's the rest of you?"

She didn't want to be talking about herself, but about him. How to turn the subject?

"English. A Mormon missionary named Jared Fanning came through the jungle preaching his faith. He and my mother fell in love and that was that. How about you? Where do you come from?"

He didn't seem to hear. "Got the blue eyes from him, I take it."

"Him and the Spaniard in the woodpile."

"Huh?"

"That's what my mother used to say. The conquistadors were big on raping the natives. My father is blue-eyed and my mother is brown-eyed, but she must carry a blue-eye gene. Since brown is dominant, the blue recessive was never expressed in her family. But apparently I caught her recessive. Match that blue allele with my father's and you have a brown-skinned, blue-eyed girl: me."

"You mentioned growing up in Utah, and by your reaction to my A.M. libations, I take it you're a Mormon."

How are we still talking about *me*?

"Was. Raised LDS but I never bought into it."

The older she'd got, the harder she'd found it to believe. The Church was filled with good, decent, hardworking people, but its origin was simply too hard to swallow. Her mother had converted before the marriage in Salt Lake City, but Laura was pretty sure she hadn't fully invested either. When her mother would take her on trips down here to visit her maternal grandparents, she'd become a different person in her own land—more relaxed, more fun.

"What are you?" she said before he could ask another question.

He smiled. "Devout agnostic. So if you're not Mormon, what are you now? A teetotaling Baptist?"

"Undecided." She glanced at him. "Tell me, Mister Hayden, does that add or detract from my status of being 'too perfect' a match for this assignment?"

"Call me Rick. Stahlman insists on the 'Mister' formality, but I don't see him all that often. Two weeks straight of 'Mister Hayden' from you will wear me out."

She thought: Your chopped-up sentences and dropped pronouns and articles are already wearing me out.

"Okay, Rick." She wasn't crazy about it—especially since it appeared he'd lied on his résumé—but she could see his point. "But you didn't answer my question."

"Can't see how your beliefs matter. What gets me is that here we are right where you did your bioprospecting. What is that, anyway?"

He had the box open now and was uncoiling bubble wrap from what looked like—

"Is that a gun?"

"Nope. It's a glazed Krispy Kreme."

Okay. She deserved that. Dumb question.

"What caliber?"

He held it up. Big, boxy, with a black matte finish. "Glock .45."

She'd seen plenty of .45-caliber wounds on her autopsy table. Few victims survived a center-of-mass hit from that size bullet.

"How did you manage to ship that here?"

"If you know who to ask and can afford the fee—which Stahlman paid—it's easy. Bought it from a guy who runs a sports shop in the city. Took care of everything."

He ejected the empty magazine and began loading it from a box of shells that had accompanied the weapon. Its label read *Federal Hydra-Shok® JHP*.

"Hollow points?"

He nodded. "You've seen what they do once they get inside, I assume."

"Not pretty. Who are you planning on shooting?"

"No plans of shooting anyone at all. Hope to keep it that way. But you know what they say: A gun is like a parachute; if you really need one and don't have one, you'll never need one again."

"A lot of firepower there."

"Yeah, well, if it comes down to using it . . . I don't like to have to shoot somebody twice."

The remark sparked an instant flare of annoyance. "Wouldn't want to inconvenience you."

He gave a derisive snort. "Why the chip on your shoulder?"

Did she have a chip? The SEAL lie, maybe. Get over it, Laura.

"It just sounded so high-handed." She lowered her voice to mimic him. "'I don't like to have to shoot somebody twice.'"

He barked a laugh. "Okay, I can see how you could take it wrong. I meant that not putting your target down with the first shot means that he has a chance to fire back and put *you* down. I'll phrase it better the next time."

She caught the snarky edge but let it slide.

"It's okay. I'll be fine."

"That's what I'm here to guarantee." He looked around as he continued loading the magazine. His fingers seemed to know what to do and were acting on their own. "Lots of empty land. Forget Louisiana. This could be Indiana or Illinois—without the cornfields."

"The government develops the coast of Quintana Roo, but ignores the interior. None of the money they make at all those resorts—and they make a ton—filters to the natives."

"Your people."

"Yes. My people. Maya. We were here first. Then the Spaniards came."

"You're getting all grumpy again. I can tell."

"Well, why not? This was their land. They deserve a piece of the pie."

"Deserve?" He snorted again. "'Deserve' is something people make up in their heads. Like 'fair.' There is no 'fair,' only what people agree is fair and can enforce. People don't get what they deserve, they only get what's coming to them."

This was interesting. Not in a good way—she hated the sentiment—but it offered a peek past his bluff, soldier-of-fortune façade.

"Hey, the Maya are good, decent, peace-loving people—"

"And 'good, decent, peace-loving people' tend to get just what's coming to them."

"Oh? And what would that be?"

"You see that roadkill we just passed? That's what's coming to good, decent, peace-loving people."

She remembered whizzing by a lump of brown fur on the shoulder and felt herself getting steamed.

"Nice view of the world, Mister Hayden."

"An eyes-open view. I didn't make it that way. And just because I see it doesn't mean I like it. The people in power make the rules. But look around: Do you see your good, decent, peace-loving people in power? No. Why not? Because they don't run for office. Or if they do, they lack that core of ruthlessness necessary to win." He glanced at her. "You strike me as a good person. Would you run for office?"

The question took her by surprise, as did the "good person" remark. Yesterday he'd called her "good people." Sincere? Or just stroking her?

"I-I've never even considered it."

"I rest my case. You'd rather be bioprospecting. Which I still don't understand."

Okay. She was glad to get off this topic—whatever it was.

"It involves lots of terms—ethnobotanist is a favorite—but it comes down to investigating how native peoples use local plants and such to make medicines. Some of those folk medicines really work, and there are firms out there that want to develop them into commercial products and make lots of money."

"Sounds like PhD work. How does an MD get involved?"

"When she's just 'too perfect' not to be involved."

He gave her a wry smile. "Am I ever gonna hear the end of that one?"

"Not while I'm around. Anyway, when I was in my fourth year of med school, someone heard from someone who'd heard from someone—you know how that goes—that I was half Mayan and spoke Yucatec. An ethnobotanical research company—"

"There's a mouthful."

"—approached me and offered *big* bucks if I'd help investigate medicinal plants and practices in Meso-america. The money was too good to turn down. I could put off my residency—I'd been planning on neurology—and build up my résumé along with my savings while possibly making a breakthrough discovery. I mean, the anti-lymphoma drug vincristine was developed from the rosy periwinkle found on Madagascar. If I could come up with something like that . . . well, the positives far outweighed the negative of delaying my residency. In fact, if I was successful at all, I could name my residency."

"And did you?"

"Make the breakthrough discovery?" She shook her head, saddened by the memories. "Turned out the company that hired me was more into biopiracy. They'd find something useful, patent it, and license it to one of the big pharmas without giving a dime back to the people they'd stolen it from. I blew the whistle on them and got out."

He pointed to her. "See? You're one of the good guys. And now you're back, hunting for the panacea." He waved at the surrounding countryside. "You think it might have originated here?"

"No. Because—and I thought I'd made this crystal clear to Mister Stahlman—I don't believe it exists."

He finished loading the magazine, then shoved it into the Glock's grip. She noticed that he didn't chamber a round before stowing it in the glove compartment.

"*Some*thing is going on."

As he spoke he pulled a large, black-handled jack-knife from the box. He unfolded and refolded a wicked looking four-inch blade, then stowed it in a side pocket of his jacket.

"I won't argue that," she said. "And I'll admit that

I don't have an answer as to what is *really* going on. But I'm not going to fill the void with a mythical cure-all."

"You ever think that the panacea might exist because we're able to have the opinion that it can't?"

"Can't what?"

"Exist."

Was she hearing right?

"Could you repeat that?"

"Okay. Did you ever think the panacea might exist because we're able to have the opinion that it *can't* exist?"

It made even less sense the second time.

"Just what is that supposed to mean?"

He sighed. "It's complicated."

Was this one of the "interesting conversations" Stahlman had mentioned?

"We've got plenty of time."

"Nah." He looked almost embarrassed. "Let's keep our eye on the prize." He checked his phone again. "We're headed for . . . " He shook his head. "No idea how to say this. Don't your Mayan folk believe in vowels?"

"We have lots of vowels. Show me."

"Not while you're driving. But at least I can pronounce the name of the medicine man or *curandero* we're supposed to see."

"It's *ah-men* in the old tongue."

"As in 'amen to that'? Anyway . . . " He squinted at his phone's screen. "This guy's name is Mu—"

"Mulac? I know him."

Rick gave her a wide-eyed stare. "And there it is."

"What?"

"One degree of separation again. Why should I be surprised you know this guy? This whole scenario has been arranged."

So he was back to that now? "You said that yesterday. It was ridiculous then and it's ridiculous now."

"Really? Guy who was terminally ill returns from Maya country in perfect health and dispenses an 'impossible' cure to an incurably ill little boy known to a certain deputy medical examiner who happens to be half Mayan. The healer guy dies as a result of what looks like foul play and ends up on the autopsy table of said deputy ME who happens to have traveled extensively in the area where the dead man visited and just happens to know the medicine man to whom the dead man has been connected."

Put that way, Laura found it . . . startling. More than a little.

"Okay, you've got a point. An amazing string of coincidences, but nothing more. I mean, how could anyone *arrange* that chain of events?"

"Not talking about just anyone."

"Then who? God?"

He looked uncomfortable. "Not sure I want to get into this."

They reached the junction with Route 293 then. She turned onto it, heading on a northwest course along the narrower, two-lane blacktop.

"Go ahead. We've still got a ways to go before we go off road. Hit me."

"When do we hit the jungle?"

She gestured at the trees crowding closer to the road. "This is it."

He stared out at the leafy hardwoods of various shapes and sizes. "Really? You call this a jungle?"

"It *is*. You were expecting ferns and palms—a rain forest, right?"

"Well, yeah."

"Rain forests are a subset of jungles, but not all jungles are rain forests."

"Duly noted. So I shouldn't expect to see monkeys swinging from branch to branch and I can't grab a banana whenever I feel like it?"

"You might catch sight of a spider monkey, but banana palms prefer wetter feet than they can get here. Rain on the peninsula averages maybe forty, fifty inches a year—about the same as Long Island. Enough for hardwoods like these. The really tall ones with the big buttress roots you see are ceiba trees, the smaller ones are baalché and copal."

"Spoken like a true ethnobotanist."

"Right. But now let's get back to how this was all *arranged*."

"Okay. But prepare yourself for some weirdness—at least what most people would consider weird."

She shook her head. "You wouldn't believe the weirdness I've seen people do to themselves and to each other. It takes a lot to weird me out."

"This'll leave everyday weirdness in the dust. So here goes: What if . . . what if humanity's sentience, our consciousness, our self-awareness is an anomaly?"

"An anomaly?"

"Yeah . . . an aberration. What if we started out genetically geared to be dumb forest dwellers, hanging from trees and eating insects and fruit? But something went wrong. Some errant gamma ray got through the magnetosphere and collided with some proto-chimp's chromosomes and its brain started to change."

He sounded erudite, and that surprised her—like he'd done some research.

"That's not a terribly far-out what-if," she said. "It might very well have happened that way, though probably not. But I can go with it for the sake of discussion."

"Doesn't have to be a gamma ray. Can be a random mutation—anything that changes a primate's genome and affects its brain. Now, those brain changes, through millions of years and stages of developmental modifications and evolutionary dead ends, they eventually result in a *mind*—sentience, sapience, self-awareness, reasoning, imagination."

He'd changed as he spoke. The flat, almost dead eyes had come alive. Wherever this was going, he was into it.

"Okay," she said, "the hominid chain leads to *Homo sapiens*. Us. That's pretty well accepted."

"Right. But the next is a bit of a leap for most people: What if sapience and self-awareness are an anomaly in the universe?"

"Okay. Stop right there. That's hard to buy. No, impossible to buy. The universe is unimaginably huge. Our galaxy alone contains over four hundred billion—that's with a 'b' as in boy—stars. If you imagine the Milky Way as the continental U.S., our sun, Sol, is the size of a white blood cell in Colorado. As for the universe, with its *billions* of galaxies—again with a 'b'—the experts figure there are a septillion stars out there."

"Never even heard of a septillion."

"Think of a ten with twenty-four zeroes after it. With that many stars, and all the possible planets circling them, I don't see sapience and self-awareness being the least bit rare."

"What about Fermi's paradox?"

"Fermi the physicist?"

"Yeah. One of the so-called fathers of the atomic bomb."

"Well, I've heard of him, but didn't know he had a paradox."

"Also known as the Great Silence. It accepts what you said about all the billions of stars and planets in our galaxy, but it asks: With all those potential civilizations out there, many so much older than ours, why haven't we heard from anyone?"

"I . . . I don't know." She'd never really thought about it.

"The conclusion I draw is that we're either alone, or that sapience is extremely rare—you might say, vanishingly rare. Look, we've got a million and a half vertebrates and invertebrate species on the planet. How many are sapient and self-aware? You can make a case in a very limited sense for dolphins and some apes maybe, but only one species has built a civilization. Sure, lots of stars and lots of planets out there, and no doubt lots of species spread all over the universe, but what if the human level of sapience is so rare that when it occurs it attracts . . . attention."

"Attention from what?"

"From larger intelligences—'intellects vast, cool and unsympathetic,' as Wells put it."

"H. G.?"

"The same."

"A *War of the Worlds* scenario? You're not seriously going there."

He shook his head. "Nothing so trite or obvious. You've heard of the Chinese curse, right?"

"'May you live in interesting times'? Sure."

"A multipart curse. That's only the first of three. The next one is 'May you come to the attention of those in authority.'"

She hadn't heard that one. Like the first, in typical Asian fashion, it could be taken in either a positive or negative way. But since it was a curse . . .

"Yeah, I can see that. Better to stay off the radar."

"Exactly. But what if our sapience has brought us to the attention of 'vast, cool and unsympathetic' intellects in authority?"

A crazy concept . . . and not a comfortable one.

"Your what-ifs are starting to creep me out."

"Just asking questions."

"Are you talking about God . . . or gods?"

He shook his head. "Bad word. 'God,' whether uppercase or lowercase, conjures up the supernatural and the spiritual. Gets you into religion or H. P. Lovecraft territory, and that just muddies the water. I'm talking about entities, vast intelligences. Don't dress them up any more than that."

This was so off the wall, but Laura had to admit he had her attention. "Okay. We've been noticed by . . . entities. Now what?"

"That's the big question. Here we are, an aberration that calls itself *Homo sapiens,* a curiosity on the radar and under the cosmic microscope. How are we viewed? Simply as curiosities? Or as playthings . . . toys?"

"Curiosities, I would hope. Where's all this going?"

"Right back to this panacea we're hunting. You yourself have said it's scientifically impossible."

"It is."

"Impossible is merely an opinion."

"No, impossible is impossible."

"Like putting a man on the moon and bringing him back alive?"

"Okay. I stand corrected. Many people were of the opinion it was impossible when they should have said 'not feasible.' Because in theory nothing about a round trip to the moon broke the laws of physics and biology. A panacea smashes them to bits and pieces."

"Then why are we driving through a Mayan jungle?"

Okay, now she was on more comfortable ground—her turf.

"Because this is how science works. Stahlman says it exists, I say it doesn't and tell him to prove his position. He says I can find it here and is willing to make it very much worth my while to look for it. I've come to investigate and prove him wrong."

"But you've seen cures you can't explain."

"True. But I have limited data on those 'cures' and so I'm here to expand my knowledge base."

"That doesn't change the fact that you're looking for something you say cannot exist."

"No, I'm looking for something that may be real but is being passed off as something that cannot exist—a medical breakthrough being passed off as a cure-all. Big difference. That unknown something might not have the unlimited scope of a panacea, but might well have limited properties that could prove to be a boon for some field of medicine."

She realized she was back to a form of bioprospecting.

He said, "But what if a true panacea does exist?"

"It can't."

"Go with me. What if it does? Would you use it?"

"Of course. To cure the incurable is a doctor's dream come true."

"Well, *a healer's* dream, anyway." His eyes were virtually sparking now. "Know the third part of the Chinese curse?"

"No. But I'm sure I'm about to learn."

"'May you find what you are looking for.'"

"Really?"

"Really. Sounds good but has an ominous ring."

It certainly did. Enough to send a chill through her. In fiction, finding your heart's desire never turned out well. Probably worked the same in real life.

"I don't see how a panacea could be something bad," she said.

"Even if it's from outside?"

"*Outside?* What's that supposed to mean?"

"A true panacea would upset the order of things. Think about it. We're talking about breaking the laws of biology and even physics. That's why you keep saying it's impossible. So if it *does* exist, it can't be from here. Has to be from somewhere else."

"You're getting all fantasy and science fictiony again."

"Not fantasy or fiction of any kind if it's real. Something like that, something that breaks all the rules, has to have been introduced from somewhere else—from *outside*. And for what purpose? Just to see how the playthings deal with it? Or is there an agenda . . . one we can't comprehend?"

Something in his tone struck her. On the surface it sounded like proselytizing, but she detected something else. A note of . . . what? Desperation? Almost as if he was trying to convince himself as well as her.

"What do you know—or *think* you know?"

He shook his head. "Know? *Don't* know, that's the problem. But I've seen . . . "

"Seen what?"

"Nothing. I'm going to shut up now."

"Come on. You can't cut off with a statement like that."

"Hey, look," he said, craning his head to look up through the windshield. "A helicopter. We should have rented ourselves one of those."

"Don't try to change the subject."

"Forget it," he said, leaning back. "Just funning with you."

She didn't believe him, not for a nanosecond. But she'd seen the walls go up and the shades come down. She wasn't going to get any more.

"'Funning,' eh? Like your 'vast, cool and unsympathetic' intellects?"

"Exactly. Although you're the intellect here. I'm just the muscle."

Laura wondered about that. She'd already caught him in one lie. How many others hid beneath that blunt exterior?

"You do realize that mental institutions are full of

people with ideas like the ones we just discussed, don't you?"

He nodded. "And that's a shame, isn't it. Because if you say you can't eat pork because the creator of the universe told you not to, fine. If you say there's a part of you no one can see that's immortal and will be reincarnated in a new body after you die, cool. If you say the earth was created in six days back in four thousand four BC, some school boards even consider making that part of the curriculum. If you—"

"Okay, you've made your point."

"I rest my case."

What a strange man he was turning out to be. A lot deeper—and a whole lot weirder—than she'd imagined. Obviously he'd given this trip and its purpose a whole lot of thought, but from such an unusual angle.

Something in his past—something he'd experienced or thought he'd seen—had skewed his take on reality. That made her a little uneasy. She preferred a travel companion thoroughly grounded in the real world to someone who thought humanity was the plaything of "intellects vast, cool and unsympathetic."

But she was stuck with him.

3

After a bumpy ride through the jungle, Laura finally found her way to the village.

"Gotta tell you," Rick said as they pulled up to the outskirts, "this isn't at all what I expected."

A cluster of huts lay ahead, stippled with afternoon sunlight, yet he was looking out the rear window.

"How so?"

"When you think Mayans, you think stone—or at

least I do. Stone houses, stone temples, stone walls. These may have thatch roofs, but they've got solid walls and look like, well, houses."

"They may not have central AC, but the twentieth century has had its influence."

"But not the twenty-first?"

"Not yet."

He looked around through the rear window again.

"That's like the fourth or fifth time you've done that. What are you looking for back there?"

He shrugged. "Just wondering if we were followed."

"We've had the road—or maybe I should say 'path'— all to ourselves."

"If you say so." He gestured to the village. "Where is everyone, by the way?"

The village looked pretty much the same as the last time she had been here, except it had been bustling with life then.

"I don't know." Laura reached for the door handle. "Let's go take a—"

"Hang on," he said, gripping her forearm. "Give me a minute."

He pulled out a couple of his zip ties and began looping them around his belt near his right hip.

"What are you doing?"

"Forgot to send a holster down. Bear with me. Be done in a sec or two."

When he finished fiddling with the ties, he fished the pistol from the glove compartment and chambered a round.

"You really think that's necessary?"

"Hope not. Hate to find out it is and not have a round in the chamber."

Okay, that made sense.

Slipping the pistol through the zip ties, he covered it with the flap of his safari jacket and got out of the car.

The heat and humidity enveloped Laura and clung like Saran Wrap as she stepped out on her side. They met by the front bumper.

"How's it look?" he said, smoothing the jacket. "No telltale bulge?"

She noticed a slight bulge, but she was looking for it.

"That's amazing. All with zip ties."

"Thousand and one uses, I tell you." He looked around. "So here are the houses. Where are the people?"

"Let's go find out."

They walked through the silent village without spotting a soul. Something was wrong. Laura felt it along the back of her neck.

On the far side, in a small clearing to the west, they found what appeared to be the entire population standing in a circle around something hanging from a branch of one of the larger ceibas.

Laura stopped in her tracks. "Is that . . . ?"

Rick's hand went inside his jacket but he kept walking.

"Yeah." His head was swiveling like a turret as he made a full turn while remaining on the move. "Human. And three guesses who."

Laura felt her heart's tempo pick up as adrenaline began to flow. She'd expected that 536—whoever they were—would be involved, but not . . . this.

She forced her feet forward. She didn't need three guesses, or even one. The body hung by its neck and was charred black. Just like the body she'd posted on Wednesday. Rick had been concerned about being followed. Apparently the 536 sect had arrived first and had their way with Mulac.

When the villagers spotted Rick approaching they cowered. A couple even started to run.

"Do not be afraid!" Laura called in the Yucatec dialect. "We mean no harm!"

Rick held his hands up, empty palms out for all to see.

The crowd parted for them and they stopped before the blackened corpse, swaying in the gentle breeze. The flies were making themselves at home. Close up she could see that he'd been strung up with wire.

"There a reason no one cut him down?" Rick said.

Laura hadn't even thought of that. She felt as if she were in a bad dream.

She put the question to the villagers. After some hesitation, one woman said in Yucatec, "A tall man and a short man come and they do this."

Laura gave her a closer look. She thought she knew her from a previous visit—the most outgoing of the customarily reclusive villagers. She looked much older now. What was her name?

"I know you. Tlalli, right? Remember me? I came to talk to Mulac years ago."

"Yes. I knew you right away. You look the same."

She thought, Oh, after marriage, a baby, and divorce, I doubt that, but . . . she meant the blue eyes, of course.

"You said two men did this?"

"Yes. They told us we had to leave Mulac there for three days. They said if we cut him down before that they would burn the village and we would all end as Mulac."

Her gut crawled. Oh, God. This was getting worse by the minute. She scanned the tree line and the brush. Were they still around? Suddenly she was glad for Rick and his big Glock.

When she translated, Rick walked over to the ceiba and used his knife to unknot the wire. Then he eased the body to the ground. It came to rest facedown.

Forcing herself forward, Laura squatted next to Mulac and tried to shift her mind into professional gear—become a medical examiner rather than a shocked and frightened traveler.

She'd met him only once, but even if she'd known him well, IDing him would have been difficult. It hadn't been a smooth meeting. Mulac had been very secretive, inhospitable, even hostile to her presence. He'd ignored most of her questions and had refused to show her any of his medicines.

His remains weren't as badly burned as Hanrahan's. On Mulac's back she still could trace the outline of a familiar tattoo. She couldn't tell if he'd been tortured before he died, or if he'd been alive when set ablaze.

She looked at Tlalli for an answer. "Did they . . . ?" She didn't know the word for torture. "Did they hurt Mulac before they killed him?"

"Yes," she said, nodding vigorously. "Hurt him bad. Then they hurt Itzel."

"Who's Itzel?"

Tlalli called to someone and another woman brought a little girl forward. She had a bloody cloth wound around her right hand. The other woman—her mother?—began to unwrap it.

I don't think I want to see this, Laura thought.

The bandage fell away to reveal four bloody finger-tips. Laura gasped when she realized the fingernails had been ripped off.

She glanced at Rick. His face had gone white.

He turned away. "Cover that," he said through clenched teeth. "*Now.*"

Laura motioned to the woman to take the child away.

Rick's reaction surprised her, because previously he hadn't seemed to react to anything. Mulac's charred, hanging corpse hadn't fazed him. But the child's muti-lated fingers . . . the sight of blood?

Maybe he was human after all.

"It's okay," she said when the child was gone.

Rick turned around. His color had improved but his eyes, if anything, were flatter and deader than ever.

"Tortured him and that didn't work," he said, his voice low and vibrating with rage, "so they tortured a little girl to get him to talk." He looked at the villagers. "Someone said a tall man and a short man came. Ask which one hurt the little girl."

She did and Tlalli answered.

"The short one," Laura translated.

Rick only nodded.

"What are you thinking?" she said.

"Nothing." He took a deep breath and nodded toward Mulac. "Is this guy—*was* this guy a panacean like Stahlman suspected?"

Laura nodded. "He has the tattoo."

A number of the villagers started babbling at once, terrified, some wailing.

"What's their problem?"

Laura listened and caught the gist of their concerns.

"You cut Mulac down and they're worried the men will burn the village as they promised."

"Well, I'm not about to string him up again. And you can tell them to bury him or whatever they do with their dead. The men who did this won't be back."

"How can you be so sure?"

"They left his body hanging here for one reason: you. To let you know they've got the lead in this and you might as well give up and go home."

"Well, that's about all that's left to do, isn't it?"

Home . . . it sounded so good. Stahlman could keep his money. She'd expected a certain amount of risk, but not torture and murder.

Rick looked around at the villagers. "Somebody's got to know something. Anyone hear what Mulac told the 536ers? And do you see that girl who was in the photo with Brody?"

Laura didn't see her. She asked Tlalli what Mulac told his killers before he died but she said no one had heard

anything but his screams. But when Laura pulled out
the photo and showed it around, the villagers shut
down.

"What's wrong?" Laura said.

Tlalli handed back the photo. "The bad men . . . they
have same picture."

That struck her like a blow.

"The same? With both people?"

Tlalli nodded.

But the papers had published only the half with
Chaim. How—? Oh, hell. When 536 hacked her computer they must have found the original scan. Dear God,
the photo had helped lead them straight to Mulac . . .
and now Mulac was dead. A wave of guilt swept over
her. She hadn't sent that photo to the papers, but still . . .

She shook it off. She could play the blame game later.

"Do you know the man?" she said, pointing to Chaim.

"We all tell the men that we don't know."

"But you do?" When Tlalli hesitated, Laura said,
"You know you can trust me. I've been here before and
never hurt anyone."

After a long pause, Tlalli said, "Chet."

Okay. Right. Chaim's nickname.

Tlalli added, "But Mulac say, he doesn't know him,
even though they say Chet is dead. Is that true? Chet is
dead?"

"It's true, I'm afraid," Laura said. "Why was Mulac
trying to protect a dead man?"

She touched the woman in the photo. "Because Chet
is with Ix'chel here."

Now they were getting somewhere.

"And who is Ix'chel?"

"Mulac's sister."

Now she understood why Mulac had denied knowing Chaim in the photo—because if he knew Chaim,
they'd expect him to know the woman as well.

Laura looked around. "Where is she?"

"She works in the city."

"Chetumal? Has anyone told her?"

"Atl went to tell her. He will bring her back when he finds her."

"Finds her?"

Tlalli shrugged. "We do not know where she lives."

"But she comes back from time to time?"

"Many times. She helped her brother with his medicines."

When Laura relayed all this to Rick, he said, "Well, if she helped her brother, we should probably wait around for her." He cocked his head and looked at her. "You don't look too sure about that."

She rubbed her moist, shaky palms against her upper arms. She wasn't easily rattled—medical examiner work had toughened her—but this had left her deeply shaken.

"I'm not sure of anything right now."

"Yeah, things got ugly real quick, didn't they. Look, this is your gig, so it's your call. You want to quit, we get right back in the Jeep and haul ass back to the airport."

Laura clenched her jaw. He'd said *quit*. She hated that word. Why'd he have to say *quit*?

"You think we're in danger here?"

"We'd only be a target if we knew something 536 doesn't know. Since that's not the case, I'd say we're safe."

That was small comfort, but . . .

"But that could change after we talk to Ix'chel," she said. "We might learn something they want to know."

"You let me worry about security. That's why I'm here. Your job is the panacea." He spread his hands. "Stay or back to the States?"

Oh, hell.

"Stay."

"Fine. Gonna take a walk through the village and check out the perimeter. Just to get familiar. Why don't you make more friends with the locals. Maybe someone knows something useful."

"I'm going to check in at home first."

She accompanied him as far as the Jeep, then watched him stroll off.

There he goes, she thought, leaving a trail of cast-off verbs and pronouns in his wake.

She sat in the Jeep and turned on its satellite phone. First, call home.

"All's well?" Steven said after she'd had a little talk with Marissa. *"You find your healer?"*

"Yes."

How much to tell him? Couldn't say he was murdered and set on fire, maybe burned alive. He'd freak.

"Any help?"

"Unfortunately he looks like a dead end."

Oh, my God! Did I just say that? I didn't mean—

"Oh, hell. Too bad. What next?"

"Trying to figure that out. I want to talk to his sister. She's supposed to show up later. Maybe she knows something helpful."

Finally—a string of completely true sentences.

The call ended with Steven's usual exhortations to stay safe and her usual assurances that she would. She wished she could feel just half as sure as she sounded.

Next she called her voice mail. One message:

"Hey, Doc, it's Phil. I know you say this guy saved you from a mugging and all, but the more we dig into him, the shakier his story looks. Turns out he wasn't a SEAL at all—in fact he was never even in the Navy. In case you didn't know, you've got to join the Navy to be a Navy SEAL. That's the bad news. But listen, lots of guys try to make themselves look

*more interesting by, shall we say, enhancing their past.
The good news is, it looks like he's an ex-cop from
Sausalito—that's the other side of the Golden Gate
from San Francisco. He was in the Marine Patrol out
there. Nowhere near as glamorous as being a SEAL,
but hey, it puts him on the right side of the law. Joined
young and took an early retirement. No black marks
against him. I'm trying to see what he's been up to
since he quit but that takes a little longer. Get back
to you soon as."*

Laura shook her head as she exited her voice mail.
Okay. Rick was lying about the SEAL thing. She didn't
like being lied to, but it wasn't a malicious lie, and he
wasn't lying to hide anything. Like Phil said: enhancing
his background. Maybe that helped his business. But
she was surprised Stahlman hadn't scoped that out before hiring him.

So instead of an ex-SEAL she was being shepherded
around by an ex-cop. Not so bad, she guessed. He'd handled that Glock like he was very comfortable and familiar with it. And Rick's deviations from the truth weren't
the problem; 536 was the problem. She hoped Rick was
right about them being gone.

She saw him approaching from down the road and
stepped out to meet him.

"Well?"

He shook his head. "No sign of anybody who
shouldn't be here. But I got to thinking." He reached out
a hand. "Can I see your bag a minute?"

She hesitated, then handed it to him. He promptly upended it, spilling its contents on the hood of the Jeep.

"Hey!"

"Don't you think it strange that 536 reached our destination ahead of us?" He began pawing through the
empty bag, one hand inside, the other outside, squeez-

ing the leather. "And just happened to be looking for the same *curandero*? That means either Stahlman or his guy James is tipping them off—unlikely—or they've been listening in. I realized you're never without this bag, so—ah!"

"What?"

He held up a black button. "You were bugged. That 536 mugger wasn't just after your phone. He planted this."

Laura couldn't hide her shock. "That's spy movie stuff."

"Not anymore. You can buy these gizmos online. Don't have much range so I doubt they've been able to listen in since we took off from JFK. But if they are . . . " He cocked his arm and hurled it into the jungle. "Let 'em listen to the crickets now. Or whatever passes for a cricket in these parts."

Laura was about to respond but stopped at the sound of a revving engine behind her.

A battered, topless Jeep Cherokee appeared, racing toward them. Rick's hand snaked inside his jacket as he grabbed her upper arm and gently but firmly pulled her behind their own Jeep. The Cherokee didn't even slow, however. Laura saw a young Mayan woman with a tear-streaked face in the passenger seat.

"Ix'chel," she said.

"Sure?"

"Ninety percent. I recognize her from the photo with Chaim. Of course she'd been smiling then."

They followed the Cherokee on foot as it raced through the village. It finally slowed to a halt near the crowd of villagers clustered about Mulac's remains. The young woman leaped out and ran. She didn't have to push her way through; the villagers parted for her. Laura saw her drop to her knees beside the corpse before she was closed from view.

Her wails of grief were wrenching to hear.

"Yep," Rick said, eyes and voice flat. "Guess you're right. But I don't think we'll be getting too much out of her tonight."

Poor girl, she thought.

Laura wasn't sure she even wanted to talk to Ix'chel now. Bad enough to lose your brother, but in such a horrible way.

"We can spend the night in Chetumal and come back in the morning," Rick said. "Or . . . "

"Or what?"

"Or stay here."

"Really? It looks like rain and, in case you hadn't noticed along the way, we didn't pass any motels."

"Got the Jeep."

The Jeep? Was he kidding?

Then she thought about it. They were outsiders here. If they spent the night on the outskirts of the village, they might seem less so. Maybe Ix'chel would be more willing to open up to her.

"We'll be safe?"

He patted the spot where he kept the Glock. "Oh, yeah."

"How will we work it?"

"You can have the backseat. Looks fairly comfortable."

Yeah. She could handle that. She wasn't quite as flexible as her younger self, but she'd slept in less hospitable spots during her bioprospecting days. The problem was sharing the car with Rick. Not that he gave off a lechy vibe—he didn't—but his weird worldview made her a little uneasy with him. Just how stable was he?

"Fine for me. But even if you could fit up front, I don't see you draping yourself across that center console."

"I can doze off anywhere, anytime, in any position.

Sleeping on a semi-reclined cushioned car seat is a piece of cake."

"Really?" Laura had to say it. "Something you learned in your SEAL training?"

He nodded without looking at her. "Yep."

Liar.

4

Brother Miguel called after sunset.

"*We're going to spend the night near the village*," he said.

"Why?" Nelson's grip tightened on the phone. "Have you found something?"

"*No. But it looks like the Fanning woman and her bodyguard or whatever he is are staying, so I figure we better do the same.*"

"Do you think she's on to something?"

"*Not yet, but it looks like some relative of the* curandero *showed up.*"

"The girl in the photo?"

"*We couldn't get close enough to make an ID, even with the binocs. And then the sun went down and so an ID is out of the question until morning. Looks like your gal and her guard dog have called it a night.*"

"This 'guard dog' . . . do you expect any problems with him tomorrow?"

"*He found the bug, so we can't listen in. But mostly he looks like a* zurramato."

Nelson hated when people threw in foreign slang.

"Which means?"

"*He's a dumbass.*"

Nelson thought of the missing and silent Simon. "Do not underestimate him."

"*I don't underestimate anyone. He did a reconnoiter,*"

as he should, but he's out of his element down here. Maybe he's good in a city, but out in the wild, in the jungle? Passed within twenty feet of where me and Jorge were perched. Not a clue we were there, watching his every move."

"Well, watch *her* every move tomorrow."

He had very much wanted Fanning out of the picture. But with nowhere to go from here, he found himself in the ironic position of rooting for her, hoping she'd stumble onto something that would turn a cold trail warm.

5

The rain came not too long after sunset and lasted maybe an hour. Rick had settled the doc into the Jeep before it began. With the doors locked and the windows open less than an inch, it became stuffy, but not unbearable. He'd harbored a faint hope the doc would fall asleep, but no such luck. Still, he couldn't let that stop him. Work to do.

As soon as the rain let up, he checked to make sure his Glock, his knife, and his flashlight were all where they were supposed to be, then opened the front passenger door.

"Where are you going?" she said from the backseat.

"Gonna take a little walk."

"I can't sleep either. I'll come with—"

"Uh-uh." The last thing he wanted. "Gonna do one last patrol before I settle down for the night."

"You're leaving me alone?"

Scared? he thought. No shame in that.

She'd just seen the charred remains of a man who was tortured and murdered for what he knew—or *might* know. Smart to be scared.

"Won't be far. Stay here with the doors locked. Anybody bothers you, or looks like they're even *thinking* of bothering you, lean on the horn. I'll be here in a flash."

"Okay. But don't be long."

"Back ASAP."

Just as soon as he conducted a little business with a couple of guys hiding in the jungle.

As he speed-walked down the road—really nothing more than two ruts flanking a line of weeds—sticking to the center so he wouldn't splash, he thought about the change in the doc's attitude toward him. He'd expected some hostility—after all, she hadn't wanted him along—but that seemed to have morphed into suspicion. Why? She learn something she shouldn't?

His name, for instance? Wasn't using the one he'd been born with, but "Rick" was close enough for it to *seem* like his. Nah. His real name was buried too deep for her or anyone else to ferret out. Had to be something else. He was wrapped in so many layers . . . had one of them slipped?

Worry about that later. Concentrate on the bad guys now.

He knew where they'd set up watch. He'd been studying the sides of the road as the doc had driven them toward the village. Sunlight had flashed off a field glass lens on the way in, and again when he'd done his walk-around. That walk-around had also revealed a place at the edge of the road where the underbrush had been crushed and then reset upright to hide the damage. Fixed up well enough for the casual passerby, but not for anyone looking for a spot where someone might have driven off the road.

The rain had been a boon, because water was still dripping and splashing from the zillions of leaves around him, masking his approach. The clouds were blowing off, leaving a starry sky. The moon would rise soon. Had to get this done before then.

He'd numbered the steps to the village from the break in the brush. He'd subtracted the Jeep's distance from the village, and now found the spot with little trouble.

Here came the hard part: reaching them without giving himself away. He was sure they were armed and just as sure that they'd shoot first and ask questions later if they spotted anyone sneaking up on them.

Crouching low, taking it slow and easy, feeling his way in the dark, he followed the crushed vegetation until he heard the murmur of low voices and the sound of dripping water splashing against metal—on the roof and hood of a car. Those big drops were a big help.

Edged closer and came upon the rear end of a Land Rover. The dashboard lights provided the only illumination, silhouetting two heads. Smoke drifted into the air through the open windows. Rick recognized the smell. The one in the passenger seat was sucking on a J. As Rick watched, the guy on the driver side tilted a bottle up to his lips. Just a couple of working stiffs relaxing after a hard day in the torture-murder trade. They were talking in Spanish so it didn't matter that he couldn't make out all the words.

Now the hard part: subduing them for a little Q & A. He couldn't brace both of them in the front seat with just the Glock. One would try something in the dark and everything could go to hell in seconds. Had to get them out in the open first.

Squatting by the bumper, he pulled his pistol and placed it in his lap, then pulled his knife. He left it folded as he gripped it in his left hand with the butt protruding half an inch beyond the heel of his palm. He raised his free hand and raked the metal of the rear hatch with his fingernails. Five quick scratches: 1-2-3-4-5. Then again. And again.

One of the men—sounded like the guy in the driver seat—stopped the other from speaking. Rick scratched again. More words were spoken, then the driver's door opened. Rick grabbed the Glock as one of them approached.

Just as the driver stepped around the rear corner, Rick leaped to his feet and started counting seconds.

One . . .

Whatever the driver had been drinking had slowed him down, allowing Rick to deliver two sharp backhand blows, *yawara* style, with the butt end of the knife to the side of his head.

. . . *two* . . .

His knees buckled, leaving him vulnerable to a solid kick in the balls.

. . . *three* . . .

As the guy went down with a groan, Rick raced around to the passenger side and jammed the muzzle of the Glock against the other one's cheek.

. . . *four* . . .

By the dashboard light he could see a semiautomatic in the passenger's right hand and his left reaching across to the door handle.

"Drop it!" Rick shouted, hoping the guy knew some English. "Drop it on the floor right now or you're dead!"

After seeing what that little girl had suffered, he almost hoped the guy did try something. Maybe that came through. The gun thudded to the floor.

Rick yanked open the door. "Out!"

The guy complied and Rick noticed that he was shorter than his pal. He kept that in mind as he prodded him toward the rear of the Rover where his moaning buddy lay on his side in the fetal position, hands between his legs.

"Hands and feet," he said to short stuff, handing him

a pair of zip ties and then pointing to the guy on the ground. "Behind the back, double figure eights. I'm sure you know how it's done."

When the first guy was tied, Rick forced the second down onto his belly, put a knee in his back, and zip-tied his wrists and ankles. Then he checked the first. The ties were looser than he liked so he remedied that.

Now he could relax a little. He pulled their wallets from their pockets, then hauled the pair around and up so they were sitting with their backs against the rear bumper.

"Okay, *señors*." Rick pulled out his flashlight and flicked the beam back and forth between their faces. "What have we here?"

The taller one looked a little fuzzy. Most likely had a concussion. Two sharp shots to the temple will do that. His bruised *cojones* had to be adding to his misery.

Short stuff's eyes flicked left, right, up, down, then repeated the circuit. He was scared but not showing it. This obviously had not been part of the plan.

"I assume you're members of 536, right?"

Neither spoke, so he opened their wallets. The taller guy, the one with the swollen *cojones*, was Miguel Herrera. Short stuff was Jorge Medina.

"Lost your voices? No problem."

He leaned Miguel forward and checked his right arm. There it was: *DXXXVI* in blue ink. Jorge's arm had a tattoo of a Mexican Day of the Dead skull, but no number of any sort.

Okay. Now he had a pretty good idea who gave the orders and who followed them. Miguel was 536, and Jorge was either a wannabe or a hired hand. According to Stahlman, the members of 536 were zealots who could pretty much be counted on to go to their deaths without giving up anything. So Rick would start with Miguel.

The flashlight provided only limited illumination, so he

stepped around to the driver's side, reached in the open door, and turned on the headlights. Then he dragged Miguel to the front of the car, followed by Jorge, and leaned them against trees with the light in their eyes. Both wore light cotton pants and guayaberas—Miguel's white, Jorge's yellow.

"Let's get past what I already know: You were sent here to find out whatever Mulac knows about the panacea. So was I. You got here first and killed the guy during the course of your interrogation or shortly after. So, since I can't question him, I'm left with you guys. Who wants to start?"

As expected, deadpan stares and silence.

"Okay. We'll let the coin decide." He pulled a quarter from his pocket. "Heads Miguel, tails Jorge."

Flipped it, caught it, and checked it in the headlight. It showed tails.

"Heads it is! Miguel wins!" He pulled out his flashlight and inspected the branches on the surrounding trees. "Let's see . . . "

Found one about seven feet off the ground that was an inch thick near its base. Perfect. He used the sawtooth edge of his knife blade to cut it off five inches from the trunk.

Next he locked a zip tie around Miguel's neck—not too tight.

"That's your collar."

Then he looped a second tie through the first at his nape.

"And let's call that your leash." He placed himself squarely before Miguel. "Okay, Miguel, I'm asking you . . . just you: What did Mulac tell you about the panacea?"

"*Chingate!*"

"Don't understand much Spanish, but I've heard that before, and it's not very nice. That your final word?"

"*Besa mis huevos!*"

"Guess that settles it then."

He dragged Miguel by his neck to the tree where he hauled him to his feet. He lifted him under his sweaty arms until the loop of the leash tie hooked over the cut branch, then let him hang.

With his air cut off, Miguel began twisting and kicking—as well as anyone could kick with his ankles tied. Rick waited until his face was good and purple before grabbing him by the hips and lifting him just enough to relieve the pressure on his throat.

"We'll try again: What did Mulac tell you about the panacea?"

Miguel gasped a few times, then answered. His voice was barely audible. "*Chingate!*"

"Okay. Gave you a chance." Rick let him drop and stepped over to Jorge. "Guess that leaves you."

Jorge didn't respond. His wide-eyed gaze was fixed on Miguel's writhing struggles behind Rick. Rick didn't need to look around to know what was happening. Instead he slapped Jorge's cheek.

"Hey! I'm talking to you."

"You just gonna let him die there?" he said in heavily accented English, still staring.

Rick hadn't expected anything out of Miguel, so no loss.

"He made his choice. What's yours?"

Jorge said nothing but his eyes widened further as the sound of Miguel's struggles stopped.

As Rick began looping a zip tie around Jorge's neck, he broke out of his trance and tried to roll away—"No-no! Please, man!"—but Rick locked it around him like a collar.

"Talk."

"Wh-what do you want to know?"

"You've heard the question twice already."

"The *curandero,* he told us nothing, man! Nothing!"

Rick heard a sound and glanced behind him. Miguel's cotton pants were darkening as his sphincter released.

"You mean you tortured him and he said nothing?"

"He say all sorts of shit but nothing that Miguel want to hear. He tell us he got lotsa cures that he be glad to show us how to make but Miguel was only interested in one, some kind of cure-all. Mulac said he didn't know nothin' 'bout that one."

"Whose idea to set him on fire?"

"That was Miguel—all Miguel. He call it 'the Leviticus Sanction' or some shit."

The Leviticus Sanction . . . sounded like a Ludlum title.

"What's that supposed to mean?"

"I dunno. Never heard of it before. But it's all about burning. Miguel called it act of faith."

" 'Act of faith'? Was he kidding?"

"Hey, don't ask me, man. Miguel got all religious there at the end, asking Mulac if he repented his sins before he set fire to him."

"Burned alive?"

Jorge looked away. "Barely alive."

Rick believed him. Nothing he said could hurt Miguel now. And as intended, Miguel's corpse dangling a dozen feet away proved an efficient tongue loosener. In fact, Jorge wouldn't *stop* talking.

"Hey, listen, man, I ain't a player here. Ain't got no dog in this hunt. I'm just hired help."

"Not 536?"

"Never heard of no 536 till you started asking. What is it? Some new super-secret branch of the CIA?"

"CIA? That who you think hired you?"

"Hey, I know it was."

Now *this* was interesting.

"Miguel told you he was CIA?"

"Naw, man. He say he some cultural something with the U.S. embassy but, hey, c'mon. Who's he kidding?"

Probably no one. CIA field agents often posed as cultural attachés and the like.

"Why'd he hire you instead of bringing someone else from the agency?"

"We worked together before, and I speak Maya. How many CIA guys you think speak Maya?"

Well, there was that. But Rick also figured this little sojourn into the interior was not an official operation. Miguel was a 536 member who happened to be in the CIA. Made sense. Gave him access to all sorts of intel and the option of masking his activities in a cloak of officialdom when it proved convenient. Whatever he paid Jorge was probably billed to the Company as a legit expense.

Perfect situation. He wondered how many 536ers hid in law enforcement around the world. No way would Jorge know.

"You came, you questioned, you killed the guy—"

"Miguel called it 'sanctioning.'"

Rick knew the type. Call it something else and it became something else. Sanctioning wasn't killing, it was . . . sanctioning.

"Whatever. He's dead, but you two are still here. Why?"

" 'Cause Miguel says we stay. He the boss."

"And he never said why?"

"We watch that lady you came with. If she find anything we miss, we get her to tell us."

"And then 'sanction' her too?"

Jorge shrugged. "His boss wants her dead."

"Really?"

That explained the creep he'd had to deal with in the doc's backyard last night. Had a flash-bang and a syringe full of something.

"And you too," Jorge added.

No surprise there.

"His boss in the CIA or his boss in 536?"

"Don't know, man." He glanced over to where Miguel's corpse dangled from the tree. "You coulda asked but I don't think he tell."

"Probably not."

"Skinny white dude. Arrived this morning with some other guy, looked around, told Miguel to make her disappear, then helicoptered out."

"My job is to protect her, you know."

"Yeah, we figured."

"And I take my job seriously."

Another glance at Miguel. "I see that. But hey," he added quickly, "she got no worry from me. With Miguel gone, I'm done. I wrap his body in the back and head for Mexico City." He shrugged again. "Maybe I get some kind of reward."

"Yeah, maybe."

Time for a change of subject.

"Who hurt the little girl?"

Jorge stiffened. "What little girl?"

Rick fought to keep his voice steady and disinterested.

"The one with the missing fingernails."

"Miguel did that. He want so bad to get Mulac to tell him about the cure-all."

The villagers had been definite about the "short one" pulling out the child's fingernails. Jorge stood at least a foot shorter than Miguel.

"Kids should be off limits, don't you think, Jorge?"

"Oh, yeah, man. Definitely."

Rick pulled out his flashlight again and checked the nearby trees. He found the right-size branch the right height off the ground. As he began to saw at it, Jorge let out a whimper.

"Aw, man. I been cooperatin', ain't I?"

"Kids are innocents, Jorge. Noncombatants. They shouldn't be used for fodder and they shouldn't be used for leverage. Shouldn't be *used*—period."

Jorge flopped onto his back and began to roll himself away.

"It wasn't me!"

Rick finished sawing off the branch and followed him.

"I don't have many hot buttons, Jorge. In fact, come to think of it, I probably have just one: hurting a kid."

Rammed a knee into Jorge's back to hold him down, then looped and fastened the leash tie around the collar tie. Used the leash to drag Jorge back to the tree. What he really wanted to do was rip out Jorge's fingernails, listen to him scream and ask him if that was how the little girl sounded—*a little girl,* for fuck's sake—when he did it to her. But he couldn't allow himself to go there, because once he started, who knew when or where he'd stop?

"You don't hurt a child for anything, Jorge. And if you do, it's not a good thing for me to hear about it. Because I don't like hearing about grown-ups hurting kids."

Jorge sobbed. "Her nails will grow back, man!"

Rick had a sudden flash of flames and the screams of the burning—adults and children—and of a figure moving among the dying, a dark man, untouched and unlit by those flames . . .

. . . and he almost lost it.

"Really? Yeah, maybe her hands will look fine, or almost fine. But what about the inside of her head? What about her nightmares? You hurt . . . you *torture* a little kid like that, the hurt doesn't stop when the pain stops. The hurt inside goes on and on. Kids are helpless in this world. They need grown-ups to protect them. So when a grown-up hurts rather than protects them it's . . . well, it's unforgivable, don't you think?"

"God forgives everything, man!"

"Even hurting a little kid? I don't think there's any redemption from that."

"Sure there is!"

"Well, not from me. Because when I hear about some-one hurting a kid, it gives *me* a pain that won't go away until I do something about it, until I make sure that sick fuck won't ever do something like that again."

Jorge's scream was brief as he was lifted and hung from the branch stump.

"Give my regards to Mulac."

Rick was aware of the choking sounds, the twisting and writhing and useless kicking at the air as he gath-ered his Glock, his knife, his flashlight, and his remain-ing zip ties, but he didn't watch. He turned off the headlights and started back toward the village.

No . . . no redemption . . . for anyone.

6

The shattering of the Jeep's rear window jolted Laura from her semi-doze. She bolted upright and saw a woman raising a *macana* for another swing at the glass.

"Go!" she screamed in Maya. "Go away! Leave us alone!"

She came around the driver's side of the Jeep, slam-ming the ornate wooden club against the roof, and then bashing the side-view mirror. Laura reached up and fumbled for the overhead courtesy light switch. As she turned it on, the woman pressed her face against the side window.

Ix'chel.

"Go!" she screamed again. "You brought them to kill my brother! Go! Leave here!"

Then her shoulders slumped and she broke into sobs.

Laura sat quaking with shock and fright for a few racing heartbeats, then opened the door on the passenger side and got out, keeping the car between them.

You brought them to kill my brother . . . was that what she believed? Nothing could be further from the truth. Although, if that photo hadn't been published, maybe—

"Ix'chel," she said softly in Yucatec Maya, "I didn't bring them. They were here before me."

She had the straight, inky hair of a Mayan and wore a wrinkled white blouse and knee-length cutoffs.

She looked surprised. "You speak our language?"

Laura started to move toward the front of the Jeep. "My mother grew up not far from here, in a village very much like yours."

"Tlalli says you are a friend, that you knew Chet."

"If Tlalli said I was a friend, then why . . . ?" She gestured at the banged-up Jeep.

Ix'chel dropped the *macana* and hung her head. "I do not know, I do not know."

"I think I understand," Laura said. The strangers who had killed her brother were gone, but other strangers had stayed. "His real name was Chaim."

"Yes, I know. And I am glad you know." She looked up. "Is it true Chet is dead?"

Laura nodded. "I am sorry, but yes . . . he's gone."

"Killed like my brother?"

"Not exactly, but by the same people."

"Five thirty-six," she said through another sob.

"You know of them?"

She nodded. "How did they know to come here?"

"Chaim had a photograph of you and him."

She sobbed again and covered her face with her hands. "Oh, no!"

"That may not have been it," Laura said quickly.

"Mulac had a reputation for performing wonderful cures. That is most likely what led them here. The men from 536 tried to make him tell his secrets but he refused."

She lowered her hands. Her expression was utter misery.

"That is because he *had* no secrets!" she screamed. "The cures are *mine*! *I* am the *bruja*, not Mulac!"

She turned and ran into the darkness.

"What the hell?"

She jumped at the sound of Rick's voice. He arrived on the run, pistol in hand. She couldn't bring herself to say so, but she was *damn* glad to see him.

"Where've you been?"

"Taking care of business." He was rotating in a slow circle. "You see who it was?"

"Ix'chel."

He stopped turning. "The sister?"

"Yes. She wants us gone. She blames us for Mulac's death."

"Really? That's not going to make her exactly forthcoming when you try to talk to her."

"Tell me about it."

She translated the gist of what Ix'chel had said and Rick was as shocked as Laura that she was the real panacean here, not Mulac.

"Then maybe this hasn't been a wasted trip," he said. "Let's go find her and—"

"Let's give her till morning."

Laura had scads of questions she wanted to ask, but Ix'chel was in no state to be questioned.

"Your call."

Rick tucked the pistol away and turned on the headlights, then made a slow circuit of the Jeep.

"Damn! What did she use? A baseball bat?"

"It's over there," Laura said, pointing to the *macana* where Ix'chel had dropped it. "A traditional Mayan warrior's club."

He wiggled the dangling side-view mirror, then whipped out one of those zip ties he liked so much and began fastening it back into place.

Laura had to smile. "A thousand and one uses, right?"

He gave her a grim smile. "Thousand and *two*, actually."

IX'CHEL

1

Monday morning broke clear and warm in the jungle. Rick went off to find some water so he could clean up, leaving Laura alone with instructions to blast the horn if she needed him.

Sleep had been out of the question last night so they'd talked about how to approach Ix'chel and decided Laura should try it alone. She might have a better chance of getting the woman to open up to her on a one-to-one basis without Rick looming over them.

But first she needed to phone home.

Marissa said she'd had a great Sunday with her dad and seemed a little disappointed that she'd been handed over to the tutor this morning.

Natasha already? And then Laura remembered the two-hour difference.

When she finally ended the call, she looked around for Rick. No sign of him. Where did he go when he wandered off? Like last night. Where had he been when Ix'chel had attacked?

She took the opportunity to call her cell's voice mail. Sure enough, another message:

"Hey, Doc. Phil again. I've been digging a little more on your ex–Navy SEAL—not. Ran into a few little wrinkles and one big one. Or maybe it's not so big, but it's weird."

Oh, no. I don't need more weird than I've already got, she thought.

"I'll give you the little ones first. After he retired from the Sausalito PD he signed on immediately as a ranger in the Golden Gate National Recreation Area. I mean, he took almost no time off, which strikes me as odd, because if you're gonna retire, you want to enjoy a little R and R, at least for a while, know what I mean? But he didn't. Goes right into it, like he's had the job waiting for him."

Laura didn't think that was a wrinkle at all. After spending over twenty-four hours straight with the man, she knew he had a lot of restless energy.

"But then what does he do? He's not on the job six months when he calls in and says he's quitting and they never see him again. Doesn't even empty his locker. He heads east, lands in Westchester, and sets himself up as Hayden Investigations and Security."

That didn't seem like Rick. Something must have happened. A woman thing gone wrong? Or maybe a guy thing? He came from the Bay Area, after all. He could be straight or gay—she had no sense of his sexuality.

But either way, this message held nothing disturbing . . . at least so far. "Little wrinkles" indeed.

"Now here's the big wrinkle: I was trying to background his childhood—his high school and all that, see if he had any arrests as a teen—and kept coming up blank. It was like he didn't exist before joining the Sausalito PD. And then I found out he'd gone and changed his name."

Changed his name? Okay, now *that* was a wrinkle.

"I haven't been able to dig out what he changed it from, but have no fear—I'll get it. Kinda weird, huh? And don't think you're wasting my time—I'm sure you're worrying about that—because let me tell you,

*this is kind of fun. This guy Hayden, or whoever he
turns out to be, is an interesting duck. He's got me curious. I'd probably follow this to the end even if you told
me to stop. Because there's something in his past he
doesn't want people to know. I can smell it. It may not
be anything serious—you know, like maybe he's related
to Charles Manson or Ed Gein or something like that—
but he's hiding something. Be careful, Doc. Watch your
back. And I'll be in touch again ASAP."*

Uneasy now, she ended the call.

"Watch my back?" she muttered. "That's supposed to
be *his* job."

2

First thing after waking, Nelson checked in with his New
York office and found three messages from Dr. Forman
to call him. Forman was number two on his call list this
morning anyway. But three calls already? That couldn't
be good.

"Been trying to reach you, Fife."

"I'm in Mexico."

"Don't tell me a vacation—"

"I wish. You have news for me, I assume."

*"Your report was waiting in my fax tray this morn-
ing."*

"I'm pretty sure I can tell you the result myself in general terms." Six hundred milligrams of ibuprofen hadn't
scratched this morning's headache. "Tell me how far
gone I am."

*"I guess that means I don't have to start off with, 'I
regret to inform you . . .' "*

"You guess right. How bad?"

"Three metastatic tumors in your brain."

His stomach clenched. Three . . . dear God!

"I'd imagined one big one . . . "

"*Mets are often multiple. Do you want to know the locations?*"

"They wouldn't mean a thing to me."

"*If I remember correctly, you said you were having headaches, right?*"

"Killers."

"*A term not to be used lightly in your case. But if you get over to Sloan-Kettering they can start a course of radiation to shrink those mets. Once the pressure on the dura and meninges is relieved, the headaches will abate. You've got a lot to do and no time to waste. You need complete removal of that primary on your neck and chemotherapy for the rest.*"

"Sloan can do all that?"

"*Those guys live for it.*"

"Will it be very time consuming?"

"*You're not seriously thinking of putting it off, are you?*"

"No, of course not. I've just got to arrange my schedule . . . "

"*Count on spending a lot of time in imaging—more CTs, MRIs, PET scans, and on and on—and the radiation is done on a daily basis, so that takes time. I don't know what specific chemo protocol they'll use—not my field—but you probably won't feel like doing much while that's running.*"

"Sounds like this is going to take over my life."

"*For a while it's going to define your life, Fife. But at least you'll have one. Look, I've got to run. Call Sloan now, today, and get rolling on this. No time to waste. Good luck.*"

Define my life? Nelson thought as he hung up. I've too much else to do.

He sat there, trembling, nauseated, overcome with dread. Radiation, chemo . . . sick unto death with no guarantee of a good outcome ... and doctors, doctors, doctors.

He shook it off. He had no time for treatment now, and the only doctor he was interested in had nothing to do with cancer.

Laura Fanning ... Uncle Jim had said the Serpent had been behind her involvement in the quest for the panaceans' home—to distract him. Nelson was beginning to wonder about that. Could it be the Lord's doing? Had He brought her into it for purposes of His own?

If so, he prayed Laura Fanning was doing His bidding and digging deep into the panaceans' secrets.

3

Laura left Rick—or whatever his original name had been—with the Jeep and wandered the village, looking for Ix'chel. She saw no sign of her but did spot Tlalli who said she'd last seen her in Mulac's hut. She led Laura to a small thatch-roofed house with stucco walls. The door was open. Laura peeked and found Ix'chel puttering within.

Small bottles lined the walls, interspersed with tied bunches of dried flowers and herbs: Mulac's pharmacopoeia.

"Can we talk?" she said in Mayan.

Ix'chel looked up. In daylight Laura could now see how hollow-eyed and haggard she looked.

She shook her head. "I will not talk to anyone who is not of this village."

"I'm *almost* of this village. My mother brought me to Maya country many times to visit my grandmother before she died."

"Tlalli said you also came here looking for cures to steal."

That stung. "She said that?"

"No. But I know how it works." She gestured around at her murdered brother's quarters. "You find something that heals and you take it back home where you call it your own and make millions but give none of it back."

"That's true for others. But that's not me. And when I found out that was happening I quit."

"You came and talked to Mulac."

"Years ago, yes. But I never hurt him. I'm not one of them."

"Oh, I know that. The bad ones, the ones called 536, they are always men. But that doesn't matter. You too are here to use us."

She sensed how tightly Ix'chel had shut down. No surprise. She was hurt and grieving and probably frightened half to death—with good reason. Laura had to find a way past the wall she'd erected, get her to open up. But how?

Well, when nothing else works, try the truth.

"I'm a doctor too, you know." Ix'chel looked up. Was that a spark of interest in her eyes? "But I work only with dead people."

"You can't cure the dead."

"I try to understand *why* they died."

"Ah, *médico forense*," she said in Spanish, nodding.

"Right. I examined Chaim . . . Chet, but I couldn't find out how he died."

She frowned. "He wasn't burned?"

"Someone tried to burn him but the firemen arrived too soon and pulled his body free."

"And you couldn't find a cause of death?"

Laura shook her head. "He was one of the healthiest corpses I've ever examined. It was as if his heart simply stopped beating."

Ix'chel stared at her for a few seconds, then said, "This is exactly what happened."

That took Laura aback. "What? How can you know?"

"Because we are taught how to do it."

"By whom? Who teaches you?"

Ix'chel waved the questions away. She wasn't going to answer. "We are taught. That is all. When the Brotherhood finds us, we know we are going to die. They—"

"The Brotherhood? What Brotherhood?"

"The 536 Brotherhood. They call us witches and warlocks and their holy book says they must kill us."

"What holy book is that?"

"The Bible. It says, 'Thou shalt not suffer a witch to live.' "

Laura gasped. In the old days they hung or burned witches, didn't they? Hanrahan had been burned, and very nearly Brody. And Mulac . . . poor Mulac had suffered both.

"We know they will torture and burn us," Ix'chel said, "so we spare ourselves the pain and deny them that satisfaction by stopping our hearts."

Laura didn't see how it was possible to stop your own heart, but everything Ix'chel was saying jibed perfectly with Hanrahan's and Brody's autopsy results, and with what Stahlman had told her.

He'd said he thought 536 might have their roots in Christianity. Seemed like he was right.

Ix'chel's expression was suspicious. "You are telling me that you knew nothing of this?"

"Almost nothing."

"You came here to steal a secret—the secret of the greatest cure the world has ever known—to make yourself rich and powerful. You are worse than the Brotherhood. They are sick and twisted murderers, but at least their motives are pure and beyond greed!"

Ix'chel began to turn away so Laura blurted, "I don't want your secrets! I was sent here to find one dose—*one dose* of your medicine for a very sick man. That is all."

Her voice rose of its own accord. "I don't care about your damn secrets, because I don't believe in your 'greatest cure.' I think you're all crazy. I think the man who sent me is crazy, and I think the men who killed Mulac are the craziest of all."

Ix'chel was slowly turning back to her, so Laura lowered her voice and continued.

"I had two mysteriously connected deaths. Two men—Chaim was one of them."

Ix'chel was staring at her. "You cut Chaim open?"

"Yes. I examined all his organs. As I said, I could find no cause of death."

"You held his heart in your hands?"

Laura nodded. "Yes."

Her eyes filled with tears. "He had a good heart."

"He had a perfect heart. He and the other man were growing some sort of plant indoors, and both had similar tattoos—wait. Mulac also had the tattoo, but you said he wasn't—"

"Mulac's was fake." She turned and lifted her blouse. She was braless so no strap obscured any part of the tattoo.

"This is real."

Laura slumped against the doorframe. "I don't understand any of this."

As Ix'chel stared at her, their eyes met and Laura sensed a moment of connection.

"You really don't believe?"

Laura shook her head. "The whole idea is ridiculous."

"You do not believe . . . you truly don't." That seemed to flip a switch in Ix'chel. Her features softened. "You are a doctor who wishes to understand?" she said, brushing past Laura and stepping outside. "I cannot promise you understanding, but come with me and you will learn."

4

"This is where I grow the plants," Ix'chel said.

She'd led Laura through one of the village's cornfields—long ago cleared from the jungle—to a bare plot at its southern corner.

"Where are they?"

"Gone. I used them all."

Laura crossed her fingers. "And the medicine?"

"I've given it all away."

"Nothing left?"

"Not a drop."

Damn. She'd have to return to Stahlman without the bogus potion. Laura's face must have given away her dismay.

"There's so many who need it here," Ix'chel said.

Laura was ready to turn away and head home, but the image of Tommy Cochran's perfect knee joint flashed through her head. She had questions . . . so many questions . . .

"How do you give it out?"

Ix'chel gave her a long stare. "I cannot say. I will end like Mulac."

"I don't want your secrets but I will keep them. I'm only trying to understand."

The stare continued, then, finally, a nod. "I will tell the woman who held Chaim's heart in her hands."

Laura experienced a queasy epiphany: a heart in her hands . . . enormous significance for Mayans—no doubt imprinted on their DNA.

Still looking conflicted, Ix'chel said, "I volunteer in many of Chetumal's free clinics. The All-Mother leads me to the neediest and—"

"The All-Mother?"

"Yes, of course. The Goddess of the Earth and all that live upon it."

Stahlman had mentioned a pagan religion. This sounded like some sort of Gaia cult. Someone like Ix'chel, being Mayan, could step into that sort of belief system like slipping on a comfortable old shoe.

"She reveals the worthy to me, and I sneak them a dose of the *ikhar*."

"Your medicine?"

"Yes. The All-Mother's name for it. An ancient word."

"Why do you sneak it?"

"Because our lives are in danger if we're caught. That is why I move from clinic to clinic so that not too many cures are in the same place."

"But if your *ikhar* cures everything—?"

"Oh, it does."

"—then why don't you reveal it to the world?"

"The All-Mother forbids. It goes only to those chosen by Her."

"She tells you?"

Ix'chel smiled. "She has Her ways . . . She lets me know."

Self-delusion . . . making her own choices and attributing them to her goddess.

"And it never fails to cure?"

Her smile broadened. "Never."

Impossible. But True Believers can convince themselves of just about anything. Few things are more powerful than the will to believe.

"But without plants, how will you make more . . . *ikhar*?"

"More seeds will be delivered."

"By whom?"

She smiled. "By mail. I have a post office box in Chetumal."

Laura had to stifle a laugh. How mundane!

"Where are they postmarked from?"

"Everywhere. Usually different places in Europe. The *urschell* moves around because the Brotherhood wants her most of all."

"*Urschell?*"

"You would say priestess."

"So this is not just a local Maya thing."

"Oh, no. The All-Mother is everywhere."

"Okay. So walk me through this. The seeds arrive and you plant them here."

"Yes. We must sprinkle them directly from the packet onto the ground and cover them with earth."

"Is there anything else in the packet?"

"A little dirt and dust."

Fairy dust? Pixie dust?

Shut up, Laura.

"And then they germinate."

"When they sprout I separate them to give them space to grow. When they have flowered and begin to form seeds, it is time for harvesting. Before they drop their seeds, I pull them up by the roots and put them in an iron pot."

"Roots and all?"

She nodded. "Even some of the root ball."

"Dirt too?"

"Oh, yes. Grubs and worms are removed, of course, but the earth is the source of all life and part of the healing is around the roots. I then add water and boil the plants until nine-tenths of the water is gone. Then I strain what is left through three cloths. The liquid that comes through is the *ikhar*."

Laura shook her head. Stahlman's panacea was a filtrate of plant-and-dirt soup. Yuck.

"You do not believe," Ix'chel said, her tone reproachful.

"I told you that. Don't be angry. It's hard for the scientist part of me to accept something that cures everything. And beyond that, there must be something you're not telling me."

"What I told you is true. I leave nothing out."

She remembered what Stahlman had told her.

"I know a man who has grown the plants and tried to prepare them every possible way but never wound up with anything that works."

She shrugged. "Of course not. He needs the blessing of the All-Mother. Without that he cannot hope to succeed."

She could just see herself presenting that to Stahlman: *You've got everything right except the blessing of the All-Mother.* Yeah, that would fly.

Ix'chel said, "What does the scientist in you say about Chaim? He was sick in many ways when he came to Mulac for healing. And yet he walked away cured."

"Mulac? But you said—"

"Mulac was very proud of being the *ah-men*, the *curandero*. He could not accept that his sister knew more. At times, when the All-Mother told me that I should cure one of his patients, I would sneak in and mix some of my *ikhar* into one of the potions he was using. I think he knew this, and believed my tattoo carried healing power. He traveled to Mexico City one day and got himself one just like mine."

Laura nodded. And in so doing, signed his own death warrant.

She imagined the sequence of events: Ix'chel's cures enhance Mulac's reputation, which attracts the hopelessly sick, Chaim Brody among them, which eventually alerts the 536 fanatics and—

Wait-wait-wait! That was all predicated on Ix'chel's *ikhar* working as a panacea, and there was no such thing as a panacea.

Remember that. Remember that.

And then Brody . . . wait . . .

"How did Chaim become a healer? Where did he get his tattoo?"

"The All-Mother called him and he answered."

"But how—?"

"She called. He answered. That is all you can know."

Her expression said that she felt she'd told too much already and this was as far as she was going to go.

"He returned with the tattoo?"

"Of course."

"Can I . . . can I see yours again?"

This time she whipped off her shirt entirely, exposing her small, dark-nippled breasts, and turned her back.

Laura studied it, comparing it to what she remembered of Chaim's. She'd brought a photo of his tattoo along, but it was back in the Jeep.

"The line in Chaim's is angled the other way. Is that significant?"

"It points to the Wound."

An idea was taking shape . . .

"Do all of you . . . what do you call yourselves?"

"*Sylyk.*"

"Is that the name of your"—she didn't want to say *cult*—"your religion?"

"We are simply the Children . . . all people are Children of the All-Mother. But Children such as myself are known as *sylyk* . . . an ancient word that means healer."

"Okay. And do all of you *sylyk* go to your birthplace and face the North Star at the equinox every year?"

"Yes. It is our law."

"Then Chairn would have gone to his home during the equinox and—"

Ix'chel blinked back sudden tears. "Chaim did not have time . . . "

Laura was picturing Chaim lying on his belly in Brooklyn. If you extended Ix'chel's tattoo line and his, where would they cross? The Wound?

. . . the injury the All-Mother suffered to bring us the cure . . .

Perhaps the *source* of the supposed cure?

If she could find the source, maybe she could get a sample for Stahlman. Not that it was going to help him, but at least she would have completed her part of the bargain.

She pointed to the earth below their feet. "Could I bring my friend here, to this spot, to try an experiment?"

Ix'chel looked skeptical. "The big man? No."

"He can be trusted."

She shook her head. "I speak only to you."

Damn.

"Okay. Then let me run back for a picture of Chaim's back. I want to show you something."

"Do not take long."

Laura started toward the Jeep at a run. "Don't go anywhere. I'll be right back."

When she reached the Jeep, Rick was nowhere in sight. Their luggage lay unguarded and exposed through the shattered rear window.

"Rick? Rick!"

"Coming."

She turned and spotted him emerging from the trees near the Jeep's hood. His green T-shirt was spotted with darker patches of sweat. The veins on his glistening arms were bulging. His safari jacket had hidden how muscular he was.

"Where've you been?"

"Working out a little. Calisthenics, mostly. Found a good horizontal branch for—"

"Great, great. Do you have a compass?"

"Can't imagine traveling into the outback without one. Why?"

"I need to measure a line from a point here at a certain angle from north."

"You mean an azimuth?"

"Yes, if that's what it's called."

"What for?"

She gave Rick a quick rundown of the mythology of the panaceans—the Wound, the prayer, the tattoo, the equinox ritual.

"So she's talking," he said. "Great. You learned a lot in a little while."

"Well, I've *heard* a lot, but I don't feel I *know* much more than when we left JFK. It's all folk tales and rituals and All-Mother mumbo-jumbo."

They opened the rear of the Jeep. Rick pawed through his duffel while she searched through her bag for Chaim's belt. She found it under the photo of his tattoo. She hoped Ix'chel could decipher its symbols.

Rick held up the compass. "Which way do we go?"

Laura shook her head. "Not 'we.' Just me. Whatever trust I've established is fragile. She'll clam up if you're there."

His expression as he handed her the compass said he didn't like it. "You know what to do?"

Laura realized she had only a vague idea. "I'm going to get the angle—the azimuth—of the line of her tattoo from north."

"This have something to do with why we're here?"

"I hope so."

"We talking polar north or magnetic?"

"There's a difference?"

"Sure is. Magnetic moves around—varies from a hundred to a thousand miles or more." He tapped the compass in her hand. "This will point you toward magnetic north."

"Ix'chel mentioned the North Star."

"That's different. That's Polaris and that's polar north because Polaris is located straight up from Earth's axis."

She looked at the sunny sky. Polaris was somewhere up there right now, just not visible. She remembered hunting for the North Star as a kid: simply find the Big Dipper and follow a line up from the leading edge of its cup. The first bright star you saw was Polaris.

"I can't see stars in the day. What do I do?"

"Don't see much choice but to wait for sundown and hope it's clear."

Damn. She did *not* want to spend another night here—not with a broken rear window.

He added, "Unless our friendly neighborhood panacean has a solution."

Laura hurried off and was relieved to find Ix'chel waiting where she'd left her.

Resigning herself to another night here, she said, "Can

we come back after dark so you can see the North Star and show us which way you lie?"

"I know the way," she said, pointing. "The star is always between those two trees."

Laura remembered Polaris being higher in the sky, but maybe things were different here.

"Can you lie down now as you did before?"

Ix'chel stepped back. "Why do you want this?"

Good question. Laura gave her an honest answer. She showed her the photo of Chaim's tattoo. "I'm curious as to why the lines are different. The Wound is not a secret place, is it?"

"No . . . "

"I seek to harm no one. I want only to understand."

Ix'chel hesitated, then stretched herself out on the ground as before. But this time she kept her shirt on and simply lifted its back enough to reveal the tattoo.

If Ix'chel was right, her true north was a tad off the compass's magnetic north, which Rick said was usually the case. Making the adjustment, Laura calculated that the diagonal on her tattoo ran on an azimuth seventy-two degrees north-northeast and two fifty-two degrees south-southwest.

Laura pictured a map in her head. South-southwest took her through Campeche, Guatemala, and back into Mexico. North-northeast took her to . . . she could picture only the Caribbean course of the line. Beyond that was uncertain. Cuba and then . . . Europe.

Great. That narrowed it down.

As Ix'chel rose, she spotted the belt in Laura's hand. Her eyes widened when she saw the markings on the inner surface.

"Where did you get this?"

"Chaim was wearing it when he died. I—"

She was unbuckling and pulling off her own belt. "I

have one too. All *sylyk* have one." She held hers and Chaim's up side by side. "See."

Laura did see: two identical sequences, exactly the same size, spaced exactly the same.

"What does it mean?"

She shrugged. "I do not know, but we are to wear it always."

There's too damn much you don't know! Laura wanted to scream, but bit her tongue.

She took back Chaim's belt and said, "When will you make more *ikhar*?"

"It will be a while. The seeds must arrive and they must grow before I have plants to boil."

"No idea when the next seeds . . . ?"

She shook her head. "The All-Mother tells the *urschell* and the *urschell* obeys."

Rolling up Chaim's belt, Laura felt herself getting ticked off at the All-Mother. "What if—?"

"I can tell you no more," Ix'chel said. "I fear I have told you too much already."

Without another word or a look back, she ran off.

Laura's initial impulse was to follow her, but she saw no upside to that. Ix'chel was fleeing to the safety of her people.

Back at the Jeep, she found Rick waiting for her. She gave him a quick summary of what had gone down with Ix'chel.

She sighed. "But all in all I've got a feeling I was wasting my time. I don't think her position for Polaris was right. Too low . . . "

"Lower than when you were growing up in Utah?" Rick said. "Yeah, it would be. The farther north you go, the higher it gets, until you reach the North Pole where it's directly overhead. Move south and it gets lower and lower. Cross the equator and you can't see it at all unless you're on a mountain."

"You're just a font of knowledge, aren't you. Would you happen to have a map of the world handy as well?"

"Sorry. Just Mexico. There's always Google Maps, but I can't access that without an Internet connection."

She had the sat phone, but the screen was too small to be of much use. She noticed Rick pulling a gizmo from his pocket.

"What's that?"

"GPS. I want to pinpoint this location for future reference so we can run an azimuth through it and see where it takes us."

"Right. Then we get an azimuth from Chaim's tattoo and see where they intersect. Hopefully at this Wound, whatever it is."

I almost sound like I know what I'm talking about.

"I guess that means we head back to New York."

Back to New York . . . She couldn't wait.

"Uh-huh. Williamsburg, here we come."

6

On the drive from the village, Laura had the wheel again. As they neared the exit for the Chetumal airport on Route 186, Rick pointed to a sign indicating *Av Insurgentes* off to the left.

"That looks like the main drag. See if we can find an office supply place."

"What for?"

"Need a protractor, remember?"

Since neither of them had been able to figure out how to trace the azimuth on Google Maps, they'd decided on the retro route.

Not only was Avenida Insurgentes indeed the main drag, but they hadn't gone a mile before Laura spotted a familiar red-and-white sign.

She had to laugh. "Office Depot. I don't believe it."

She stayed with the Jeep—the broken rear window meant it couldn't be left unattended—while Rick ran inside. He emerged ten minutes later with a flimsy plastic bag, grinning like a little kid.

"Got us a protractor—a three-hundred-sixty-degree model—a ruler, world map, pens, and pencils. We're all set."

Half an hour later they were in the waiting area for the charter service that would fly them back to Cancún. Rick had filled out forms for the damage to the Jeep, blaming it on an attempted carjacking by a gang of teens. While their charter was being readied, Rick spread the map out on a chair.

"Here's approximately where we were," he said, checking his GPS and making a dot with a red Sharpie. "The longitude lines all go to true north, so if we line up with the nearest and plot your readings . . ."

He placed the circular protractor on the page and made dots at the 72- and 252-degree lines. Then he took the ruler and drew a line that connected both through the village dot. As she'd known, heading west-southwest the line passed through Campeche, Guatemala, Chiapas, and into the Pacific.

"Continuing it westward," Laura said, "there's nothing but ocean until you hit Australia."

"Let's go the other way."

He continued the line east-northeast from the village and Laura watched with dismay as it ran through Cuba, Portugal, Spain, France, Italy, Croatia, Hungary, the Ukraine, and all across Russia.

Rick grunted. "Thought this would narrow the field but I guess not."

Her feelings exactly.

"Ix'chel said the seeds are usually postmarked from

different spots in Europe, so I think that's the direction we should be looking."

She'd pulled the photo of Chaim's tattoo from her bag when they dropped off the Jeep. She laid that on the map.

"See? His transecting line runs the other way."

Rick laid the protractor on it and got a quick reading.

"Roughly one twelve, one thirteen degrees southeast."

"Just for fun, draw a line from New York at that angle."

He did. Chaim's line intersected Ix'chel's in the middle of the Atlantic.

"Well, there goes that theory," Rick said.

"What theory?"

"That the lines all cross at the . . . what was it?"

"The Wound."

"Right. The Wound. Well, unless the Wound is the sunken city of Atlantis—"

"Oh, no . . . please, let's not start with that."

"Not starting anything, but unless the Wound in is the middle of a watery nowhere, we need a new theory. And exactly why do we want to find this?"

"Maybe we can find a dose of *ikhar* there." When Rick gave her a puzzled look, she added, "That's Ix'chel's term for Stahlman's panacea."

Laura was running a quick mental review of all that Ix'chel had told her and thought she'd found their error.

"We may be operating on a false premise," she said. "The *sylyk*—that's what healers like Ix'chel and Chaim are called—have to say the prayer at the place of their birth during the autumnal equinox. Get it? The place of their birth. We're assuming Chaim was born in Williamsburg."

Rick's mouth took on an annoyed twist. "Of course. GIGO."

"What?"

"G-i-g-o. Old computer acronym for 'garbage in, garbage out.' Any calculation is only as accurate as the data entered. Verify data first and *then* calculate." He looked at Laura. "How do we find out?"

"I make a call."

He shook his head. "Imagine how many Brodys live in Williamsburg."

"Lots, but the ME's office dealt with his family. I just have to call my office."

She just hoped the family had filled in the place-of-birth blank. Otherwise, she'd have to call the Brody house.

But lucky for her, his mother had written *Gan Yosaif, Israel,* in the blank. Laura requested a PDF of the page be emailed to her.

"Israel?" Rick said when she told him. "Whoa. Wasn't expecting that. Sounds like a kibbutz."

"Kibbutz . . . isn't that some sort of communal farm?"

"You got it."

"How do you know it's a kibbutz? Is it famous?"

"Never heard of it, but *Gan Yosaif* translates to 'Joseph's Garden'—sounds like a vegan restaurant but it's a typical kibbutz name."

"Funny . . . you don't look Jewish."

"I'm not. Just know a little Hebrew."

"Really? How?"

"Just do. Let's get a ballpark on Chaim's azimuth from Israel."

Laura watched him start to draw a line on the map, but all she could think of was how the mystery man she was traveling with didn't know Spanish but did know Hebrew. Weirder and weirder.

"Not going to bother with the southeast azimuth. You can see that's going to hit Jordan and Saudi Arabia and on toward southern India. Low yield there. But the other direction . . . "

The line running 293 degrees northwest sliced through the toe of Italy's boot and straight through the Pyrenees, south of Toulouse.

Something clicked in Laura's brain when she saw that. She jabbed her finger onto southern France.

"There! That's the place!"

"What makes you so sure?"

"Ix'chel said her cult, her Children of the All-Mother, has been around for thousands of years. And Stahlman said they might be an offshoot of the old druids."

"So?"

"That used to be Gaul, a hotbed of pagans before the Dark Ages."

"And you just happen to know this how?"

"Tell me how you know Hebrew and I'll tell you how I know about pagans in Gaul."

He shook his head, his expression annoyed. "We're going to decide the next stop on this trip based on what you're saying here. Let's not play games."

He was right, damn him.

"Okay, I took four years of Latin in high school. We spent sophomore year translating Julius Caesar's *Gallic*

Wars. He talks about the Gauls being pagans and I think he mentioned one or two of their deities."

God, she could still remember the first line: *Gallia est omnis divisa in partes tres*. Some things never left you.

"Caesar called them 'pagans,' huh?" Rick laughed and shook his head. "A polytheist pot calling a pantheist kettle black. Gotta love it." He looked up at her. "Next stop Tel Aviv?"

Her throat tightened. Her heart had been set on returning to New York and seeing Marissa. But she'd promised Stahlman two weeks. Twelve more days to go . . .

"Why Israel?" she said. "Why not go straight to . . . Gaul?"

"Because 'Gaul,' as you put it, is big."

"But we've got a line going—"

"Israel is not big—about the size of New Jersey—but it stretches a whole two hundred fifty miles north to south. If I run the same azimuth from the two ends of the country"—he traced a finger back and forth across the map—"the path could take us north of the Pyrenees and place us in France, or south of them into Spain. Two different countries. We need to find Gan Yosaif and establish a pinpoint GPS locus for it, then go high-tech and recalculate both azimuths as accurately as possible." He raised his eyebrows. "So, I repeat: next stop Tel Aviv?"

She sighed. "I suppose so."

Williamsburg, here we come had morphed into *Promised Land, here we come*.

7

As Nelson admitted Bradsher to his suite, he knew immediately from his expression that he was not bringing good news.

"Is this about the Fanning woman?"

"Afraid so, sir."

"Tell me."

"She and her bodyguard just used Stahlman's credit card to rent a charter out of Chetumal."

Nelson felt a ball of ice form in his chest. That meant she'd left the village and driven all the way to the coast, and no word from Miguel in all the time she had been on the road. Unless . . .

"Did Brother Miguel call and you not tell me?"

"No, sir. Not a word from Miguel. And I've called him at least a dozen times since I got word of the charter, but he's not answering."

Nelson didn't have to say it, and Bradsher obviously felt no need either. They both knew Miguel and his hireling were either dead or disabled.

Just like Simon.

"How could this happen?"

"I don't know, sir. Miguel is—"

"—an experienced field agent. So I was told. Two tours in Afghanistan with side work. So I was told. And he was with a vicious little thug from Mexico City. So I was told. Neither of them could expect any trouble from a private security op from Westchester. 'Nothing to worry about,' right?"

Bradsher didn't look too happy having his words flung back at him.

"Something must have gone wrong, sir."

"Damn right something went wrong. This so-called dumbass—what was the term Miguel used?"

"I believe it was *zurramato,* sir."

"Well, this *zurramato* obviously got the drop on them, didn't he? Just as he undoubtedly did on Simon."

"It would appear so, sir."

"Hubris on Miguel's part, I'm sure. After all, why should he worry about a *zurramato*? Do you remember me warning about luck, good and bad?"

"Yes, sir. But unless Miguel screwed up badly—and I don't think he did—I think more than bad luck might have been involved. We heard Stahlman mention that he's an ex-SEAL."

It made sense in a way. A man worth a billion-plus like Stahlman wouldn't hire just anybody. Nelson should have paid more attention to him but, because Dr. Fanning was not supposed to survive Saturday night, he hadn't thought it mattered. Now it did.

"I want a thorough background on him. Back to year zero. If he was circumcised as an infant, I want a picture of the foreskin."

"You'll have it ASAP, sir."

Bradsher turned and left but returned less than half a minute later with his phone in his hand.

"A new development, sir. She's booked on a flight to Madrid, and from there to Tel Aviv."

Israel? Why in God's name was she going to Israel? The panacea hadn't originated there. He could pinpoint its origin and it was nowhere near Israel. Obviously she was on a wild-goose chase . . .

Should he follow? Damn her! He had tumors growing in his lung and brain. He needed to tie this up and start treatment. But he had no choice.

"She's learned something . . . or thinks she has. Do we have someone there?"

"Yessir."

"Good. Alert him. Send him her flight information

and have him keep an eye on her. Then book us to Ben Gurion."

Israel . . . what on God's good earth could have sent her there? God himself, perhaps? It was the birthplace of the Son, after all . . .

Yes . . . Nelson was sensing more of the hand of the Lord rather than the Serpent. Either way, he knew the Lord wanted him to follow.

8

"Well?" Laura said as Rick returned from a conversation with an Orthodox Jew he'd spotted waiting for the same plane to Madrid.

He shrugged. "He's Israeli but never heard of Gan Yosaif and doesn't know much about kibbutzim. Says a lot of them failed in the eighties and nineties due to some economic crisis. In short, they went broke and the kibbutzniks dispersed. He suggests we check with the Israel Land Authority when we get to Tel Aviv . . . says they administer over ninety percent of the country's land."

"I wonder if that was what happened to Chaim's folks. Their kibbutz went broke and so they came to America—or returned to America."

He shrugged. "Does it matter?"

"No. Just wondering if Chaim would have got into heroin if he'd stayed on the kibbutz."

"Does it matter?"

"Yes, it *does* matter. If he'd stayed in Israel he wouldn't have wound up on my autopsy table and Mulac would still be alive and I'd be home with my daughter."

"Chaos effect."

"What?"

"Nothing."

"You're a great conversationalist, you know that?"

"Sorry."

He stared off into space.

For a while there, as they'd been working with the map in the Chetumal waiting area, he'd been different. He'd been lively and almost fun. Almost. For the first time since they'd begun their journey at JFK, they felt like a team. Now they were back to simply two travelers with the same destination.

With nothing better to do, Laura left the first-class lounge and wandered the shops in the terminal. While browsing the English-language section of a newsstand, she spotted a somewhat familiar face.

"Will? Is that you?"

He jumped at the sound of her voice and turned. Yes . . . Will Burleigh, an internist she knew from the medical society meetings. Recognition lit his eyes. Well, not exactly *lit*. If anything he looked a little dismayed. Didn't he want to be seen?

"Oh . . . Laura. I don't believe this."

"Yeah, it's weird, huh? Haven't seen you in months, and now we run into each other in Mexico City. Where are you going?"

"South . . . to Mesoamerica."

Odd. Hardly anyone called it that. She was an exception. So apparently was Will.

He didn't look good—pale and drawn. He had a worn baseball cap jammed down on his salt-and-pepper hair. A fresh scar peeked over the top of his turtleneck collar.

"Not the usual tourist destination—unless you're looking for fun in the sun in Cancún."

He shook his head. "No fun. Just a miracle." He glanced at his watch. "Oops. My plane's boarding. Gotta run. Safe trip wherever you're going."

And then he was hurrying off.

How odd. A miracle? She was hunting the same thing. And he seemed to have the same level of hope as she about finding one: zero.

In the newspaper rack she found an English-language edition of *People* and brought it back to where they were seated.

Rick was on the phone. He handed it to her as she dropped into her seat.

"Stahlman wants to speak to you."

His voice sounded wheezier than before. *"I'm terribly sorry for what you've been through. I know you didn't bargain for this and you must believe I had no idea it would turn out this way."*

"I'm sure you didn't."

"Are you sure you want to continue? I feel terrible and I'm willing to prorate the amount I promised you if you want to quit."

That word again.

"That's very generous . . . "

"I don't think I could forgive myself if anything happened to you."

How true was that? The man had a terminal diagnosis. He wanted to live. No question that he didn't care about the financial cost to himself, but what about the personal cost to others? Well, really, what did it matter what he thought?

"I'm going to see this through."

The words startled her. They were accurate as to how she felt, but they'd come out on their own.

He didn't respond immediately; then, *"That's very brave. I chose you because I felt you perfect for the job. I didn't know how perfect. Your courage and determination are a lagniappe."*

Was it courage? She didn't feel brave. Her mother always told her what a stubborn child she had been

growing up. Was that what this boiled down to? Stubbornness?

No. More than that. She sensed it went back to those
two perfectly healthy corpses, refusing to give up their
secrets. And Tommy's perfect joints. This trip was an extension of all that—an assault on an enigmatic onion.
She wouldn't be happy until she'd peeled away all its
layers of mystery and had her answers.

Not sure how to field the compliment, she said,
" 'Lagniappe' . . . you don't hear that too often in conversation."

*"My word of the day. Call me when you've done
what you have to do in Israel. And be careful."*

"Will do."

"He gave you an out?" Rick said as she handed the
phone back.

"He did."

"And you didn't take it?"

"As I'm sure you heard."

"Yeah."

He looked at her, gave her a quick, silent nod, then
resumed his thousand-mile stare.

Laura flipped though her *People* and she realized she
recognized only one out of ten celebrities in the whole
magazine.

Finally she broke down and tried for conversation
again.

"So . . . here we are, embarking on the next leg of our
wild-goose chase."

He snapped out of his reverie and came back from
wherever he'd been drifting.

"You still think this is all futile, then? Even after what
Ix'chel told you about Chaim being cured?"

She shrugged. "Chaim got sick unto death, Chaim got
better—I don't dispute that. The mystery is what happened between. I promised Stahlman two weeks and I'll

give him twelve more days of my best to unravel that mystery. And then I'll have to tell a very sick man that I couldn't find his cure."

"But if you do find it, what will you tell *yourself*?"

The question took her by surprise—not only for its perceptiveness, but because she had no answer.

She looked at Rick and saw he'd already resumed his deep-space stare.

"Thinking about your 'vast, cool and unsympathetic' intelligences?"

He pulled back to the airport again. "Guess you could say so. But only indirectly."

"Spend much time thinking about them?"

Now *I'm* dropping pronouns. Is it catching?

"Try not to. But yeah, sometimes."

She had to say something: "Tell me, do you have something against starting a sentence with a pronoun?"

"What do you mean?"

"'Guess you could say so' . . . 'Try not to' . . . That sort of thing."

He frowned. "Never thought about it. Never realized—"

She laughed. "See? There you go again. And verbs and articles as well?"

"No kidding?" His voice went robotic. "I. Will. Try. To. Speak. Your. Brand. Of. English."

"Now you're being silly. I shouldn't have mentioned it. It just popped out. Back to these intelligences. Have they got names?"

"Maybe. Probably not. They're too rare and too vast and unknowable to have names. Naming is a human thing. When we name something we've classified it, pigeonholed it, circumscribed it—made it safe. Or relatively so. I like to put myself in their place and imagine how they view us."

"Like bugs?"

His mouth twisted. "More like microbes—but *thinking* microbes. Imagine how entertaining we must be as they toy with our beliefs and emotions on a mass scale to see how we react."

Okay. She could temporarily buy into this crazy mind-set—but only as an intellectual exercise. Better than silence.

"But if they're that powerful, they could simply wipe us out if we don't respond as they wish."

He shook his head. "You're getting Old Testamenty there, in the cranky Yahweh mode. If sapience is a rare aberration, they're gonna want to preserve us. If they wipe us out, the toys are gone, and where's the fun in that?"

"Okay, so assume you're one of these intelligences . . . what do you do?"

"Well, the key word is 'unsympathetic.' By that I don't mean they have ill will toward us, just that they don't *feel* for us. They've no compunction about hurting us just to see how we react and recover. As for me, as an unsympathetic intelligence, I'd want to set some rules. Every game has to have rules."

"Like?"

"Okay, you can't simply insert an idea into the heads of a population. That's too crude. Lacks style, no élan. You have to manipulate events in a way that sparks the idea. Once that idea is fixed, then you watch where it goes."

"Sounds complicated."

He shrugged. "It is, and it isn't. Maybe they're playing with chaos theory."

"That's the second time you've mentioned chaos."

"Is it? Oh, yeah. About Chaim leaving Israel. Just a toss-off about how a seemingly unrelated event in Israel—the failure of a kibbutz in the nineties—triggered enormous changes in your life decades later."

He was right, wasn't he. A long chain of causes and effects leading directly to her . . . She found it disturbing.

"Is this where you tell me it was arranged?"

He laughed. "You think I know? I'm just juggling ideas. And that brings me back to chaos theory, which is most easily appreciated in predicting weather."

"You mean like the butterfly flapping its wings in Brazil causing a tornado in Kansas?"

"That's the famous example everyone gives. It's exaggerated but it sets up the paradigm that in a complex system like weather, small variations in initial conditions can have huge effects down the line. Look how El Niño, created by the temperature of a relatively small area of the Pacific off the west coast of South America, influences droughts and tornadoes and hurricanes in and around the U.S."

"So chaos theory would apply to the complex system of a globe-spanning race of sapient beings. Namely us."

"You got it. Maybe these unsympathetic intelligences like to introduce an anomaly here and there to see where the ripples go."

Now she saw where he was heading. A crazy, almost psychotic conversation, but she couldn't deny she was enjoying it. How many men—how many *people* of either sex—could spark a conversation like this? She couldn't remember ever meeting anyone like him.

"An anomaly like a panacea?"

"Exactly. Maybe they introduced it to a pagan cult and waited to see how its spread would affect human civilization. But the cult kept it to itself and doled it out to only a lucky few. That's got to piss off the U-I's."

U-I's? she thought. Oh, unsympathetic intelligences.

"Why?"

"No chaos effect or ripple effect into the larger system because their panacea was kept under wraps, leaving the system unaware of its existence. The experiment was a failure."

"Fine. No fun for them. But I'm still not sure I get this whole event-manipulation thing."

"They wait a couple of millennia—an eye blink to them—and no chaos effect. So they start manipulating events to get this thing out in the open. The result is Doctor Laura Fanning on her way to Mesoamerica, and then to Israel."

A chill ran through her. "You think they *want* me to find it?"

"Of course they do. And it works even better to have it revealed *now* rather than back in the Iron Age or whatever. Because *now* the sapient microbes have *science* and we're gonna be faced with something that breaks all our carefully constructed theories of biology and physics. The ripple effects through all of science and eventually human civilization will be enormous."

Yes, Laura thought, nodding. Widespread availability of a panacea would cause . . . she could barely comprehend it. Agree with him or not, he was a thinker, this guy.

" 'Enormous' doesn't touch it," she said. "The effect of no disease, and no premature death from disease, will change *everything*. Old religions will fall before the panacea, new religions will spring up around it, the social order will convulse with all these extra old folks around, the course of history will be corkscrewed."

"Or just plain screwed."

She remembered something he'd said yesterday. "Is that what you meant by 'Did you ever think that the panacea might exist because we're able to have the opinion that it can't exist?' "

"Uh-huh. Science has worked for centuries to make sense of the world around us. We've had theories which we've confirmed enough to call knowledge. We can say that this is the way things work, and then along comes the panacea and it breaks all those rules. The Garmin GPS of human knowledge says 'Recalculating route,' and that starts an intellectual chain reaction leading who knows where?"

Laura sat back and shook her head. "This sounds suspiciously like intelligent design."

"No-no. Just the opposite. More like intelligent disarray or intelligent disorder. It's like seeing something as orderly and productive as a beehive and saying, 'I wonder what would happen if we stole the queen?' And then you do just that. Or on a human scale, it's, say, 1963 and you've got a cold war between two factions of your microbes, the commies and the capitalists. Let's take a guy connected to the commies and nudge him to kill the leader of the capitalists and see what happens. That sort of thing."

"I see why you want to keep the word 'unsympathetic' in there. And I see where this is going. Endow this hate-filled little Austrian with an enormously seductive and persuasive speaking voice and see where it takes him."

"Now you've got it. But that pales in comparison with introducing a true panacea to humanity." He was staring at her. "Which brings us to the big question."

"Which is?"

"If you find the panacea, what will you do?"

For an instant she seriously considered her answer, then shook herself.

"A moot point, Rick. It doesn't exist."

"Imagine it does, and you find its secret, and it's up to you to reveal it to the world or keep it hidden. What do you do?"

What was he doing . . . asking out of curiosity? Or probing her ethics, taking her measure? It made her a little uncomfortable. But she'd engaged in the topic, so she figured she owed him an answer.

She thought of the turmoil the panacea would cause in every facet of human civilization. And yet . . .

"Okay, assuming it exists, I think I'd give it to the world."

"Despite the consequences?"

"I don't think it would be my right to withhold it. And if I did, every time I heard of a child dying from a supposedly incurable illness, I'd feel responsible. I couldn't live like that."

"So it's all about you?"

"That's not fair." She was getting a new, unsettling perspective on Rick. "Let me turn this around. Let's say the panacea exists and I found it. Would you stop me from giving it to the world?"

"What kind of question is that?"

"What kind of answer is that? You're starting to worry me. If I lift up your sleeve, will I see a 536 there?"

He laughed but his head shake was emphatic. "You've seen my arms. But it comes down to this: I was hired to watch your back during your travels and return you safely to Mister Stahlman. And that is what I will do."

She still hadn't learned where he stood on this admittedly moot question.

She said, "Let me rephrase: If you found the panacea, would you give it to the world?"

"I probably wouldn't be able to answer that until I had it in my hand."

"You're really doing your damnedest to avoid an answer."

"Okay, that scenario would put me in a position to frustrate the U-I's, and I've got to tell you, I'd be sorely tempted not to play the game. I might even destroy it."

"And condemn untold millions to premature death?"

"I wouldn't be condemning anyone to anything. The operative word there is 'tempted.' The jury's still out on what I'd finally decide."

"But the very fact that you'd even be tempted . . . "

"You're operating under the assumption that a panacea would be a good thing for the human race."

She couldn't help making it personal . . . thinking of Marissa if her stem-cell transplant hadn't worked.

"Ultimately, yes. Lots of turmoil in the beginning, but in the long run—"

"Nothing from outside can be good in the long run. And in the long run you'd only be rewarding the U-I's. Enabling them. And encouraging them." He shook his head. "Don't you want to thumb your nose and raise a middle digit?"

"I might . . . if I believed in these vast intelligences. But I don't. Just as I don't believe in the panacea. This is a fun intellectual exercise, Rick, but no more than that. Right?"

"A guy named Charles Fort spent much of his life documenting weird, inexplicable occurrences. His conclusion: 'We're property.' "

"Oh, I can't buy into that," Laura said.

"Maybe by the time we finish this you will."

Not likely, but she remembered something else he'd said.

"You started to say something yesterday. You said, 'I've seen . . . ' but you never finished. What did you see?"

He stood. "I think I'll hit the bar for a drink. What can I get you?"

"Conversation over?"

"The topic's run out of steam, don't you think? What can I get you?"

She sighed. After the last twenty-four hours, she could use a drink—a stiff one. But she didn't do well with hard liquor, and since she was operating on next to no sleep, she'd be snockered.

"A Pinot Noir if they have it, otherwise a glass of Cab. I'm not particular."

He nodded and strolled away.

What had he seen—or thought he'd seen—that he wouldn't talk about? Was that why he'd dropped everything in California and moved across country?

She pulled out her smartphone—no need for a sat phone here—and dialed her voice mail. One message. Now what?

"Hey, Doc, Phil again. You're not gonna believe this. Your not–ex-SEAL changed his name to Rick Hayden from—wait for it—Ramiz Haddad. Can you believe this? He's some sort of Arab. I've never seen the guy. Does he look like an Arab? Anyway, now that I have his birth name, I can go deeper into his background. I'll be back in touch as soon as I find something."

After ending the call, Laura sat and stared into space pretty much as Rick had done.

An Arab? Rick didn't look a bit like an Arab. And he spoke Hebrew.

What the hell was going on?

9

"I found her," Bradsher said.

Nelson was seated in the Avianca area of Benito Juarez International Airport, awaiting their connecting flight to Miami. He knew Fanning was also in the airport and had sent Bradsher in search of her. For some reason he could not fully explain, he wanted to see her in the flesh.

"Where?"

"Near the Iberia gates. She's with Hayden."

"You mean Ramiz Haddad."

Bradsher had backgrounded this so-called nobody ex-SEAL and learned he wasn't a SEAL at all but an ex-cop from the sleepy town of Sausalito who had changed his name from Ramiz Haddad to Rick Hayden. It made some sort of sense because one could see why he'd think he'd have a better chance of advancement in a little town like Sausalito with an American rather than an Arab name.

The reason didn't matter. What mattered was that this Haddad, who wasn't a SEAL at all, had somehow neutralized Miguel and Jorge. Nelson had informed the Company's Mexico City office of the situation and they were sending someone into those jungles to find Miguel. His satellite phone's battery had not yet run out and so they'd been able to ping it and triangulate on his signal for an approximate location. But that meant only that they'd be able to find Miguel's phone. It didn't mean he was with it.

Nelson had a terrible sense of events spinning out of control—not that they'd been exactly under his thumb in the first place, but the tumors, Stahlman entering the picture, Simon gone, Miguel and his hireling in the picture and then out of it, Fanning heading to Israel . . .

The Serpent's work, or the Lord's?

Nelson sighed and rose from his seat. "Show me."

"Are you sure?"

Bradsher didn't know the connection between Fanning and Uncle Jim; Nelson was content to leave it that way.

"We've sent three men against her and none has returned. She's the target but her companion is frustrating our every move. So, yes, I'm quite sure I want to lay eyes on both of them."

Bradsher led him to the gate where passengers awaited their Iberia flight to Madrid. They stopped near a cell phone kiosk.

"She's over there, by the window."

Searching out of the corner of his eye, Nelson found her—jet-black hair, trim figure. A surge of rage flowed through him as he watched her blithely flipping through a magazine. Uncle Jim may have forgiven her, but he could not.

"Where's her guard dog?"

Bradsher looked around. "He was seated next—here he comes."

A tall man, a drink in each hand, was winding through the other passengers. His face was turned away at first, but became visible when he sat.

Nelson felt as if he'd been punched in the chest. He grabbed Bradsher's arm.

"No!"

"What's wrong?"

"I know him."

"How? Who is it?"

"One of our own. Or at least he used to be."

His presence explained so many things.

Why him, of all people?

This was terrible. Worse than terrible. This was the absolute worst.

Because Nelson knew all too well what this man was capable of.

1

By the time they found Gan Yosaif—or what was left of it—the sun was resting on the horizon, readying to slip below.

Just as well. They needed night to find Polaris.

They'd chosen another Jeep, but Rick—or should she think of him as Ramiz now?—had driven this time while Laura navigated them south into the Negev Desert. He pulled to a stop before a broken gate that hung canted from a single hinge across the dirt road. A weathered sign dangled next to it. The word on the left had been obliterated, leaving . . .

$$...\text{גן}$$

"That's the word for garden," Rick said. "This must be it."

Beyond the gate, on a rise, they could make out a few buildings.

"Good thing I talked to that guy in Mexico City," he said, getting out and stretching. "We'd have never found this place on our own."

No argument there. Gan Yosaif was on no map.

They'd spent the latter part of Monday and most of today in airports and airplanes. When they arrived in

Tel Aviv they bought the most detailed map they could find, and searched through guide books, but Gan Yosaif might as well have been on a moon of Jupiter.

So they took the Orthodox fellow's advice and visited the Israel Land Authority, but had to travel to Jerusalem to do so. The trip took less than an hour and turned out to be in the general direction they needed to go anyway.

It didn't take the woman at the ILA long to pinpoint Gan Yosaif for them. The location remained in her records but was no longer on the maps because it was among the many kibbutzim that had failed decades ago.

She directed them south into the Negev to a point east of Rahat and south of a tiny town called Dvira. When she asked why they were looking for a forgotten kibbutz, Rick had told her it was the birthplace of a recently departed dear friend. Laura could almost admire the glib way he mixed fact and fiction on the fly. The woman warned them to be careful since Gan Yosaif was just a couple of miles from the Arab sectors of the West Bank.

"I can't believe it," Laura had said as she'd watched Jerusalem recede in the rearview mirror. "We rode through Jerusalem and I didn't see a damn thing except the inside of a government office."

Rick shrugged. "Didn't miss much. I've been here before. Mostly a jumble of old buildings. Most of Israel's historic sites are just old buildings. Great if you like that sort of thing. Personally, I hate them."

"Are you kidding me? Israel is more than old buildings."

"No argument there. Mostly desert—as you'll appreciate for the next couple of hours."

"You, sir, are a Philistine—and I use the term advisedly."

"Good choice, considering the locale."

"Do you know how much history has happened here? The course of western civ was determined by events that occurred—or are believed to have occurred—right here a couple of millennia ago. Ever think about that?"

"All the time. I think about something out there taking notice of a preacher wandering around the Jerusalem area back then, and watching the Romans torture and kill him because he was getting too popular, and then after he's dead and buried, that something starts thinking—"

"Oh, no. You're not . . . "

"Yeah, that something starts thinking, 'Hey, what would happen if I raised this guy from the dead? Wouldn't that cause a major freak-out?' Which, of course, it did."

"Probably no one more freaked out than that poor preacher."

"Right. But it's a perfect example of the chaos effect we were talking about. That isolated anomaly in Palestine—"

"You mean *belief* in that anomaly."

"Whatever, it's had an enormous effect on the complex system of human history over the past two thousand years."

And so it had gone, across miles and miles of desert . . .

Rick dragged the kibbutz gate open enough to admit their Jeep, then drove them through. They passed spindly olive trees and overgrown date groves until they came to a cinder-block building with peeling paint and a collapsed roof. It backed up against a silo of some sort. Or was it a cistern?

She opened her door and was about to step out when Rick said, "Wait."

He turned the Jeep around so it faced down the driveway.

"What's that for?"

"In case we need to make a quick getaway."

She didn't like that. "What are you saying?"

"Just that I like to be prepared."

Wary now, she stepped out. The sun was already gone. She'd read somewhere that night comes fast in the desert. No kidding. That sun had dropped like a stone into a pond. She could already feel the temperature falling, but her legs appreciated the chance to get out and walk around.

With the motor off, the silence crashed in. She heard the faint rustle of the wind through the olive branches, the ticking of the cooling engine, and nothing more. The sense of isolation lay thick on the forbidding terrain. A little creepy out here.

"Speaking of prepared," she said. "You didn't happen to get a special shipment like in Chetumal, did you?"

He'd sent his pistol back to America from Chetumal, saying he wouldn't even think about trying to sneak a weapon aboard an El Al flight.

"I wish. Didn't have time. But even if I had, it's so much more difficult to ship a weapon into Israel. The country's a freakin' fortress."

She looked around. "I wonder why this place failed."

"Debt, I gather," Rick said from the other side of the hood. "A failure of will, a failure of economics, or maybe a little of both. A kibbutz is a commune, you know."

"Like the hippies in the sixties?"

"Somewhat, but a lot better organized."

"How many hippy communes left, you think?"

He shrugged. "Don't know. Can't imagine many. From what I've read they were mostly organized around free love and drugs. The original kibbutzniks here were serious about communal farming, and you joined one to work, not to get high. There's still hundreds of them left and they're responsible for a lot of Israel's agriculture."

She looked around. "What do we do until the stars come out? Explore?"

"I'm going to record our exact latitude and longitude just to get that out of the way. But feel free to wander."

She looked at the dilapidated buildings and decided against exploring. She didn't believe in ghosts, but the place looked haunted, almost menacing.

She could phone home again. She'd had to wait until three this afternoon when they were in Jerusalem to call—at just barely eight A.M. back in the States—and Steven had assured her that everything was fine, although Marissa seemed to be feeling her mother's absence more and more. Laura promised to be home as soon as possible. She'd checked her voice mail then but nothing more from Phil.

Instead of wandering, what she really wanted to do was confront Rick about his identity problem. But was twilight in the middle of nowhere the right time and place to do that?

Probably not.

Not that she feared him. In fact, despite the incongruities in his personal history, she took comfort in his presence. Not because he seemed devoted to her; more devoted to the job of protecting her—a matter of pride or a sense of duty. Still, she couldn't imagine being out here on her own.

"Can I ask you a personal question?"

"No."

She ignored that. "Is there a woman in your life?"

"Isn't that a personal question?"

"No, just a curiosity question. Is there?"

"Are you applying for the job?"

"Hardly. Answer?"

"No, no woman in my life. Satisfied?"

"How about a man in your life?"

A soft chuckle. "Just Stahlman."

"Has there ever been a woman in your life?"

"Now *that's* personal."

"Okay, why isn't there one now?"

"Also personal, but I'll just say that relationships are overrated and leave it at that."

Spoken like a man who can't find a woman willing to put up with him. She tried to imagine living with him . . . and failed.

He took his GPS reading and made his notes, then reached across the hood toward her.

"Have you got that pic of Chaim's tat handy?"

She reached through the Jeep window and pulled the photo from her shoulder bag.

"It's too early, isn't it?" She looked at the sky where the sun's rays were fading but not yet gone. "There's a star up there but I don't think that's north."

"You're half right," he said, taking the photo. "That's not north, but that's also not a star. That's Jupiter."

"How do you—? Oh, right. SEAL training."

"You got it."

She wanted *so* badly to challenge him.

He pulled out his compass, took a reading, then laid the photo on the hood and aligned it at an angle.

"We should find Polaris over that way when things get darker."

2

Bradsher looked agitated as he entered Nelson's suite in the Sadot Hotel. Since it was only a short shuttle ride away from Ben Gurion Airport, he'd decided to center their operation here.

"Close the door and tell me what you've got."

He spread his hands. "Brother Miguel and his hireling are no longer with us."

The news came as no surprise, not after seeing Fanning's travel companion, but Nelson's headache suddenly worsened.

"Details?"

"The men we sent spotted a cloud of birds circling an area of the jungle. They found them there, both strangled, hanging from trees near their car. The birds and apparently some of the jungle cats had been at them."

"Time of death?"

"They estimate Sunday night or early Monday morning. They drove the remains back to Mexico City. I don't know what they plan to do with—"

"And we don't care. Who do they think did it—natives in retaliation, or Hayden?"

Nelson knew the answer but he wanted the available facts.

"Isn't he really 'Haddad'?"

"He's neither, but we started with Hayden so let's stick with that."

The Haddad name hadn't clicked until he'd recognized Fanning's bodyguard. Then it all came crashing together. The real Haddad's body had been found a while ago during a dredging operation near Treasure Island in San Francisco Bay. If not for the dredging, the body would have remained in the muck forever. Not much left of him after years in the water. He'd been identified by dental records.

The Company had suspected Haddad of terrorist ties and he'd been under close observation, especially after he quit the Sausalito force. But then he dropped off the radar. At least that was the official story.

Nelson had had no inkling until now that his identity had been usurped. Apparently the Company had known, but they'd buried the information behind high-level clearances.

Why, Lord? Why him of all people?

"I wish you'd tell me his real name."

"As soon as you have the proper clearance, I will gladly tell you."

"Yessir. As for Miguel, the men who found him commented on the method. They felt it would be highly unusual for the natives to use—"

"Zip ties?"

Bradsher's eyes widened. "How did you know?"

Nelson shook his head. Could this get any worse?

"He always had a thing for zip ties. Very creative with them. Were the bodies burned?"

"No, sir."

Well, at least he hadn't tried to make a mockery of the Leviticus Sanction.

"The question is, did he learn anything from Miguel?"

"No signs of torture on either, sir. I'm sure Miguel would say nothing even under extreme circumstances, and the hireling knew nothing."

"And yet . . . something sent them off to Israel . . . to a dead kibbutz."

"As you said, sir, Israel's a dead end. They're doing nothing more than sucking up our time and attention and resources. The desert is a perfect place to eliminate them and have done with it."

Bradsher didn't see the Lord's hand in this, nor Nelson's place in His plan. For he was becoming more and more convinced that the Lord had a plan for him—specifically for him. But Nelson couldn't voice that. Not yet. Not until he was sure.

"You're probably right. But she's following some sort of trail, one we didn't even know existed. Let's give them a little more time and see where it leads."

3

It didn't take long for the clear desert sky to fill with stars. No moon, but the combined light from more stars than she had ever seen at one time was bright enough to light the ground and even cast faint shadows.

"Isn't that the Milky Way?" she said, sweeping her raised hand along a massive, mottled arc of light and cosmic dust stretching across the sky.

"Yep. See that thickened brighter area? That's downtown Milky Way, the galactic hub. They say there's a massive black hole there."

She'd heard that and for some ridiculous reason it always made her uncomfortable. Not as if she was ever going to get near it. She continued searching the sky until she spotted a familiar configuration.

"The Big Dipper. Look."

"Got it." He pointed. "Follow the edge and there's Polaris."

He pulled out a flashlight, angled the photo to align the tattoo's staff toward the star, then used his protractor.

"Two hundred ninety-three degrees west," he announced, as if addressing an audience. Then, motioning her closer, he leaned farther across the hood and lowered his voice. "Don't react to what I'm about to say, okay? Don't look around, just concentrate on the photo."

Her immediate instinct was to straighten up and look around. It took every ounce of will not to.

"Why? What's—?"

"We've got company."

She had to ball her fists to keep herself from looking.

"Where?"

"They're behind the building. Slowly, casually, we're

going to get back in the Jeep and roll out of here. Got that? Slowly, casually. If they think we're unaware of them, they might let us go."

"Wh-who are they, 536?"

"Maybe. But since we're about two miles from the West Bank, I have another prime suspect when it comes to sneaking around in Israeli territory at night. Now . . . " He lifted the photo and raised his voice. "Okay! That's that! Back to civilization!"

Laura's knees felt a little wobbly as she straightened and stepped toward the passenger door. This wasn't like Mexico where Rick had been armed. She found herself thinking about Marissa.

What will happen to her if I'm killed? Steven won't be able to—

Her fingers were just brushing the door handle when the night suddenly came alive with incoherent shouting as four figures raced toward the car.

"Hands up," Rick told her. "No sudden moves unless someone starts shooting, then hit the dirt."

Laura had a quick impression of camo pants, sweaters, ammo vests, and head scarves, and then she was shoved up against the Jeep and roughly patted down. Whoever was doing it took extra time with her buttocks and between her thighs.

Then more shouting in a language she didn't understand, and a lot of pushing and shoving until they were both backed against the decrepit block building.

The Jeep headlights came on, blinding her and pinning her to the wall.

One of their attackers had found the car rental agreement and their passports and was on one knee by the headlights, inspecting them. He wore a white-and-blue keffiyeh, Arafat style, and appeared to be the leader. At least the others seemed to defer to him.

He rose and said something to his companions. Whatever it was, they laughed and grinned. After a little back and forth chatter and more laughter—what was so damn funny?—the leader approached.

"Tourists?" he said in heavily accented English.

"Yes-yes!" Rick said. "We're tourists! Please don't hurt us!"

"We will not hurt you. We—"

"No!" Rick wailed, his voice breaking. "You're going to cut our heads off! I've seen the video!"

What was he saying? Cut their heads off? Why give them ideas?

"Be calm," the Palestinian said. "We only—"

"Please!" he shrieked, dropping to his knees and pressing his hands together in prayer. "I beg you! Take her! Go ahead! You can have her! Just let me go!" He dropped his head almost to the ground as he held his folded hands aloft. "*Pleeease!*"

She'd known him only for a couple of days, but this was so un-Rick, it had to be an act. She didn't *like* the act—*take her . . . you can have her . . .* seriously?—but decided to play along.

She stared at him with feigned disgust. "You sniveling bastard!"

Apparently the lead Palestinian felt the same. He snarled something and kicked Rick in the ribs. The rest happened too fast to register. She saw a blur of motion and suddenly Rick had hold of the leader, pulling him down and turning him around to face his men, then using him as a shield as he opened fire from behind him.

Rick's words echoed back to her: . . . *someone starts shooting . . . hit the dirt . . .*

She dove for the sand and scrabbled out of the headlight glare. Two of the three silhouetted targets fell quickly, but the third was able to return fire—quick, three-round bursts from some sort of assault rifle slung over his shoulder. She saw the leader Rick held buck with the impact of the slugs meant for Rick. The top of his head exploded.

As the shooter ducked away from the Jeep, Laura realized he was heading straight for her. She tried to scrabble away but he caught her under an arm and started to lift her, obviously to use as a shield against Rick.

No way.

She had a little girl waiting for her.

She grabbed a handful of sand and hurled it at his face. He'd been looking and firing at Rick and didn't see it coming. He recoiled as it hit his eyes. She raked those eyes with her fingernails for good measure. He cried out in pain and released her. As she fell back, a bullet caved in his throat and another took away part of his face.

Rick shoved his human shield aside and ran toward the Jeep. He quickly checked the first two men and stripped them of their weapons. None of the downed men was moving, certainly not the one closest to her.

"You okay?" he said, hurrying over.

"Wh-wh-what just happened?"

"We just got ourselves out of a nasty jam."

"We?"

"Nice move with the sand and going for his eyes. Gave me a clear line of fire."

A delayed reaction from her adrenaline surge was making her hands shake as she brushed them off and rose to her feet. She looked down at the bloody, ruined throat of the one who had tried to grab her. She'd seen too many dead people to have a corpse bother her, but this one did. He'd been blown away right in front of her.

She leaned over and retched but nothing came up.

"You okay?" he said as she straightened.

"No, I'm not okay. Your bullets passed about three inches from my face."

"An inch is as good as a mile."

His too-casual attitude was pushing her shock and confusion to anger—a too familiar place for her.

"What were you thinking? There were four of them and one of you. They weren't even pointing their guns at us!"

"Best time to make a move. And anyway, I didn't like their plans for us. They were going to hold us for ransom."

"How do you know that?"

"The head man said 'These two will be valuable.' "

"You speak Arabic too?"

"A little."

Who *was* this man?

Oh, right. Ramiz Haddad. And not a reach to think a man born Ramiz Haddad would speak some Arabic. She still had trouble buying that Arab bit. If he was an Arab, she was Mongolian. But that was secondary now. Even tertiary . . .

"Stahlman would have paid."

"These yokels wouldn't be looking for money. They'd be looking to trade us for their terrorist buddies in Israeli prisons. That type of negotiation, if it gets done at all, can take months. And besides . . . "

"What?"

He stopped at the Jeep's passenger door and turned to face her.

"According to their chatter they had more than just a 'hostage situation' in mind."

"What's that supposed to mean?"

"They had plans for you."

"Me? What do you mean?"

"Well, first off, they were each going to take turns with you before they took you back across the border. The leader had firsties."

"Wait . . . what?"

He sighed. "They were each going—"

"Okay, okay. I got that." She swallowed. "Really?"

"And they were going to make me watch. They thought we were lovers."

So that was what the laughter had been about. In the back of her mind she'd detected a lascivious twist but had been too scared to fully grasp it.

"And back in the West Bank," Rick was saying, "they were going to set you up in a room for themselves and their friends to visit until the trade was worked out."

. . . that type of negotiation, if it gets done at all, can take months . . .

Laura looked down at the corpse at her feet and delivered a kick to its torso.

"Bastards!"

Rick opened the door as she approached. When she'd settled into the seat she began to shake all over.

"Hold on to those," he said and dropped their passports and rental agreement onto her lap.

She watched him step over the bodies as he hurried around the front through the light.

"How did you manage to kill all four of them?" she said when he'd slipped behind the wheel.

"I didn't. I dropped only three. They took care of their fearless leader for us. I'm glad he had Kevlar under his sweater, otherwise those AK rounds would have gone through him and into me."

Their fearless leader . . . the one who had *firsties*. She shuddered.

"The first two were easy. I've always been a good shot—no brag, just one of those things that comes easy for me. Before they even realized what was happening they were dead. Surprise is like a hidden weapon. It freezes them for a second or two as they try to adjust to the sudden change in their situation. In an eyeblink they went from having total control to having someone shooting at them."

"But so fast."

"Not so. I think I'm slowing down. I wasn't fast enough to keep that last guy from reaching you. Whatever, I had to drop them as fast as I could while I still had the surprise. Grabbing their buddy's sidearm was the last thing they expected from a wimpy tourist, but they weren't going to stay surprised long."

She couldn't help a tiny smile. "Speaking of wimpy . . . you're a terrible actor."

"You didn't buy it?"

"Don't quit your day job."

She flashed back to his quickness, the ruthless accuracy of his fire.

If he wasn't an ex-SEAL, what *was* he?

He started the Jeep and headed down to the gate. But when he reached it, four sets of headlights flared and shadowy figures raced toward them, shouting in a foreign language.

"Oh, no!" she cried. "More of them?"

"Raise your hands and relax," Rick said. "That's Hebrew they're shouting."

4

"Daddy, I'm cold."

Steven looked up from his laptop. Marissa stood in the doorway to the den with her arms wrapped across her chest. Natasha, her homebound instructor, stood behind her.

"She feels warm to me, Mister Gaines."

He motioned Marissa forward. "Come here, honey. Let me feel."

He noticed her face was flushed and when she reached him he pressed his hand against her forehead. Hot and dry.

"Definitely warm. Let's go get the thermometer."

"I'll get it," Marissa said.

Steven followed her to the linen closet—he'd expected the bathroom—questioning her along the way.

"Sore throat? Cough? Congestion?"

"Nope."

"Tummy hurt? Feel like you're gonna throw up?" He hoped not. Just the smell of vomit made him want to hurl himself.

"Nope."

"Okay. Besides cold, what do you feel?"

"I hurt all over."

That sounded viral.

She pawed through the second shelf of the linen closet and pulled out something that looked like a small flashlight.

"That's not a thermometer," he said. "That's a nose-hair clipper."

Natasha had trailed along. "It's one of those forehead thermometers," she said.

Steven let Marissa take the lead with the thing. He didn't know what to do and she loved being in charge. She fiddled with it for a second, then pressed the tip against her forehead.

"This is the way Mommy does it." She held it there for what couldn't have been more than a second, then looked at the little window on the handle. "One-oh-one-six."

He didn't like the sound of that.

"That wasn't anywhere near long enough."

"Oh, no," Natasha said. "That's all it takes. It's the greatest thing. Accurate too."

"Really? Let me see."

Sure enough: *101.6°F.*

"Well, that's not good." He still couldn't buy that it could work that fast. "Let's try again. Show me how to do it."

He followed Marissa's instructions, but held it against her forehead for a good five seconds. No matter. He got the same reading.

Okay. He had to make some decisions.

"You," he said, pointing to Marissa, "are to get under the covers where it's warm. I'll get you some Tylenol." He turned to Natasha. "And I guess you've got the rest of the day off. Figure on tomorrow too, maybe longer. I'll call you when she's over this."

She nodded, looking disappointed. He imagined the state DOE paid her on a per diem basis for homebound instruction. Couldn't be helped, though. Marissa's immune system was fragile on her best days. Now that she was sick, he needed to keep traffic through the house at a minimum.

The good news was that the visiting nurse was due at two . . . ten minutes from now. She'd check Marissa over, maybe draw some blood . . . do all the things nurses do.

Almost nine P.M. in Israel now. If he didn't hear from Laura soon, he'd call her.

5

Laura couldn't sit still. She paced the small interrogation room while Rick sat behind the scarred wooden table, leaning back in the chair, arms folded across his chest. He sat so still he could have been asleep with his eyes open.

She tried not to look in the mirror as she paced. First off, she'd had a peek at her reflection and she looked old and haggard in this harsh light. Hell, she *felt* old and haggard as well. Second, she was ninety-nine percent sure it was one-way glass—like in every TV interrogation room she'd ever seen.

"Why are they keeping us? We're Americans. We're allies with Israel, probably its best friend in the world."

Rick stirred and said, "Haven't mistreated us."

"No, but if they're going to hold us they could put us in something other than this smelly little room. We were the victims out there."

"We were picked up by *Yamas* and they've got four dead Palestinians to explain. They're thorough about these things."

She stopped pacing.

"Hamas?"

"Whoa! Whoa! That's *Yamas* with a Y. *Hamas* is on the other side—the suicide bombers."

"All right, who's *Yamas* and how do you *know* this stuff?"

"Don't know for certain about *Yamas*, but the signage on the way in indicated that this is a Shin Bet station—that's Israel's FBI—and *Yamas* is their border division. So it's a pretty good guess. And to answer your question, I've had some business over here from time to time."

"With the Israeli FBI?"

"You do know they're listening to every word, don't you?"

"I guessed that."

"Well, they probably wouldn't like me talking about it."

All right, she'd had enough.

"Who *are* you, damn it! Because I know—"

He held up a hand. "Whatever you know or think you know is wrong. Which is all the more reason to keep it to yourself. Please."

The *please* got to her. She'd never heard him say it. Not once. And it took her by surprise.

Okay. She'd say nothing. Now. But later . . .

The door opened behind her. She saw Rick stiffen as he looked past her. She turned and saw a short, fiftyish man with bushy salt-and-pepper hair enter the room. He wore a gray suit, a white shirt, and no tie. He nodded to Laura and indicated the chair next to Rick.

"I am Noam Chayat," he said in English that carried a faint British accent. "Please be seated."

Laura complied, but had to ask, "Why are we being held here? We were the victims."

He smiled as he lowered himself into one of the facing chairs on the far side of the table. "You are very amusing."

"You think this is funny?"

She felt Rick's hand rest on her thigh and give it a gentle squeeze. What was he telling her? Back off?

"No," Chayat said, "but you must understand, we find four armed men, quite efficiently shot to death, and the killers claim to be victims."

"But—"

Another gentle squeeze from Rick. "He knows."

Chayat nodded. "Yes, I do. The four who attacked you were members of a raiding party from one of the Izz ad-Din al-Qassam brigades."

"Hamas," Rick said.

Chayat nodded again. "We had been tracking them. We found explosives behind one of the buildings. I am sure they must have been as surprised to encounter you as you were to encounter them."

"Not nearly," Laura said.

"We had been hoping to capture them alive. We have questions, they had answers. Those answers died with them."

"Sorry," Rick said. "Doctor Fanning had nothing to

do with the shooting. You can check her hands for GSR. They're clean."

"Yes. I gathered that." He pulled a U.S. passport from his pocket and opened it. "Richard Hayden. Who are you, Mister Hayden?"

Exactly what I want to know, Laura thought. She did not need the thigh squeeze to know not to voice that thought.

"I do private investigations and security back in the States."

"A private detective who dispatches four seasoned brigade members with one of their own weapons. I must say I am impressed."

"I got lucky."

What? Laura thought. Not going to mention you're an ex-SEAL?

And then she almost jumped out of her seat.

Good God, if Phil is right and Rick's real name is Ramiz Haddad—what if Chayat finds out he's an Arab?

What if he already knows?

"Yes. Very lucky. Why are you in Israel?"

"Doctor Fanning and I are here to pay our respects at the birthplace of a mutual friend, Chaim Brody. We paid our respects to his Maya girlfriend in Mexico and then came here to visit his birthplace in the old Gan Yosaif kibbutz."

Laura nodded in agreement. She realized Rick's scenario would fit the itinerary in their passports and was as good a story as any.

Chayat opened another passport—hers. She stared at it, resisting the urge to lunge across the table and snatch it from his fingers. She could go nowhere without it— couldn't get on a plane, couldn't even rent a hotel room. She was no *one* without it—especially in Israel. She wanted it back.

"You are a medical doctor, Ms. Fanning?"

"Yes."

"This is a very odd excursion you two are on, but it is not for me to judge. However, I am having difficulty with the way your arrival in an abandoned kibbutz coincided so perfectly with the raiding party's. Almost as if it had been planned."

"I can assure you," Laura said, "it was anything *but*."

"Neither of us have any connection to any Arab groups," Rick said. "Or Israeli groups, for that matter. At least I don't." He looked at her. "Laura?"

She shook her head. "Not a one. Just an awful case of being in the wrong place at the worst possible time."

"I guess I will have to accept that," Chayat said with obvious reluctance. "I back checked on your movements since your arrival—including your stop at the ILA—and they've been nothing but direct and straightforward. It's just . . . "

Laura waited for him to continue but he left the word hanging. Something about Rick's change of name?

"Just what?" she finally said.

"It's just that these four brigade members had strange scars on their arms."

Rick's grip on her thigh tightened. Laura kept an equally tight grip on her composure. And on her words. Casually now . . .

"Oh? Strange how?"

"Nothing. Forget it."

"You've got me curious now," she said. She started to improvise. "Certain teenagers in the U.S. make slices in the skin of their arms. It started with some disturbed kids and became a sick fad for a while. They line them up, like stripes. Something like that?"

He shook his head. "No, these appeared to be a Roman numeral, of all things." He fished a slip of paper from his pocket and pushed it across the table. "Have you ever seen the like?"

Rick's hand closed like a vise on her thigh as she stared at the sheet.

DXXXVI

"No," she managed. "Can't say as I have."

"On all four of them?" Rick said, finally relaxing his grip.

Chayat nodded. "All four."

"Wait," Rick said. "If I remember my Roman numerals, that means five hundred thirty-six. Wasn't Mohammed born in the sixth century? Could that be his birthday?"

"The accepted date of his birth is five-seventy."

Rick leaned back. "Well, that kills that theory."

Laura wanted to applaud. A brilliant bit of misdirection.

"Even if it were Mohammed's birth year," she added, getting on board, "why would Islamic terrorists write it in Roman numerals? I mean, didn't the hated crusaders use Roman numerals? How would they even *know* them?"

Chayat shrugged. "The very same question I am asking myself. Most incongruous and perplexing. But of no concern to you." He retrieved the slip and handed Laura her passport. "You are free to go, Doctor Fanning."

She snatched it from him and clutched it between her breasts. Got it! Now she knew how Gollum felt. She noticed with concern that Chayat kept a grip on Rick's passport. She stood and waited.

"You can go, Doctor Fanning," he repeated.

"What about Mister Hayden?"

"I would have a few words alone with Mister Hayden."

"Why?"

The Arab thing again?

He glanced up at her. "You may wait in the arrival area."

the left. When it steadied itself, he turned
ainst the edge.

at this from another angle. Doctor Fan-
ght forensic skills to the quest. They have
directions we don't understand. She has
elt that we've somehow missed all along."
re reason to believe she'll beat us to it."
eason to believe she'll *lead* us to it." He
hat sink in. "Think about it: A lone woman
to succeed where generations of our broth-
. . . simply because she is a woman."
owned. "How so?"

he panaceans are women, and we've long
are led by women. So who better to work
ugh their layers of deception than another
ve?"

a divine symmetry at work here. The Ser-
o thwart God's plans. When Eve accepted
n the Serpent, she sabotaged God's Plan of
Humanity. Because of her act, God changed
banished Mankind from the Garden into
ess and suffering. And ever since the Day
at, the Serpent had been trying to thwart
ment. Nelson saw delicious irony in a
ing the Serpent's scheme.

en so looking forward to her demise, but
he must delay that pleasure for a higher
y . . . that was the key word. He was con-
at the Lord was guiding her—and Nelson
—so for now he would back off and simply
ath she traveled. But when that path came
ich it eventually must, she would be called
r the debt she owed.

They locked gazes for a few heartbeats. He wasn't
going to budge, and arguing would only delay their
departure—if indeed they would be allowed to depart.
Besides, he held all the cards. She broke off and turned
toward the door.

"Don't be long," she said with a bravado she didn't feel.
"I want to be on a plane out of here as soon as possible."

She closed the door behind her, walked down the
short hallway, and wound up in a small room with an
armed man in a green uniform seated behind a desk.
Saying nothing, she took a seat and waited. The shock
of learning that their attackers carried the *DXXXVI*
tattoo vied with a nightmare vision of seeing Rick being led out of that room in handcuffs a few minutes
from now. The world seemed upside down.

What would she do if they arrested Rick? Call the
American embassy? Hell, she didn't even know what
city it was in. Tel Aviv? Jerusalem?

She decided to worry about that if and when she
had to.

She watched the border policeman out of the corner
of her eye. Did he have *DXXXVI* branded on his arm
as well?

6

After Laura was gone, Chayat stared at him a long time.
Rick stared back.

"Who are you, Mister Hayden? Really."

Rick didn't know where this was going, but he saw
no other course than to play it like everything was on
the up and up. Which it was. The details, however, were
not up for discussion.

"Just what it says there," he said, pointing to his passport. "I don't know what I can add to that."

Chayat offered him a tolerant smile. "No, you are something else. When I called in the situation at Gan Yosaif, word quickly came back to go through the motions and let you go. I don't know who you know or what you know, but that is most unusual."

Yeah, unusual as all hell.

But he kept his expression bland. "I assure you, Mister Chayat, neither the doc or I are involved in anything sinister."

"Oh, I'm quite sure that's true about 'the doc.' But you . . . you are a different story. Word did not come down to go easy on the American couple. It came down to go easy on you . . . on Richard Hayden."

"Somebody at the American embassy?" He sounded like he was clutching at straws, and he was. He didn't get it.

Chayat shook his head. "Much too quick for that. No time to query the embassy and have them formulate a reply, especially at night. This came from within. Someone above my clearance level recognized your name and pulled on the reins."

"Someone in Shin Bet?"

He was nodding now. "Where else? You have a friend high up. Any idea who?" His hand shot up, palm out. "Not that I want you to tell me. I'm just curious as to whether you know who it might be."

Rick was sure Chayat was dying to know, but since everything was being recorded, he preferred to remain in the dark.

"I can tell you with all honesty, sir, that I haven't the faintest. As my passport shows, I've never been to Israel before."

Right . . . as far as that passport showed.

"I have any number of passports," Chayat said. "How many do you have?"

"Just that one."

Very true . . . now. But

Chayat slid the passp

for removing four threa

say that I wish you had

but that would be less th

Hayden. Or whoever yo

Hiding his relief, R

walked out.

The knock on the door

turned out to be Bradsh

"Shin Bet is going to

admitted him.

"Any clue as to why t

"Clues, yes. They had

a map with an azimuth

They had the degrees of

butz but hadn't plotted

"Have you?"

Bradsher nodded, h

They cross in the neighl

"Really."

Nelson leaned back.

ancient abbey was in t

the panacea . . . and the

Bradsher said, "The r

the perfect place to set u

Nelson held up a ha

wanted now.

"Not yet. Let her run

"Sir?"

Nelson felt the need

suite's desk but had to g

a slight tilt

and leaned

"Let's lo

ning has br

taken her

this encode

"All the

"It's also

paused to le

might be al

ers have fai

Bradsher

"Many c

believed the

her way th

daughter of

He sense

pent existed

the apple fr

Paradise fo

His plan: H

a life of sic

of Banishm

God's puni

woman und

He had l

now he kne

purpose. De

vinced now

through her

observe the

to an end, w

to account

Laura used the waiting time to phone home. Ten thirty here meant midafternoon there.

"I'm glad you called," Steven said. *"Marissa's running a fever."*

Aw, no.

"Any other symptoms?"

"No. One-oh-one point six degrees, chills, and tired."

"Sounds viral."

"That's what the nurse said."

"Is it Grace?"

Grace was experienced with transplant patients and had been on the scene during Marissa's first weeks home. Child and nurse had bonded, and Marissa was completely comfortable with her.

"Yes. She gave her Tylenol and her temp's down. She's sleeping now. Grace drew some blood too."

"Great. Is she still there?"

"Yeah. Want to speak to her?"

She discussed Marissa with Grace. Everything pointed to a simple viral illness, but Laura had an ongoing fear of Marissa contracting HCMV—human cytomegalovirus. Her little girl had tested negative before the transplant, which left her susceptible. In a normal child her age, HCMV would be a nuisance infection—a mononucleosis-type syndrome—or might not be noticed at all. Get sick or feel a little crummy, then get better with no specific treatment. Close to eighty percent of U.S. adults had had the infection by age forty.

But in an immunocompromised child like Marissa, HCMV could prove fatal.

So Laura told Grace to add a HCMV DNA PCR assay to the tests being run on her blood samples. Just for peace of mind. The PCR was the fastest test. If any cytomegalovirus DNA showed up—even a trace—it meant that Marissa had contracted the infection.

Laura said, "I hope to be on a flight tomorrow." To France if things managed not to go to hell here, otherwise straight to JFK. "I'll call as soon as I land in Paris. If the PCR is positive, I'll book a flight home immediately."

"I tell you what I'll do," Grace said. "I'll put a stat on the order and leave my number. As soon as the results come in, I'll have them call me, then I'll text you."

"You're the best, Grace."

"Just looking out for my little sweetie. I'm sure she'll be fine. You take care now and we'll talk sometime tomorrow."

Laura decided to ride Grace's optimism to a calmer place. She'd had everyone who came into repeated close contact with Marissa screened. She, Steve, Grace, and Natasha all carried CMV antibodies. Odds against Marissa having CMV were high. She'd go with that.

Next call was to her voice mail. Since that was empty, she called Deputy Phil directly.

"Hey, Doc. Great to hear from you. How're things in Mexico?"

If she told him she was in Israel he'd have a thousand questions. So . . .

"Fine. Any new word on our friend?"

"Sorry. I keep running into dead ends. That could be because they are dead ends, or it could mean they were blocked for a reason."

Was Phil getting paranoid now?

"What reason, for instance?"

"Don't know. And I don't want to sound prejudiced or anything, but if the guy wasn't an Arab, I might not be so gung ho. But I still remember seeing the smoke from the Towers from all the way out here that day. You

don't forget something like that. So I'm taking nothing for granted."

"You have options left?"

"Yeah. The sheriff's department's had a lot of contact with the feds during these joint task force operations. I'm going to see if someone can do me a favor."

"Don't get into any trouble."

"Don't worry. I won't. See you soon."

At the moment, no one wished that more than Laura.

Rick appeared—alone, no handcuffs. He waved his passport then stopped at the desk where he collected the keys to the Jeep.

"Let's go," he said, walking by her.

She caught up to him at the door. "What did he want?"

"Just a few minor irregularities with my passport," he said, looking straight ahead as they exited the building. "Nothing serious. We're free to go."

"Fine. But where are we going?"

"To Ben Gurion."

Thank God.

"And from there?"

"That's up to you." He glanced at her. "Europe or U.S.?"

"Southern France, I guess."

"You *guess*?"

"I'm assuming that's where the lines cross."

"'Assume'? I *assume* you've seen *The Bad News Bears*."

"I have, and the quote you're about to reference is from the sequel."

"Really?"

"Really."

She knew having a daughter into baseball would pay off someday. Marissa could recite the entire script . . .

and she *loved* to be able to say *ass* without being reprimanded.

"Since we can't be sure yet of the path of the new azimuth, we'll need some time with the map before we decide whether we fly to France or Spain."

The Jeep's lights blinked as he used the key fob to unlock it.

"Let's not do it here," she said.

"Amen to that."

They wasted no time putting themselves on the road to the airport.

As they rolled along, Rick said, "We okay?"

"With what?"

"With what went down at the kibbutz."

"Does it matter?" The words came out with more of an edge than she'd intended.

He shrugged. "Won't change my job description, but things will run smoother if we're both on the same page."

"And what page would that be?"

"That I'm gonna do whatever's necessary to get you back home safe, and making that happen will be easier if you're not perpetually ticked at me."

Laura had never believed the end justified the means, but the end in this case . . . home safe . . .

"Oh, hell, I don't know. I guess you did the right thing. It's just . . . " She ran out of words.

He gave a low laugh. "Why should I be special, right?"

"What's that supposed to mean?"

"Well, you seem to be mad at everyone."

She hadn't expected that sort of perceptiveness from him.

"It's that obvious?"

"Uh, yuh. Like some sort of grouchy alien."

"Oh, so I'm an alien now?"

He nodded. "Yup. From the Crabby Nebula."

She had to laugh at that, and it broke the tension.

She leaned back and sighed. "I don't like it but I can't help it. Seems I've been that way since Marissa got sick. I mean, why her? She didn't do anything to deserve leukemia. I wanted to point to a cause."

"The blame game."

"Right. I wanted a vaccine, a toxin, a pollutant, a medication, a food additive, even a relative to blame. Anything. But I had no target for my anger, so I guess I've been spreading it around." She looked at him. "Say, what about your vast, unsympathetic intelligences? Can I blame them?"

He shook his head. "I doubt they micromanage. They're more into the drop-a-rock-in-a-tranquil-pond school of mischief. How about God?"

"Which one?"

"Take your pick."

"I'll pass. Must be nice to say 'Let go, let God,' or 'It's God's will.' That's a comfort I'll never know. The best I've got is 'Shit happens,' but it happened to my Marissa and it's left me royally pissed off."

"As that Hamas guy who grabbed you found out."

"Let's leave that story back at Gan Yosaif."

"Fine, but what do you think about those Hamas guys carrying the 536 brand?"

Laura shook her head. "I was thinking about that while you were alone with What's-his-name—"

"Chayat."

"—and no matter which way I turn it, it doesn't make sense from any angle."

"Right. No sense at all in Islamic radicals carving Roman numerals on their arms, unless . . . "

"Unless what?"

"Unless 536 is everywhere, unless its membership supersedes national and religious and ethnic boundaries."

"But Stahlman said it had Christian origins."

"Stahlman could be wrong."

She remembered Chayat's puzzlement: *I am having difficulty with the way your arrival in an abandoned kibbutz coincided so perfectly with the raiding party's . . .*

She'd assumed it was simply a matter of terrible luck. Now she wasn't so sure.

"You think they were there to intercept us? To stop us from finding the panacea?"

It no longer mattered that she didn't believe in it. Others obviously did—passionately—and seemed ready to go to extraordinary lengths to keep it secret.

He shrugged. "What else can we think? But how the hell did they know where we'd be?"

"Well, someone put a bug in my bag. What's so hard about putting a tracer in our Jeep?"

"But a GPS tracer can tell them only where we are, not where we're going. Those Hamas guys were practically waiting—oh, hell."

"The land office?"

"Right. A 536 member in the ILA would have known."

"But didn't you say the raiders were talking about us as hostages?"

Rick's remark about the leader calling "firsties" on their planned gang rape still turned her stomach.

"Right. 'Firsties' and ransom. No other issues. But maybe they thought they could use us as a two-fer: stop us from tracking down the panacea *and* use us as bargaining chips for the return of some of their own."

She leaned back and closed her eyes. "So everybody's against us. The panaceans don't want anyone outside their cult to know their secrets, and 536 doesn't want us to find them either."

"The panaceans are simply hiding from us and everyone else. We're lucky you were able to connect with Ix'chel."

You held his heart in your hands? That had been the tipping point for Ix'chel.

"Right," Laura said. "Thanks to her we know next to nothing rather than absolutely nothing."

"Yeah, but 536 on the other hand . . . looks like they want us off the playing field, and they're not afraid to play rough."

"I can't wait to get out of here."

"You think Europe will be any safer?"

She straightened and looked at him. "Won't it? I mean, it'll be more civilized—no deserted communes and deserts and terrorist raiding parties. That has to be better."

"Don't count on it. Got a feeling Mexico and Israel make up the proverbial frying pan. Next stop . . . "

"The fire?"

"The fire."

9

When they reached Ben Gurion they dropped off the Jeep and found an empty corner of an El Al terminal where they spread out their world map. The line from Mesoamerica into Europe was already there, as was the test line from Israel. All they needed was the new azimuth from Gan Yosaif. Rick pinpointed the GPS coordinates of the kibbutz and was about to draw a line from there at 293 degrees northwest when shadows fell over them.

Laura looked up to see two airport security cops—a man and a woman, both young—staring down at them. Both were armed and dressed in light blue uniforms with dark blue trim and epaulets. Each had a shoulder walkie-talkie.

"What are you doing?" the woman asked in English.

A simple answer popped into Laura's head—one that had the benefit of being the truth. She put on her brightest smile and said, "We're plotting the location of our next destination."

Her smile was not returned. "Are you ticketed passengers?" the man said.

Rick tapped the map and picked up the ball without hesitation. "Not yet. That's what this will decide."

"Come with us, please."

This hadn't been the plan. Now what? More trouble with Rick's passport and its "minor irregularities?" But the encounter turned out to be a good thing.

They were escorted to a room in the security area where they explained their quest. The woman security guard wrote down the GPS loci and the azimuths, then walked out. Twenty minutes later she returned with a surprise for them.

"We have a computer program that plotted it out," she said, handing Laura a slip of paper. "Here are the coordinates where the azimuths cross."

Laura looked at the numbers and degrees and minutes and seconds.

$$1° \ 21' \ 36'' \ E$$
$$42° \ 47' \ 38'' \ N$$

They meant nothing to her.

"Where is it?" she said.

"Nowhere—quite literally."

"Can we be more specific, perhaps?" Rick said.

"Midi-Pyrenees. In the mountains south of Toulouse and northwest of Andorra."

Rick frowned. "France?"

"Southern France!" Laura said, giving him a knowing look. "Part of ancient Gaul, to be exact." She turned to the woman. "Thank you. You've just decided our next destination. Looks like we fly to Paris."

The two cops did not seem willing to take this at face value. They escorted Laura and Rick to the ticket counter where they stood by and watched them buy their first-class tickets to Charles de Gaulle on the first nonstop out Wednesday morning. They then guided them to Terminal Three's King David Lounge.

Rather than go through the hassle of leaving the terminal and renting hotel rooms for the dwindling hours before they'd have to be up and about for their six A.M. flight, Laura and Rick settled into a corner of the first-class section of the lounge to spend the rest of the night.

Laura pulled out the slip of paper and looked at the coordinates again.

"If my theory is right, this should be the location of the so-called Wound."

"Approximate location," Rick said. "Totally ballpark."

"But that cop lady said she had a computer program that—"

"GIGO, remember? We're talking about protractor readings taken off some woman's bare back and off a photo of a tattoo on someone else's back as they were lined up with the North Star. A degree or two off this way and a degree or two off that way, and we're talking a target area totaling hundreds of square miles."

Annoyed, she waved the paper. "Then what good is this? Why did we spend all this time and effort and endanger ourselves if this isn't the location of the Wound?"

"It doesn't tell us the exact location, but it puts us in southern France, and gives us an approximate area to search . . . *if* you're right."

Always that little dig . . .

"Ix'chel said it points to the Wound."

Rick shrugged. "Then we'll go with that."

Laura didn't see any other options.

Rick pulled out his phone. "Gonna give Stahlman a call and bring him up to speed. Maybe he's got some ideas."

"Let me have a word when you reach him."

When she had the phone, Laura dug into her shoulder bag and pulled out three folded sheets from her notepad.

"Mister Hayden updated me," Stahlman said. *"This is turning out to be an extraordinary quest. I'm expecting you to tell me you're quitting."*

"Why do you keep nudging me to quit?"

"I'm doing nothing of the sort—anything but. It's simply that, according to Mister Hayden, just hours ago you were in jeopardy of what could justifiably be termed 'a fate worse than death.' We both know you didn't sign up for that. So I'll restate my previous offer of prorating—"

"I'm not quitting."

The words had popped out as if on a direct line from her subconscious. What was that all about? She'd narrowly escaped abduction and gang rape tonight. If she had a lick of sense she'd take Stahlman's offer and head for home.

But as much as her heart pointed toward Marissa, another part of her needed to see this through.

Why? Was she starting to believe in the panacea?

No way. But . . .

"You continue to amaze me. I confess to be in awe of you."

Nice to hear, but she didn't need to be stroked. Stahlman needed a cure, but she needed a solution to the mysteries of Chaim and Tommy. She'd been sent to find *something* and people were trying to stop her. That didn't sit well with her stubbornness gene, she guessed. She'd find the Wound and see where the trail took her from there. If it ended there, so be it. But if she found another signpost, she'd head in that direction.

"Are you recording this call by any chance?"

"No, but all I have to do is press a button."

"Good. Press it. I translated Ix'chel's poem on the flight to Madrid. Maybe it'll make sense to you."

After she'd finished her recitation he said, *"Makes no sense to me."*

"Join the club."

"Look, I'm going to put someone on finding you an authority on the pagans of Gaul and Aquitaine you can consult when you get to France. Save the poem for him."

"Gotcha."

"Let me speak to Mister Hayden again."

While Rick talked to Stahlman, Laura texted Steven her flight plan: due to land de Gaulle at 10:05 tomorrow morning, Paris time, which would be four A.M. East Coast time. She'd call when it was sevenish in New York.

Rick pocketed his phone and said, "Aquitaine? Where's Aquitaine?"

"Right next to Midi-Pyrenees, I believe. Caesar had a battle or two in Aquitania in his *Gallic Wars,* if I remember correctly."

He was staring at her. "How do you remember that at all, correctly or otherwise?"

"Beats me." Truth: She hadn't the faintest idea where she'd pulled it from. "But whatever, I've got this feeling we're getting close."

"To what? The Wound? We don't even know what that means."

"But maybe some history nerd in Paris can help us figure that out. The Wound is key to the panaceans' mythology. Find that and we'll have a big leg up."

"Let's hope."

He slouched back in his chair and closed his eyes. Laura had seen a sign—in both Hebrew and English, thankfully—about shower facilities. She availed herself of those to clean up, then napped as best she could. She dreamed, and in her dream she was firing Rick's Glock at charging CMV particles that wanted to take Marissa hostage.

10

Bradsher cleared his throat as he put down his phone. "They're on an early flight to Paris tomorrow."

"Then get us on a late flight tonight. I want to be there first."

"It might not be necessary, sir."

"Why not?"

"As you know, we've been monitoring her phone. From what we've gathered, her daughter is sick."

Nelson waved this away. "Children get sick all the time. And isn't her husband with the child?"

"Yes, but the child had a recent stem-cell transplant for leukemia and an otherwise simple infection can turn serious very quickly." Bradsher smiled. "A common virus might accomplish what Miguel could not."

"You mean take her off the trail? But we no longer want that." If it wasn't one damn thing it was another. "How real is that possibility?"

"According to her last phone call, Doctor Fanning expects to learn of the lab results on her daughter when she lands in Paris. If the results are bad, she'll head straight home."

"We can't have that," Nelson said. "Returning to the States will derail her quest. And I have a feeling she's on to something."

"We can control the results," Bradsher said. "No sweat."

Nelson waved him to silence. Changing results would be easy—everything was stored in computers these days. But that wouldn't stop the child's condition from worsening. They'd accomplish only a brief delay in Fanning's abandoning the hunt, and that was no accomplishment at all.

"Can we control her phone?"

"We're already in her phone. Not a big step from there. How much control do you want?"

"No voice communication to or from the States. Only texts. And the same with Hayden, in case she wants to borrow his for a call home."

"Easy."

"Then I want to control every text that enters or leaves her phone."

"That can be done but it will require someone on standby twenty-four/seven."

"Then make it so."

"Will do."

Glory filled him as his role in this divine drama took on greater and greater definition. Here was a glimpse at why the Lord had included him: to keep Laura Fanning on the path He had set for her. The Serpent had sickened her child to bring her home. Nelson would see to it that its foul plan failed.

"Oh, and speaking of monitoring her phone," Bradsher said, "she's had a deputy from the Suffolk County Sheriff's Department looking into Hayden."

"Interesting. How's he doing?"

"Not bad. He ferreted out the Haddad/Hayden connection. Now he says he's going to use a 'fed' contact to help dig further."

Nelson couldn't help but smile. "Good luck with that. That information is buried *deep*."

Bradsher's expression showed a mixture of hurt and annoyance. "Yessir."

"Too bad. The truth might drive a wedge between the two of them. We might be able to exploit that gap if it proved necessary."

And that gave Nelson an idea.

"Once we get to France, give me all you've got on this deputy sheriff."

France . . . he really should be headed back to New York and Sloan-Kettering . . .

But damn the tumors, primary, metastatic, and otherwise, the final phase was going to need his personal touch, more than a little micromanagement.

After all these years of frustration, he sensed they were approaching the home stretch and he wanted to be in on the kill.

And it *would* be a kill—multiple kills.

The Leviticus Sanction was overdue for a workout.

THE YEAR WITHOUT A SUMMER

1

Damn-damn-damn!

Steven glanced at the clock/radio/iPod port next to Marissa's bed: *1:08*. Add six hours and that meant it was seven A.M. in Paris. Another three hours before Laura landed and he could get hold of her.

Marissa coughed again, and once again Steven laid a hand on her forehead. He didn't need the thermometer to know she was burning up, but he grabbed it and pressed it against her forehead anyway. He checked the readout:

102.4°F.

Christ! He'd given her Tylenol about an hour ago but it hadn't dented the fever one bit.

Okay. He couldn't take this anymore. Brookhaven Medical Center was just up the road. He'd take Marissa to the emergency room there and have her checked out. He didn't know how Laura would react to that, exposing her to a roomful of sick people and all, but he saw no other option.

Nurse Grace had said it looked like an everyday virus, and maybe it was. But the cough bothered Steven—that and the fever he couldn't break. What if it was pneumonia? What if the fever kept going up?

Throughout Marissa's life he'd deferred all medical questions and decisions to Laura—so comforting to have an expert on the premises or available at all times—but now she was thousands of miles and a number of time zones away, and incommunicado to boot. He felt totally at sea, with no land, not even a marker buoy in sight.

He needed help—now.

He pulled out his phone, speed-dialed Laura's cell, then listened to her outgoing message.

"Hi, this is Laura. I'll state the obvious: I can't answer right now, so leave a message and I'll get back to you ay-sap."

After the beep he said, "Laura, it's me. It's one A.M. and Marissa's burning up. I can't break her fever so I'm taking her up to Brookhaven where they can check her out. I know you won't get this till you land. Hopefully everything will be squared away by then and we'll be back home. Call me back right away. Talk to you soon."

He knew she was waiting for test results on Marissa's blood so he had no doubt she'd check her texts and voice mail as soon as she landed.

Marissa stirred as he bundled her in her bed comforter and carried her downstairs.

She opened her glassy eyes and said, "Mommy?"

"No, it's Daddy, sweetie."

But oh, man, does Daddy wish Mommy were here.

2

Bradsher turned on his phone as soon as the plane's wheels squeaked on the Charles de Gaulle runway. Nelson glanced at his watch. He'd set it back to Paris time immediately after takeoff. It read 9:03—they'd landed two minutes early.

A long flight. The Company had managed to snag two first-class seats on the last Alitalia jet out of Ben Gurion. It involved a two-hour layover in Rome, but it did land them an hour ahead of Fanning. Nelson had wanted to arrive first, and here he was.

Bradsher leaned close and whispered, "Monitoring reports that the doctor's husband left her a voice mail. The child's fever is up and he's taking her to the emergency room."

Not good, Nelson thought. But nothing that couldn't be remedied.

He'd had the techs leave Fanning's voice mail only half blocked: People could leave messages but she could not access them. When she checked she'd hear, "No new messages."

Incoming calls to her home number and her husband's cell were being monitored. Any call originating from France, or any European country, for that matter, would trigger an uncompletable-call message. Any calls to her phone from the U.S. would receive the same message.

Text messages would be blocked in both directions and rewritten accordingly.

"Erase it," Nelson said.

"Will do. Want to substitute something?"

Nelson knew they had the technology to perfectly duplicate the pitch and tone of any voice over the phone. But nuances of speech and inflection were something else. An ersatz message might pass muster between acquaintances, but not spouses. Fanning and her husband might be divorced, but they'd known each other too long for Nelson to trust synthesized speech.

"No. Just make it disappear. If the child is fine and returns home, we'll unblock everything and they'll chalk up the missing message to a tech glitch. But I don't want any distractions getting in her way. I want her *focused*."

"Got it."

He watched Bradsher's thumbs fly as they tapped out a message.

"Where to next?" Nelson said when he finished.

"We have a car meeting us. We'll head south to a place called Ballainvilliers. It's about an hour's ride, more or less, depending on the traffic. We have a farmhouse there."

Nelson knew all about the farmhouse. The Company had crammed it with monitoring equipment so it could keep tabs on various radical Islamist groups in and around Paris, and on a few choice French officials as well. That hadn't been enough to stop the *Charlie Hebdo* and the subsequent massacres but it would allow Nelson to monitor Fanning's movements.

"What about living quarters?"

"We use the Relais des Chartreux Hotel on the border of Ballainvilliers and a neighboring district, Saulx-les-Chartreux. We have reservations. If you want to stop there first . . . "

"I would. We have an hour before Fanning lands. I'd like to be settled in by the time she does."

Nelson let Bradsher take the lead on an expedited trip through customs, then through the airport to the ground transportation area where a black Mercedes sedan awaited them. Once they were settled in the rear and the driver had them on their way, Nelson removed a sheet of paper from his computer case. He'd written a password on it. He handed it to Bradsher.

In answer to the agent's questioning look, he said, "Guard dog."

Bradsher looked puzzled for an instant, then his eyes widened. "I've been cleared?"

"I would think the answer to that is obvious, don't you?"

"Yes, yes, of course."

"But wait until later to read it."

Pickens hadn't officially cleared Bradsher yet, but Nelson had no doubt he would. The Company found the episode embarrassing, and with good reason, so it restricted access. But Bradsher would be dealing with the man—indirectly and, inevitably, directly soon enough—so he deserved to know what he was up against.

But Bradsher wouldn't be alone on the learning curve. Nelson was working on a way to inform Fanning of her guard dog's true identity. His original plan was to get the same information into the hands of a certain Suffolk County deputy sheriff and have him tell her. But with her phone blocked to calls and voice mails from the States, that wasn't going to work. No worry, he'd come up with a way.

As they drove through Paris, Nelson was only dimly aware of the mix of the familiar and unfamiliar— something called Flunch followed by a McDonald's, and then a KFC followed by a Pomme de Pain. He began to feel strange. A slight nausea. He'd never been prone to car sickness, but this could be what it felt like.

Eventually they came to a low-slung hotel behind a high hedge. He was aware of a red canopy emblazoned with *Relais des Chartreux Hotel*. He began to notice wavy lines of light sparkling in his peripheral vision as he found his room and keyed open the door. Bradsher said something to him as the door closed but it seemed to come from down a long hallway.

The sparkly lights brightened until they consumed his vision. He felt his body shaking like a sapling in a storm, and then the world exploded.

3

"You have no new messages."

Laura ended the call and tapped her phone against her thigh as the plane taxied to its gate.

Okay. She'd expected that. It was four A.M. back

home and no news was definitely good news in this case. The only reason Steven would call her was if Marissa had taken a turn for the worse. She imagined them both sleeping soundly—Marissa in her bed and Steven, all uptight and worried he'd miss something, snoring in a chair in her room.

No text from Grace either, but she hadn't expected one. Way too early for PCR results. Polymer chain reaction tests weren't like a CBC or a glucose; they took time. But the CMV PCR result was what Laura most wanted to hear.

Negative . . . please be negative.

"Wow," Rick said, staring at his phone.

"What?"

"Long-winded message from Stahlman. Better listen for yourself."

"Bad news?"

"Not at all. Just something he could have said in two or three sentences." He tapped his phone's screen. "Here. Let me replay it."

She put it to her ear and heard Stahlman's voice.

"Good morning, Mister Hayden. I trust you had a comfortable flight. After our conversation last night, I rattled some cages on this side of the pond and had contacts wake up a few people over there. It seems the fellow you'll want to speak to is an historian named Jacques Fontaine at Université de Toulouse-Le Mirail, but he won't be available until tomorrow.

"Not wanting to waste time, I gave the matter some thought and realized that a shooting star is prominent in the tattoos, so why not combine astronomy and Gaul and see if there was a comet or meteor shower that had some significance back in those days.

"So I've contacted a certain Doctor Simon Duval of the Paris Observatory and put him on retainer to help

in any way he can. However, although the observatory itself is in Paris proper—on the Left Bank, as a matter of fact—anyone you might wish to talk to is rarely there. All the astronomers cluster in a satellite campus in Meudon, a suburb on the exact opposite side of Paris from the airport. It's only a five- or six-mile trip, so you should be able to cab there with no problem. Call me after you've spoken to Duval."

Laura handed the phone back to Rick.

"Gonna save this one," he said, tapping the screen. "I'll never remember those names and places." He turned to her as he stowed it in a pocket. "Well?"

"Well, what?"

"Wanna talk to an astronomer?"

What she really wanted to do was sleep. Turning this way and that in an airport lounge was no way to get a restful night's sleep. She'd managed to doze during the flight, and though the first-class seats were wide and reclined almost flat, nothing beat a bed.

"Do I have a choice?"

"You're the boss. You look beat."

"I *feel* beat. Why don't *you* look beat? Oh, wait. I know. How did you put it? You can doze off anywhere, anytime, in any position. Your SEAL training, right?"

"Right."

This was not the time or place, but she was determined to call him on that before the day was up.

"Let's get it over with," she said. "I just hope I can stay awake while he's talking."

"I'll keep nudging you."

"As long as it's just a nudge. No more of that thigh stuff."

"Sorry. Didn't know any other way to keep you quiet without Mister Shin Bet knowing."

"What made you think you had to keep me quiet?"

"People being interrogated don't realize how much they give away in what they consider innocent chatter. You think you're making idle conversation, just filling in the uncomfortable silences that interrogators purposely leave, but all the while you're giving away the farm. Best course is a short, to-the-point answer. Or if you've got to talk, *you* ask questions. Interrogators hate that."

"And you know this how?"

"SEAL training, what else?"

She balled her fists. Soon, Mr. Haddad or Mr. Hayden . . . very, very soon . . .

4

Where the fuck was Laura and why the fuck wasn't she answering her phone?

Steven was ready to hurl his cell across the emergency department. Either that or scream. But that would frighten Marissa.

He looked at her, supine on the gurney, an IV running into her left arm, sound asleep but restless. Every so often she'd have a coughing fit.

He'd seen the concern in the ER doc's face when he'd told him she'd had a recent stem-cell transplant. He'd ordered blood work and a chest X-ray.

In the meantime Steven had left Laura three voice mails and hadn't heard a word back. Maybe if he texted—

"Glad you're here." The ER doc was stepping through the curtains, his expression grim. "We're going to have to move your daughter."

"You're admitting her? Is that necessary?"

"Afraid so. The X-ray shows pneumonia. But Brookhaven isn't the place for her."

He felt his blood turning to ice. "What? I don't . . . "

"A regular child, no problem, but an HSCT patient . . . " He took a breath. "She needs a PICU."

His numbing brain took a few seconds to process the familiar acronyms: human stem-cell transplant . . . pediatric ICU . . .

"ICU?"

"Your daughter is a sick little girl. I called her oncologist and he wants her in Stony Brook Children's. They have all the pediatric subspecialties she's going to need."

Steven looked at Marissa, a sleeping angel, and back to the doctor. "She's that sick?"

"Not yet, but she could be. If she takes a bad turn— I'm not saying she will, but she could if she's got the wrong kind of infection—I want her where they can do everything for her."

"'Wrong kind of infection'—you mean like CMV?"

The doc looked mildly surprised. "So you're aware of that. Yes, that's the bogeyman we're worried about."

"My wife's a doctor. She mentioned it. She even ordered some sort of test for it. Unfortunately she's in France at the moment."

"It wouldn't happen to have been a PCR, would it?"

"That sounds familiar."

"Great. Wherever she is, she did the right thing. Good to know a PCR is already cooking. They take a while. Where'd she have it sent?"

"Here, I think."

"Super. I'll check with the lab and get started on the transfer."

"By ambulance?" He wasn't going to let Marissa out of his sight. "I'm riding with her."

"Of course."

But the first thing he had to do was get hold of Laura.

Since ur not answering my voice mails im trying text. Im in brookhaven ER with marissa shes got pneumonia and theyre shipping her to stony brook picu. Please call. She needs u! we both need u!

Where the hell *was* she?

5

Nelson awoke to an insistent knocking on his door. Bradsher's voice came from the other side.

"Sir? Sir, are you all right?"

Something pressing against his cheek. He opened his eyes and saw carpet. The floor! He was facedown on the floor.

What am I doing on the floor?

Slowly, painfully, he rolled over. What happened? He felt wetness and looked down at the dark splotch that had spread over his groin area. Had he—?

Yes! He'd wet himself!

"Sir? Is everything okay?"

Couldn't let Bradsher see him like this.

"I'm—" He had to clear his throat. "I'm fine. Just fell asleep is all."

"We have a text to deal with, sir."

"Give me a few minutes. I need to take a quick shower to . . . to freshen up."

"Okay. I'm in two-eleven. Ring me when you're ready."

"Two-eleven. Right."

"I accessed his file, by the way."

File? Whose file? Nelson's thoughts were too scattered and jumbled to remember or care, but couldn't let Bradsher know.

"Anything interesting?"

"*Disturbing, to say the least.*"

"Talk to you later."

Using the bed for support, he struggled to his knees. The room wobbled a little but not too badly. The worst was the foggy feeling. He'd need to pull himself together before he faced Bradsher. He had decisions to make . . . nuanced decisions, and nuances were not his strong point in this state.

He pushed himself to his feet and stood swaying as he considered his current state: a visual aura followed by a period of unconsciousness accompanied by loss of bladder control. He knew the explanation.

He'd had a seizure.

He felt over his limbs and ribs. No major tenderness. He hadn't broken anything. He ran his tongue across his teeth—he hadn't bitten it. And he felt oriented—he knew this was Wednesday afternoon and that he was in a hotel south of Paris.

A minor seizure, he guessed. Major enough to cost him bladder control but not enough to cause serious injury.

His freshman-year roommate at Penn State had been epileptic. He'd been well controlled on medication but Nelson had looked up the condition. They hadn't got along and parted ways at the end of the year. Nelson was glad he'd never had to witness a fit.

And now he'd just had one himself.

The three tumors in his brain were the only explanation. Dr. Forman had even mentioned seizures as a possible complication if Nelson left them untreated. But he'd had no choice. He couldn't stop for radiation and chemotherapy now. Tumors be damned, he had to see this through to the end, no matter what.

By some miracle his jacket and shirt had stayed dry,

but that didn't matter. He'd worn one of his wool gabardine suits for the plane ride, and it was dry-clean only. Good thing it was one of his cheaper suits. He might be able to find further use for the jacket, but he'd have to discard the pants. Luckily, he'd brought a spare suit.

He'd mentioned a shower to Bradsher as a delaying tactic, but now it seemed like an excellent idea. It would help clear his head, and Lord knew, it needed clearing.

6

Half an hour later, dressed in his backup suit—a Continental cut blue flannel—and his head defogged by the shower, he dialed room 211 and told Bradsher to stop by with the text problem.

While he waited, he composed himself. A seizure . . .

Are you testing me, Lord?

Uncle Jim's words came back to him: *Every affliction has a purpose, every trial is part of His Divine Plan.*

Was the melanoma part of that plan? Nelson had become aware of it shortly after he'd become aware of the return of the panaceans. Coincidence? How long had it been there? He had no way of knowing. Had the Lord caused it to appear? Were the tumor and the panaceans connected somehow?

Show me, Lord. Give me a sign.

Bradsher arrived then, cutting off further speculation. Nelson gathered his wits as Bradsher displayed the message from Dr. Fanning's husband on his phone screen.

"Apparently the child is quite sick," Bradsher said.

"So it would seem. We can't let Fanning see this message. She'll immediately abort her trip and head home."

"Kill it then?"

"Of course."

"What do we substitute?"

Nelson glanced at the clock. "It's not yet seven A.M. in the city. She won't be expecting an all-is-well message this early. Let's wait and let her initiate contact. Her calls will be blocked. After a number of tries, she'll text. Have them watching closely. And speaking of the good doctor, where is she?"

"We tracked her to the suburban campus of the Paris Observatory."

"Observatory? As in looking-at-the-stars observatory?"

Now here was a surprise.

"Yessir. The astronomers have a campus not terribly far to our west."

"Do we have anyone inside?"

"No. So we're limited to keeping close watch and tracking where she goes from here."

Nelson wasn't sure whether to be relieved or not by yet another unexpected development. When he'd heard she was headed to France, he suspected she'd found the location of the Brotherhood's abbey and would make a beeline for it. But apparently she was more interested in the sky.

In the heavens . . . the Lord's domain.

Yes . . . all was becoming clear.

7

At the observatory's Meudon campus they learned that Dr. Duval would not be available until after lunch, so they drove around until they found a quaint little restaurant just off a traffic circle in a woodsy setting: La Mare aux Canards.

"The Sea of Ducks?" Rick said, squinting through the windshield at the sign.

Laura had to laugh. "Sea is m-e-r. *La Mare aux Canards* translates to 'Duck Pond.' You know Arabic and Hebrew but you don't know French or Spanish?"

"I know enough of each to be dangerous. German is my best non-English tongue. I can speak it like a native."

Laura sent Rick inside to snag a table while she phoned home. She couldn't hold off any longer. The local time had reached one P.M. and she was sure Steven would be awake by now. She'd added the U.S. country code to her home number on the speed dial and so she thumbed that.

She was rewarded with a message telling her that her call could not be completed as dialed. She tried twice more and heard the same message. She switched to Steven's cell number and the same thing happened. She called the operator and even he could not get through for her.

Rick wandered back out. "I've got us a table on the terrace. You coming in?"

"I can't get through to home."

He handed her his phone. "Try mine."

She did but received the same message.

"Damn!"

"International calling can get weird at times," he told her. "You have a data package?"

"I signed up for everything before I left."

"Try texting then." He left her and headed back inside.

Why not? She hated typing on the tiny screen so she used her phone's voice-to-text app to dictate a message to Steven's number and watched the words appear:

> *Steven I can't get a call through. How is Marissa? Call me as soon as you get this. I'm on tender hooks waiting to know.*

She'd said "tenter" but noticed the software changed it to "tender." Without bothering to correct it, she sent the message and watched to see if it would bounce. But no, it went out with no problem. She headed inside and they directed her to the terrace where Rick was studying a menu under a large canopy.

"Guess what they specialize in?" he said as she seated herself.

"I'll take a wild guess: Donald and Daffy?"

"Not to mention Huey, Dewey, and Louie."

"You just did."

"I never knew you could eat duck so many ways. They even stuff their hamburgers with foie gras."

"Not hungry anyway."

Too worried for that. She placed her phone beside her forks where she could keep an eye on it. She ordered a club soda while Rick ordered a Campari and soda.

"How continental," she said.

"When in Rome . . . or Paris, for that matter . . . "

She stared at her phone, willing it to ring. Why wasn't he replying? And then, just as their drinks arrived, the text chime sounded. From Steven. At last!

But why a text and not a call?

Didnt you get vmail this am? Marissa fine. Fever broke in night now cool as can be. Still asleep. What up with ur phone. Tried to call just now but no ring no vmail.

No ring no vmail . . . she couldn't get incoming calls either? This sucked. She dictated back:

Great news. So relieved. I'll check in on a regular basis. Have Grace text or email me the lab results when she gets there. Tell Marissa I love her.

"Good news, I gather?" Rick said as she replaced the phone on the table.

"Fever's down. That's good but we're not out of the woods yet. It could spike again. If she goes a whole day without another fever, there's a good chance we're home free."

"Good. Now relax and have some quack-quack."

"You know, I just might."

Her appetite was back.

8

Steven stood in the hall outside Stony Brook's PICU and scanned through his messages. They'd made him turn it off when he was inside. So far he hadn't seen them do anything here that they hadn't been doing at Brookhaven, but at least she had a lot of professional people hovering around her, and that was good.

Because Marissa looked bad.

He'd grown used to her pallor over the years—anemia in leukemia was often profound—but now she seemed to be fading into the sheets. And that cough . . . it sounded like pieces of her lung were going to come up.

Here—a text from Laura.

Got your message. Tried to call but calls not going through. Stony Brook PICU? She's that bad? I'm sick about this. Did the CMV PCR come back? I'm checking Air France and United and any carrier who can get me back fastest. Will let you know. Give her my love. Tell her Mommy's on the way.

Thank God! he thought. Laura will make everything right.

CMV test not back yet but they suspect thats what it is. Hurry Laura. We need you here.

He turned off the phone and rushed back inside to tell Marissa the good news.

9

"What am I supposed to make of this?" Dr. Duval said, staring at the photo of Chaim's tattoo.

The professor reeked of cigarettes and wine. Sixtyish, goateed, and rather slovenly, he was not at all what Laura had expected. His office was situated in the north wing of the Agence de l'Observatoire, an old stone building with an impressive observatory dome jutting up from its center. His cluttered quarters, with its star maps and Hubble photos tacked to the walls, looked like a student project straight out of Set Design 101. But at least he spoke English, so she wouldn't have to translate everything for Rick.

"Sense, hopefully," Rick said. She could tell that already the professor was not on his list of favorite people.

She unfolded her English version of Ix'chel's poem and placed it before him.

"It goes with this."

> 'Twixt the house of the fallen godmen
> And the tomb of the fallen star
> That slew summer,
> Auburon lies drowning.
> He sleeps,
> Martyred and imprisoned
> Yet mocking his oppressors.

> *He sleeps in the Wound,*
> *Midmoon from the godmen gate*
> *Where five men stand above his door.*
> *His guardian leg shall bear you to new life.*

His lips moved as he read it.

Finally he looked up. "You are joking me, yes? This is supposed to cause me to talk about aliens?"

"Aliens?" Laura said. "No, it—"

"'Fallen godmen' . . . what can that be but aliens? This is a hoax?"

"No joke," Rick said, anger peeking through in his tone. "This tattoo? It's on the back of a dead man—murdered because of it. Mister Stahlman has paid you to help us, I believe?"

Duval pursed his lips. "Oui, but—"

"This is *not* a hoax. Trust us."

"This 'tomb of the fallen star' that's mentioned," Laura said, trying to get the meeting back on track. "That indicates a crater to me. What do you think?"

He nodded. "Very possible. Especially since there is this falling star in the tattoo. That could be a meteorite or a comet."

"The 'Wound' mentioned farther down . . . couldn't a crater from a meteor impact be considered a wound in the Earth?"

. . . in the All-Mother?

"One could look at it that way, of course."

"How big would the crater be?"

Duval gave a classic Gallic shrug. "The ancient Vredefort impact crater in South Africa was three hundred kilometers across before erosion set in. And the Chicxulub crater in—"

"Of course!" Laura said, giving herself a head smack and looking at Rick. "We were just there. It's off the north coast of Yucatán."

"Exactly," Duval said. "One hundred eighty kilometers across."

"I've heard of that," Rick said. "Not by that name, though. The 'dinosaur killer,' right?"

"Correct. That was believed to be an asteroid."

"How about France?" Laura said. "Any impact craters here?"

"None recognizable as such. We had the Rochechouart impact but that was two hundred million years ago and we can only estimate its size. Probably twenty kilometers when it was fresh." He tapped the poem. "But here is what jumps out at me: 'the tomb of the fallen star / that slew summer.' That could be a clue."

"How so?"

"L'année sans été," he muttered.

"Pardone?"

"The year without summer . . . just two hundred years ago, I believe. Let me see . . . " He stepped to a bookshelf, ran a finger over a row of spines . . . "Ah!" He thumbed through it as he returned to the desk. "Here. In 1816, the famous year without a summer."

Much too recent, Laura thought, but still . . .

"Was that impact-related?"

He shook his head. "No, volcanic. Due to the Mount Tambora eruption in the Dutch East Indies the year before. It caused crop failures, famine, and food riots in Europe and North America."

"I've never heard of that," Rick said.

Duval's expression said he wasn't surprised, but tact won out. "We are much more interested in global warming these days. This was global *cooling*."

Laura said, "Can you think of any other years without summer?"

"How far back do you wish to go?"

"How about back to the time of the druids and such here in Gaul."

"No . . . I don't recall any . . . " He twisted his goatee for a few seconds, then straightened. "Wait."

He sat, moused his computer awake, then clicked through a number of screens.

"Yes. Here it is. You will find no direct recording of the event—druids and their ilk did not believe in writing things down—but I saved an article about later accounts because the astronomical event they described was so singular and amazing. Texts from the thirteenth century mention tales of fire in the sky over sixth-century Gaul. They say the sky 'burned' for days."

Laura leaned in for a look but the screen was all small-print French. "What would cause that? A meteor shower?"

"Perhaps, but nothing like the Leonids and Perseids that we watch from our backyards. This must have been a huge flock of meteors—big ones. It might even have been a comet that broke up in the atmosphere and caused multiple impacts. Whatever made the sky burn back then had huge climatological effects."

Laura was suddenly excited. "Enough so that this 'fallen star . . . slew summer'?"

"Oh, I should say so. Most definitely so. For after the fire came the cold. Crop failures all over the western world caused mass starvation. Those coincided with the Justinian Plague and, for all we know, triggered that plague. The end result was the fall of the Roman Empire and the start of the Dark Ages."

"All from a 'fallen star'?"

Duval gave a small, sad smile. "Civilization is much more fragile than we think."

"So any idea when this happened?" Rick said.

"A very good idea. The druids and pagans kept no written records but the Romans were obsessive. Multiple sources record the cold temperatures and crop failures and famines, and from that they can estimate the year of impact of your 'fallen star.'"

"And when would that be?"

Duval leaned closer to the screen. "It says 536 AD."

10

Nelson had acquiesced to a tour of the monitoring station as a courtesy to the agents in place. Not that he needed it—he knew the make and model of every drone stored in the detached stable.

Interpol and La Sûreté were well aware—unofficially, of course—of what went on in the farmhouse and even called on its occupants for help from time to time when they needed to peek in on the activities of certain Islamist factions in and around Paris.

The tour over, he and Bradsher now sat in the tiny office that had been accorded Nelson for his time in France. He had offered his hosts no details of his mission beyond the fact that they were tracking the movements of a pair of Americans currently in country.

The most immediate concern, for Nelson at least, was how to *keep* both those Americans in country.

"What we need," Nelson said, "is to create a plausible scenario for her husband wherein Doctor Fanning is trying desperately to get back to the States but is frustrated at every turn. We'll feed piecemeal accounts of her travails to him via text messages."

"How long do we want to drag this out?" Bradsher asked as he scribbled on his pad.

"As long as we have to."

"What about the doctor's end?"

"I believe we have her covered. So let's see what scenario we can concoct to delay her return."

While Bradsher mulled that, Nelson considered the message he would compose from her deputy sheriff friend. He had accessed her voice mail and listened to the man. He was sure he could duplicate the tone of his chatter in a text.

Hey, Doc. Tried calling but can't get through. And your voice mail is all screwed up. Keeps booting me out. But that's okay. Have I got news for you. Wait till you hear this . . .

Oh, yes. No problem there.

11

"You're sure of that date—536?"

As Laura spoke she stared at Rick who stared straight back. She was certain his shocked expression mirrored her own.

"Quite," Duval said. "From all accounts that was another année sans été." He peered again at the screen. "I have a paper here from Cardiff University that says examination of tree rings—from multiple sources such as oaks pulled from Irish bogs and ancient American pines—show that plant growth around the world virtually ceased between 536 and 545 AD. It also mentions Chinese scrolls from that period referring to a 'dust veil' obscuring the skies. Roman and Greek records from the time mention a 'dry fog' that blocked out much of the sun's heat." He looked up. "The plume effect from a comet exploding in the atmosphere would do just that."

"Would that be described as the 'sky on fire'?"

"Mon Dieu, yes. All the fragments would incandesce as they shot through the atmosphere."

"Then where might we find the impact craters?"

Another Gallic shrug. "There might not be that many, if any. Comets are called 'dirty snowballs' because they are mostly ice and dust. A collision with Earth's atmosphere would vaporize the water and scatter the dust. The fragments would set the sky on fire, as it were, but much of the matter would remain in the atmosphere, causing the 'dry fog' described in the sixth-century accounts."

"So there'd be no 'Wound,'" Laura said, feeling some of her initial elation fade.

Duval raised a finger. "Ah, but there might. Some comets are 'snowy dirtballs' in that they have a rocky core. If that was the case with this comet, then yes, enough matter could survive the fall to impact the surface."

"Any ideas where to look?" Rick said.

Duval spread his arms. "The whole world. Just because you see bright lights flashing through the sky does not mean they will impact nearby. France—or Gaul, back then—has the Atlantic to the west and the Mediterranean to the south. A watery impact could have a tsunami effect but leave no noticeable crater."

Laura wandered to the office window and stared out at the wide lawns. The Meudon campus was large and peaceful. A few low buildings clustered here and there within the bordering trees, but most of the space seemed devoted to lawns.

Okay, what do we have?

A jaw-dropping astronomical event occurred in 536 AD and changed the course of western history. The people chasing her and Rick had named their group/cult/order/whatever after the year of that event. She had good reason to believe from the poem's reference to a "fallen star" that "slew summer" that the same event caused the "Wound" mentioned in the poem. The professor said the comet might not have left an impact crater but Laura was sure it had. Else why would the lines from the tattoos cross in southern France?

She turned back to Rick and Duval.

"Let's assume that this particular comet had a rocky core and that it landed in France with enough force to cause a 'Wound.' Where might we find that?"

He raised his hands in supplication. "You are asking the impossible from me."

She glanced at Rick with a raised eyebrow. "Impossible is an opinion." This earned a smile.

Duval said, "An impact crater in the populated areas would be well known and catalogued. We have nothing like that. So your crater would have to be in a remote region."

"The Pyrenees, perhaps?"

He nodded. "The Pyrenees would be perfect. But like everything else on the planet, the Pyrenees have been extensively photographed from space and nothing like what you are looking for has been spotted. If it had, geologists and astronomers would have been all over it."

"You're depressing me," she said.

"I am sorry. But think about it: Your crater would be almost fifteen hundred years old by now, and long since reclaimed by the forests. With all the erosion and overgrowth in that time, you could walk right through it and think of it as a small valley and nothing more. Unless . . . "

Was this dour Frenchman offering a ray of hope?

"Unless what?"

"Unless it became a lake. If the impact occurred on a hillside with considerable runoff, or opened an underground spring, it eventually would have filled with water."

Laura gave herself another head smack. "That's it! Why am I so stupid? 'Auburon lies drowning . . . He sleeps in the Wound.' Duh! It's been right there in front of us all the time: The Wound is an impact crater that's become a lake!"

"Do not become too excited," Duval said. "The Pyrenees have hundreds of lakes—perhaps thousands of them. When you look on a map you will find all these puddles of water named Estany This and Estany That."

"What's 'estany' mean?"

"It is Catalan for lake or pond. And on the French side you will see Lac de This and Etang du That."

"You're a regular Debbie Downer," Rick muttered.

"What is this 'Debbie Downer'? I do not know this."

"Thousands?" Laura said. "Really?"

"Perhaps I exaggerate. But many, many, many lakes."

Laura pointed to the snake on the tattoo. "Any areas particularly known for snakes?"

Duval shook his head. "I would not know."

"What about the name Auburon?" Rick said. "Does that point us to any locale?"

"It is Old German or Frankish. Old Gaul and Aquitaine were full of Franks during the sixth century." He twisted his goatee for a second or two, then added, "Perhaps I can suggest one thing that might narrow your search for this Wound. If it is not a lake, I tell you now that you will never find it."

"You call that help?" Rick said.

"No-no, wait. I am not finished. If this Wound is now a lake, it will be round, and it may have an island at its center."

"Really," Laura said, interested now. "Why do you say that?"

"Large impact craters often contain a central peak. I do not think—in fact, I am sure you will not find a very large crater. But if the impact was caused by superheated rock, heated to the point where it was molten, there might have been enough central upwelling to leave a peak.

When the crater filled with water, the peak would become an island."

Laura no longer had any doubt that they were looking for a lake in the Pyrenees. Finding a lake with a central island would narrow the search—*if* they could find
any such lake.

"Do you know of a directory of lakes in France? Or
better yet, in the Midi-Pyrenees region?"

"I believe there is. In fact, I am sure I have seen one.
But the lakes are listed by name. Your lake would have
to have a name to be listed. Do you know it?"

"No."

"Then the directory will be of no use to you. But your
lake might not even have a name. It might be in some
remote area where the locals refer to it merely as 'the
lake.'"

Definitely a Debbie Downer . . . but he was only stat-
ing facts. She turned to Rick.

"Any ideas?"

"Google Earth."

"You've got to be kidding. That could take forever."

He shrugged. "I don't see that we have a choice. At
least we have a starting point with the coordinates that
Israeli gal gave us. Find that spot and do a widening
grid search from there. I've played with Google Earth
before. We settle on a magnification that will let us spot
any lake-size body of water, then use the maneuvering
arrows to slide back and forth and up and down. Lines
of latitude and longitude can serve as our grid. It'll be
tedious as all hell but we can take turns. Unless of course
you have a better idea."

Try as she might, Laura couldn't come up with one.

They were looking at major drudge work, but she
realized she didn't care. She was *into* this now—fully
invested in the search. Were Rick's loony ideas conta-

gious? She preferred to think her new fierce determination was being fueled by the intellectual challenge of assembling this jumble of disparate pieces into a coherent whole.

"Google Earth, here we come."

12

Sent by Laura Fanning 18:02 GMT/UTC/DST + 2:00

> *Tried calling again but keep getting bounced. Can you call ATT and see what's the problem and can they fix? I'd much prefer speech to text. Since I haven't heard to the contrary, I'm assuming and hoping that Marissa is fine. I guess you guys are having lunch around now while I'm looking for a restaurant for dinner. After that we plan to spend the rest of the evening poring over Google Earth. Thanks again for taking care of Marissa. Give her my love.*

Received by Steven Gaines 18:09 GMT/UTC/DST – 4:00

> *Tried calling again but keep getting bounced. Can you call ATT and see what's the problem and can they fix? I'd much prefer speech to text, especially with Marissa sick. How is she? I'm going absolutely crazy here. I've spent the whole day running from ticket counter to ticket counter and going online. I cannot get a flight out of here today or tonight. I managed to grab a seat on an early am nonstop tomorrow that gets me in to Newark of all places at noon your time. Tell Marissa I love her and I'll see her tomorrow.*

Received by Laura Fanning 18:11 GMT/UTC/DST + 2:00

*Hi mommy. It is me marissa. Daddy says to tell you
i am feeling great. Natasha is here and we are doing
geography. Where are you so I can find you on the
map. I miss you. Love marissa*

Sent by Laura Fanning 18:14 GMT/UTC/DST + 2:00

*Hi, honeybunch. I'm so glad you're feeling good. You
had me worried there for a while. I'm in Paris. When
you find it on the map look really close and you'll see
me waving at you. Love you. See you soon.*

Sent by Steven Gaines 18:22 GMT/UTC/DST – 4:00

*With all the NYC flights out of Paris u cant get a seat?
Thats completely crazy. But okay. Ull be here noon tomorrow. Thank god. Dont want to scare u but things
not good here. The pcr test u ran came back positive.
Shes got cmv. Still dont know what that is but docs
say not good. Guess I dont have to tell u that.
I wish u had wings. We need u here. Hurry, hurry,
hurry.*

13

Rick entered *E 1° 21′ 36″* and *N 42° 47′ 38″* into Google
Earth and Laura found herself looking down on an
empty mountainside nearly a mile above sea level in the
Ariège department.

" 'Middle of nowhere' . . . no question about that."

Professor Duval had directed them to the Hotel Victor
Hugo a few towns away—an old-style, four-story structure with cranky plumbing and small rooms, but suitable
for their purposes. They ate so-so sushi in Masaki, the
Japanese restaurant on the ground floor, then were di-

rected to an Internet café where they rented the biggest
screen in the place and prepared to burn their eyes out of
their sockets.

They had an immediate false alarm with a lake just
north of the coordinates. The label said *Etang de Lers*.

"What does that mean?" Rick said.

Laura hadn't a clue. "*Etang* is a pond or lake. *Lers . . .*
" She shrugged. "It's not round but let's take a look."

"I'll be damned," he said as he zoomed closer. "It's
got an island."

Could it be? Could those crude azimuths have crossed
within a mile or two of the Wound? It seemed impossible, too good to be true . . .

Arranged?

The island sat near the southern shore and supported a stand of trees. It looked nothing like a central
peak from an impact. More like a peninsula from the
shoreline that had been cut off by rising water. If the
water level dropped, it would become a peninsula again.

Plus Etang de Lers had a blacktop road running past
it, a snack bar on the north shore, and was surrounded
by photo icons.

"Not the Wound, that's for sure," Rick said. "Looks
like a tourist stop. A swimming hole in summer and a
snowmobile spot in winter."

They took turns, searching clockwise in a grid pattern
as they moved out from their starting point in an ever-
enlarging square. For what seemed to be the longest
time they found no lakes. Then, as their search slowly
expanded toward the west, they found many, all labeled
etang instead of *lac*. From the air the lakes stuck out
reasonably well, appearing dark blue, almost black
against the greens and browns of dry land. Occasionally the white blur of a cloud would be reflected on a
surface.

"I never knew lakes came in so many shapes," Laura

said as she relinquished the mouse and rubbed her eyes. Over two hours at this now with nothing to show.

"And how few are round," Rick said.

True. Most were freeform style, their shape dictated by the terrain surrounding the depression where they'd formed. But not one lake so far, no matter what the shape, had possessed a true island, central or otherwise. Laura was convinced this was a hopeless exercise, but didn't want to say so. She believed in keeping mum unless you had something better to offer. She didn't.

"Hey, here's something," Rick said.

She leaned in as he zoomed down on a blue-black circle.

She looked for a label. "Where's its name?"

"Doesn't seem to have one. Looks about half a mile across . . . and . . . is that an island in the middle?"

She gripped his shoulder and squeezed. "Yes! Smack-dab in the middle!"

He glanced at her hand and she realized what she was doing. She let go.

He zoomed past the limits of the image's resolution, then backed up until it sharpened.

He browsed the shoreline. "No name . . . no one's posted photos around the edge . . . no snack bar, no road unless this brown line is what passes for one. Might be a couple of houses here among the trees, but if that's what they are, they're pretty rustic."

The view moved across the water to the central island. As he moved down on it, the image blurred again.

"We've maxed the resolution," he said. "And there's only an aerial view. Nothing from the side."

"If there's anything on that island, it should be trees. But what's that brown splotch?"

He looked at her. "A building of some sort? Holy shit. Could it be?"

Laura was nodding, barely able to contain a surge of

excitement and exaltation. "The 'house of the fallen godmen'! Could be! Could very damn well be!"

She stared at the blurry image as Rick scribbled down the coordinates.

"We started in the middle of Nowhere and now we're in the hinterlands of Nowhere. There's not even a road. How do we get there?"

"No problem. Let's get back to the hotel."

14

Bradsher put down his phone.

"That was our man tailing them. He checked their computer after they left the café. They cleared their history in Google Earth but—"

Nelson held up a hand. "Let me guess: They've located the Abbey."

"They might have. He got a few peeks at their screen and they were searching that area of the Pyrenees. Which calls Doctor Fanning's value into question."

They sat in their makeshift office in the farmhouse. Nelson's head throbbed and his vision had gone blurry. He seemed to be viewing Bradsher through a foggy window.

"What makes you say that?"

"She's headed to the Abbey. We are familiar with every nook and cranny of the Abbey. What can she find there that we don't already know?"

He could see that Brother Bradsher still had a lot to learn. As an agent he was excellent at taking care of the leaves, but in the course of keeping each one shiny and green, he tended to lose sight of the tree.

"First off, she *found* the Abbey. That in itself is an accomplishment."

"But meaningless to our purposes."

The tree! Nelson wanted to shout. Look at the *tree*!

"Allow me to finish, please."

"Sorry, sir."

"My point is, she found the Abbey without looking for it. She's obviously looking for what the pagans call the Wound." The idiocy of the name never failed to assail him. Logically consistent with their personification of the Earth as a deity, but a planet couldn't be wounded. "That means she's been following the pagans' mythology, and has found the place where they first conspired with the Serpent to create their hellish potion."

Even through the Vaseline blur, he could see Bradsher's expression fairly shouting, *So what?*

"Tell me, Agent Bradsher, when has anyone else done that? Ever? We've kept it out of the lake directories and off the maps. However, there's only so much we can do about satellite photos. But still, we don't know of anyone outside the Brotherhood, the panaceans, and a few local yokels who know about the lake and the Abbey. And we know of no one who has gone looking for it and found it except . . . Doctor Fanning. So what does that tell you?"

Bradsher took on a slightly chastened look. "It tells me that she might be on to something . . . that she might have information we do not."

Yes, that could be so. But obviously it hadn't occurred to him that an unseen hand might be guiding her. Not the Serpent, for the Serpent's goal was to keep the source of the panacea hidden. That left the Lord.

Nelson wanted to share this with Bradsher, but a full explanation would mean revealing his cancer, and he wasn't ready to do that. Not yet.

"Possibly. We know she was crisscrossing azimuths in Israel and they led her to the Wound. Who knows?

She may find another azimuth to follow from the Wound itself."

"Why don't we simply grab her and find out what she's got?"

The *last* thing Nelson wanted—the Serpent would rejoice if they did that. But he needed a mundane rationale.

He shook his head. "This goose is laying golden eggs. Why kill it?"

"I didn't mean kill—"

"Not literally, no." At least not yet. "She is following a trail and we are right behind her, step for step. If we interfere, we may compromise her vision, we may interrupt the flow of information someone might be feeding her. Right now she is working for *herself*. In my experience, people expend their best efforts toward their own goals. If we snatch her she will wind up working for *us*—and under duress, for that matter. We will see nowhere near the same level of commitment."

Bradsher was nodding. "You're saying she's like a hunting dog, and they work best off the leash."

"Exactly."

Maybe there was hope for him yet.

Nelson pulled a sheet of paper from his pocket and slid it across the table.

"I want you to text this to the good doctor's phone."

Bradsher read it and frowned. "Aren't you afraid it might throw her off the scent?"

Nelson had to smile. "Sticking with the bloodhound motif, I see. No, I don't see that happening. She is not doing this for him. She'll press on. I'm preparing for the future when we may have to make a move on her."

"You think she'll be more vulnerable without her guard dog."

"Immensely so. You read his file. You've seen what he's capable of."

"*Formidable*," he said, using the French pronunciation.

"Right. So our best course is to divide and conquer." He waved at the message. "Text that off right away."

15

Laura had her shirt halfway unbuttoned in prep for a shower when her phone emitted its text-message chime. *Phil* lit the screen.

She hesitated. The only reason he'd be messaging her was more info on Rick. Laura didn't want to hear anything negative. She was starting to like him. Not in *that* way. As a companion. They'd progressed from barely speaking to a comfortable camaraderie. Yes, he'd lied about the SEAL thing—and kept on lying about it—but was that such a big deal? He was smart and quick and their backgrounds were different enough so that their knowledge bases complemented each other. He was proving an asset on the search.

Not to mention how he'd saved her from God knows what in Israel.

She sighed and picked up the phone. Whatever. She'd never considered hiding one's head in the sand a viable option.

Hey, Doc. Tried calling but can't get through. And your voice mail is all screwed up. Keeps booting me out. But that's okay. Have I got news for you. Wait till you hear this.

Oh, crap.

My contact with the feds did a little digging and came up with yet another name for this guy. Get this: His

*real name is Garrick Somers, and he's ex-CIA. He was
a suspect in a mass murder but they couldn't pin it on
him. They caught him selling classified info to Israel
but couldn't make the charges stick so they finally
booted him out. He was never Ramiz Haddad, and
Rick Hayden is an identity he adopted to allow him
to hide in plain sight. Apparently he made his share
of enemies while in the CIA. I'd drop this guy, doc. I
mean put some real distance between you and him.
He sounds like big-time bad news.*

Shaken, Laura read it again. And then a third time,
stumbling over "suspect in a mass murder" and "selling
classified info to Israel."

She'd seen him kill, and do so with cool efficiency.
And even though they'd been questioned in Israel, they
seemed to have been sent on their way rather quickly,
considering the dead bodies he'd left behind. Could that
have been a little payback for passing off U.S. secrets in
the past?

Okay. Enough pussyfooting around. She'd kept her
mouth shut about the SEAL thing and the name change.
No more. Time to beard the lion, and she knew the location of his den.

Rebuttoning her blouse, she strode down the hall and
rapped on his door. She wondered for an instant if this
was wise. He was a killer, after all. But oddly enough,
she didn't fear him.

He opened the door and stood there in his jeans and
white undershirt.

"Hey. Something wrong?"

"Yeah," she said, thrusting the phone at him. "This.
Read it."

Frowning, he took the phone and checked out the
screen. His frown deepened. Finally he looked up at her.

"Who sent you this?"

"A friend who's been looking into your background."

"My background? Why?"

Why? Good question. Was finding him off-putting at first a good reason?

"I made it clear that I didn't want you along, but when Stahlman insisted, I wanted to find out why he was so stuck on you."

"Did you find out? Because I'd like to know too."

There. He was doing it again. That disarming attitude that he was in the woods too.

"No, but I found out everything else."

"Sure as hell did."

That took her aback. "You mean it's true?"

"Most of it."

"The traitor part too?"

"Not that part." He leaned out and looked up and down the hall. "Look, um, could we talk about this inside?"

Alone in a hotel room with him. Was she crazy not to be afraid of him—*still* not afraid of him?

"Will I be safe?"

"You really have to ask that?"

She saw the hurt that flickered across his face, but she couldn't help that. He hadn't been straight with her.

"How about we step outside and talk—just until I get the truth from you."

He sighed. "Fair enough, I guess. Let me put on a shirt."

He handed back her phone and didn't close the door all the way. He returned half a minute later in the shirt he'd worn earlier and a heavy bottle dripping ice.

"Champagne?"

"Hey, it's France, and Stahlman's paying." He held up a pair of flutes. "They sent two glasses. Want some?"

"No." She immediately reconsidered. "Yes. I could use something."

They went downstairs and stood on the sidewalk as the traffic on Rue Lazare Carnot sped by. He filled the two flutes, handed her one, then clinked his against hers.

"To setting the record straight."

"I'll drink to that." She sipped her Champagne. A bit tart, but she liked the bubbles. "So far you've been anything but straight with me."

"As straight as I could be."

"Come on. That whole SEAL thing? You weren't even in the navy."

He put the bottle on a window ledge and leaned back against the wall. He kept his voice low.

"No. I was a CIA field agent. But I took the full SEAL course and qualified."

"So that's why you're not listed with any team?"

"Right. I'm an unofficial SEAL. If I *had* been in the navy, I would have been on a team."

"But why take SEAL training?"

"Because I was going under—deep under—and no one was going to have my back. You learn a lot of deadly stuff as a SEAL. I wanted the skills to get myself out of a jam should the need arise."

"Did it?"

His eyes went flat as he took a sip of Champagne. "It did."

"What about selling secrets to the Israelis?"

He shook his head. "Never happened."

"Then what—?"

"Framed—very cleverly framed. I'll capsulize a long, torturous story. I was assigned to go under in Germany. A bunch of native-born Germans, total Aryan types who would have made Hitler proud, adopted Islam as their religion. A very radical form of Islam. Sounds crazy, I know, but they had their reasons. I was to infiltrate them. My way in, believe it or not, was through Israel."

"Now *there's* a back door if I ever heard one."

"Not so crazy when you realize that Mossad—that's Israel's CIA—has had quite a presence in Germany since the Munich Olympics. They keep watch on the Islamist groups there. They had connections with these Aryan Muslims and got me into places where I could bump into them. I speak perfect German with a very slight Swiss accent. We hit it off and I was in. But it turned out they'd discarded radical Islam by that time and were into something else, something way-way out."

"Like?"

"That's not part of the Israeli story. I wanted you to know how I got connected with them. When my Germany assignment was over, I was debriefed by Mossad and I kept in touch with a couple of their people after I returned to the States. Didn't know it then but keeping in touch would lead to my downfall. Some documents wound up in their hands and all the evidence pointed to me."

"Aren't we allies?"

Rick grabbed the bottle and refilled her glass. She hadn't realized she'd emptied it. Where did it go?

"We have intelligence that we don't share with them. They have intelligence that they don't share with us."

"They stole it and framed you?"

"The Israelis stole it but someone on our side framed me. Don't ask me why, I don't know. My friends in Mossad couldn't say anything without risking their guy who'd done the real stealing, so they zipped their lips."

"And left you twisting in the wind."

He shrugged. "I don't blame them. They had to choose one of us to protect. They chose their own."

"Is that why we got off so easy in Israel?"

He nodded. "That's my guess. Chayat said word had come down from on high to go easy."

Laura didn't know if she believed that. The reason

could be because they owed him for the stolen intelligence. But what of all that stuff about that Sausalito cop?

"Were you ever in San Francisco?"

"Absolutely. Spent some time there after Germany."

"Posing as Ramiz Haddad?"

He smiled. "No. *Watching* Haddad. One of my jobs was tracing his international contacts. He was a member of the Sausalito Police but also attached to a jihadist cell in Frisco. He changed his name to Rick Hayden and used his runs in the Sausalito Marine Patrol to check out the supports on the Golden Gate Bridge."

"Oh, no. He wasn't thinking of . . . "

"Oh, yes he was. Took retirement and applied for the Golden Gate National Recreation Area Rangers. Message intercepts concerned a plan to blow up the bridge and he was to learn the best places to set the charges. Then the Israeli problem broke and things got messy for me. Ramiz/Hayden disappeared about the time the Company and I parted ways, so I decided to assume his identity."

"What does that mean exactly—he 'disappeared'?"

"You know—vanished."

"I don't—"

"Look. He stopped being a jihadist. What else do you need to know? I didn't want to be bothered by the CIA or anybody else, so I became Rick Hayden. The high-ups knew what I was up to and they buried it. I didn't want contact with anyone from my CIA life and they didn't want anyone contacting me, so it was a good solution for all concerned."

"If you say so."

Once again her glass was empty and once again she let him refill it. Good stuff.

"Who's your source, by the way?"

She smiled. "If I tell you, I'll have to kill you."

Now why the *hell* did she say *that*?

He shook his head. "Not funny."

"Okay, he's with the local sheriff's department."

He looked shocked. "Really? You're not kidding?"

"Why would I be?"

"Because when I say the high-ups 'buried' my identity switch, I mean they entombed it. I don't believe someone from the Suffolk County Sheriff's Department, even with the help of a friendly fed, could gain access to my file. Someone's feeding him."

She didn't like the sound of that. "What do you mean?"

"Someone wants you thinking bad thoughts about me."

"Why?"

"So you won't trust me—that pops first to mind."

"I don't under—"

"You know we're not alone in this, right? That 536 has had its eye on us the whole time? The guys at Gan Yosaif had 536 tats, someone tailed us from the observatory, someone was watching us in the Internet café."

"You're paranoid."

He pointed to her phone. "That last text was meant to drive a wedge between us. If we split up, they've got you all to themselves."

She liked the sound of that even less.

"Did it work?" he said.

"You mean, are we split? It depends."

"On what?"

"On this mass murder he mentioned. What about that?"

He paused, took a deep breath. "That crazy German cult I told you about. They had this old book and they were doing unspeakable things in an effort to raise someone or something called 'the Dark Man.' They all died in a fire—men, women, children, all burned to death. Nowhere near as many as Waco, but a good number. No question about arson, either. The fire had been deliberately set. I survived so I was suspect."

She couldn't imagine him hurting a child, especially after the way he reacted to the little Mayan girl who'd been tortured.

"That was the night I saw something . . . something I'll never be able to explain."

"You mentioned that before. What was it?"

"A man, or rather a shape—oblong and upright—moving through the flames. I could hear the screams of the dying but he or it seemed impervious to the flames, seemed to be wallowing in the screams."

"Was he wearing PPE?"

"You mean firefighter gear?"

She nodded. She'd once had to perform a post on a firefighter who'd been trapped in a blaze so hot even his gear hadn't been able to protect him.

"No. He . . . it was black. The blackest black I've ever seen. Surrounded by fire but it didn't reflect the light from the flames. Seemed to absorb it."

"The Dark Man you mentioned?"

"I don't know. That was their thing, not mine. I never read the book. I'm glad I didn't."

She didn't know what to say. He seemed genuinely disturbed by it. It must have been an awful experience to still affect him this way.

"Dark matter."

"What? I've heard of that."

"The thought just hit me. It's the stuff between the stars that's supposed to make up most of the mass of the universe. They say it doesn't emit or absorb or reflect energy. It's just there."

"I'm supposed to believe dark matter was walking through the flames?"

Put that way, it did sound ridiculous. But she was just trying to help.

"Or it could it have been some sort of illusion, a trick of the heat and flames."

He drained his glass. "Sure. That sounds good. Let's hope so, okay?"

"But—"

"Enough of me. I'm tired of talking about me. In fact I hate talking about me."

"Okay, fair enough. But one more thing about you: What am I supposed to start calling you? Garrick? Or Gar?"

"Oh, please no. Neither. Garrick Somers is gone. I've been Rick Hayden long enough to think of myself as Rick. So leave it Rick."

"But if you were framed, don't you want to clear your name?"

"Nope. Don't care. And which name? Rick Hayden's name is clean. That's all I have to care about."

"Well, don't you at least want to know who framed you?"

"Oh, I know who. This Company guy I used to butt heads with all the time. He hated my guts and I'm sure he was behind it. Name was Nelson Fife."

LEANDER

1

Laura awoke with a name running through her head.

Fife . . . Nelson Fife. It hadn't clicked until after she'd left Rick. No relation, she was sure, but the same last name as James Fife, the man she'd run down as a teen.

She hadn't thought about him in years and wondered if he was still alive. Hearing the name had awakened that awful memory.

Driving along, two weeks with her driver license, applying mascara in the rearview mirror when she blew through a stop sign and hit a man. She could still hear the sound of his head smashing against the windshield.

She'd been a basket case. She visited him in the hospital every day until he was transferred back east. He still hadn't regained the use of the left side of his body when he was released. The prospects of his ever recovering that were virtually nil.

The relentless guilt over James Fife was why she had gone to medical school, why she had originally wanted to be a neurologist—to help people like the man she had crippled.

And look at her now: a pathologist traipsing around her third continent in four days, chasing a wild goose. How far she'd wandered from her goal.

She was glad Rick had mentioned that name. She'd forgotten about James Fife, and she couldn't allow that. Ever.

2

"They've chartered a helicopter to Midi-Pyrenees," Bradsher said as he entered Nelson's makeshift office in the farmhouse.

"'They'?"

"Doctor Fanning and Hayden or Somers or—"

"Call him by the name on his passport—for the sake of consistency if nothing else." He rubbed his temples. "She's still with Hayden?"

"Most definitely."

He slammed a fist on the table and the noise shot a bolt of pain through his brain. He had another blinding headache but he'd lasted through the night without suffering another seizure.

"Damnation! *Why?* Is it something sordid? Have they become intimate? Is that it?"

Somers/Hayden had always had a way with women, and many, many notches in his belt.

"They spent some time talking on the street after I sent your text. I assumed she was confronting him. They spent the night in their own rooms but were back together for breakfast early this morning. Doctor Fanning made some calls—she speaks fluent French—and just moments ago the two of them took off from Charles de Gaulle in a pontoon-equipped five-seater Colibri EC120."

Nelson nodded in grudging admiration. "They're not wasting a minute. They'll land on the lake within a stone's throw of the Abbey. Is that drone team in Toulouse?"

"They arrived last night as per your instructions. I just sent word that they are to head into the hills and await instructions. They have the coordinates of the Abbey."

He hit the table again, but more gently this time. "This means that if and when we have to deal with her, we'll have to deal with him as well."

"I'm sure we can handle him."

"I'm sure we can too. It's just that he's well trained and will not go quietly or easily."

"You said you'd tell me your history with him."

"Did I?" Nelson couldn't remember.

"Yes. And since we've nothing to do until they arrive at the Abbey, I thought now might be a good time. They've got a couple of hours in the air and their copter doesn't have the range to make the trip without refueling."

Nelson leaned back. Oh, why not?

"One of my projects as an analyst was a group of German nihilists, the kind who would have been kicked out of the Baader-Meinhof gang of the seventies for being too violent. They popped onto the Interpol—and consequently the Company's—radar when they proclaimed their conversion and devotion to the Wahhabi branch of Sunni Islam. Garrick Somers—our present-day Rick Hayden—was assigned to infiltrate them to see if he could get wind of any schemes of mass destruction ahead of time. Hayden's father spent years working for Schelling, a Swiss pharma giant, so he was raised in Geneva where he grew up with German as a second language."

"Perfect for the job," Bradsher said.

"Right. But here's where the story gets interesting. By the time he'd infiltrated the group they'd abandoned Wahhabism for something much darker. What mattered to the Company was that, whatever rites this crazy cult was practicing, they did not involve terrorism or a threat to the U.S. or its interests, so my recommendation was that Hayden be pulled."

Bradsher leaned forward. "I have a feeling that's not the end of the story."

"Not by a longshot. He refused to leave. He refused to say why, just that he hadn't finished the job. I suspected he'd gone native."

"Joined the cult?"

"Exactly. And that posed a threat to other agents, of course. We had an extraction team ready to move in when the old farmhouse the group called home—much like this one—exploded and burned. We knew they'd stored explosives and incendiaries of various sorts, and something or someone must have set them off. Since our man was the only survivor, we suspected him, but couldn't prove anything."

"Was that the 'mass murder' mentioned in his file?"

"Yes. Eleven adults—six men and five women—and fifteen children under age ten."

Bradsher gave a low whistle. "Children."

"Yes. He was brought home but never seemed to adjust. PTSD, I assume. Then he was suspected of selling intelligence to his old friends in Mossad. Again nothing could be proven so he and the Company decided both parties would benefit if they went their separate ways. As a parting shot, he killed Ramiz Haddad—who had changed his name to Rick Hayden—and assumed his identity."

"We know that?"

Nelson nodded. "That we know. Haddad's death was no loss to the gene pool. He had ISIS connections and was stockpiling explosives—only a matter of time before he attempted a catastrophe. The Bureau was upset because they were watching him in the hope of following him to a bigger fish, but *c'est la guerre*."

That's my story and I'm sticking to it, Nelson thought.

He wasn't about to tell Bradsher or anyone else that Hayden had nothing to do with the intelligence that wound up with the Israelis. Or that Nelson had arranged all the evidence to point to him.

As the analyst who had been collating the intelligence Hayden reported from Germany, Nelson debriefed him on his return. The man had been a mental and emotional basket case, babbling about some "dark man" he had seen in the fire and spouting one blasphemy after another. Totally unreliable. A major security breach waiting to happen. Nelson had decided it would be better for the Company if he were booted out. When the opportunity presented itself, he hadn't hesitated.

And now he wanted a change of subject.

"What about the doctor's communication with home?"

"We're on it around the clock, though we don't expect her to call home until it's at least one P.M. here. Maybe later, depending on how long she stays in the hills. No cell service up near the Abbey."

"You have messages set to go?"

Bradsher nodded, smiling. "We have a terrible storm front coming through that will cancel all flights. So even if the husband suggests she charter a flight home, it's no use."

Nelson knew the weather forecast was for a beautiful day.

"This could all go to hell if the husband checks the weather on the Continent."

"I can't see him doing that," Bradsher said. "He's too involved with his sick daughter. She's not doing well."

Nelson might have felt a pang of guilt for keeping a mother in the dark about her daughter's illness, but this was Laura Fanning. She deserved it.

Besides, Dr. Fanning's presence back home would not improve the child's prognosis one iota. And no matter where the trail led, Laura Fanning would not see her daughter again, would not be heading home . . . ever. He was convinced now that the Lord had cast him in

the role of Moses and was using her as a Pillar of Fire
to lead him to the Promised Land.

As for her daughter, the child was with good doctors
and her fate was in God's hands.

Let go, let God.

3

"Looks like we won't be alone there," Rick said as they
paddled toward the island.

Their helicopter had stopped in Toulouse to refuel,
then followed the pilot's GPS locator straight to the coordinates Rick had copied from Google Earth last night.

Where they'd found themselves hovering over the
Wound.

Not a cheap ride by any stretch, but Stahlman was
paying for it.

The copter settled on the water where Rick inflated
the raft they'd brought along. The pilot drifted and
smoked while they headed for the island. Laura sat in
the bow, paddling, while Rick paddled and steered from
the rear.

"What do you mean?" she said.

He pointed over her shoulder at the rowboat tied to
a sapling near a short set of steps carved into the rock
of the island. He'd noted a couple of crude wooden
boats pulled up on the lake shore as they'd landed, but
hadn't noticed this one until they'd approached.

"Somebody's here ahead of us. Is that a fishing rod
leaning out the stern?"

"Looks like it," she said. "But why are there crosses
on the building? I thought we were dealing with pagans."

Rick had been staring at the boat. He raised his gaze
and, yes, those were crosses.

The building appeared to be a single-story rectangle

fashioned of beige stone blocks. From this angle they had a good view of the narrow end that appeared to be the front of the structure. The entrance was a round arch with a prominent keystone. A simple Christian cross had been carved into the stone blocks above it. He could see three similar arches along the building's right flank, and each of those sported a cross as well. A narrow tower, open on the top, rose from the roof near the front end.

A bell tower?

"I'll be damned," he said. "A church."

Laura was shaking her head. "Who in their right mind would put a church on this tiny island in the middle of a lake in the middle of nowhere?"

"Why do you assume they were in their right minds?"

"Good point. But—wait. It looks more like a monastery." She gave him a wide-eyed look over her shoulder. "The 536 Brotherhood?"

A monastery made more sense. The original purpose of monastic orders was to retreat into prayer and study, cloistered from the temptations of the world. As for 536 . . .

"Who else could it be?"

She lowered her voice. "But the panaceans directed us here."

"While 536 was trying to keep us from getting here. Makes sense now."

She was shaking her head. "No, it doesn't. It makes no sense at all. None of this makes sense. If this is some sort of revered place to the panaceans, why would 536 build a monastery here?"

"To purify or sanctify the site? Or maybe just to get in their pagan faces."

They were closer now and he could see how the place was overgrown with vines and the bell tower had partially collapsed on a side.

"But whoever built it doesn't appear to be devoting much effort to upkeep."

"It looks abandoned," she said.

That it did. All the better.

"Aim for the boat," he told her. "We'll tie up next to it and use those steps."

"I've got a big question about that boat."

"Yeah?"

"Like whose is it?"

"Only one way to find out. Unless you want to turn back. Your call."

He knew her answer in advance, but felt he should offer the option.

"You're kidding, right?"

He smiled. This gal was not a quitter.

"Okay. But let's do a quick reconnoiter first."

He could tell she was anxious to get up to the monastery, but he insisted on paddling all the way around first. He wanted to minimize the chance of an ugly surprise once they left their boat.

He steered them to starboard as Laura paddled her heart out. She wasn't very adept with the oar but she'd insisted at the start on grabbing one and helping. He liked that in a woman.

He liked a lot about her. Especially the fact that the text she'd received last night hadn't sent her running off in a panic. She was just too damn smart and levelheaded for that, and it had to be driving 536 nuts.

What he didn't like so much was her backgrounding him. He hadn't expected that. And he should have. As ME she worked with law enforcement and he should have anticipated that she'd want to learn more about the guy she was traveling with and would know just how to find out.

He'd underestimated her, but not as bad as 536 had with that text.

He'd been shocked by its accuracy. It hinted that whoever was birddogging them from 536 had deep connections into the government, and into the Company itself. Garrick Somers had proved an embarrassment to the CIA and the higher-ups had wanted him not only gone but forgotten.

Not that he blamed them. After what he'd seen and done in Germany, he'd returned with as bad a case of PTSD as any of the downrange casualties of the Iraq and Afghanistan theaters. But he'd tried to hide it. Being up front would mean he'd have to talk about it. And he couldn't talk about any of it, especially the night of the fire.

When Fife framed him for the Israeli leak, Rick had known his time was up. Fife probably thought he was doing the Company a favor, but he'd done Rick a bigger one.

Knowing that surveillance of Ramiz Haddad would lapse when Rick left, maybe long enough to let him place his explosives around the Golden Gate supports, he'd terminated him, sent his body to stay with Davy Jones, and adopted the Rick Hayden identity.

The new persona worked psychological magic. Garrick Somers had suffered horrendous mental trauma, and now Garrick Somers was gone. Rick Hayden had done nothing to be ashamed of. As Rick Hayden he'd slept peacefully for the first time in years.

It had shaken him when Laura asked if she should start calling him Garrick or Gar. No way. Garrick Somers was gone, and Rick wanted him to stay gone. *Nobody* wanted Garrick Somers back.

On the far side of the island they spotted the fisherman: An old guy with long gray hair and a ratty white beard who sat with a line in the water. He peered at them from under the wide brim of a straw-colored, sweat-stained slouch hat, then waved.

Rick and Laura waved back.

Laura called out, *"Pouvons nous venir à terre?"*

"I speak English," he replied in a high-pitched, fragile voice. "And this is not my land. So . . . yes, of course."

"What did you ask him?" Rick said as they continued their circuit.

"If we could come ashore."

They tied up to the same shoreline sapling the rowboat had used. Rick led the way up the steps.

"Welcome," said a voice from within the shadows of the entry arch, pronouncing the "W" as a "V."

Rick instinctively put himself between the building and Laura. He had a hunting knife he'd picked up in Paris, but he left it in its sheath on his belt.

"How did you know we spoke English?" he called back.

The old man stepped into view with his fishing rod over his shoulder. He had a bent spine and wore a ratty sweater over faded denims. Muddy, unlaced boots completed the picture. Looked harmless enough, but Rick had a sense of something not quite right about him. He couldn't go so far as to say *wrong*, just . . . not right.

"Voices carry over water. I was listening to you on your way in."

Definitely a German accent.

"Were we right?" Laura said, stepping forward. "About this being a monastery?"

His clear blue eyes fixed on her from the shadow of his hat brim. "You are . . . ?"

"Laura Fanning . . . from the U.S."

He smiled. "I knew the *where* from your accent. I am Leander." He looked at Rick. "And you?"

"Rick." He leaped right to the important question: "Are you here alone?"

A crooked smile. "I was until a moment ago."

"You speak English pretty well for someone who lives in such an isolated area." An idiotic statement, he knew, but he was looking for a way to get the codger to spill.

"I speak French and German and Spanish as well. I have traveled much but I always return to this area. It is home." He looked from Rick to Laura and back again. "I cannot remember the last time I saw anyone else on this island. It is good to have company."

"How's the fishing?"

"The smallmouth bass are excellent."

Laura gave Rick a nudge and a look. "Can we talk about the monastery?"

"Yes, you were right," Leander said. "It is a monastery of sorts."

Rick gestured to the climbing vines, the crumbling masonry. "Looks more like 'was' a monastery."

He shrugged. "When is a monastery no longer a monastery?"

"When it has no monks."

Leander glanced over his shoulder at the building. "It has no monks . . . at least not for as long as I have been alive. It is more properly an abbey. Men come and visit, but no one stays." He turned to Laura. "I heard you mention 'panaceans.' Where did you learn that term?"

"We were told it applies to a certain group of pagans we've been tracking. Also called the Children."

"Pagans . . . Oh, these parts have been home to many pagans, and heretics too—followers of Arius back in the day. But the Romans and the Franks and the monks converted all they could and killed the ones they couldn't."

"We have a poem from the panaceans," she said, pulling the paper from a back pocket. "Would you mind taking a look at it?"

She's not wasting any time at all, Rick thought.

"I do not mind."

"Don't you need glasses?" she said, handing it to him.

"Not if the light is good." He angled it into the sun-light and read aloud.

> *" 'Twixt the house of the fallen godmen*
> *And the tomb of the fallen star*
> *That slew summer,*
> *Auburon lies drowning.*
> *He sleeps,*
> *Martyred and imprisoned*
> *Yet mocking his oppressors.*
> *He sleeps in the Wound,*
> *Midmoon from the godmen gate*
> *Where five men stand above his door.*
> *His guardian leg shall bear you to new life."*

"Have you ever heard that before?" Laura said.

He handed it back to her. "Of course. Everyone around here knows 'The Song of Auburon.' It originated in these parts many, many centuries ago, although this is the first time I have seen it in English. The original was in Catalan, I believe."

"A monastery with no monks," Rick said, thinking aloud. Leander's reading had caused pieces to start clicking into place. "Holy crap! Is this 'the house of the fallen godmen'?"

Leander nodded. "Yes . . . if the old tales are true."

"But . . . " Laura was looking around. "Where did they fall from?"

"Grace," Leander said simply. "Come."

He stepped back under the arch and motioned them to follow. Of its own volition, Rick's hand found the handle of his knife. Leander stopped before the dark rectangle of an open doorway. Rick looked for signs of life or movement down the shadowy hallway beyond. All quiet.

Leander pointed to a number carved into the stone above the door.

DXXXVI

Rick tensed. "Well, I guess that settles that."

"But why did they build it *here*?" Laura said.

"You do not know the story?"

"No. But you're going to tell us, right?"

"Of course. It is no secret. We have passed the story from generation to generation." Leander pointed to a block of stone outside to the right of the arch. "There. Let me sit and warm myself in the sun while I tell you."

They followed him and stood by as he settled himself.

He squinted up at them. "Tell me what you already know."

"We know of the comet that caused the sky to burn in 536 AD, and the piece of it that landed here."

Leander nodded. "The 'Wound' of the poem. That was what Auburon's people called it. They had come from the north and mixed with the Visigoths, but they worshipped the All-Mother. Being a pagan was dangerous back then, so they pretended to follow the teachings of Arius, who preached that Jesus was not an aspect of God in the Trinity, but a separate being created directly beneath God. But even though Arians were themselves considered heretics by the pope and the rulers of the Church in Rome at that time, they fared better than pagans. The Church had absolutely no use for pagans. Thus the pretense. When they saw the fire in the sky they thought the Christian God was attacking the All-Mother."

Laura was shaking her head. "And we assume life was so simple back then."

Leander smiled. "Anything but. Imagine what a terrible time that must have been: A veil has covered the sky, obscuring the sun after the firestorm that caused the Wound. On the day of the summer solstice, a heavy snow falls. Summer does not come and the crops mostly fail. Auburon keeps his family from starving by hunting the diminishing small game and eating the stunted, deformed plants growing around the rim of the Wound which is slowly filling with water. He pulls up the cold-resistant plants and takes them home to eat. Half delirious with fever from an infected wound on his leg after a hunting accident, he dumps his plants into a boiling pot."

"How do you know all this?" Laura said.

"My father told me the story when I was a child, just as his father told him, and now I am telling you. Auburon should not be forgotten. The next morning he has no fever and the wound has healed. A miracle! Or could it be the tea he made? He is a farmboy who learned healing ways from his mother. After experimenting, he discovers that a tea made from the whole plant has great healing properties. He becomes revered among the locals and his reputation grows."

"The first panacean," Laura said.

"Yes. And everything is fine until the Church arrives."

"Here we go," Rick said. "The 536 Brotherhood rears its ugly head."

"They were merely Benedictine monks then. It is a few years after the impact when Friar Hugh arrives from the Montecassino monastery in Italy to establish a new abbey in Gaul. Via the good word of the pope—named Vigilius by then—Hugh's party has the blessing of King Chlothar, who provides troops to guarantee safe passage from Toulouse to Aquitaine. Each Benedictine monastery at that time was autonomous and Hugh and his followers want to establish a more ascetic life-style than Montecassino's."

"I smell fanaticism," Laura said. "Or fundamentalism at the very least."

Rick nodded. Just what he was thinking. He'd been keeping watch on their surroundings as Leander spoke. He couldn't shake the sense of something off about the old dude.

"You shall see. This was the frontier of the Church and Friar Hugh and his fellow Benedictines saw themselves as pioneers blazing new paths for the Glory of God. They chose southern Gaul because they figured the recent years of empire-wide cold summers and famine would make it easy to convince the local Visigoths, mostly followers of Arianism, to convert to the Trinitarian beliefs of the Byzantine Empire. It was also safer than heading east, because shipments of grain from Egypt had brought plague to Constantinople and it had spread across the Mediterranean from there. Even Emperor Justinian was not spared, although he survived his illness."

Laura glanced at Rick. "Duval called it the Justinian Plague. The start of the Dark Ages."

"Yes," Leander said, nodding. "The Dark Ages . . . and men like Friar Hugh helped bring the darkness. A short time after his arrival he hears of a local known as Auburon who performs miraculous healings. In fact, the local Arians call him 'Saint Auburon.' This does not sit well at all with Friar Hugh. He tells the accompanying soldiers to bring this Auburon to him."

"I'm guessing the rest isn't pretty," Laura said. "Not with 'martyred and imprisoned' in the poem."

Leander smiled. "Did you never question the order of those two states of being? I mean the fact that 'martyred' precedes 'imprisoned' in the poem?"

"I assumed it was for purposes of rhyming or meter in the original."

"We shall see. In his innocence, Auburon explains to Friar Hugh that he performs neither miracles nor witchcraft. It's just a tea he brews from the plants along the rim of the hole God made when the sky rained fire. He leads them to the crater—filled with water by now—where Hugh sees the twisted plants. The friar tells him this isn't God's work. The night of fire was the work of Satan—the Serpent—to undo God's Holy Church. After the night of fire, the Serpent stifled the light of God's sun, causing years of darkened skies without summers, famine throughout the empire, and now plague. These deformed plants are the legacy of the Serpent's attempt. Were Auburon not a heretic, he'd know that. Hugh orders him imprisoned. But there is no prison, so he is tied to a tree."

"Okay," Laura said. "It's reversed in the poem. Imprisoned first."

"We shall see. During the night, a Frankish soldier named Paschal, tasked with guarding the bound healer, shows his prisoner the leprosy on his lower leg. He's been hiding it from his fellow soldiers. Auburon instructs him how to make the tea. Paschal follows the directions and drinks. The leprosy is gone by the next day, but Paschal has to watch in horror as Auburon is burned alive, and then drawn and quartered for heresy and witchcraft and pretending to be a holy man."

"Paschal," Rick said. "We now know the name of the second panacean."

Leander turned to him. "You are quite correct. But now we come to the abbey. Friar Hugh becomes the abbot of his new order. The construction is slow work because it's being built on the high uplift in the center of the crater. Some of the block can be quarried from the uplift itself, but so much else has to be brought over by boat. He chose to consecrate the uplift in order to purify and sanctify this mark of Satan's work."

"Ah-ha!" Rick said, nudging Laura. He couldn't help it. "Told you."

She gave him a look. "You love being right, don't you."

"I do, I do, I do."

"Because it's such a unique experience?"

He laughed. "That was harsh."

Yeah, he really liked her.

"May I go on?" Leander said.

Rick raised his hands. "Yeah. Please. Sorry."

"But Hugh cannot seem to stamp out the local pagans and their healings. He has started calling them panaceans. But whenever he finds and executes one, another pops up.

"It is during the abbey's construction that Friar Hugh—far removed from the orthodoxy of Rome—develops the peculiar theological underpinnings of his new order. He instructs his fellow monks—once Benedictine but now a long way, both physically and spiritually, from their order—in his new interpretation. He agrees with the Church teaching that, even though man was born to suffer, we are doing the Lord's work when we ease human suffering. But we are to help alleviate only *some* suffering. The pagan potion, though it cures disease, is really Satan's work, created to subvert God's punishment for the transgressions in Eden. Man was banished from the Garden to know death and disease and hunger and despair. The panacea undoes God's will. Because of their growing fixation on the Banishment, they start to refer to Satan as 'the Serpent.'"

"That's a majorly twisted view of Genesis," Laura said.

"I don't know," Rick said. "It's logically consistent with the Garden of Eden myth."

"Oh, you would think that," she said. "Because it's also consistent with your myth that it's evil because it comes from *outside*—wherever *that* is."

"We don't need to go into that now," Rick said, but her words pierced like a knife.

Was he another side of the 536 coin?

"Please?" Leander said. "May I finish? Hugh and his fellow monks dedicate themselves to stopping the evil the Serpent began in the year 536. They brand themselves with the date so they can never forget."

"This explains so much," Laura said. "They don't want the panacea for themselves—they want to keep *anyone* from getting it."

"Yes, and to that end, Friar Hugh decides to destroy all the plants around the crater. He calls on a postulant, a former Frank soldier who left the army to join the 536 order. He instructs him to rip up all the plants that the panaceans use for their potion and burn them. He cannot seem to stop the pagans, but if he destroys the raw materials for their sacrilegious potion, he'll have rendered them powerless. The postulant says he'll start immediately. But the postulant's name is Paschal who, you might remember, was cured by Auburon. He and others like him have become a fifth column among the friars. In fact, he has been overseeing the quarrying of stone from within the upwelling for the abbey's foundation. He tells his fellow panaceans to dig up whatever plants they can under cover of night and move them and their soil to a remote place in the mountains where they can grow in safety."

"And so it began," Rick said. "A secret war lasting a millennium and a half. And we're in the middle of it."

"How are you in the middle?" Leander said.

Laura shook her head. "Another long story."

Leander slowly rose to standing. "I would love to

hear it but this old man's bladder is full. I will relieve it on the far side of the abbey. Do not go away."

"Not on your life," Laura said. She turned to Rick as the old man tottered away toward the abbey's left flank. "Well, what do you think?"

"I think we just struck the mother lode of panacean lore. That old dude has answered a lot of questions. But can we trust him?"

"What do you mean?"

"Something off kilter about him. I wish I could say just what. And I don't like him going off by himself."

Laura smiled. "Why don't you peek around the corner and see if he's really relieving himself."

"Don't think it hasn't occurred to me."

But he'd take a pass on that. Instead he pointed to the abbey. "'The house of the fallen godmen.'" Then to the lake. "'The tomb of the fallen star.'"

"Right. But Auburon sleeps 'twixt' . . . somewhere between . . . where would that be?"

Rick knew the poem by heart by now. " . . . *mocking his oppressors . . . He sleeps in the Wound . . . Midmoon from the godmen gate . . . Where five men stand above his door.*" He looked around. "The 'godmen gate' could be the front door to the abbey. But what's 'midmoon' from that?"

"A half moon? " Laura said.

"Yes! A hundred-eighty degrees."

He hurried along the abbey's right flank to its rear wall—a blank stone expanse with a cross carved into the block. Not even an arch. He was hoping to find some sort of statue or monument—any sort of structure. But all he found was brush.

"Check the ground for a trapdoor or something," he said, parting the brush.

"You don't think they'd make it easy to find, do you?"

"Or look for remnants of statues—namely the 'five men' who 'stand above his door.' Auburon should be beneath."

"Nothing but dirt and rock here," Laura said.

Yeah, she was right. Damn it.

He stepped to the water's edge where they'd seen Leander fishing.

"Wait. 'Auburon lies drowning.' " He pointed toward the water. "He's down there."

"But no statues of five men. How about carved into the bank?"

Rick leaned over for a look. "Nothing but blank rock."

" 'Five men stand above his door,' " Laura said. "What if that means five man-lengths? People didn't grow much above five feet back then. Could he be in some sort of crypt down there . . . twenty-five feet down?"

"Damn right, he could. *Martyred and imprisoned . . . Yet mocking his oppressors.*' It all fits. His first disciple, Paschal, was in charge of the quarrying. They placed him right under the abbey where he could thumb his nose at them for eternity."

"It fits, but is it true?"

He began shucking his jacket. "Only one way to find out."

"You're not thinking . . . "

"Unless you can come up with a better way, this is the best I've got."

"We should have brought some scuba gear."

"No one wishes that more than yours truly." He wasn't concerned about free diving two dozen feet. The SEALs had put him through a lot worse. The temperature could be trouble because Rick knew, just *knew* that water was going to be cold. Too cold and his muscles would seize up. "My kingdom for a drysuit."

"Maybe I should get Leander . . . "

"Let him empty his bladder in peace. It takes old guys a while."

As he stripped down to his cotton boxer briefs, he heard Laura groan behind him. Her voice had a husky sound.

"There are some things one cannot unsee."

He laughed. "Don't tell me I have skid marks!"

"Just get this over with."

He grabbed the Maglite Mini from his jacket pocket. The water looked clear and the high sun would add a lot of light near the surface, but he might need it twenty-five feet down. Not waterproof, just water resistant, but he figured it would last longer down there than his breath.

He picked up his hunting knife.

"Are you expecting to run into a shark?" Laura said.

"Never know. Maybe a kraken."

Nah . . . he dropped it.

"Be careful," Laura said.

He looked back and saw her concerned expression. She cared? Nice to know.

"See you in a couple of minutes."

He looked down at the still surface of the water, maybe five feet below. If Laura's calculation was right, he'd find something twenty feet or so below the surface. He filled his lungs to capacity then slowly released the breath four times. Taking a final deep breath, he turned on his Mag and dove in headfirst.

He'd been mentally prepared for the cold but the shock nearly drove the breath from him. This couldn't be just mountain runoff. Had to be a cold spring at work here.

He kicked straight down, stroking with one arm and aiming the flashlight with the other. He saw the opening almost immediately: a black square, three feet on a side, cut into the rocky wall of the upwelling. Definitely not natural.

He hesitated only a second before gliding into it, Mag thrust before him. He expected to find a coffin or some skeletal remains, but the passage made a sharp upward turn. He followed it. He doubted he could turn in the confines of the passage, so getting out would take longer than going in. He decided to allow himself a dozen or so more feet before he started backing out.

The flash beam—don't fail me now—reflected against something ahead. The end of the passage? He stroked on, wondering at the purpose of the passage, when he suddenly broke the surface into air.

Air?

Yeah. No light, but air—stale and musty. He pulled himself out of the water. Not exactly warm here, but positively balmy compared to the lake. He spent a moment shaking off the water and rubbing his skin to warm it. He figured he was under the abbey. Which would put him *'Twixt the house of the fallen godmen . . . And the tomb of the fallen star . . . That slew summer.*

He flashed his Mag beam around. So where was Auburon sleeping?

He had barely begun his search when he heard a deep scraping sound above him.

4

As he stared at the monitor, Nelson willed his blurred vision to clear, but with only minimal success. He sat in a darkened room—the low light helped his headache—in the rear of the Ballainvilliers farmhouse with Bradsher and two of the local field agents.

"What am I looking at?"

"Per Agent Bradsher's instructions," said an operative he knew only as Henry, "the drone team drove into the hills this morning and set up near the designated coordinates. The hover drone reached those coordinates just as you walked in."

"Ah, yes," Nelson said, recognizing the Abbey in the center of the wide view of the lake.

He felt a twinge of vertigo as the camera panned around.

"There's the helicopter they arrived in," Henry said. "I'm going to follow the shoreline."

Nelson was pleased to note that none of the Serpent's plants grew along the shore. The Brotherhood had been efficient and effective in eradicating them from the locale.

"There's some sort of ruin on the island. It looks religious, what with the crosses and all. Are you two familiar with the location?"

"Vaguely," said Bradsher.

Henry was not of the Brotherhood and the less he knew the better.

"Tell me again why we're watching these two?"

Nelson didn't feel up to it so he nodded to Bradsher.

"That's on a need-to-know basis," Bradsher said. "But I can tell you that she's a medical doctor who has been hired by a very rich man with an anti-American agenda."

"We talking Soros-type money here?" Henry said.

Bradsher kept his eyes on the monitor screen. "You didn't hear that from me."

"Well, as long as this is budgeted through your account and not mine, I don't need to know. The two Interpol guys running the drone won't even ask. They love playing with it."

"There's the doctor," Bradsher said as the view swung around to the rear of the Abbey. "But where's . . . ?"

Henry said, "She's staring at the water and appears to be standing beside a pile of clothes. Could her companion have gone for a swim?"

"It certainly appears so," Nelson said.

He glanced at Bradsher who looked equally baffled.

"Oh, wait," said Henry. "Here comes someone."

Nelson leaned closer. A bearded old man was walking up behind Dr. Fanning. That certainly wasn't Hayden. Nelson had never seen him before.

"Who in God's name is he?"

5

"Where is your friend?"

Laura jumped at the sound of Leander's squeaky voice. She'd been so intent on watching the surface of the lake for Rick's return that she'd forgotten about him.

She pointed to the water. "He's looking for Auburon's tomb."

The old man's already high-pitched voice jumped an octave. "In the lake?"

"Well, we figured that particular spot is 'midmoon from the godmen gate,' so he dove in to see."

"But the water is so cold. Such impulsive behavior. He should have spoken to me first."

"There's nothing there?"

Leander stepped to the edge and stroked his scraggly beard as he peered at the water. "How long has he been down?"

Laura wished she'd looked at her watch before he dove in. "Two minutes, maybe?"

"Well, then, let us hope he has found it."

Laura grabbed his arm, thin and bony through the fabric of his shirt. "Found what?"

"The passage to Auburon's tomb."

"What are you talking about?"

He turned and motioned to her to follow. "Come. And you should bring his clothes. If he is alive, he will be cold."

"*If* he's alive?" she said around a stab of panic. "What do you mean?" Laura picked up Rick's clothes and hurried after Leander as he began walking toward the front of the abbey. "Wait-wait-wait! What do you mean?"

"The water is cold and the passage is narrow. He is your lover?"

"No. No way. He's just helping me search."

"You care for him." Leander was not asking a question.

Laura thought about that. She guessed she did care about him. Else why this anxious squeezing in her chest? He'd started out aloof and annoying, but he'd proved reliable and good company, despite his weird take on the world.

"It's a professional relationship but he's become a . . . a friend."

"He is a good swimmer?"

"I don't know." She couldn't resist. "He says he swims like a SEAL."

"'Like a seal.' An odd choice. Most people would say 'fish.'"

"Nope. Like a SEAL."

She prayed he'd been telling the truth about that.

She followed Leander through the front door of the abbey. Just across the threshold he stopped and picked up a very modern oil lamp.

"You've come prepared," she said.

"I have explored this place many times."

As he pulled out a little butane lighter to fire up the lantern, Laura considered her position of being alone in a dark, deserted abbey in the middle of a lake with a strange old man who just happened to be waiting on shore when they arrived. In a sci-fi movie he'd turn out to be Auburon himself, resurrected by the panacea. Or in a B-grade thriller he'd turn out to be the leader of 536 and would either attack her or imprison her.

She looked at Leander's bony limbs and bent back and figured she could handle him. And anyway, this wasn't a movie.

Still, she'd be careful not to let him get behind her.

Then she had another thought. "Can I see your back?"

"You are looking at it now, I believe."

"No, I meant the skin on your back."

He glanced at her. "You think I carry the panacean tattoo?"

"I don't know what I think right now."

"The tattoo . . . is that how you found the abbey?"

"We were looking for the Wound. Can I see?"

He turned his back to her. "Suit yourself."

Laura lifted the back of his sweater to reveal unmarred skin, as smooth and white as a baby's behind.

"Satisfied?" Leander said.

"I'm satisfied you're not with the panaceans. Can you roll up your sleeves?"

He complied: no tattoos.

But who *was* he with, if anybody? He was like a tour guide. He came on like a local codger who liked to fish and tell stories about the history of the area's private landmark, and maybe that was all he was. But Rick had said something about Leander was "off kilter" and Laura was getting a feeling too that maybe he was more than he pretended to be.

Which meant she was starting to think like Rick, and maybe that was not such a good thing.

Which was why she made him lead the way down the abbey's central hallway. Open doorways, their doors long gone, lined the passage, leading into small rooms—

cubicles really. Each had a single window that opened through the right or left flank of the building. Daylight filtering from the rooms lit the hallway, but still left it gloomy.

"Here," Leander said, stopping before the only darkened doorway. "You are strong?"

"I guess so . . . relatively."

She worked out, did the weight circuit at the local gym when she could get there. She didn't carry a lot of muscle, but what she had was toned.

"Good," he said. "I am not."

The door opened onto a narrow stone stairway. He held the lamp high with one hand and steadied himself against the wall with the other. No handrail here.

"Where are we going?"

"Down. To find your friend."

The steps ended in a small, stone-walled room.

"This used to be their larder," he said. "Cool all year-round."

"But—"

"See this tilted stone?" he said, moving to the corner. "We must lift it."

The square stone ran about two feet on each side and did not lie flush. One edge angled up an inch or so above the floor line. Leander stood the lantern next to it as he knelt.

"Help me. I cannot do it myself."

"Where is my friend?"

"If all is well, he waits below in the subcellar."

That was enough for Laura. She dropped Rick's clothes, knelt beside Leander, and hooked her fingers against the edge. Together they pulled upward. The stone began to move, scraping against the sides of its neighbors. The damn thing was heavy and Laura feared she was losing her grip when the stone suddenly began rising on its own.

"I hope you're who I'm hoping you are," said a familiar voice from below.

Laura's throat tightened at the sound.

Oh, come on. I couldn't have been *that* worried.

"Rick! You're all right!" He helped push the stone the rest of the way aside, then raised his head into the light. "I also hope you brought my clothes."

"I did." She shoved them through the opening. "What's down there?"

"I haven't had time to find out." He looked at Leander. "You could have told us about this hole in the floor."

"You did not give me a chance. And besides, you did not tell me you were hunting for Auburon."

"Yeah, well . . . let me get something dry on and I'll help you down. We could use that lantern." Less than a minute later he was back. "That's better. Who wants to be first?"

"I'll help you through," Laura told Leander.

He shook his head. "I was down there many times in my younger days. I do not—"

"Uh-uh," Rick said. "I'm not leaving you up there with that stone. No offense, and sorry to sound untrusting, but uh-uh."

Laura could have said that the stone was too heavy for the old guy to move, but maybe he'd been only feigning feeble.

The old man sighed. "Very well. There is no trust left in this world, is there."

Laura helped him slide through the opening.

"You're a light one," she heard Rick say from below.

Okay, maybe he was just as feeble as he looked.

Laura handed the lamp down, then slipped her legs into the hole and began lowering herself. Rick's hands clamped on her hips, guiding her down, and she liked the feeling.

Far too long since you've been with a man, Laura.

"He is over here," Leander said, once they were all settled.

He lifted the lamp and led the way over the broken, uneven rocky floor. The light didn't penetrate far into the gloom.

"From what you told us," Rick said, "it doesn't sound like much was left of him."

"His flesh had been cooked and his skeleton torn asunder, but all the parts were there. His friends and family gathered them up and buried them."

"Then how'd they get here?"

"Paschal's work. He found this hollow in the stone of the upwelling and decided to play a trick on the friars. When the foundation of the abbey was complete, they exhumed Auburon's remains and sneaked them in through the same passage you used. And thus the odd sequence in the poem: martyred before imprisoned." He lifted the lamp higher. "Here we are."

Laura stepped forward and looked at the skeleton. It had been laid out on a raised flat expanse of stone. She hadn't expected any flesh and found none. Nothing left but bone. Obviously the poor man's pieces had been laid out in anatomical fashion and that was how they had remained . . . except for one of his legs.

"Where's his right femur?" she said.

"His thigh bone?" Leander stepped around the head to the far side of the body. "That was moved over here."

Laura followed but stopped short, stunned. The femur stood upright in a niche in the rock. It looked just like the staff in . . .

"The tattoo!" And then she remembered what had been wrapped around the staff/femur in those tattoos. "Are . . . are there snakes here?"

She hated snakes but she would not—*not* go all girly and leap into Rick's arms.

"Snakes?" Leander said. "No. Why would there be? There is no light here. Nothing for them to eat."

"Then why is there one on the panacean tattoo?"

"You told me you used the tattoo to find this place. Have you not asked?"

"We'd have loved to," Rick said, "but pretty much everyone we met with except one was no more able to tell us than your friend Auburon here."

Laura remembered asking Ix'chel, but she hadn't had any idea.

Leander looked puzzled. "What? I do not—oh, I see. That is too bad. The work of the 536 Brotherhood, I presume?"

"You presume right."

Laura still couldn't fit all the parts of the tattoo into a coherent whole.

"Okay, I get the bone acting as a staff—that represents their martyr. And the shooting star is obvious now that we know what we know. But the snake?"

Rick said, "Didn't Stahlman tell us that snakes go with Asparagus or whatever his name, the god of healing and all that?"

"Asclepius—yes. But that's from another culture. It could be Asclepius, but I find it jarring."

"Maybe it is a symbol for something else," Leander said.

"Well, what else have we got?" Rick sounded disgusted. "We have the tattoos and we have the poem. We're missing something. We need another piece or we're stuck. We're sure as hell not going to find a dose of the panacea here in this dump."

"That is what you are after?" Leander said. "The panacea?"

"Just one dose."

"Do you believe in such a thing?"

Rick's reply faded out as Laura cudgeled her brain.
One more piece . . . Rick was right . . . one last piece
and the puzzle would be complete. She could feel it . . .
so close . . .

"I am such an idiot!" She began tugging at her waist.
"The belt . . . Chaim's belt!"

She pulled it off and held it up to the lamplight. "Does
this mean anything to you? Anything at all?"

The old man leaned closer and peered at the string of
letters. Finally he shook his head. "Nothing I see here
makes sense."

Rick took it from her. "Could it be a scytale?"

"Italy?" Laura said.

"No. Scytale." He spelled it for her. "Part of the you-
know-what training was codes, and a scytale is just
about the oldest cipher there is. Before you say anything: Yes, we did classroom stuff too. The ancient Greeks
used it. You wrap a piece of cloth around a cylinder and
write the lines of the message along the length of the
cylinder. When you uncoil the cloth from the cylinder, it
looks like gibberish."

Laura felt a tingle of excitement. "Which is exactly
what we have here."

"To decode, you wrap it back around a cylinder—but
unless you use the same-size cylinder, it's still gibberish."
He looked past her. "And I think I know just the cylinder we're supposed to use."

Laura followed his gaze . . . to the femur. Of course.
It made sense. That was why the snake was coiled
around it. As Leander had said, *Maybe it is a symbol for
something else.* And then she remembered the closing
line of the poem.

"'His guardian leg shall bear you to new life.' Look
at it standing there, like it's on guard. That has to be
what the last line means."

Rick looked at Leander and pointed to the bone. "Do you mind?"

Leander shrugged. "It is not mine. However, it does belong to local history, so please be careful."

"I will."

Rick squatted next to the bone, removed it from its niche, and began wrapping Chaim's belt around it.

"Look at the way they're lining up. Got your trusty notebook, Doc? We'll need to write this down."

Laura pulled her pad and pen from her shoulder bag and knelt beside him. Leander stepped closer and held the lamp over them.

"This L here looks like it starts things off. Copy that line."

Laura transcribed the first three letters, then . . .

Rick turned the bone and Laura copied the letters that rotated into view. Then the third line—containing a single letter—and then the fourth, fifth, and sixth.

"Okay," Rick said. "What've we got?"

$$L \quad \overline{i} \quad \overline{X}$$
$$O \quad i \quad i \quad i$$
$$A$$
$$\overline{i} \quad \overline{i}$$
$$X \quad L \quad i \quad V$$
$$O$$

"Roman numerals."

"Okay," Rick said. "L-I-X is—"

"Fifty-nine." Laura scribbled it in her notepad as she deciphered the Roman numerals. She showed the result to Rick. "This is what it says. I kept the line over the numbers, though I don't know what it means."

$$\overline{59}$$
$$03$$
$$A$$
$$\overline{2}$$
$$44$$
$$0$$

"That was an old-old way of indicating a decimal point," Leander said.

"Really?" Laura quickly reworked the figures. "I'll be damned."

$$59.03$$
$$A$$
$$2.44$$
$$O$$

Rick laughed. "They're coordinates. But it needs north, south, east, west to make sense."

"If that's the case, and if I remember my Latin correctly, *A* would stand for *aquilo* which means north, and *O* for *occasus*—west."

"Two-plus degrees west," Rick said, squinting. "That's somewhere in England."

She wrote again: *59.03 N, 2.44 W.*

A wave of exultation swept over her. "We didn't know where to go from here. Now we do. Next stop: England."

Rick held up a hand. "Wait a minute, wait a minute. This doesn't come from Auburon's time."

"What do you mean?"

"Another thing we studied was maps. I mean we were

all over maps, and the classes came with some history lessons. These coordinates are latitude and longitude. One of the things we learned was that although latitude was calculated in BC times, no one figured out accurate longitude until centuries after our friend here was dead. These coordinates are recent—I mean, relatively speaking."

"So these must be recent coordinates of . . . what?"

Rick closed his eyes. "Okay . . . two and a half degrees isn't far enough west for Ireland, so it's gotta be the U.K. Sixty degrees north is pretty far up there. So we're talking Scotland, I'll bet."

"Oh, no. Are you thinking what I'm thinking?"

He opened his eyes. "Not Loch Ness. Please don't let it be Loch Ness. That would be too, too corny. That would make this all a big joke."

"Well, isn't that consistent with your view of this whole thing—that it's all a cosmic joke?"

"The panacea is the joke. But these coordinates were laid down by humans—the people we're searching for."

Laura had an awful thought. "But what if it's all misdirection?"

"Then we're fu—screwed. And we're fools."

From above and behind them Leander said, "I'm sure this is an interesting conversation on some level, but the chill down here has prompted this old man's bladder to empty again. And since I don't want to insult the inhabitant by relieving myself in his sepulchre, I would appreciate help back to the surface."

"Of course," Laura said. She looked at Rick. "I think we've got all we're going to get out of this place. You agree?"

He nodded and began unwrapping the belt from the femur. "Our work here is done, pardon the cliché."

He placed the bone upright in its niche again as she wrapped the belt around her waist. Then they made their way back to the hole in the roof of the subcellar. Ten minutes later they were standing in the midday sun watching Leander shuffle around to the far side of the abbey.

"Oh, man," Rick said, spreading his arms to catch the rays. His hair was still wet from his swim. "Does that feel *good*."

"Scotland . . . " she said. "Leander said the All-Mother worshippers came from the north and mixed with the Visigoths. Scotland would fit."

She glanced at her watch. Not one P.M. yet. Marissa and Steven would still be asleep. Even if it were later, she knew she had little chance of finding cell service out here.

"Well, will you look at that," Rick said, pointing up.

Laura looked but didn't see anything. "What?"

"Follow the shoreline, right near the tops of the trees. We've got company."

And then she saw it: a dark object with an odd shape gliding through the air.

"What is it?"

"A drone—hover model. And you can bet it's got a camera trained on us."

"Who, 536?"

"Stahlman says they're high-tech. But this . . . " He shook his head. "They've gotta be well connected to do this."

"What do you mean?"

"Think about it. Counting the U.S., in the last week we've been in four countries on three continents and they've been in every one as well. You'd almost think they had someone in my old outfit keeping track of us."

"The C—?"

His hand shot up. "Uh-uh. Voices carry, remember? But yes, that's who I mean."

"That's comforting. I—"

"Nothing like relieving oneself against the wall of this abbey," said Leander as he returned from his rest stop.

"You've no love for the friars, then?" Laura said.

He shrugged. "They were gone from here long before I was born. I have no love for interlopers in general. They came here, killed people, and set up house as if they were entitled."

"Isn't that the story everywhere throughout history?"

"It is. And I will gladly pee on those buildings too, if given the chance."

Rick laughed. "You're okay, Leander."

The old man put his hands on his hips. "Well, I suppose you'll be leaving now. Thank you for your company. I do not get much of it."

"Thank you for all the information," Laura said.

She felt a little bad that she had harbored doubts about him. Just a harmless and lonely old man.

"Safe trip," he said, "wherever your next stop may be."

Yes, Laura thought. Wherever that may be.

She couldn't wait to get to their maps and find out where they were headed.

6

Sent by Laura Fanning 13:52 GMT/UTC/DST + 2:00

STILL getting bounced from the phone. Did you call ATT? Texting is fine in a pinch but I'd prefer to hear Marissa's voice. The good news on this end is that I think I'm entering the last phase of the journey. Tell Marissa I rode on a helicopter today and visited a crater where a comet hit over a thousand years ago. It's now a lake. Tonight we head out to Scotland and to-

morrow we visit one of the Orkney Islands. Have Natasha help Marissa look them up on the map later. Thanks again for taking care of her, Steven. As usual, give Marissa all my love.

Received by Steven Gaines 14:02 GMT/UTC/DST – 4:00

STILL getting bounced from the phone. Did you call ATT? I need to TALK about this. I DON'T BELIEVE WHAT'S HAPPENING! I reached the airport early and was on line to board when the flight was cancelled. Can you believe this? There's some huge front pushing through and it's going to be storming here all day! I'm trapped and I want to scream! Going to try to get a night flight but everybody else in the airport is trying the same thing. I'll let you know what happens. Meanwhile get back to me ASAP on Marissa's condition. I'm so frustrated I don't know whether to cry or kill someone.

Sent by Steven Gaines 14:07 GMT/UTC/DST – 4:00

This is unf***ing believable. Oh look my phone is censoring me. Just great. Marissa not good. The pneumonia's getting worse. She seems a little confused at times. I know u want to be here more than anything. I know theyre not telling me everything or maybe softpedalling it all. Theyll be straight with you cause ur a doc too. I get the feeling the cmv is out of control. We need u here. I think hearing ur voice will do her a world of good. Please find a way home asap. Please.

Received by Laura Fanning 14:10 GMT/UTC/DST + 2:00

The last phase? Thats kinda bittersweet. Marissa and i are having a great time. I think we needed a little more bonding and this has been just the ticket. I guess what im saying is, do whatever u have to do over there and don't worry about us. She misses you but shes fine. Orkney islands? Can you bring me back one of their single malts? I hear theyre excellent. Marissa wants to know if ur going to loch ness to see Nessie.

Sent by Laura Fanning 14:13 GMT/UTC/DST + 2:00

No time for Loch Ness, I'm afraid. Glad you two are getting on so well. Can't wait to get home. See you soon.

Received by Steven Gaines 14:15 GMT/UTC/DST − 4:00

No flights until tomorrow and I'm on standby!!! Can you believe this? I'm sitting in the airport crying like a baby. I can't handle this anymore. I think I'm going insane.

7

"Fanning and company have booked a flight to Glasgow," Bradsher said. "They're heading for the Orkney Islands."

"The Orkneys? Why the Orkneys?" Nelson held up a hand. "Rhetorical. I know you haven't the faintest. But if they're going, then so are we."

Bradsher said, "I had a feeling you'd say that. Orly is closer than de Gaulle and I believe British Airways flies out of there. I'll check."

"Wherever she goes I want to be right behind her. So make this our last commercial flight. I want military from here on in."

"Yessir. In that case, we'd be better flying into Heathrow and driving up to Mildenhall."

Mildenhall . . . Mildenhall . . . then it came to him: The base in Sussex shared by the U.S. Air Force and the RAF.

"Good thought. Have one of the Brothers in the U.K. get up to Glasgow and follow their every move. I want to be on top of them when they reach the Orkneys, and I want heavy firepower along. Who knows what we'll run into?"

"I'll get right on it."

"One more thing: Any word on who that old man might be?"

Bradsher shook his head. "With that floppy hat we had no clear shot at his face, so recognition software is off the table."

"Not important now. Book us to Heathrow."

Nelson was sure the trip to the Abbey had something to do with Brody's belt. Something had been written on it. But what? Did all the panaceans wear such a belt? The irony was not lost on him: Had the Leviticus Sanction not involved burning, they might have had one of those belts for themselves all this time.

Well, no matter now. The Lord had compensated for the Brotherhood's error and shown Dr. Fanning something that sent her scurrying off to Scotland.

A bolt of pain shot through Nelson's head as Bradsher held up his smartphone.

"Message from Israel, sir. Look who's coming to England later today."

Nelson's vision had blurred with the pain but he didn't want to let on that he couldn't read the message.

"Yes. I see."

"He'll be handy to have along if we confront the panaceans tomorrow. Shall I invite him?"

Israel . . . Nelson had a pretty good idea who he was talking about.

"Yes, of course. He'll make things interesting."

Bradsher left and Nelson was finally alone.

. . . if we confront the panaceans tomorrow . . .

If Nelson's instincts were right, the Lord had guided Fanning to the location of the panaceans' lair and she was headed there. So that might well happen.

The big question: Would they have any of the panacea available? And if they did, should Nelson partake? He had been told all his life that the panacea was anathema. But Nelson had asked for a sign from God. If he found a dose, would that be the sign? He was convinced so, for partaking would allow him to continue his service to the Lord.

The moral dilemma had been growing in his heart since watching Fanning wander the grounds of the Abbey—sacred ground that had put her close to the Lord. Had He inspired her there?

He shook off the doubts and questions. The option might never present itself, rendering all this angst wasted.

Nelson had to let Fanning lead him to the panaceans' lair, then step in and destroy their means of production . . . and send any of the pagans he might find to their ultimate punishment. And Hayden with them. That man certainly could not be allowed to continue as an ongoing liability.

As for the doctor herself . . . if things went as he hoped, tomorrow would be her last day on Earth.

CLOTILDE

1

"Another middle of nowhere," Rick said as their boat plowed through the swells near the western border of the Orkney Islands. "What did you call it last night?"

Laura clung to a chromed railing in the cockpit. "The Orkney Triangle."

Back at the abbey, Rick's estimate off the top of his head of the location of the coordinates on the belt had been on the money as far as being in Scotland, but he'd underestimated how far north they'd have to go. It turned out that 59° 3' north and 2° 44' west was situated in a seemingly empty expanse of sea in the center of a triangle formed by Stronsay, Shapinsay, and Auskerry Islands—practically in the North Sea.

"The good news is," he said, "I've never heard of ships disappearing here."

They'd chartered a flight from Glasgow to Kirkwall yesterday and spent the night at the Ayre Hotel. First thing this morning, Rick had headed for the docks and rented a twenty-eight-foot cabin cruiser, ostensibly for a leisurely cruise of the channels between the islands. He'd had to demonstrate his prowess at the helm before they'd let him take her out, and he passed with flying colors. His vaunted SEAL training, she guessed.

She said, "The bad news is, there's nothing here. Why does every destination have to be in such remote locations? Interior Quintana Roo, the Negev, the Pyrenees, and now somewhere among the Orkneys."

Laura pulled her Windbreaker tighter around her. She'd worn it to fend off the chill wind. The sky was clear and she wouldn't have needed it onshore, but out here on the water was a different story.

Her fatigue magnified the chill. Too many time zones, too little sleep.

Rick said, "Well, Paris and Meudon weren't exactly wildernesses."

"They weren't exactly destinations either. More like stops along the way."

They followed the Kirkwall-Lerwick ferry out of Kirkwall harbor and east through the channel south of Shapinsay Island. Soon they were losing sight of land behind with nothing ahead but the ferry and open water.

"Approaching the two-degree, four-minute mark," Rick said, eyeing his GPS. "Time to turn north."

Unease nibbled at her. No land ahead, none visible behind, and only empty sea to the north. They were leaving the comfortable wake of the ferry and striking out on their own.

"Are we crazy?" she said.

"Could be." He gave the wheel a slow turn to the left—okay, port. "But the coordinates sit north of here. We either head there or head back. Your call."

She stamped her foot. "Why do you always *do* that?"

"Do what?" He looked amused.

"Put the decision on me."

"First off, just to see you stamp your foot. Second, because this is your show. I'm here to help you get it done and see that no one gets in your way. I'm glad to point out options when I see them, but in the end the choice has got to be yours."

"I'd feel a lot different if there was something on the map, but there's nothing. *Nothing.*"

He nodded. "Well, not completely nothing. We saw white on one of the photos. That could have been foam from shallows or something under the surface."

"Like what? You're thinking we reach those coordinates and the *Nautilus* surfaces and Captain Nemo welcomes us aboard?"

"Or maybe he works for 536 and this was all a ruse to get us out on the water where he can torpedo us."

"How comforting. Just when I was starting to enjoy your company."

"Comfort is my middle name. Hey, wait—*starting* to enjoy my company?"

"Drive."

What if she'd been wrong about the coordinates? What if they got there and found nothing? That was what frightened her. Because she was out of options. Out of clues. Out of trail markers and direction arrows. She'd have to go back to the States and pray she ran into another panacean—a live one—and hope he was in a talkative mood.

She watched the ferry cruise away toward the Shetland Islands, way up in the North Sea.

"How far from here do you think?"

He shrugged. "A league or two, I'd say."

"You're expecting me to ask how far a league is, aren't you?"

He grinned. "Who, me?"

It just so happened she knew. Back in Mesoamerica a league was the distance a man could walk in an hour, but here at sea: three nautical miles—the average distance to the horizon when viewed at sea level. She knew because she'd had to look it up for Marissa when they'd watched *20,000 Leagues Under the Sea*.

"So if it's not visible now, it should be soon."

He nodded with approval, although she sensed it might be the grudging sort. "You got it. The sea-level haze out here will interfere a bit. I saw a pair of field glasses in the galley. Why don't—?"

"Good idea."

She hurried the three steps down to the cabin. It had a small kitchen and two very uncomfortable looking bunks. The binocs hung on a hook. She grabbed them and bounded back up to the deck.

She spotted a bulge on the horizon almost immediately. She blinked. Could it be?

"Got something," she said.

"Where?"

"One o'clock."

"Changing course thirty degrees to starboard, Captain," Rick called out. He leaned forward, squinting over the windshield. "Thar she blows!"

"Don't say that."

"Just kidding."

"No, I mean, what if it really is just a whale?"

"Helluva big whale if it is, and why the sudden pessimism?"

She shrugged. "Not pessimism. It's just that we saw nothing but water on the maps and the satellite photos. We found the lake when we had only a vague idea where it was. This time we've got the actual coordinates—or at least I think we do—and nothing's there."

"No," Rick said, pointing. "Something's definitely there."

She had to agree. She didn't need the field glasses now to see the growing mound on the horizon. No, not a mound, more like a plateau—a very low plateau. And not a perfect plateau, either. Something bulged at its center.

"Could there be a house or a cabin on it?"

Rick nodded. "We've found *something*. Don't know if it's what we're looking for, or why it doesn't show up from orbit, but it's something."

Laura fought the excitement bubbling inside. She couldn't let her hopes get too high. But the fact that this place had somehow hidden itself from the satellites had to mean something.

As they neared she saw rocky cliff walls maybe twenty feet high. And all along the top of that wall . . . something flapping in the breeze.

"What is that?" Rick said. "Laundry?"

She looked at him. "Tell me you're kidding."

"Of course I am. But what is it?"

"Well, if we can find a way up those cliffs, we can figure it out."

"Gotta be a way." He throttled down to an idle and they coasted to within a hundred feet of the sheer walls. "Let's take a tour."

He spun the wheel to starboard and they began to cruise the perimeter of the oblong hunk of rock.

"It's tiny," Laura said. "Can't be more than two hundred feet long."

"And half that wide. I—" He pointed. "Hey, what's that?"

She saw what he meant: a vertical gap in the rocks at the north end. As they floated closer she saw a narrow cove penetrating the wall at an acute angle to the shoreline.

"It's like a micro fjord," she said. "And look—there's a boat in there."

Rick piloted their craft into the rocky alleyway. A similar cabin cruiser, maybe a few feet shorter but much more weathered and worse for wear, rocked on its moorings at a tiny dock snug against the end of the little fjord. Beyond that sat a small shed and a rickety staircase running up the wall.

"Problem solved," Rick said as he cut the engine.

But Laura became aware of another engine as the sound of theirs stopped.

"Is that other boat running?" she said.

Rick shook his head. "No. It seems to becoming from that little shed there." He vaulted onto the bow and fended off the nearest piling. He tied the bow line then jumped onto the worn, makeshift dock. "Toss me the stern line," he said.

Laura did just that, and once they were moored, she joined him on the dock where she followed him to the shed. He pulled open the door to reveal a running generator hooked up to a fifty-five-gallon drum of diesel fuel.

"Look," Laura said, pointing to the gray pipe she saw running up the wall and diving into the rock near the top. "Somebody up there needs electricity."

He nodded to the stairway that zigged, then zagged to the top. "And there's our way up to join them. I'll go first."

"Why you?" Not that she really cared, just . . . why?

"Because, number one: Going first is my job. And number two: Because if it will hold me, it'll hold you."

She pointed to the weathered launch. "It obviously held whoever arrived in that."

"This is not up for discussion."

She let it go. He had his macho on, and arguing with him was only going to delay things.

He stepped on the first step and jiggled the railing. The whole stairway vibrated.

"Wish me luck," he said and started up, moving quickly and smoothly. It took him only a few seconds to reach the top. "It's got lots of rot but it's sturdier than it looks. Come on up. You've got to see this to believe it."

Laura hurried up with no problem—all that blather for nothing—but froze when she reached the top.

"What the . . . ?"

The first thing Laura thought of was a Christo art project. Back in 2004 she'd trained into Manhattan to see his "Gates" installation in Central Park. This reminded her of that, except the rectangles of fabric were blue-gray instead of orange and tethered at all four corners eight to ten feet above the ground. She hadn't been at all impressed by Christo's thing—she couldn't bring herself to call it art—but this was mind blowing.

"It . . . it looks like it covers the whole island."

"I'm sure it does," Rick said. "And I think that's why it doesn't show up on Google Earth. All this fluttering fabric looks like water from space. Not gonna fool high-res spy cams, and it can't hide the surf when the seas get rough—that explains the foam we saw on one of those photos—but it does make it hard to find."

Beneath the fabric lay a carpet of green. But not grass . . .

Laura knelt and examined the plants. "These are like the one Stahlman showed me . . . the ones the panaceans grow."

"I thought they looked familiar. I guess we've found the place we're after . . . or at least were still on the right road."

She rose and looked around. "Which way do we go?"

"Well, since we end up in the drink if we head north, let's try south."

She gathered that was his way of saying *Dumb question* without using those exact words.

"That boat didn't drive itself here," he added. "Gotta be some sort of dwelling."

"Then why can't we see it? This island can't cover more than an acre."

"Less, I'll bet. All we can do is look. I suggest we follow this narrow little strip of earth where the plants don't grow." His voice took on a pedantic tone. "Now why wouldn't they grow there? Hmmm . . . could it be that someone travels that path to and from the dock? What do you think?"

"I think you're getting on my nerves. Let's go."

He hesitated, patting the hunting knife on his belt. "Wish I had something better than this."

"If this is the home of the panaceans—or one of them—I don't think we have to worry. So far we haven't seen any violence from them, defensive or otherwise."

"It's not the panaceans I'm worried about."

"I don't see that you or I can do anything about that now. We're here. Let's go."

He nodded. "Let's."

The narrow path led them around a small hillock and stopped at a door.

"It's a freakin' hobbit house," Rick said.

She had to agree: An arched stone wall with a door and two windows was set into the hillock.

"No wonder we couldn't see it," she said. "Its back end is all plants."

The door opened and a woman stepped out. She looked maybe seventy with long silver hair and bright blue eyes. She wore a monkish robe tied at the waist.

"Good morning," she said, smiling. "I was expecting you sooner."

Laura had noticed Rick's hand darting toward his knife, but it dropped to his side as they both stared, dumbfounded.

Laura found her voice first. "Wh-what?"

"What took you so long?" she said.

Something familiar about her. The hair, those eyes . . .

"You wouldn't happen to have an older brother, would you?"

She hunched her back and stroked an imaginary beard. "You mean Leander?" she said in a perfect imitation of his creaky voice.

Laura laughed. "Yes! That's him!"

"No," she said, shaking her head, "I have no siblings of either sex."

"Then . . . ?" Suddenly Laura got it. "That was *you*?"

She nodded. "Yes . . . me with a beard. I am Clotilde."

"I knew something was off about you," Rick said. "But what were you doing around the side of the abbey if you weren't peeing against the wall?"

She smiled. "Giving you time to decode the poem. You needed to do it on your own."

"You knew we were coming to the Wound," Laura said. "You were waiting for us. How?"

"We've been following you. I disguised myself because I knew we would be watched." She looked around. "Just as we might be right now. Come in, come in."

As expected, with no windows except the two in front, the interior was dark, but an array of oil lamps lit the long front room. Wooden planks for walls, floor, and the bowed ceiling, with curved beams arching overhead like ribs.

Rick had to stoop to keep from getting clocked by those beams.

"Give me a ring and call me Bilbo," he said, looking around. "Oil lamps? What's the generator for then?"

"I have other uses for its current."

"With all those plants out there," Laura said, taking it all in, "I have to assume this is Panacea Central. I expected something a little more elaborate."

"We're not centralized about anything," Clotilde said. "This is just one of our farms."

"That's probably smart," Laura said. "But why the Orkneys?"

"This is home. The original Orkadians were worshippers of the All-Mother. We lived and thrived here five thousand years ago. We raised the stones of Stenness for Her, and dedicated the Ness and the Ring of Brognar to Her. But the climate changed, became too cold for farming, and we had to move south. But now it's warming again and here we are."

"So are we," Laura said. "And I guess you know why."

Clotilde nodded. "Yes. The panacea, as you call it."

"What do you call it?"

"*Ikhar*. It's from the old tongue."

The term Ix'chel had used.

"Does it really work?"

"You examined the remains of the boy who had the arthritis . . . "

"You know?"

"I told you we've been watching. When one of our *sylyk* is murdered, we take notice. When two . . . "

"This panacea," Laura shook her head. "I . . . I can't grasp it."

"From outsi-ide," Rick singsonged in a low voice.

Laura ignored him. "Is it real? Tell me—please."

"The *ikhar* is real."

"But how does it work?"

Clotilde shook her head. "We do not know. We know only that it does."

"*What* does it do?"

"It rights what's wrong."

"That doesn't make sense."

It made sense to Rick, she knew, because he had an answer. But she could not accept that answer any more than she could wrap her mind around a cure-all.

"Does it have to make sense?" Clotilde said.

Yes, dammit!

"But that means if you had an endless supply you could live forever."

The old woman shook her head. "It cures what is wrong at the moment. It resets your health to maximum."

Sounds like a video game, she thought.

"But," Clotilde was saying, "it would not prevent you from catching, say, malaria from a mosquito bite the very next day. Yes, you might live longer because you are no longer suffering from a particular malady, but aging is not a malady. It is a natural process."

"It doesn't lengthen telomeres, then?"

"I have no idea what you just said. I do know that your cells get tired and they stop functioning. The All-Mother sets a limit for you at conception. You cannot undo what the Goddess has planned."

Laura realized this pagan was talking about genetic limitations on lifespan, something science was only beginning to understand, but which Clotilde was attributing to her deity.

She tried a new tack.

"Okay. Just say I accept all that. Why hide it from the world then?"

"Because that is the way the All-Mother wishes it to be."

That's not an answer! Laura wanted to shout, but bit it back. Not an answer to her, who didn't believe in this All-Mother, but apparently all Clotilde needed to know.

"She doesn't want you to share it with the world?"

"We do share it."

"Barely. Only on a strictly limited basis."

"Because that is the way—"

"—the All-Mother wants it. I get it."

"I'm with the All-Mother," Rick said.

Laura could only glare at him.

"I'm serious," he went on. "Making it freely available to the world would be aiding and abetting."

Now was Clotilde's turn to look puzzled. "Aiding and abetting whom . . . or what?"

"Vast, cool and unsympathetic intelligences," Laura said. She didn't add *as imaginary as your All-Mother*, though she wanted to. "But let's not get sidetracked here. I'm requesting a single dose to take back to the States."

"To analyze it?"

"No, to give to a very sick man."

"I do not think the All-Mother will object, but first we must deal with the members of 536 who are about to arrive."

Dimly through the earthen roof and the stone front wall, she heard the rhythmic thrum of a helicopter.

Laura's heart sank. "We led them here."

"Well, we knew they were following us." Rick didn't seem surprised. "I was hoping we could get on and off before they caught up."

"But the ocean was empty and the sky is all clouds. I thought—"

Rick poked a thumb skyward. "Eyes in the sky. You can't hide these days." He turned to Clotilde. "Any idea how many?"

"Three from 536," she said, "plus the pilot."

"How do you know this?"

"We are more than you would think. We have eyes on them. Please do not resist. They are heavily armed and I do not wish any bloodshed."

"There *will* be bloodshed," Rick said. "These guys leave dead bodies everywhere they go."

Clotilde held out her hand. "Give me your knife, please."

"I don't think so."

"Having it will only tempt you to use it. They will have guns and will outnumber you. You will die." She fluttered her fingers. "Please."

After a moment's hesitation, he pulled it from its sheath, gripped it by the blade, and passed it to her handle first.

"I hope I don't regret this."

"You must trust me to handle them," she said, slipping the knife into a drawer. "The All-Mother has foreseen this. She has been guiding me and will continue to do so. Do what they tell you to do and all will be well. The All-Mother will see to it."

Oh, well, Laura thought, that makes me feel *so* much better.

Outside, the *thrum-thrum-thrum* grew louder.

2

The pilot's voice crackled in Nelson's headphones. Even with the volume turned up to maximum, he could barely hear him over the noise of the helicopter's engine and rotors.

"I can't land!"

Nelson could see why. All that camouflage fabric and the poles that supported it would foul the rotors if they tried to put down. The fabric might fool the commercial satellites but it hadn't fooled the Company's or NSA's recon birds. Bradsher had been able to follow the course of Hayden's rental launch from hundreds of miles up—even through the fog.

"You'll have to use the winch," the pilot added.

The winch . . . this Huey was primarily used for rescue, so it had a heavy-duty winch installed on the right side of the cabin. Riding that down was not quite the last thing Nelson wanted to do, but very nearly. His head felt ready to explode and the insane noise of the copter only made things worse.

But he said, "Fine. Let's just get on with it."

"I'll go first," Bradsher said.

In less than two minutes he had the cabin door slid open, the winch arm extended, and himself in the harness. He swung out over the AGM-114 attached just below the hatch and made the short, twenty-foot descent look easy. He unslung his HK MP-5 and held it at ready as the winch rolled back up.

"This doesn't change anything," Nelson told the pilot. "Follow the plan we outlined."

He nodded and gave a thumbs up. "Got it."

Nelson descended next. Chayat, also armed with an MP-5, followed. As soon as the Israeli undid the harness, the copter roared away. It would hover off the south end of the island and await instructions.

Nelson praised the Lord for the relative peace and quiet as he slipped off his headset and stowed it in a pocket.

"Infrared scanning indicated some sort of habitat that way," he said, pointing.

"I believe I see it already," Chayat said.

Indeed . . . straight ahead an older woman stood in a doorway set in a stone wall, set itself in an earthen mound. She was beckoning to them.

"Come! I've been expecting you."

"Be very careful," Nelson said as he led the way forward. "Be ready to shoot on an instant's notice. We don't know how many are in there."

The infrared had detected a generalized heat signature but, because of the insulation supplied by the thick layer of dirt over the structure, individual signatures were not appreciated.

Nelson stopped before the woman. He didn't bother showing his credentials. What for? They carried no weight here.

"How many people besides you are present?"

"Two others. I believe you are familiar with them both, Brother Fife."

The use of his name jolted him but he refused to acknowledge it.

He pointed to the open doorway behind her. "Lead on."

He stood aside and let Bradsher and Chayat follow her with their assault weapons ready, then stepped in behind them.

Dr. Fanning and Hayden stood a dozen feet back from the door, both sets of hands in plain sight.

"Fife?" Hayden said. "Jesus Christ! You're behind this?"

Nelson pointed to him. "Pat him down and cuff him. Take no chances with him."

The only reason Nelson did not have Bradsher and Chayat drag Hayden outside and terminate him immediately was because that would inject panic and fear and anger into whatever followed. Much easier to have a semi-civil conversation-interrogation, learn what he could, then start adding to the body count.

Wisely, Hayden offered no resistance. Chayat kept the muzzle of his weapon pressed under the ex-agent's chin while Bradsher searched him and then cuffed his hands behind his back.

"Look!" Bradsher said, his expression fierce as he held up a handful of zip ties. "These are what he used on Miguel." He leaned into Hayden's face. "I can't wait till I have a little one-on-one time with you."

"Gee, that's just what your mother said the last time I saw her."

Bradsher reddened and punched him in the face, rocking his head back.

Hayden shook it off and said, "Your mother punches harder than that."

Bradsher cocked a fist, but before he could throw another punch, Nelson said, "Step away from him. Now."

Bradsher reluctantly complied.

Nelson couldn't lecture Bradsher now, but couldn't he see that Hayden's childish remarks had succeeded in getting him riled? That had been the whole purpose: Emotionally riled people make mistakes.

"I know what you were doing," Nelson said, stepping before Hayden and unbuttoning his own shirt. "If you think you can turn the tables on me, think again. I am always one step ahead of you."

"Like when you framed me for selling intel to the Israelis?"

How did he figure that? Nelson thought. No matter.

"*Someone* sold it. I still don't know who, but no matter. Someone needed to be blamed. The Company was better off without you so . . . " He shrugged.

Hayden mimicked his shrug. "I was ready to get out anyway. The accusations were the convincer. It all worked out, so no hard feelings."

No hard feelings . . . His eyes said otherwise.

Nelson continued unbuttoning his shirt.

"What is this?" Hayden said. "A strip-tease?"

"No. I want to show you something." He pulled it open to reveal the device taped to his chest. "This is a monitor-transmitter. It monitors my heartbeat. If that heartbeat should stop, or if this should be removed from me, a signal will be transmitted to the helicopter hovering outside, causing two AGM-114s to fire at my last known location."

"Hellfire missiles?" he said. "Isn't that overkill? I mean, just a little?"

He began rebuttoning his shirt. "Mutually assured destruction. I know you were nearly suicidal when you returned from Dusseldorf, but I also know your sense of duty. You wouldn't want anything to happen to Doctor Fanning on your watch, would you?"

Hayden shook his head and lowered his voice nearly to a whisper. "Hardly a deterrent when it's clear that you and your two goons will be the only ones leaving this island alive."

Was the man a mind reader? No, the options were narrow and obvious.

"Not so," Nelson said. "The jury is still out on the good doctor."

That ought to keep him from trying anything stupid.

Hayden raised his voice again. "You were always a son of a bitch, Fife. But I didn't know you were crazy too. You're really a member of 536?"

"Most of my life."

"And this Israeli too?"

Nelson turned to see Dr. Fanning staring at Chayat. She said, "Weren't you . . . ?"

Chayat smiled and bowed. "Noam Chayat, at your service."

"But you said you were with . . . what was it?"

"Shin Bet. I am. But my first loyalty is to the Brotherhood."

She shook her head, obviously baffled. "But . . . but you're an Israeli and 536 is Christian."

"Bereshit, the first book of our Torah, is Genesis in your Old Testament. You learned of mankind's banishment from the Garden from us."

"Then it was you who sent those raiders after us."

He laughed. "Hardly. Your naïveté is so charming, Doctor Fanning."

She looked puzzled. "I don't get it. You're telling me those dead men did *not* have '536' branded on their arms?"

"Of course not."

"Why would you lie about that? For what purpose?"

"To keep you off balance."

"Enough chatter," Nelson said. "The Lord singled out Doctor Fanning to be our Pillar of Fire, leading us to our goal." He turned to the woman. "To a priestess of the cult."

"We don't use that term. We prefer a more traditional designation: *urschell*."

"I don't care what you call yourself. I am more interested in where you are in the hierarchy of your cult."

"I suppose I am at the top."

The high priestess herself. This was getting better and better.

"Do I have to tell you why we are here?"

"Call me Clotilde," she said with a sweet smile.

She did not seem the least bit nervous or apprehensive. In fact, she seemed completely composed and relaxed, as if welcoming friends for coffee and cake. That bothered Nelson.

"I call you pagan and witch, and I've come to put a stop to your sacrilege."

"Gimme a break," Hayden said. "Did we just walk onto the set of a Syfy Channel film?"

Clotilde shook her head. "There are too many of us. You cannot stop us. You may stop me. But someone else will take my place. We shall go on."

We'll see about that, Nelson thought.

An obvious candidate for the Leviticus Sanction, she would not be leaving the island either.

"I've also come for the secret of your potion."

"You mean that after all the *sylyk* you've killed, you still don't know the secret?"

Was she toying with him?

"No, we don't. Especially since your members now seem to be able to stop their own hearts."

Dr. Fanning said, "I still find that hard to believe."

Clotilde nodded. "The Brotherhood would subject our *sylyk* to the tortures of the damned. If they get caught they know they are going to die horribly, so they have the option of avoiding the pain and ending it right there."

Nelson raised a hand. "Never mind that. Is sudden death what we can expect from you as well?"

"Perhaps. But I am not a *sylyk* and I have no problem telling you the secret. I am one of the few who knows it."

"What do you mean?"

"The *sylyk* couldn't tell you the secret, no matter what you did to them, because they were never told." Clotilde shook her head sadly. "Centuries of torture . . . all that pain inflicted on people who could not divulge a secret they did not know."

She's lying, he thought. She must be.

"But they make the potion."

"They simply follow instructions."

"We have followed those same instructions—to no avail."

She smiled. "So . . . you have tried to make the cure. I thought it was an affront to God, an act punishable by death."

"Do not question my commitment, woman. It has merely been a matter of 'know thine enemy.' The more we know about your infernal potion, the more efficient we can be in combating it."

"If you say so."

Nelson waited for her to go on, but she merely stared at him.

"Well?" he said finally. "What have we been missing?"

"You have killed the *sylyk* and burned their bodies, you have uprooted their plants and cultivated them in your own plots, you have followed the instructions for boiling and filtering, just as they described them to you between their screams, but the result was no more effective than a sip of water."

Nelson's pounding headache, blurred vision, and queasy stomach had drained his meager reserve of patience.

"Tell me something I *don't* know."

"The answer has been written on the back of every *sylyk*."

"The tattoo?" Dr. Fanning said.

Clotilde turned to her. "You know the meaning of the shooting star and the staff. What is left?"

"The snake?"

The old woman shook her head. "It is not a snake."

Fanning said, "I thought it was meant to represent the message on the belt."

Nelson leaned closer. "I know about the belt, but what message?"

"It doesn't matter now," Clotilde told him, somewhat dismissively, he thought. She turned back to Dr. Fanning. "Do you know the origin of the staff of Asclepius?"

"He was the Greek god of healing. He's always pictured with a snake coiled around his staff. And one of his daughters was . . . " Nelson saw her glance his way. "Panacea."

Clotilde nodded. "What most people don't know was that the creature wrapped around the staff was originally a worm."

"I'm sure this would make a fascinating lecture sometime," Nelson said, "but what does it have to do with—?"

"It has everything to do with the 'infernal potion,' as you call it. Humans in ancient times were plagued by parasites, and worms were the most common—in the gut and under the skin. Ancient doctors couldn't do much for intestinal round worms and tapeworms, but they had a way of ridding people of the ubiquitous *Dracunculus*— the guinea worm."

Dr. Fanning was nodding. "It's confined to Africa pretty much. I've never seen a case in the flesh, but I've seen pictures."

"Yes, confined to Sudan and Chad and thereabouts now, but in ancient times they were a plague all around the Mediterranean. You could see them moving under the skin."

Nelson swallowed bile. His already queasy stomach threatened to heave. "What does this—?"

Clotilde continued as if he hadn't spoken. "Doctors of those times would make a slit in the skin ahead of the worm's path and when its head appeared, they would grab it and remove it from its victim by slowly winding its body around a stick. It could take a while because some worms run as long as a man's arm."

"You're kidding, right?" Bradsher said, looking a little green.

"Not a bit. Doctors used to advertise their services by painting a stick wrapped with a worm outside their homes. Now, as to what all this has to do with the *ikhar* . . . follow me."

"Follow you where?" Nelson said.

"Downstairs . . . to the farm."

As she stepped to the rear of the room and opened a door, Nelson raised a hand. He had to maintain control of the situation.

"Wait. Stop right there. You don't go anywhere—you don't even move until I tell you to."

Clotilde folded her arms across her chest and stared at him. "Whatever you say, Brother Fife."

Nelson stepped to the doorway and looked down the stone steps. A warm glow filtered up from the space below. The moist air rising along the stairs was redolent of earth and a vague rot.

He motioned to Bradsher. "Go see." He pointed to Chayat, then to Hayden. "Do not take your eyes off him. Do not hesitate to shoot him dead."

A few seconds after Bradsher had descended the steps he called back up.

"It's empty. Nothing here but a dirt floor and lots of lights."

Nelson looked at Clotilde. "Doesn't sound like much of a farm."

"Ask your man if he notices anything unusual about the soil."

"I heard that," Bradsher said from below. "Yeah . . . it's full of holes."

Nelson got it then. "A worm farm?"

She bowed. "Exactly. The key to the 'secret ingredient' you've been seeking." She cocked her head toward the doorway. "Shall we?"

Nelson could think of nothing he wanted more right now, but he couldn't allow any sloppiness. He pointed to Chayat again.

"Take him down first."

That would put Hayden downstairs with the two armed men. No way could he be allowed to stay up here with a single guard.

After they had passed and were well on their way down, he made a flourish to Clotilde and Dr. Fanning. "Ladies first."

At the bottom of the stairs he found an expanse of moist earth lit by lamps suspended from the ceiling timbers.

"All this," he said, amazed, "for worms?"

"They are the key, Brother Fife. I don't know if the comet brought the seeds of the plant with it, or if something within it caused a change in the plants around its impact site, but I do know that these earthworms were changed and are crucial."

He stared at the expanse of earth and realized the Lord had been with him when he'd requisitioned the AGM-114s. Pickens had been dubious at first, but once Nelson convinced him that the U.S. had a chance to lay exclusive claim to the panacea, and that the missiles would be used only as a last resort to protect that exclusivity, the assistant director pulled every string necessary to get them approved.

The Hellfire missiles were two more things that would not leave this island.

"Do you see that bag on the table to your left?" Clotilde said. "Would you kindly hand it to me?"

Nelson checked inside and saw a powdery substance. "What's this?"

"Bread crumbs. Very fine bread crumbs. May I?"

He dug his hand inside to make sure nothing was hidden there, then handed it to her. She withdrew a handful and scattered the crumbs over the soil, like she was spreading seed. She replaced the bag on the shelf.

"Watch."

So saying, she went to the near left corner where a thick block of wood had been partially buried in the soil. She lifted a large wooden mallet with both hands and slammed it down on the top of the block. The sound echoed through the underground chamber. Nelson felt it vibrate through his shoes.

"What are you doing?"

"Wait," she said, and struck the block twice more. "Now . . . watch."

For a moment, nothing happened, then glistening pink tendrils began to poke up from the mossy surface and wriggle free of the dirt, more and more appearing and slithering around until the earthen patch was alive with them.

Somewhere to his left he heard Bradsher say, "Gross."

Nelson could not disagree.

"Trained earthworms," he said. "How quaint."

"They have mouths but no teeth. They eat almost anything but mostly feed on dirt and the organic matter, living and dead, within it. The tiny bread crumbs are a treat. They devour some, roll around in the rest and that way take them back into their tunnels. Worms are crucial to plant growth. Did you know that in the average acre of land, sixteen thousand pounds of soil pass through the guts of its earthworm population?"

Nelson felt his thin patience fraying to the breaking point.

"Is this some sort of delaying tactic?"

"You asked for an answer. I am giving it to you."

"But we know they are not part of the process since your instructions to your minions are to remove all worms before boiling."

The old woman offered a tolerant smile. "I will get to that, if I may continue. All that soil passing through the guts of the earthworms is left behind in the form of nutrient-rich castings. It is the castings of these particular worms, excreted after they've fed on the plants from around the crater, that are the source of what you call the panacea."

"Worm shit?" he heard Hayden say through a laugh. "You gotta be kidding me! The cure-all is worm shit?"

"You're lying," Nelson said. He waved to the worms. "This is all an elaborate misdirection."

"No, Brother Fife. The misdirection is telling the *sylyk* to remove all insects and worms and grubs. Instructions for making the elixir include boiling some of the dirt in the root ball, but by telling them to discard the worms, we make them appear worthless, when in reality it is their casts in the soil that yield the panacea. That is why anyone who steals the plants will be frustrated."

Mute with shock, Nelson could only stare at the thinning mass of worms as they slithered back into their tunnels. Mutated earthworms . . . that was the key? The reason all the acres of those foul plants the Brotherhood had planted over the centuries yielded nothing?

"So . . . " he said, finding his voice, "your minions never knew?"

Clotilde shook her head. "They have no need to know. We, the *urschell,* send them packets of seeds from various post offices around the continent—never the same twice. Unknown to the *sylyk,* tiny cocoons of the mutated worms are included along with the seeds. When the seeds are planted, so are the cocoons, which hatch as the seeds germinate. We tell them they must uproot the plants before they drop their seeds. Once they've used up one crop, they must wait for a new packet to start another."

How very clever, Nelson thought with grudging admiration. *They hold the reins on supply, and eliminate demand by keeping the panacea's very existence secret. That is how they've maintained control for fifteen centuries.*

The situation was perfect for the Lord's purposes. People must never learn of the panacea's existence. If they knew, they would clamor for it, riot for it, and flock to the Serpent for it.

And that, he supposed, was reason enough to terminate Dr. Fanning. Avenging Uncle Jim would be simply a bonus. But he would let her know about her victim before she died.

"And here is the result," the woman said, stepping over to a shelf and lifting a flask of cloudy fluid. She held it up and looked at Nelson. "What so many have died for. Their blood is on your hands."

She unstoppered the flask, took a shot glass from that same shelf, and began to pour the fluid into it.

"What do you think you're doing?" Nelson said, stepping closer.

She tossed back the liquid. "I know I will be going to the All-Mother very soon. I wish to arrive in good health." She looked over at Fanning and Hayden. "Perhaps I can offer some to your prisoners?"

"Absolutely not."

"He doesn't want you to waste it," Hayden said.

He'd saved Nelson the trouble of saying it.

"Wait," Dr. Fanning said. "Are you planning to . . . kill us?"

"Of course he is, dear," the old woman said.

"But we're no threat to you."

"Ah, but you are," Clotilde said. "He can't leave a witness to his crimes."

Nelson felt a familiar rage expand within him. "Doctor Fanning has her own crime to answer for."

She looked baffled. "What?"

"The man you ran down in Salt Lake City. You not only robbed him of the use of the left side of his body, but his career and his life's mission as well."

"What on Earth are you . . . ?" The light dawned in her eyes. "Fife . . . James Fife."

"Yes!" he said, exalted now that he could finally confront her. "My uncle. The man who raised me."

Fanning shook her head, her expression dismayed. "Your uncle . . . I'm sorry. I've never stopped regretting that."

He didn't believe her—not a word of it.

"Empty words. You've suffered no consequences, while he's stuck in an East Meadow nursing home, suffering every day. That scale needs balancing."

He waited for delicious fear to fill her eyes, but instead he saw tears pooling along the rims of her lids.

"Oh, no," she whispered, her voice quavering. "That poor man."

He fought the sudden evaporation of his exaltation. No . . . crocodile tears. She couldn't fool him. He'd—

"Brother Fife," Clotilde said. "I ask you again: May I give them a wee dram to send them to the Goddess in good health?"

He forced himself to focus on the here and now. "And I tell you again: no."

Clotilde gave him a level stare. "You don't look well, Brother Fife. As a good hostess I'd offer you a taste, but I know you won't take it."

Nelson could not take his eyes off the bottle. There it

was . . . the cure for his headaches, his blurred vision, his seizures . . . his cancer.

And then he realized that God had put him here on this island, in this cellar, with this high priestess of evil, for a purpose.

"Oh, but I will take it. I accept."

He saw Clotilde's surprised expression, heard gasps of shock from his fellow brothers.

"Sir!" Bradsher said. "You mustn't!"

He turned to them. He wished he'd found a way to reveal this before, but the circumstances had never been right.

"I have cancer. It has spread through my body. The Lord has led me here so that I may be cured. It is the only way I can go on serving Him. And I must go on serving Him. For this is not the end of our holy task. You heard her: She said they are many and that someone would take her place to continue their foul work. I can't stop now. There's too much of the Lord's work yet to do. And besides, the sin is not in taking the panacea, but in making it."

"Wow!" Hayden said. "Your moral and ethical muscles must ache like hell from the contortions you just put them through."

The words stung but Nelson held firm. Bradsher and Chayat looked unconvinced, however.

"Don't you see the Divine Plan in this?" he said. "Using the Serpent's scheme against the Serpent itself? Can't you almost hear God laughing at the irony of it?"

When he turned back to Clotilde she was holding the shot glass out to him. Without hesitation he poured the liquid onto his tongue. It tasted awful and his stomach was already protesting, but he forced it down.

"I want some for my brothers." He raised a hand to stifle their protests before they could start. "You two are here for a reason. Would you be so arrogant as to think that your presence is not part of a Divine Plan as well? Do you think that all the little day-to-day decisions that brought you here were entirely your own? You don't know what might be lurking beneath your skin, ready to bring you down before you complete your holy purpose. You were guided here and I command you to partake of this cure."

With obvious reluctance, they took turns—Chayat first, stepping forward and quaffing the potion while Bradsher kept his weapon trained on their prisoner. Then Bradsher's turn.

"And now," he told them, "we will be cured of whatever illness is hiding within, and will be healthier, hardier tools in the hand of the Lord."

Hayden said, "Aren't the rest of your 536 buddies going to be up in arms when they hear about your little tea party here? Or will they want in too?"

"I have handled this operation on a need-to-know basis."

"I see. Covering your ass: If you fail, only a few know, right?"

The man had struck uncomfortably close to the truth. But Nelson had an answer for him.

"Not at all. A compact operational unit is much more easily managed and fine-tuned."

He noticed Clotilde staring at him. She said, "It works overnight, so you will not reap any benefit until tomorrow. But in the meantime . . . "

An alarm rang through his head. "In the meantime what?"

"Is the cancer in your brain?"

He saw no harm in telling someone who would very shortly be on her way to hell.

"Some of it."

"You may feel some strange sensations as the *ikhar*

shrinks those tumors and the displaced tissues move back into their original positions."

He shook his head. "I know why you are doing this. You think that by putting me in your debt I will forsake my duty and spare you. And under more mundane circumstances I would be inclined to show you mercy. But the choice is not mine. Your sentence was passed when you sided with the Serpent. I will see it carried out. You cannot buy me off."

"I believe you and your kind are the serpents. We exist to heal, you exist to destroy."

Nelson clapped his hands. "Enough blather. Time to end this."

He'd learned what he needed to know. And he had two Hellfire missiles ready to wreak havoc. Only a hundred pounds each, but so effective. Their armor-piercing capabilities would take them through the front wall. Their explosive payload would destroy everything above and below ground here. And since they'd use only a smidgen of their solid rocket fuel traveling from the helicopter, the resultant fire would incinerate the three bodies, the worms, and everything else in this structure—a Leviticus Sanction for everyone involved.

But what to do before he fired the missiles? Terminate them or let the Hellfires do the job? Shooting meant leaving bullets in the bodies and that—

His legs gave out on him and he dropped to his knees. Was this what she had warned him about? Despite his best efforts, he couldn't remain upright and started falling toward the floor. He tried to put his arms out to cushion the blow but they suddenly weighed tons. He landed hard on the floor, banging the side of his head.

He saw Bradsher start toward him but his legs gave out as well. Brother Chayat's legs were crumbling too, but as he was falling he turned his MP-5 in the direction of the old priestess. Hayden rammed him with his shoulder before he could bring it fully around and the weapon erupted in a short burst that tore up a section of wall. Then Chayat was down.

What happened? Why couldn't he move? He tried to say something but only inarticulate sounds came out. Only one explanation: They'd been poisoned.

"What the hell?" Hayden was saying as he stood over Chayat.

Dr. Fanning was kneeling next to Bradsher. "They're alive but . . . "

"Paralyzed," Clotilde said.

"How?"

"That wasn't the *ikhar* in that bottle. It is something derived from a plant supplied by the All-Mother. Much like curare."

"But I saw you drink from the same bottle."

"In preparation for this day, which I sensed would come sooner or later, I have been sipping a little every day, getting my body used to it."

"Mithridatism!" Dr. Fanning said. "I've heard of it but . . . " She shook her head. "Incredible."

"I had more than usual today," the old woman said. "I must sit down."

She slumped onto a bench against the wall.

"Hey, Doc," Hayden said. "Unlock these, will you? The key's in the pocket of the one who punched me."

Nelson lay helpless as he watched her release Hayden. When he was free, he removed Bradsher's and Chayat's weapons and leaned them against a wall. Then he approached Nelson, rubbing his wrists as he squatted next to him. He lifted Nelson's arm and released it. Nelson could slow its descent, like falling through water, but not keep it from dropping.

"Curare and its cousins block nicotinic acetylcholine at the neuromuscular junction," Dr. Fanning said, watching.

"How's that in English?"

"Skeletal muscle paralysis."

"It's not going to kill him, is it?" Hayden said. "Because you heard the man: If his heart stops, a couple of Hellfires will pay us a visit."

"Heart muscle is different from skeletal muscle so it's not affected." An instant of panic flashed across Dr. Fanning's face. "Oh, but it can kill at high doses. Paralyzes the diaphragm."

Clotilde shook her head. "We do not kill. These did not receive fatal doses."

Hayden said, "Good. But we've got to get you out of here. And by that I mean off the island. We can't be sure more 536 goons aren't on the way. Doc, can you help her to the boat?"

"Sure. But what are you going to be doing?"

"I'll just be tidying up a bit before I join you."

"Do not harm them," Clotilde said as Dr. Fanning helped her to her feet. "The All-Mother decides when Her children are to return to Her soil. We have nothing to say in the matter."

Hayden held up his hands. "Hey, I've done some things I'm not proud of, but I've never stooped to beating up on a paralyzed man, and I'm not going to start now."

Nelson tried to shout that he was lying and not to leave him with this psychopath, but his tongue was limp and his mouth hung open and immobile. All he could do was grunt.

"I should hope not," said Clotilde.

Hayden said, "Collect their phones, Doc. We'll use the signals to confuse anyone looking for them."

Nelson felt a tugging on his coat, and soon Dr. Fanning spoke.

"Help me get Clotilde up the stairs and we'll take it from there."

Nelson listened to their shuffling footsteps recede, then a single set returned.

"Fife, Fife, Fife," Hayden said, squatting beside him again. "There's irony here in that we both know the panacea is from Outside, except we both have wildly divergent ideas about the nature of that Outside. We both want to keep the panacea off the record books—you, because it upsets your god's plan; me, because it breaks too many rules and upsets the balance of nature. Pretty close, huh? We could have been allies if you and your pals weren't such assholes. Where we part company is that I can live with the All-Mother crowd's narrow-band approach of a cure here, a cure there, but no-rule-changing revelation. Your bunch could have accommodated them. But you can't, can you? It's all or nothing for you guys. You've got to run around killing anyone who disagrees."

Nelson couldn't tell him that the Lord would never compromise with the Serpent.

"On the subject of kill, though . . . I have a dilemma. I can't leave you around to hound the doc. You tried to kill her before, and you were ready to kill her today, and you'll be looking for another chance as soon as you get your muscles back. But I promised not to harm you. So what do I do?"

He wanted to promise that he'd leave her alone—promise anything—but could only grunt.

"You don't say? Well, listen, I want you to get used to the idea that you're not getting out of here alive. Despite my promise, this is where your train stops. And it's not revenge or anything like that. Getting kicked out of the Company was the best thing that ever happened to me. So it's not for me. It's for her. The doc. She's one of the good ones, and we've got to do what we can to keep the good ones around."

Hayden rose and stepped over to Bradsher. He pulled his damned zip ties from Bradsher's pocket and used them to bind his wrists and ankles, then he used a third to tie the wrists to the ankles behind his back. He hog-tied Chayat the same way.

"Just in case Clotilde's magic potion wears off too soon."

Then he picked up one of the MP-5s and hefted it as he returned. He bent and pressed the muzzle against Nelson's temple.

"So easy."

Do it! Nelson wanted to scream. Stop my heart! Go ahead! Do it so you'll burn in here before you pass on to an eternity of burning in hell!

"But a promise is a promise." He straightened and looked around. "Gotta be a way."

Something seemed to capture his attention but Nelson could not tell what it was.

"I just got a crazy idea, Fife. It might not work, but it will be beyond awesome if it does."

What . . . what could that twisted mind be thinking?

"Yeah. Let's try it."

Laying down the MP-5, he grabbed Nelson's wrists and began dragging him across the floor, through the small pool of saliva that had drooled from his gaping mouth. He couldn't see where they were going, but he soon recognized the mossy surface and the dead leaves.

The worm farm?

Finally he released him and Nelson found himself with a close-up view of dozens of worm holes. He felt zip ties go around his wrists and ankles. Hayden didn't hog tie him, however.

"As I said, Fife, this may not work. But sooner or

later we're all gonna be worm food. Let's see if we can make it sooner for you."

What was he talking about?

He watched Hayden walk out of his field of vision, then heard the big mallet slam against the wooden block—once, twice, three times—and felt the ground vibrate with each blow.

"Wish I could stay and watch, but gotta run. Save a spot for me in hell, Fife."

And then the sound of his footsteps ascending the stairs.

Fife wished he could laugh. The idiot! Did he think the worms were going to eat him? They had mouths the size of pinholes, and no teeth!

He sent a prayer of thanks up to the Lord. Surely He was watching over him. It wouldn't be too long—a few hours at most, certainly—before the paralysis wore off, and then he'd be able to walk out of here and continue the hunt.

A ridged worm, pink and glistening, emerged from its tunnel and wriggled across the moss. Soon it was joined by others. In minutes the surface was acrawl with them. Pink squirming tubes filled his field of view. Disgusting, yes. But completely harmless.

He began planning Hayden's fate when he caught up with him. He needed to think like Dante and make the punishment fit the—

A worm began to crawl into his right nostril, the one against the moss. Did it think it was a worm tunnel? He managed to snort it out. Thank the Lord his diaphragm still worked. Well, he'd be dead if it didn't, but—

The worm was back again, or maybe another had taken its place, but whatever it was, this time it was crawling into his mouth. Dear God, he couldn't push it back with his paralyzed tongue, couldn't spit it out with his jaw slack and hanging open. But his taste buds still worked and the foul flavors of the dirt and mucous coating on its skin made him want to gag. But he couldn't gag. He couldn't do anything but let it crawl around in there.

And then another joined it. And then one in his right nostril and another in his left as well. He tried to snort them out but it didn't work this time. It felt like they'd expanded their bodies to wedge themselves in and keep from being expelled.

More slithered between his slack jaws. Attracted by the warmth and moisture? More and more until they filled his mouth, cutting off his air.

And now he knew the Lord was punishing him for his sin. Adam and Eve all over again, and he'd unwittingly followed in the footsteps of Adam. He saw that now. Clotilde had been Eve, holding out the poisoned apple from the Tree, only today she'd disguised it as a cure for his ills. He'd fallen for the temptation, rationalized a reason to take the fatal bite, with death and damnation as the result.

He thought of Uncle Jim's scourge and wished now that he'd used it. Maybe he could have avoided giving in to the temptation.

More worms . . . couldn't breathe . . . choking . . . air . . . no air!

Help! Someone, please help! Air! *Aaaiiirrrr!*

3

Second Lieutenant Jason Lowery, USAF, was hovering his trusty old Huey as ordered just off the coast of this strange little island and thinking this had to be *the* weirdest mission he'd ever run. His three passengers had introduced themselves by first name only. Sure as hell not military. If they weren't spooks, he was Hillary Clinton.

He was also sure he'd never know how they wrangled two Hellfires for his bird, which was usually equipped for rescue and nothing more. But there they sat, racked port and starboard, just outside the sliding cabin doors. They weighed only a hundred pounds each so they had no effect on the bird's handling, but he wasn't comfortable with ferrying around that amount of explosive payload. What were the spooks planning to do with them?

He'd stationed his bird at the south end of the island, facing east into the wind. He had no idea what was going on down there under all that fluttering fabric. They could be playing ring-around-the-rosy for all he knew. The fog was thinning. He could rise above it into the midday sunlight, but he wanted to maintain a direct line of sight to the island. He figured less than an hour for the sun to burn it all off.

And just as that thought passed through his mind, the Huey shuddered and jolted as both missiles ignited and launched with simultaneous roars. He watched in shock as they raced east for fifty yards, then looped around in a one-eighty turn that pointed them directly at the center of the island.

What the hell was *that* all about?

He hadn't the faintest, but he knew if his passengers were anywhere on that island he'd be heading back to Mildenhall alone.

4

"Where *is* he?" Laura said as she watched the crest of the cliff at the end of the cove.

"We only just got here," Clotilde said.

Laura didn't want to mention it, but it had taken a

while to get the old woman down those steps. She probably wouldn't have bounded down on a good day, but she'd just taken a dose of a neuromuscular toxin, and despite having built up a tolerance in her system, it had weakened her.

They waited in the open aft of the rented launch, Clotilde seated on the bench against the transom, Laura standing by the captain's chair, listening to the rumble of the engine. Rick had left the keys in the ignition, so she had started it to let it warm up.

"You mentioned a strange word back at the farm," Clotilde said. "Something about a myth."

"A myth? No, I—oh, you mean mithridatism. It's named after some ancient king who took small amounts of poison every day to inure himself from its effects."

Clotilde shook her head. "I thought of it as merely a form of immunization. I never knew it had a name."

"It doesn't work with every poison. Won't help at all with cyanide, for instance."

Finally Rick appeared, leaping onto the staircase and pelting down the steps at a mad pace that shook the whole structure. He ran down the dock and immediately began untying the mooring lines, bow first, then the stern. He leaped onto the aft deck just behind the captain's chair.

"You've got her running!" he said with a tight grin. "You're the best!"

And then he kissed her on the forehead, taking her totally by surprise. The casualness of it . . . like he did it every day. What was up with that?

Without breaking stride he squeezed behind the wheel and hit the throttle. Laura had to grab the top of the seat to keep from falling back with the sudden acceleration. Something in his frantic pace bothered her.

"Why the big hurry?" she said as they roared toward the sea.

"You telling me you want to hang around?"

"Not a bit, but you look like the hounds of hell are on your tail."

"'Hounds of hell,'" he said with that same tight grin. "You could be half right."

"You did not harm him, did you?" Clotilde said from the rear.

"No. I promise. He was alive when I left him."

"That doesn't mean he wasn't bleeding to death," Laura said.

He raised an *I-swear* hand. "I did not injure him in any way. I left him in the same condition as you saw him—facedown on the floor, alive, breathing, not bleeding. I just . . . moved him."

Laura wasn't sure she wanted to hear this.

"Where to?"

"That worm playground."

She didn't see what that accomplished. Why would he . . . ? Oh?

"You didn't happen to bang that hammer, did you?"

Clotilde had worked her way from the transom to the co-captain seat. "You called the worms?" she said.

Laura looked between the two of them. "What will that do?"

"It will bring the worms to the surface," Clotilde said.

"I know that. But, well, it's not like they're going to eat him, is it?"

The old woman shook her head. "That is impossible. They will crawl all over him, but they cannot harm him."

Laura couldn't imagine what that had to feel like and didn't want to try.

Then she saw Clotilde's eyes narrow. "Unless . . ."

Just then the island exploded behind them.

At least it seemed to. Laura watched a huge fireball

mushroom into the air. Bits of the camo fabric—from tiny rags to full sheets—swirled and fluttered like angry birds. Bit and pieces of the struts that once anchored them pinwheeled from the sky and rained on the water astern, peppering the waves with splashes big and small.

The missiles Fife had mentioned . . . Hellfire missiles that would launch when his heart stopped. This meant . . .

Rick whooped. "Made it! Far enough to be safe from the shrapnel, close enough to the cliff to be shielded from the shock wave!"

Laura only stared at him. So did Clotilde. Finally he noticed and sobered.

"What?"

Laura shook her head. "Didn't you promise—?"

"I did. I regretted it almost immediately, but I held to it."

"That explosion means Fife's heart stopped."

"Yeah, that's what he told us, but I didn't stop it."

"But you knew the worms would . . . " Laura glanced at Clotilde. "What? Choke him?" She couldn't imagine any other way it could happen.

Clotilde nodded, looking angry. "To use the All-Mother's creatures like that . . . you had no right."

"Hey, if the worms did it, they were only doing what comes naturally. I couldn't know they'd—"

"But you hoped!"

"Well, yeah, I thought it was a possibility, but, you know, remote. Hey, really. Why am I getting all this heat? The guy was going to kill us all in cold blood and cremate us with those missiles. Turnabout is fair play, don't you think?"

"I don't know what to think, Rick."

And that was true. Fife had been the leader. Apparently

he'd been giving the orders all along, which meant he'd ordered Mulac's torture and murder.

She couldn't say he hadn't had it coming to him, she simply didn't like being a party to the three deaths back there.

"Well, think about this," Rick said. "The worms may have done him in, but if he hadn't synched those missiles to his heart, his two buddies would still be alive. So maybe we should thank him for being so paranoid. Because of that, you won't have to be looking over your shoulder every moment now."

"What do you mean?"

"I don't know how much these 536 guys network, but you heard him say he'd kept this operation pretty much under his hat. The passing of him and his team has probably knocked you off the 536 radar. And that's a good thing, don't you agree?"

"One of his crew said you used your zip ties on someone named Miguel. What did he mean by that?"

"I wouldn't pay too much attention to crazies like that."

"Who is—or was—Miguel?"

Rick was silent a moment, then he sighed. "A Company man."

"CIA?"

He nodded. "A 536er too, just like Fife, only Fife was in charge. Miguel and a hired hand from Mexico City tortured Mulac. And burned Mulac. And hung Mulac. And they were waiting to see if you learned anything they missed. If you had, they planned the same for you. Oh, and they ripped out that little girl's fingernails too."

A blast of hate suffused Laura. A child . . . doing that to a child.

"And you . . . ?"

He shrugged. "I just did my job."

"You killed them?"

"I'm supposed to protect you, so . . . "

"When?" She could think of only one occasion when he would have had the time. "Sunday night? When you went for that 'reconnoiter'?"

He nodded. "They gave themselves away earlier in the day when they were spying on you."

Spying on me . . . dear God.

"And you did it with zip ties?"

"Um, yeah, but don't ask for details. The details don't matter. What matters is they won't be torturing *curanderos* or little girls or deputy medical examiners or anyone else ever again."

"Good."

Rick's head snapped around. And Laura herself was surprised she'd said that, but she wasn't about to take it back.

"Anyone who can torture a little girl is capable of anything. They have to be stopped."

"Well, we finally agree on something."

"I guess we do." She wasn't exactly overjoyed with that idea. "But just that one thing."

When she thought about it, Rick was one scary guy. He'd come out and told her that he'd killed this Miguel and whoever was with him. And he'd done it with zip ties. She couldn't imagine how, but it didn't sound like he'd been fighting for his life. It sounded more like an execution. And then he'd returned all cool and calm like he'd been out for a quiet stroll. What sort of man could do that?

Yeah. One scary guy. So why didn't he scare her? Why wasn't she appalled?

She realized with a pang that she wasn't the same Laura Fanning who had left Long Island on Sunday

morning. And what day was today? God, she actually
had to think about it. Friday? Yeah, Friday. Six days on
the road, as that old song went. Six days over which she
felt like she'd lived six years. It would be so good to get
home.

Wait.

"Clotilde," she said, turning to the old woman. "Did
you save a dose of the *ikhar*?"

She nodded and patted a pocket of her robe. "I did
not know how long we would be gone so I grabbed
some on my way out."

"And you'll let me bring a dose back to America?"

"I said I would, did I not?"

Laura gave Rick a look. "Well, sometimes you can
hold to the letter of a promise while circumventing its
spirit."

Rick only smiled.

But the important thing was she'd be home with her
Marissa by tomorrow.

5

"Nurse!" Steven called from Marissa's bedside. "Nurse!"

He'd just arrived and the Marissa in the bed now was
nothing like the Marissa he'd left earlier.

His shock must have been obvious because a nurse
he'd never seen before hurried to his side. Her name tag
read *H. Sayers, RN*. She had chocolate skin and glossy
black hair pulled straight back from her round face.

"What's wrong?" she said.

"Look!" He bent over the bed. "Marissa? Marissa?"

She opened her eyes but they didn't seem to focus.
"Mommy?" she said in a slurred voice.

"What's wrong with her?"

"I called Doctor Franks. He's going to talk to you."

"Franks? Never heard of him."

"He's a neurologist."

"Neurologist? She's got pneumonia."

Nurse Sayers looked uncertain.

He heard his voice rise on its own. "Tell me what the hell is going on!"

"She . . . she's developed meningitis."

"What? Oh, no! How can that be?"

"As Doctor Franks will tell you, it's not that uncommon in a post stem-cell transplant with CMV."

Marissa's lids had slipped closed again. He couldn't take his eyes off her waxy face. He tried to speak, failed, tried again.

"Is she going to die?"

Sayers didn't answer.

"Is she going to die?" he repeated, managing with supreme effort not to scream.

"That is not for me to say, Mister Gaines."

He wanted to throttle her, then realized the hospital probably had rules about how much a nurse could say—hierarchies and protocols and all that shit. Not her fault. Spare the messenger.

"All right, who *will* say or who *can* say?"

"That would be Doctor Franks. I expect him back shortly."

"What can *you* tell me?"

"I can tell you that she's comfortable. She's not in any pain."

Because she's dying, he thought, the inescapable realization shredding his heart. My little girl is dying.

And where was Laura? Where the fuck was Laura?

"Always wanted to try haggis," Rick said.

Laura looked at him over the top of her menu. "Really? Why?"

"Because it sounds so awful I want to be able to say I've eaten it."

"From what I've gathered, it doesn't sound like you've led a life devoid of things to talk about."

"That's just it—Can't talk about them. But nothing to keep me from talking about haggis."

"If you survive it."

"Well, there's that, isn't there."

It had taken them a while to find their way back in the fog. When they spotted a ferry heading west, they figured the odds favored Kirkwall as its destination and they were right.

For most of the trip she'd been watching her Droid like one of those smartphone-obsessed dweebs who annoyed her so much back in the real world. As soon as she had service she tried to call, but still couldn't get through. So she texted that she'd be home tomorrow, and would follow up with her exact time of arrival after she was booked. She heard back almost immediately from Steven that Marissa couldn't wait to see her.

As soon as they'd settled up the fees on the cabin cruiser, Laura had wanted to head straight for the airport and back to Heathrow. But Clotilde was still weak from her dose of poison and needed to rest. She didn't feel right leaving her—she'd brought trouble to the old woman's door and they owed her big-time for getting them out of it.

Oh, well, she'd still be home tomorrow, just later than she'd hoped.

She and Rick already had rooms at the Ayre so they booked Clotilde one too. While she hit the sheets for a rest, Rick and Laura hit the pub for a meal. She hadn't eaten since last night. Food had been the last thing on her mind all day, but now that they'd completed their quest, she realized she was famished.

"You know," she said, closing the menu, "I'm hungry enough to eat haggis myself."

"Dare ya."

"You're on. You eat it, I'll eat it."

Rick tried to order them each a glass of Champagne but they sold it only by the bottle. So he ordered a bottle. Neither of them knew much about Champagne and the pub didn't have any selection to speak of, but they'd both heard of Moët so they settled on that.

"To bringing home the panacea," he said, lifting his flute and extending it toward her.

She didn't know if she could drink to that. And besides . . .

"I thought you were on board with keeping its existence under wraps . . . refusing to play their game."

"I am. But it's only one dose, so it remains out of sight."

"How about 'to bringing home what we came for'?"

He smiled. "Doubting Thomasina. But fair enough."

They clinked glasses.

"Still refusing the panacea Kool-Aid, huh?" he said after he'd downed half his glass in one gulp.

"I've seen some cures—or what look like cures—that I can't explain, but accepting the existence of a panacea . . . " She shook her head. "I still can't go there."

"Then what are you bringing Stahlman?"

"Exactly what he sent me for."

They finished the Champagne—Rick downing two glasses for every one of hers—before the haggis arrived, so Rick ordered a Burgundy to go with dinner. He called it a French Pinot Noir and said Pinot Noir went with everything, even haggis.

Turned out he was right. The haggis itself looked awful but she found it edible if she kept sipping Burgundy with it and didn't think about the ingredients.

They ate and talked about where they would go and what they would do once they got back home. Rick had a feeling Stahlman would keep him on or at least on retainer, while Laura figured she'd stay with the ME's office and watch over her suddenly wealthy daughter.

Rick finished his meal first—naturally—and helped clean her plate when she'd reached the bursting point.

"We've got nearly half a bottle left," he said. "We can polish it off upstairs."

Seriously? What was this?

She remembered the kiss on her forehead a few hours ago. Just a quick peck, really, but it presumed a familiarity that she didn't share.

Or did she?

She'd grown comfortable with Rick. And why not? They'd been through a lot. Despite all his secrets, all the things in his past he couldn't or wouldn't speak of, she knew he had her back. How many other men could she say that about? She couldn't name one. Oh, Deputy Lawson might go to bat for her, but only as far as the law allowed. Rick, on the other hand, seemed a law unto himself.

He seemed to sense her hesitation. "I'm not gonna try to jump your bones. You should know that by now."

Would that be so bad? said a voice somewhere inside.

No, no, no. Don't go there.

"I guess I do. My room. Let's go."

"Well," he said, raising a couple of fingers of Burgundy in one of the room's squat tumblers, "if you won't toast to the panacea, will you toast to 'intellects vast, cool and unsympathetic'?"

She raised the glass he'd poured for her. "Why not your Dark Man? At least you saw him."

Any warmth that had grown in his eyes over dinner vanished as if it had never been.

"Don't joke about that. Don't ever joke about that."

His cold vehemence struck her like a blow.

"I'm sorry. I was just—"

He started to rise. "I'd better go."

"No. Please." She pushed him back, not believing she did that. "I was just trying to get you talking about yourself."

"The me that existed before I became Rick Hayden is gone. Nothing to discuss."

"Then what about the cult?"

"No! They were . . . I want to say animals but that's not fair to animals. Human monsters is more like it. They're best forgotten." He started to rise again.

"Oh," she said, making one last desperate try. "That's too bad. Because I think I can explain that total blackness you saw."

"Not that dark matter idea."

"No. It has to do with how we see."

He sat back down. "I'm listening."

She gathered her thoughts. She was going back to medical school classes for this. She hoped she remembered right.

"Light is part of the electromagnetic spectrum. We perceive less than one percent of the wavelengths—the so-called 'colors.' The color we see is the wavelength the object reflects. A lemon is yellow because its skin reflects the yellow wavelength. Black is black because it reflects *none* of the visible spectrum. What you're seeing then is a *lack* of color."

"But this was beyond black."

"Okay. So imagine a surface that absorbs not only all the visible but all the invisible as well: ultraviolet and infrared and X-rays and gamma rays. It reflects absolutely nothing. What would that look like?"

Rick's eyes had lost focus, as if he were looking into the past.

"Like a hole in reality."

Laura's chest tightened. Yes . . . she hadn't thought of it that way, but she imagined that would be exactly what it looked like.

"Do you think what you saw might have been one of the vast, cool and unsympathetic intellects?"

He shook his head. "Doubt it. Maybe just a manifestation, maybe just its pinky fingernail, maybe a trick of the light."

She didn't want to mention the Dark Man again so she said, "Was that what this cult thought it was after? A hole in reality?"

"They found an old book from the early nineteenth century by some crazy German. It's a description of the practices of obscure religions all around the world—all the continents and lots of isolated islands. They let me take a look at a copy they'd Xeroxed off. I got through a couple of pages and"—he shuddered—"that was it. I couldn't go any further."

"Like what?"

He waved a hand. "You don't want to know. Like you said the other day, there's some things you can't unsee. Well, there are some things you can't unread."

"But you stuck with them?"

"Last thing I wanted, but I felt I had to. They had explosives and combustibles. They hated everything, Laura. They had this crazy idea that if they could raise this Dark Man or bring him across, he could be their WMD. I was cool with that sort of wild-goose chase. As long as they were chasing phantoms, they weren't making bombs."

"So this evil book was actually serving a good purpose."

"Wait," he said. "Around this time the Company decided to pull me out. Since the group had dropped Wahhabism, Langley didn't think they were a threat to the U.S., but lemme tell you, they were a threat to *everybody*. I flew home to make my case for continued surveillance but I might as well have been talking to myself. They pulled me."

"So what did you do?"

"I flew back on my own . . . and I saw what they'd been up to while I was away."

"What?"

"Children . . . they'd found something in that damn book and they were doing things to little kids."

Did she want to hear this? She didn't think so. But she had to ask.

"What sort of things?"

"Hurting them, maiming them in awful ways . . . this was how they would draw the Dark Man . . . kept the kids in a barn behind the farmhouse . . . I went . . . " He cleared his throat. "I went a little crazy, started tearing up the farmhouse. Some of the combustibles they had stored ignited. I managed to get out. They didn't."

"The farmhouse fire that Fife's text mentioned?"

An absent nod. "And then the barn with the kids blew apart in a massive fireball. One second it was there, the next it was an inferno."

"Oh, no!"

"The German crime-scene crew later reported that the barn had been rigged to explode, with the trigger in the house."

"But why?"

"I'm just guessing, but I imagine they figured that if they were ever raided, they couldn't allow anyone to see what they'd done to those kids. So they had some sort of switch they could throw that would incinerate the barn and everything in it. The damage to the house must have triggered the barn detonators. And that's when I saw that thing, that hole in reality."

Laura tried to picture the scene . . . and failed.

She looked up and saw him rubbing his sleeve across his reddened eyes. "Fifteen kids . . . and I killed them."

"But you didn't set those charges, those monsters did."

"If I'd simply backed off and called the cops . . . "

"But the children would still be dead, right? The arrival of the cops would have triggered the barn bombs, right?"

"I suppose."

"Have you ever told anyone about this?"

"No. You're the first. Sorry to lay it on you." He wiped his eyes on his sleeve again as he rose. "I don't drink like I used to. Out of practice, I guess."

"You mean you've been carrying this around since . . . ?"

It explained so much about him, especially his reaction to the tortured little Mayan girl.

He shrugged and looked uncomfortable. "I don't know about carrying it around. I just . . . I should go."

Laura shot to her feet and found herself swaying. She was much more out of practice than Rick in the drinking department.

"No, wait. You can't leave like that." On their own, her arms slipped around him and she squeezed against him. This man needed a hug. "You tried to do the right thing and it went horribly wrong. You've got to let it go."

His arms went around her back, but lightly. When was the last time a man had held her? Too long . . .

"I thought I had. I'd convinced myself the dark shape I'd seen was just a hallucination, but then this panacea business popped up and brought it all back."

She lifted her head to look at him. "Then 'too-perfect' me came along and everything seemed 'arranged.'"

He smiled. "I'm glad you did. I'm glad I was along to help you out. But I've decided you're not too perfect. You're simply perfect."

Somehow their lips met, a touch as gentle as it was brief.

"I probably should leave now."

The "probably" struck. Yeah, he was probably right, but she wanted to try that again.

So instead of backing away she leaned into him and they kissed again. More firmly this time. Laura felt a sigh half escape. A sudden pounding on the door cut it off.

"Laura! Laura!" Clotilde's voice.

"What the—?"

"Laura, open up! Emergency!"

She broke from Rick and yanked open the door. A distraught Clotilde stood there, hands clasped between her breasts.

"What's wrong?"

"Your daughter—she is in hospital. Very sick!"

"What? What are you talking about?"

"My people there have learned that she was hospitalized three days ago."

Three days? No way. The initial shock and fear began to fade.

"No, that can't be. If her last name is Fanning, you've got the wrong girl. Her name is Gaines. I've been in touch daily. She's fine."

Clotilde's eyes narrowed. "You've spoken to her?"

"No, the phones won't—oh, dear God."

"Fife?" Rick said.

"We think so," Clotilde said, nodding.

Laura backed up a step, looking from one to the other. "Wait—what?"

Clotilde held up a smartphone. "Brother Fife's. You left the 536 phones with me. I found texts from him telling someone what texts to send you from your husband and to your husband from you." She looked at Rick. "I even found a fascinating text concerning your companion."

The horror was seeping through.

"But why?

"To keep you on the trail of the *ikhar*."

"The son of a bitch," Rick said. "I hope that lays to rest any lingering guilt about his passing."

Laura couldn't care less about Fife.

"Marissa . . . how bad?"

"Gravely ill. An infection. Something called—"

"Please don't say CMV."

Clotilde nodded. "That is what we have heard. She is at a place called Stony Brook."

Laura knew what that meant. But even though she was in good hands . . .

"I'm going to lose her." She looked around for shoulder her bag, grabbed it, and began to push past Clotilde. "Gotta get back. Now."

Clotilde stepped aside and let her pass. Laura noticed Rick close behind her.

"You don't have to—"

"Yeah, I do."

"I just quit Stahlman," she said.

"I didn't. But that's not the point. You're gonna need me."

"I'll be fine."

"Trust me. You're gonna need me."

Right now all she needed was to get to Marissa.

MARISSA

1

"Uh-oh," Rick said as they stepped out into the midday sunlight—blinding after all those hours in terminals and on the plane. "I was afraid of this."

"What?" Laura said.

She was running on fumes now. They'd abandoned their luggage at the hotel and rushed to the Kirkwall airport where someone made a few calls and found a pilot to fly them to Heathrow. They looked for the first flight to the New York metro area—JFK, Newark, no matter—and lucked out with a Virgin flight to JFK, landing just shy of noon.

Laura had tried to call Steven while they waited at Heathrow but his phone was still playing games. So she called the medical center, got connected to the PICU, and learned the whole story: admitted early Wednesday followed by steady deterioration. CMV pneumonia complicated by cerebral edema secondary to CMV meningitis. Every relevant specialist and subspecialist on the pediatric staff had tried to halt her downhill course, all with no success. She'd slipped into a coma and the prognosis was grave. She didn't have long.

Rick had dozed off immediately after the first-class dinner Laura couldn't eat and she'd wished she could do the same—the trip would have gone so much faster. But sleep was out of the question. He'd bullied them to be first off the plane but Customs and Immigration would not be rushed. She'd felt her control slipping with the delay. Once they were finally cleared they'd run through the cavernous Terminal Four to the public transportation area.

Rick pointed to a familiar-looking van, idling in a no-idling zone. "Stahlman's here. Shit."

Laura didn't see the problem. "What's wrong? He can drive us to Stony Brook."

"Yeah. Maybe. Let me do the talking here."

"I'm perfectly capable of—"

"Just follow my lead, okay?"

She wondered what had him so concerned as she matched him stride for stride toward the van.

Stahlman's driver—James, was it?—stepped forward. "Do you have luggage?"

"The boss inside?" Rick said.

James gestured toward the open side panel. "He awaits."

She followed Rick inside with James close behind. The door slid shut behind them.

"What the—?" Rick said, turning. "Where is he?"

"Mister Stahlman awaits . . . at home. He is too sick to greet you in person. He sent me to bring you to him."

"Fine," Rick said. "But we've got a stop to make first."

"That won't be possible, I'm afraid. Mister Stahlman said I was to bring you both directly from the airport."

"We don't have his panacea," Laura said. "I'm sorry."

Rick touched Laura's upper arm. "Come on, Doc. We'll grab a cab."

James said, "Wait." He had a gun in his hand.

"Whoa-whoa!" Rick said

Oh, God, this was insane. This couldn't be happening. A gun at an airport. She glanced through the van's windows, hoping for a cop, but they were too darkly tinted for anyone to see inside.

"My daughter is dying!"

James's expression was tortured. "I'm sorry, but my boss is dying."

"I told you," she said, "I don't have it!"

Rick stepped around Laura and put himself between her and the gun. "We've got a sick kid to visit. And anyway, you're not crazy enough to start shooting at an airport, are you?"

"I don't want to, Rick, but Mister—"

Laura didn't see what happened then. All she could see was Rick's back, but there seemed to be an instant of struggle and the next thing she knew, Rick had shifted to the side and had a pistol muzzle jammed up under James's chin.

Somehow, she wasn't surprised.

"Didn't think so," Rick said. "But you know *I'm* crazy enough, right?"

James looked frightened. "Look, this wasn't—"

"Your idea? I know that. That's why you're going to turn around and put your hands behind your back."

James hesitated, then complied. Rick fished something from his pocket—a zip tie—and bound James's wrists, then sat him down.

"Thousand and three uses," he said as he secured his ankles.

She remembered what he'd said back in the Orkneys: *You're gonna need me . . .*

"How did you—?"

"SEAL stuff."

"But how did Stahlman know to be here?"

"I booked our flights with his credit card. I'm sure he's been tracking every transaction."

"But why would he send someone to . . . to kidnap us?"

He rose. "If I'm gonna put myself in his head, I think it's a good bet he knows about your daughter—known about her all along."

"And didn't tell me?"

"The last thing he wanted you to do was call off the hunt and rush back to the States. Now he thinks you're back to give the panacea to your daughter instead of him."

"If I had any, the bastard could have it all!"

"We need to talk about that. But right now let's get moving. I'll get us out of the airport, you navigate from there. Never been to Stony Brook so you'll have to point the way."

She estimated the distance as about the same as to her home—around fifty miles. An hour at least.

"Get us to the LIE," she said. "And hurry."

2

As Rick steered them out of JFK, she called the PICU.

After introducing herself as Marissa's mother and clearing the confusion over the difference in last names, she said, "How's her coma?"

"Level seven—that's counting a two on eye responses, a one on verbal, and four on motor responses but slipping there. Her condition is deteriorating quickly. Are you nearby? Your husband has been frantic."

Laura didn't bother adding *ex*. She was running through what she remembered about the Glasgow classification of coma levels. A one meant no verbal responses; a two on eyes meant they opened in response to pain. She didn't recall much about the motor scale. Too long away from live patients.

"Doctor Lerner, the pulmonologist, has ordered a respirator for her."

Her heart sank. "Aw, no."

"Her O-two sat has been dropping steadily and he says it's time."

She ended the call and Rick said, "Worse news?"

A sob blocked her throat, then broke free. "I'm going to lose her!"

He said nothing as he reached over and squeezed her hand.

They headed up the Cross Island Parkway and finally onto the LIE. The speed limit was fifty-five and the speedometer read sixty-eight as they raced east, but it felt like they were crawling.

"Can't we go faster?" she said.

"I'm pushing it as much as I dare. We get stopped, it'll waste lots more time, especially with a guy tied up in back."

Oh, right. She'd already forgotten about James. All she could think about was Marissa.

Hold on, honeybunch. Mommy's coming.

Midday traffic wasn't bad and they made good time to the Northern State Parkway, but still had a ways to go.

"Here," Rick said.

She tore her gaze from the road and saw that he was holding out three vials.

"What?"

"The panacea. Clotilde slipped them to me as we left the hotel."

"But—"

"Just listen to me for one fucking minute, okay?"

He sounded angry. He'd always used a euphemism for "fucking" until now. Okay, she'd listen.

"Go ahead."

"I know you think you've got to be all scientificky and always ask the next question and all that, but you've been doing more denying than questioning. You've closed your eyes to firsthand evidence. You knew that kid with arthritis, you knew how bad he was, and you autopsied him yourself and found no trace of it. Then there's

Chaim's medical records versus what you found on autopsy. You can't explain it but you can't deny it's fucking *there*. So accept it."

"But—"

"No buts! You have *got* to put all that aside and give Marissa a dose of this worm juice."

Worm juice . . . seriously?

"Can I get a sentence in?"

"Go ahead."

"My 'but' was to say that I was just thinking that I'm so desperate, if I had a dose of Clotilde's tea, I'd give it to Marissa."

He blinked. "You would?"

"Damn right!"

Worm juice . . . Marissa's immune system had already crashed. To add a dose of that bacteria- and mold-laden soup would be—

Stop it.

Not my life—Marissa's.

And so acceptance had passed beyond permissible to obligatory. If Marissa's condition was anywhere near as hopeless as the PICU nurse had described, nothing could make her worse. And if the chances of the *ikhar* working were one in a million—in a *billion*—how could she *not* give it to her?

"Desperate times," she said. "Marissa's got nothing to lose."

"And everything to gain."

She took one of Clotilde's little tubes from him and held it up to the light.

How many had 536 killed and burned because of this . . . what? What did she call this cloudy goop? She was reminded of that famous line from *The Maltese Falcon*: the stuff dreams are made of.

"All the preposterous and unimaginable noise around

this stuff. Fife's god made me a guide to Clotilde—called me a human pillar of fire—while Clotilde's All-Mother led me to her, and your vast, unsympathetic intelligences arranged my participation. It all comes down to *Laura Fanning: tool.*"

"One way of looking at it."

She wrapped her fingers around the vial, forbidding herself to hope. Hope was a trap, an empty promise, a surrender. She could not allow herself to hope. Not even a little. But she would give Marissa the worm juice.

And then a thought struck like a bullet. "Oh, shit!"

Rick jumped in his seat and jerked the wheel. "What?"

"The respirator! They're going to intubate her!"

"That'll keep her alive, right?"

"But she won't be able to swallow."

"Fuck it!" Rick said and floored the accelerator.

Laura grabbed her phone and called the PICU again. "Has Marissa been intubated yet?"

"No, but the team is on its way."

"Don't let them do that!"

"I'm sorry, Doctor Fanning. Your husband signed the consent and her O-sat just dropped below ninety."

Oh, hell . . . below ninety. Still . . .

"Let me speak to my husband!"

A pause, then, "He seems to have stepped out. Perhaps to wash up. He's been at her bedside all night."

"Damn-damn-*damn*!" She ended the call and pointed ahead. "Here's our exit."

She directed Rick onto Nicolls Road and northward to the medical center.

As they approached the front entrance, Rick called back over his shoulder. "If I cut you loose, James, can I count on your best behavior?"

"It's a little late for anything else, don't you think?"

"That's my man." He turned to Laura and handed her

a second tube. "I'm keeping one for Stahlman. I'll get it to him as soon as you finish inside."

"I'm not a fan of Stahlman's right now."

He may not have blocked her from learning of Marissa's condition, but he'd withheld what he knew.

"Neither am I. But I hired on to get you back safe with a dose of that stuff for him. I'm only half done."

Duty . . . staying true to his word . . . finishing the job. Instilled or inherent? She suspected the latter.

"And let's face it," he added. "You'd have *zero* options right now without him."

Good point. But if Marissa was intubated, she'd be back to zero.

As soon as Rick pulled to a stop just short of the entrance, he jumped out of his seat and went back to snip James's ties.

"Wait one second."

But Laura couldn't wait—not while Marissa was somewhere within those walls.

As she opened her door and hopped out, she heard him say to James, "Hang here for a bit and maybe we'll both come through this smelling rosy."

Then she was racing inside. She wasn't familiar with Stony Brook's layout and had to ask directions to the PICU. When she reached it, she skidded to a stop before the doors. She didn't want to see this.

Rick caught up to her then, stopping beside her but saying nothing.

"You don't have to come in," she told him. "In fact, I'd rather you wouldn't."

His expression was grim. "Tell you the truth, I'd rather not myself. But I've got a feeling you're gonna need me."

"You keep saying that."

"I'll stop as soon as I'm proven wrong." As she started

forward, she felt his hand grip her shoulder. "Give me a signal when you're ready to make your move."

"What?"

"They'll most likely have CCTV in there. If so, put yourself between Marissa and the camera. I'll make sure no one's watching."

A camera . . . that hadn't occurred to her.

With Rick close behind, she pushed through the doors into the beeping, blinking, wheezing cocoon of an ICU. She didn't have to ask which bed was Marissa's because she immediately spotted Steven's blue-and-red Rangers jacket draped over a chair to the right of a bed holding a child she barely recognized.

So pale, eyes closed with lids so dark and sunken.

A woman in scrubs bustled toward her. "Can I help you?"

Laura continued forward. She tried to answer but words wouldn't come.

"Ma'am, you just can't come in here." Her name plate read *H. Sayers, RN*.

"I-I'm Marissa's mother."

"Doctor Fanning? I spoke to you before. We—"

"What level?"

"Six—she's down to one on eye response. I'm so glad you made it."

"Swallow reflex?"

"Still there the last time we swabbed her mouth." She pointed to a man and woman in scrubs behind the nursing station. "The intubation team is here."

Laura froze. For the first time she noticed the ventilator on Marissa's left, next to the bed on the far side from Steven. If she was going to do this, she had to act now.

She glanced around for the camera and found it—up near the ceiling and angled toward the side of the bed opposite the still dozing Steven. She caught Rick's eye and gave him a quick nod.

He winked and ducked behind the nursing station where he began pulling open random drawers.

"Where's the good stuff?" he shouted. "Show me the good stuff!"

Nurse Sayers made a beeline for Rick. "Sir! Sir! What do you think you're doing?"

Laura moved in the opposite direction, unstoppering the vial as she neared the bed.

Sayers's voice well behind her now: "Wait! Stop! You can't go in there!" Other protesting voices joined her. "Help! Call security!"

"Just want a little taste!" Rick shouted.

Squeezing between the silent ventilator and the bed, placing her back to the camera to block her hands and Marissa's head, she tilted her daughter's chin up and parted her jaw. She then tipped the vial and poured its contents into Marissa's mouth, then sealed her lips.

Marissa made a choking sound, then coughed, but not before swallowing.

"Laura!" Steven said, looking confused and concerned as he came up behind her. "You're back!"

"Finally. In time, I hope."

She turned to see Rick watching her as he struggled with Sayers and two other nurses, one male. She gave him another nod. Smiling, he wrenched free and headed for the doors.

"You people are no fun. I'm outta here."

Watching him go, she realized she could love a man like that.

Steven looked baffled as he tried to grasp the situation by the nursing station, then he turned to Laura. "You've got a hell of a lot of explaining to do."

"You don't know the half of it."

Nurse Sayers hurried over to her. "Do you know him?"

"He foilowed me in."

Steven was turning in a slow circle. "What just happened here?"

"I wish I knew," Laura said. "I wish I knew."

THE IKHAR

1

"I still don't understand about the phones and the texts," Steven said.

She'd spent the rest of Saturday afternoon and much of the evening trying to explain it as best she could. Why wouldn't he just drop it for now?

Midnight had come and gone and now on Sunday morning they were seated on either side of Marissa's bed, each holding a hand. Activity in the twilit PICU had dropped to sleep-time level. Laura had convinced a very reluctant Dr. Lerner to hold off on the ventilator a little longer.

It hadn't been easy. Her heart had quailed when he'd shown her the X-rays. The CMV pneumonia was steadily taking over her lungs. Most adults were immune to the virus, so chance of spread to others was low. But Marissa had never been exposed to it, and it had overwhelmed her compromised immune system, clogging her airways. Even on nasal oxygen, her pulse ox was running only 89 or 90 percent. Lerner told her when—Laura had noted that he didn't say "if"—her oxygen saturation dropped to 88, he'd be obliged to intubate her and start the ventilator.

"I barely understand it myself," she told Steven, "but this isn't the time or place to discuss it."

He shook his head, accepting the fact, but obviously not liking it.

Really, Steven? Our daughter is slipping away before our eyes and you want to discuss phones?

"I take it you didn't find what you were sent for."

"What do you think?"

She couldn't tell him she'd dosed their daughter with—what had Rick called it?—worm juice.

Right. Tell him *that*.

A nurse came over and checked the pulse oximeter on Marissa's index finger. She took it off, looked at it, frowned, then replaced it.

"Something wrong?"

"Just checking."

That hadn't been a just-checking frown. Laura watched her return to her desk, lean over one of her monitors, and frown again. Laura had to go see.

"What's up?" she said when she reached the desk.

She hoped her MD degree still carried some weight.

"Oh, Doctor Fanning." Her nameplate read *J. Philips, RN.* "I . . . I'm just wondering about the oximetry reading."

"There's a problem?"

"Her O-two sat appears to be rising."

Laura clutched the counter as the room seemed to sway.

"What's it reading?"

"Ninety-two."

Okay. Not a dramatic jump. Just two or three points up from where she'd been running. Laura would not allow herself to step into that abyss called hope.

She noticed a paper clip on the counter and grabbed it before she returned to Marissa's side.

"What's going on?" Steven said.

She considered her reply and decided it would be cruel to give him hope.

"She seems to be holding her own. No ventilator yet."

"Yet," he said with a sour expression. "Yet."

If he'd had hope in the past day or so, it had slipped through his fingers like a gambler's savings.

She straightened a loop of the paper clip and waited until no one was looking. Watching Marissa's eyes, she dug the tip into the web between the child's thumb and forefinger. The hand withdrew—still at level four on the motor scale—but the eyes remained closed.

No change.

Yes, best not to hope.

1:07 A.M.

For the fourth time in less than hour, Laura approached the nursing station.

"Any change?"

"Um, yes," Nurse Philips said, her expression uncertain. "Pulse-ox jumped to ninety-four."

Up another two percentage points. That was with continuous oxygen flowing into her nose. She'd have nowhere near that on room air, but still . . . it meant her red cells were carrying more oxygen to her tissues.

"This isn't supposed to be happening," the nurse muttered. "Doctor Lerner said—"

"Yes. He told me too."

Laura couldn't trust herself to say more. She feared she'd break into hysterical laughter. Because this was insane. And yet it was happening. Hope was becoming insistent . . . insistent as all hell.

"Ventilator time?" Steven said when she returned to the bedside.

She shook her head. She had to tell him. "Her oxygen saturation has actually improved."

His eyes widened. "Could she be . . . ?"

"Don't go there, Steven."

Not yet.

As he slumped back in his chair on the far side of the bed, Laura dug the paper clip into Marissa's hand again.

She jerked her arm, moaned, and briefly opened her eyes.

"Oh my god!" Steven said. "Did you see that? Oh my fucking god! Nurse! Nurse!"

Marissa had just risen from a six to an eight on the coma scale.

Was she coming out of it . . . *really* coming out of it?

2:31 A.M.

Marissa became the focus of all attention in the PICU. The third shift was much smaller than the first, but every nurse on duty kept stopping by to check on the little girl who was defying all the dire expectations.

"She's a real fighter, isn't she," said an older nurse who studied her from the foot of the bed.

"You can't imagine," Steven said.

Which was the expected response. Marissa really was a fighter. She'd fought through the pain and side effects of all the leukemia therapies that had failed without ever a hint of wanting to give up. But this was different. The CMV had dealt a death blow. Something else was bringing her back.

With all the traffic around the bed, Laura hadn't tried poking her again.

"Call her name," the nurse said.

Laura leaned close. "Marissa? It's Mommy. Can you hear? Marissa?"

She opened her eyes.

Laura balled her fists. That put her another point up the scale.

Nurse Philips appeared at the bedside. "Pulse ox is up to ninety-six." She sounded as if she'd just run around the building. "I called Doctor Lerner and he ordered a portable chest. He's on his way in."

3:12 A.M.

Laura stood behind Dr. Lerner where he sat at the nursing station. She stared at the monitor screen over his shoulder.

"This is impossible," he was saying. "I've never seen anything like it."

"Impossible is an opinion," Laura muttered.

Lerner turned to Nurse Philips. "You're sure the film didn't get mislabeled?"

"No, look," Laura said, pointing to the tube visible in her little chest. "The central line is in exactly the same place as the last film."

Dr. Lerner had yesterday's portable and this morning's side by side on the computer screen for comparison. Laura was no radiologist or pulmonologist, but the new film was definitely better.

"She's had fifty-percent clearing in less than twenty-four hours. That's impossible, you know. Even a bacterial pneumonia that's sensitive to an antibiotic won't do anything like that. And this is viral. There has to be a mistake."

"Pulse ox just hit ninety-eight," Philips said.

"That goes with the X-ray." Lerner shook his head. "I just . . . just . . . " He shook his head again.

You just don't get it, Laura thought. Well, neither do I. But I'm going with it. I'm—

"She's talking!" Steven cried from the bedside. "She's not making any sense, but holy shit, she's talking!"

Laura rushed over. Marissa's eyes were open and staring at the ceiling while she babbled in a hoarse voice.

". . . mayonnaise soup computer severe plate school spots lights night . . . "

"Word salad," Laura said.

"Right," said Lerner, stepping up beside her. "But it means her meningitis is abating as well. This is incredible. Just incredible."

4:19 A.M.

Marissa's oxygen saturation had passed 100 percent. She'd lapse into a sleeplike unconsciousness, then awaken and spew more word salad.

Laura had found that hope wasn't necessary now: Her little girl was getting better by the hour. Steven had fallen asleep in his chair and Laura felt herself slipping into that delicious presleep drowsiness when she heard Marissa start making sense.

"Where's Natasha? It's time for math. She should be here by now."

Her head was propped on a pillow now but remained stationary. Only her eyes moved. She seemed disoriented, but she was making sense.

"Do the Mets play tonight? No, it's December. That's silly."

Then she closed her eyes again.

Laura could no longer fight the reality of what was happening. The *ikhar* . . . whatever was in it was working. She still could not accept the All-Mother or Rick's vast intelligences, but she had to accept the *ikhar*. It was real and it was working.

SUNRISE

"Mom? Mommy!" The voice seemed to come from far away . . . from the other end of a tunnel. *"Mom, wake up!"*

Laura forced her eyes open . . .

. . . and found herself staring at Marissa's face. She was sitting up in bed. She looked unsettled but fully alert.

"Marissa? Honeybunch?"

"What happened? How did I get here?"

"You were sick."

"I was?"

"Yes. Very."

"But I'm okay now. Can we go home?"

Laura couldn't answer. She was sobbing too hard.

2

The rest of Sunday became a series of parades, starting with a parade of inexplicables.

Marissa's second chest X-ray of the day showed no pneumonia—not a trace. Her white blood count had returned to normal—*all* her labs were normal.

The second was a parade of the specialists and subspecialists who had treated her over the course of her stay, all coming to bear witness to the miracle in the PICU.

Marissa was her normal precocious, gabby self, meeting them all for, what was to her, the first time.

Laura sat back and watched the expressions on their faces as they listened to Marissa's lungs and questioned her. Most of them had visited her at one time or another during the past thirty-six hours. None of them seemed able to reconcile the bright-eyed, vivacious little girl before them now with the obtundent child they'd seen before.

Laura even heard one mutter that it was a trick—had to be a twin or something—no way was this the same kid.

How human: When you don't have an explanation for what you see, you make one up.

While Marissa was basking in the spotlight—and Steven was home grabbing a shower—Laura had a chance to look around at the other PICU patients. A sandy-haired little boy about Marissa's age caught her eye. He had the usual assortment of tubes running into him, but his color was terrible. She wandered over.

"Hi."

He looked up. "Hi." His voice was a puffy whisper. Clearly short of breath despite the oxygen cannula in his nose.

"I'm the mother of that popular little girl over there. What brings you here?"

"Heart (*puff*) went bad."

Nurse Sayers from yesterday arrived then and added, "Cory has a cardiomyopathy."

"Viral?" Laura said.

"They think so. We're getting ready to transfer him to Presbyterian for a new one."

Laura nodded. "Good place." Columbia Pres had a renowned transplant center. "They have a match?"

Sayers shook her head. "Not yet. We're all hoping."

As the nurse bustled away, an idea—an insane idea—took hold.

"Cory? You thirsty?"

He nodded.

"What kind of juice would you like?" She made a point of not mentioning water.

"Apple?"

"You got it."

Trying to look casual, Laura followed Sayers back to her station.

"Cory says he's thirsty. Looking for apple juice. Is he on fluid restriction?"

"He is, but he can have four ounces."

"I'll give it to him."

She gave Laura a quizzical look. "You sure?"

"I'm in a mothering mood and my own doesn't seem to need much at the moment."

Sayers glanced toward Marissa and her pseudo press conference and smiled. "When I was here yesterday, the general opinion was no hope. Now look at her. It's a miracle."

"It sure is."

"Well, she can spend the rest of her Sunday on a general peds floor—private room, of course."

Apparently they still considered her immune system fragile.

"You're transferring her?"

"Yeah. We need the bed and Marissa no longer needs intensive care."

Sayers measured out four ounces into a plastic cup, tapped an entry into the computer, then handed it to Laura.

"Let me know if he doesn't drink it all so I can adjust the intake/output."

"Sure will."

Laura detoured to Marissa's bed where she fished the third vial from her bag. Cory's eyes were closed so she turned her back to the CCTV camera and quickly emptied it into the juice, giving it a good swirl.

"Hey there," she said, tapping him on the shoulder. "Got your juice."

He opened his eyes and took the cup without speaking.

"The nurse wants you to drink it all."

He nodded and tossed it back. He made a face as he swallowed. "Tastes *(puff)* funny."

"I think it's the fresh kind. Better for you."

He handed back the cup. "Thanks. So *(puff)* thirsty." He looked past her. "There's my *(puff)* mom."

Laura nodded to the frazzled, distracted looking woman approaching the bed and glided back toward Marissa.

3

With Marissa on the regular pediatric floor and Steven back on bedside duty, Laura took the keys to his Audi and headed for the parking lot. She needed a long hot shower.

She found a familiar figure waiting.

"Clotilde?"

The older woman wore a baggy sweater and jeans and looked like she could be right at home at Walmart.

"Your daughter is well." A statement, not a question.

"Yes. Thank you."

"No, thank you for your faith in the All-Mother."

Here we go, Laura thought.

Something must have shown in her expression because Clotilde added, "You may not believe in Her, but She believes in you."

"To tell you the truth, I didn't believe in the *ikhar*, even as I poured it between her lips, but I had no alternative."

"And now?"

Laura sighed. "It worked."

"You credit the *ikhar* and nothing else?"

"There's nothing else *to* credit. And I am forever in your debt."

"You are in the All-Mother's debt."

Laura wasn't going there. "But you're the one who gave Rick those vials."

"Yes. Three vials. One to your daughter, one to your sponsor, and an extra in case one broke. Do you have the third?"

"I slipped it to a little boy."

A pause, then, "You were discreet?"

"Did my best."

Clotilde smiled. "You are now a *sylyk*."

"I don't know about that, but I do know I couldn't watch him laboring for breath and not use it."

"You have the soul of a healer. But you must avoid such proximity with your cures. You will draw attention."

"I don't think that will be a problem, seeing as I'm all out of *ikhar*."

"I will be sending you a dose every few months."

The responsibility shook Laura. And the fact that she was shaken made her realize that she'd drunk what Rick had called the panacea Kool-Aid: She was a believer. At least in the *ikhar*. As for the rest . . .

"I'm probably not the best choice. Most of the people I deal with are dead."

"You were taught how to deal with live ones before you devoted yourself to the dead, were you not?"

"Well, yes, of course—"

"Then perhaps it is time you changed your field of endeavor."

She'd already been leaning that way.

"Why me?"

"The All-Mother guided you to Auburon, and then to me. She smiles on you."

"Yeah, well . . . " Whatever. "Just don't expect me to get my back tattooed."

Because no way was that going to happen.

"Only if you wish." She smiled. "Expect your first shipment next month."

And with that she turned and walked away.

VISITORS

1

"Good to be home?" Laura said as she ushered her daughter through the garage door into the utility/mud-room.

Marissa trotted into the kitchen and went straight to the refrigerator.

"Super! Do we have anything to eat?"

At Marissa's insistence they'd stopped at a Burger King on the way home.

"You just had a whole Whopper and fries."

Not her child's usual fare, but this was a special occasion.

"Yeah, but I'm still hungry."

After less than a day on a regular pediatric floor, Marissa had been going stir crazy. She was still weakened from the aftereffects of the infection and of living off IV fluids instead of food, but Laura had decided she didn't need more hospital. She needed *home*.

Dr. Lerner had refused to discharge her, despite the fact that her blood picture had returned to normal. She overheard one of the doctors saying not only was it like she had never had the infection, but like she'd never had the stem-cell transplant for the leukemia.

Laura remembered Clotilde's words: It resets your health to maximum.

Lerner insisted she needed to be under observation for another day or two. Laura disagreed and signed her out

AMA. She knew what Lerner meant by "observation"—more poking and prodding and testing to see if he and his team could find an explanation for this miracle. They weren't going to and she refused to allow her daughter to be a lab rat.

Of course, it didn't hurt that the second miracle in the PICU—Cory Nicolay's overnight recovery from a severe cardiomyopathy—had drawn attention from Marissa. Laura had mentioned him to Dr. Lerner. Though not a cardiologist, Lerner had consulted on Cory's pulmonary function and been astounded to hear that the boy's ejection fraction had jumped from a disastrous 16 percent to a very normal seventy overnight.

"What are they doing in that PICU?" he'd said.

Laura had shrugged. "Must be something in the water."

She followed Marissa into the kitchen. Not much to snack on. She'd spotted ice cream in the freezer when she'd come home to shower yesterday. Why not? Marissa needed calories to regain those lost pounds. And besides, what passed for ice cream in this house was really frozen nonfat yogurt.

"Will ice cream do?"

"Yes!"

Laura placed a three-scoop serving in front of her, then sat down at the kitchen computer. She accessed Google and began searching for East Meadow nursing homes. She intended to find James Fife and visit him . . . see if she could do anything for him. The names were just starting to pop onto the screen when the front doorbell rang. Her first thought was 536—but they weren't the type to ring the bell. Still . . .

She and Marissa were alone in the house. Steven had gone back to work—he'd done nothing but hang by Marissa's side for days—and a Monday seemed like the perfect time to restart a normal schedule.

She tiptoed to the door and was relieved when a peek through the sidelight revealed a familiar—and yet not so familiar—face. And then the anger came.

She yanked open the door. "I don't think we have anything to say to each other, Mister Stahlman."

He stood there looking contrite . . . and wonderfully healthy. His posture was straight, his face pink, and not an oxygen tank in sight.

"I apologize for my callousness. My only excuse was my desperation."

"You knew my daughter was dying and—"

"But she didn't die. And the only reason she is alive is that you did not prematurely rush home to be with her. If you had, you would have arrived in the PICU empty-handed. Instead of celebrating her return home right now, you would be planning funeral arrangements."

She recognized the irony: Marissa was alive because of Fife's elaborate web of false texts and Stahlman's silence. Their lies and deceit had paid an unexpected benefit for that little girl . . . and for Laura.

She allowed a grudging nod. "That's a harsh way of putting it, but . . . touché."

"I stopped by to thank you personally and to let you know I've added another fifteen million to the account."

The amount jolted her. "Fifteen? I thought five—"

"I doubled it, remember?"

She guessed she hadn't taken that seriously. Twenty million dollars . . . that was going to take some time to sink in. She pushed it aside.

"You're looking well, which can only mean that Rick delivered the dose."

"Yes. Good man, although at the time I did not appreciate the side trip." He frowned. "You haven't seen him since?"

She shook her head. "No contact at all."

She'd wondered at that herself. They'd spent almost a week in virtually constant contact and then . . . nothing.

She missed him.

"As I said, good man . . . but a strange one."

"You don't know the half of it."

She missed his strangeness too . . . and their strange conversations.

"I probably do. But there's another reason I've stopped by. I have a proposal."

"No offense," she said, "but I'd rather be catching up with my daughter. She went to close the door. "Goodbye, Mister—"

He put out a hand to stop her. "Wait. Just hear me out. It's not really a proposal. Just an idea. I can formalize it later."

Curious now, she said, "Make it quick."

"You know Rick's theory that the panacea was from 'outside,' right?"

"He may have mentioned it."

An understatement, to be sure.

"Well, I'm beginning to think there's merit to that."

If not for her experience with Marissa and Cory in the last two days, she might have closed the door right then.

"I'll reserve judgment on that. Go on."

"Well, what if other supposedly mythical things and places and people are real and are out there in the world? I mean, what if they're not based on fantasy but on fact—like the panacea? If they're out there, I want to find them."

"Good luck with that. But what's this got to do with me?"

"Everything. I'll keep my ears out for stories that may point to one of those. When something starts to sound promising, I'll send you and Rick off to investigate it."

No way was that going to happen, but she had to ask . . .

"Why me?"

"Because you're plucky and—"

"'Plucky'? Did you just call me 'plucky'?"

He grinned. "I love that word. And it fits you to a T. You're plucky and you have a science head. Rick has a knack for getting things done. The two of you make a great team—you've proven that. And if something you bring back turns out to be commercially viable, we'll all split the profits."

She shook her head. "Once a businessman, always a businessman."

"I prefer 'entrepreneur.' Of course, if it's as resistant to analysis as that panacea—"

"What do you mean?"

"I sent the residue in the vial to a commercial lab for analysis. It crashed every machine they tried."

"Good day, Mister Stahlman," and this time she did shut the door.

Through the door she heard, *"I'll call if I have something."*

"Don't call us, we'll call you," she muttered as she headed back to Marissa.

Plucky . . . seriously?

2

Rick stood in the shadows at the rear of the backyard—the same spot where he'd dealt with that 536er the night before their trip—and watched her through the windows. The moon was scheduled to rise later and he might have to find a new vantage point then.

The second miracle cure in the Stony Brook PICU had him worried. He had no doubt what had happened

and who was responsible. He'd learned about it when he
stopped by the hospital earlier to see how Marissa was
faring. Turned out Laura had already taken her home
but the hospital was buzzing about miracles.

Not good.

He figured Fife had been using NSA's electronic monitoring to track miracle cures. His boss, Pickens, might do
the same, but Rick doubted it. He'd met Pickens years
ago; he had a rep as a guy who never stuck his neck out.
Without Nelson on point, he'd let it slide.

The Brotherhood was another matter. He didn't
know if anyone else in 536 was upper echelon enough
to access NSA data, but he'd decided to keep an eye on
Laura's place for a couple of days, just to be safe.

Or was he kidding himself?

Because he couldn't get that kiss out of his mind. If
Clotilde hadn't knocked . . .

And so here I am, not just driving past her house like
some moony teenager, but taking it a step further by
standing in her backyard like some pervo peeper.

And there *she* was, visible through the sliding glass
doors that opened onto the low rear deck, cleaning up
after dinner while Marissa watched a baseball game on
TV. Half a glass of white wine sat on the counter. The
sight of someone that special going about everyday mundane tasks caused an indefinable ache in his chest. Why?
Why the ache? For some reason he felt he might stop the
ache by joining her in there and helping out.

How crazy was that? He did not belong in there, in
the light. Out here in the dark, keeping watch, that was
his place.

Because she deserved someone better, someone who
deserved *her*.

Marissa bounded up from the TV area and into the
kitchen. As she passed the sliding glass doors she glanced

his way and froze. Then backed toward her mother, pointing at him.

How the hell had she spotted him?

He could duck away but that would only leave them frightened—the last thing he wanted. So he held his ground as Laura quick-stepped to a wall and hit a switch.

The yard flooded with light.

He waved and saw the tension go out of Laura's posture. She slid open the door.

"What are you doing out there?" she called.

"Well, I—"

"Never mind. I can guess exactly why you're there. Come in."

"No, I—"

She stamped her foot. He loved when she did that.

"No excuses. Get in here right now."

He shrugged and crossed the rear lawn, hopped up on the deck, and stepped into her kitchen.

"Marissa," Laura said. "This is Mister Hayden. He kept me safe during my trip."

"Hayden like the planetarium?" Marissa said.

Rick instantly loved her.

"You're pretty smart to know that." He extended his hand. "Just like your mom."

Her little hand disappeared into his as they shook.

"You like baseball?" she said.

He hated baseball.

"Love it."

"Cool! What's your favorite team?"

He could see himself getting boxed in as to best players and such—he hadn't a clue—so he said, "I don't have a favorite. I just like to watch whoever's playing at the moment."

As much as I like watching paint dry.

"Do you—?"

"You can talk baseball later, honeybunch," Laura said, pointing her back toward the TV. "Mister Hayden and I have grown-up stuff to discuss."

When she'd returned to her cross-legged position on the floor before the screen, Laura turned to him with a concerned expression and lowered her voice.

"Do you really think playing watchdog is necessary?"

"I honestly don't know. Fife told us he'd kept his team small, working on a need-to-know basis. If that's true, there's a good chance no one will connect you to those two miracle cures."

"I guess that was a dumb move on my part," she said as she pulled a wineglass from a cabinet. "I'm usually not impulsive, but I was exhausted and euphoric over Marissa, and I saw this little boy and I just . . . " She shrugged. "I only have white—no bubbles."

He waved her off. "That's okay. I should probably—"

She opened the refrigerator. "You should probably have a glass of wine and sit down and relax. We can talk. After all we've been through, we should get to know each other a little better, don't you think? I mean, beyond talk of vast, cool and unsympathetic intelligences and such."

He was trying to grasp the subtext here. Her words were saying they should be friends, but what was *she* saying? That she'd like it to be more? It would never work.

But he said, "I . . . I'd like that."

She poured him two-thirds of a glass and refreshed her own.

"Good. I'm quitting the ME's office, you know."

"No. I didn't know."

"Decided today. I think it's time for me to get back to seeing live patients. Going to look into a neurology residency."

"You'd be good at that."

"No, I'm much better with dead people, but I can learn. I've got motivation."

Another subtext running here . . .

"You're not going to start growing funny plants, are you?"

She laughed. "No. But someone is going to be sending me a dose every now and then."

"And you're going to use it?"

"I'm sure as hell not throwing it away."

"You'll have to be very careful."

"No worry there. What about you? Any plans?"

"Stahlman wants to keep me on retainer. He's always had irons in dozens of fires, and now he's revving back into high gear. So I suppose I'll be doing my usual—a little this, a little that."

And a lot of watching your back.

"Did he mention his idea to you?"

"About panacea-like stories and hunting them down? Crazy, huh?"

"Totally. But . . . "

Uh-oh.

"But what?"

"Remember the first part of that Chinese curse you mentioned?"

"'May you live in interesting times'?"

"That's the one." She locked her blue gaze onto him. "Seems to me it doesn't always have to be a curse."

"No . . . no, it doesn't."

Not at all.

THE SECRET HISTORY OF THE WORLD

The preponderance of my work deals with a history of the world that remains undiscovered, unexplored, and unknown to most of humanity. Some of this secret history has been revealed in the Adversary Cycle, some in the Repairman Jack novels, and bits and pieces in other, seemingly unconnected works. Taken together, even these millions of words barely scratch the surface of what has been going on behind the scenes, hidden from the workaday world. I've listed them below in chronological order. (NB: "Year Zero" is the end of civilization as we know it; "Year Zero Minus One" is the year preceding it, etc.)

Panacea is part of the Secret History.

THE PAST

"Demonsong" (prehistory)
"The Compendium of Srem" (1498)
"Aryans and Absinthe"* (1923–1924)
Black Wind (1926–1945)
The Keep (1941)
Reborn (February–March 1968)
"Dat-Tay-Vao"** (March 1968)

---

* available in *Aftershock & Others*
** available in the 2009 reissue of *The Touch*

Jack: Secret Histories (1983)
Jack: Secret Circles (1983)
Jack: Secret Vengeance (1983)
"Faces"* (1988)
Cold City (1990)
Dark City (1991)
Fear City (1993)

YEAR ZERO MINUS THREE

Sibs (February)
The Tomb (summer)
"The Barrens"** (ends in September)
"A Day in the Life"* (October)
"The Long Way Home"**
Legacies (December)

YEAR ZERO MINUS TWO

"Interlude at Duane's"† (April)
Conspiracies (April) (includes "Home Repairs"†)
All the Rage (May) (includes "The Last Rakosh"†)
Hosts (June)
The Haunted Air (August)
Gateways (September)
Crisscross (November)
Infernal (December)

* available in *The Barrens and Others*
**available in *Quick Fixes—Tales of Repairman Jack*
† available in *Aftershock & Others*

YEAR ZERO MINUS ONE

Harbingers (January)
"Infernal Night"* (with Heather Graham)
Bloodline (April)
Panacea (April)
By the Sword (May)
Ground Zero (July)
The Touch (ends in August)
The Peabody-Ozymandias Traveling Circus &
Oddity Emporium (ends in September)
"Tenants"**

YEAR ZERO

"Pelts"**
Reprisal (ends in February)
Fatal Error (February) (includes "The
Wringer"†)
The Dark at the End (March)
Nightworld (May)

* available in *Face Off*
** available in *The Barrens and Others*
† available in *Quick Fixes—Tales of Repairman Jack*

They locked gazes for a few heartbeats. He wasn't going to budge, and arguing would only delay their departure—if indeed they would be allowed to depart. Besides, he held all the cards. She broke off and turned toward the door.

"Don't be long," she said with a bravado she didn't feel. "I want to be on a plane out of here as soon as possible."

She closed the door behind her, walked down the short hallway, and wound up in a small room with an armed man in a green uniform seated behind a desk. Saying nothing, she took a seat and waited. The shock of learning that their attackers carried the *DXXXVI* tattoo vied with a nightmare vision of seeing Rick being led out of that room in handcuffs a few minutes from now. The world seemed upside down.

What would she do if they arrested Rick? Call the American embassy? Hell, she didn't even know what city it was in. Tel Aviv? Jerusalem?

She decided to worry about that if and when she had to.

She watched the border policeman out of the corner of her eye. Did he have *DXXXVI* branded on his arm as well?

6

After Laura was gone, Chayat stared at him a long time. Rick stared back.

"Who are you, Mister Hayden? Really."

Rick didn't know where this was going, but he saw no other course than to play it like everything was on the up and up. Which it was. The details, however, were not up for discussion.

"Just what it says there," he said, pointing to his passport. "I don't know what I can add to that."

Chayat offered him a tolerant smile. "No, you are something else. When I called in the situation at Gan Yosaif, word quickly came back to go through the motions and let you go. I don't know who you know or what you know, but that is most unusual."

Yeah, unusual as all hell.

But he kept his expression bland. "I assure you, Mister Chayat, neither the doc or I are involved in anything sinister."

"Oh, I'm quite sure that's true about 'the doc.' But you . . . you are a different story. Word did not come down to go easy on the American couple. It came down to go easy on you . . . on Richard Hayden."

"Somebody at the American embassy?" He sounded like he was clutching at straws, and he was. He didn't get it.

Chayat shook his head. "Much too quick for that. No time to query the embassy and have them formulate a reply, especially at night. This came from within. Someone above my clearance level recognized your name and pulled on the reins."

"Someone in Shin Bet?"

He was nodding now. "Where else? You have a friend high up. Any idea who?" His hand shot up, palm out. "Not that I want you to tell me. I'm just curious as to whether you know who it might be."

Rick was sure Chayat was dying to know, but since everything was being recorded, he preferred to remain in the dark.

"I can tell you with all honesty, sir, that I haven't the faintest. As my passport shows, I've never been to Israel before."

Right . . . as far as that passport showed.

"I have any number of passports," Chayat said. "How many do you have?"

"Just that one."

Very true . . . now. But that hadn't always been the case.

Chayat slid the passport across the table. "Thank you for removing four threats to the people of Israel. I could say that I wish you had left one alive for questioning, but that would be less than gracious. Bon voyage, Mister Hayden. Or whoever you are."

Hiding his relief, Rick grabbed the passport and walked out.

7

The knock on the door to his suite at the Sadot Hotel turned out to be Bradsher.

"Shin Bet is going to release them," he said as Nelson admitted him.

"Any clue as to why they were at that dead kibbutz?"

"Clues, yes. They had coordinates written down and a map with an azimuth plotted from Quintana Roo. They had the degrees of another azimuth from the kibbutz but hadn't plotted it yet."

"Have you?"

Bradsher nodded, his expression grim. "Roughly. They cross in the neighborhood of the Abbey."

"Really."

Nelson leaned back. Now *that* was interesting. The ancient abbey was in the Pyrenees—the birthplace of the panacea . . . and the Brotherhood.

Bradsher said, "The road back through the Negev is the perfect place to set up an ambush and—"

Nelson held up a hand. That was the last thing he wanted now.

"Not yet. Let her run, let her find the Abbey."

"Sir?"

Nelson felt the need to move. He rose behind the suite's desk but had to grab the edge as the room made

a slight tilt to the left. When it steadied itself, he turned
and leaned against the edge.

"Let's look at this from another angle. Doctor Fanning has brought forensic skills to the quest. They have
taken her in directions we don't understand. She has
this encoded belt that we've somehow missed all along."

"All the more reason to believe she'll beat us to it."

"It's also reason to believe she'll *lead* us to it." He
paused to let that sink in. "Think about it: A lone woman
might be able to succeed where generations of our brothers have failed . . . simply because she is a woman."

Bradsher frowned. "How so?"

"Many of the panaceans are women, and we've long
believed they are led by women. So who better to work
her way through their layers of deception than another
daughter of Eve?"

He sensed a divine symmetry at work here. The Serpent existed to thwart God's plans. When Eve accepted
the apple from the Serpent, she sabotaged God's Plan of
Paradise for Humanity. Because of her act, God changed
His plan: He banished Mankind from the Garden into
a life of sickness and suffering. And ever since the Day
of Banishment, the Serpent had been trying to thwart
God's punishment. Nelson saw delicious irony in a
woman undoing the Serpent's scheme.

He had been so looking forward to her demise, but
now he knew he must delay that pleasure for a higher
purpose. *Delay* . . . that was the key word. He was convinced now that the Lord was guiding her—and Nelson
through her—so for now he would back off and simply
observe the path she traveled. But when that path came
to an end, which it eventually must, she would be called
to account for the debt she owed.